Katie Galvin lives in Perth, Western Australia. Her childhood love of fantasy and magic followed her into her adult years, resulting in her writing *The Gifted* series. In the rare moments where she's not running her speech therapy business or writing, Katie can be found at the gym, with a coffee in hand or rolling her eyes at her cat's antics.

 instagram.com/katie_galvin_writing

Also by Katie Galvin

The Gifted
The Broken
The Divine

THE DIVINE

KATIE GALVIN

One More Chapter
a division of HarperCollins*Publishers* Ltd
1 London Bridge Street
London SE1 9GF
www.harpercollins.co.uk
HarperCollins*Publishers*
Macken House, 39/40 Mayor Street Upper,
Dublin 1, D01 C9W8, Ireland

This paperback edition 2025

1

First published in Great Britain in ebook format
by HarperCollins*Publishers* 2025

Copyright © Katie Galvin 2025
Katie Galvin asserts the moral right to be identified
as the author of this work

A catalogue record of this book is available from the British Library
ISBN: 978-0-00-867921-7

This novel is entirely a work of fiction. The names, characters and incidents portrayed in it are the work of the author's imagination. Any resemblance to actual persons, living or dead, events or localities is entirely coincidental.

Printed and bound in the UK using 100% Renewable Electricity
by CPI Group (UK) Ltd

All rights reserved. No part of this publication may be reproduced, stored in a retrieval system, or transmitted, in any form or by any means, electronic, mechanical, photocopying, recording or otherwise, without the prior permission of the publishers.

Without limiting the exclusive rights of any author, contributor or the publisher of this publication, any unauthorised use of this publication to train generative artificial intelligence (AI) technologies is expressly prohibited. HarperCollins also exercise their rights under Article 4(3) of the Digital Single Market Directive 2019/790 and expressly reserve this publication from the text and data mining exception.

Chapter One

Dining with a god was not as exciting as one might think.
 Not only were they terrible company, they possessed an abhorrent tendency to arrive late. Time was, after all, the commodity that they were richest in. An hour wasted was like a pinprick of light in a star-speckled sky.

Not that I minded.

Every minute they spent away from me was a minute I could spend plotting an escape from the golden-gilded prison I'd found myself. A minute I could spend daydreaming of the demise of the king of gods. A minute I could close my eyes and remember the man I loved.

Leaning into the velvet-padded chair I'd been unceremoniously chained to, I tipped my head back. The arched roof above was splintered through with golden webbing. The corrupted light that flooded the room stung at my eyes. Weathered stone curled into white pillars, each carved with an individual depiction of the gods.

Tarina, goddess of Illusions and trickery. Akmad, god of

shadows and light. Evania, goddess of peace. Kerta, goddess of war. More, many long forgotten by the mortal realm, others perfectly preserved in history tomes.

And upon the central pillar, the most monstrous of them all. Vitus, god of life.

The door creaked. I sighed, keeping my eyes on the ceiling.

'Is this how you greet your king?' that very monstrous god asked as he entered the dining hall, his voice a cluster of resentment and malice spent too long festering.

Slowly, I straightened, chains clanking. My wrists stung, chafed from three weeks of wearing them every time I was allowed out of my cell. I preferred the rawness to the golden lines carved underneath the shackles, though. 'You're no king of mine.'

He tilted his head. Skin cracked through with golden veins flared. At a wave of his hand, one of his mindless Ankurans – creatures of half-life created from corpses – scampered forward, her bare feet pattering upon golden tiles. She was around my age. Eighteen, perhaps, or even younger. Her fist flew, the stench of decay accompanying the punishing blow as it slammed into my cheek.

My head whipped to the side, a metallic taste coating my tongue. Between matted strands of dark hair, I allowed myself a handful of seconds to stare at the floor before I straightened. Blood dribbled over my lips. My eyes met Vitus's.

Then, I smiled.

This had become a game of ours after his attempts at physical torture had failed. He'd invite me to a meal. Attempt to coax me into joining his side, swaying my father to his side. Feed me pieces of information, always careful to keep the truth of our current location from me. And I'd inevitably leave bloodied but triumphant.

'What a lovely start to this meal,' I said, blood staining the golden skirts I wore. Chosen, of course, by Vitus. 'I'm starting to think you're warming up to me.'

Rage sparked in Vitus's eyes. The flesh he wore pulsed with light, fissures racing through the pale skin. King Kane, whose body Vitus now inhabited – and the man who'd once enslaved me to fight his wars – barely resembled anything mortal now. His head was bare of any hair, plain features split through with gold. Limbs that'd always been thin had become so emaciated that I often fantasised about how easy they'd be to snap. He was little more than power in a vessel threatening to break.

'Where's my dear father?' I asked, ignoring the crackling tension rising around us. Metallic-yellow light flickered over the long table. 'You seem to enjoy hearing him deny your requests to bring down the barrier. I would've thought—'

A crack thundered through the room as Vitus's fist slammed down on the table. Outside, the haze of dusk upon streets unfamiliar to me seemed to shudder with anticipation of his wrath.

My smile ticked up as I looked down. A long crack now ran from one side of the table to the other, each side tilting towards the other like opposite sides of a valley. 'What a waste. That's the third one this week.' I ran my finger along one splintered edge, clicking my tongue. 'What will you do when you run out of furniture? You've killed all the humans who might've been able to craft you more.'

'Enough.'

Even the Ankuran who'd stayed beside me shrank back, as though some mortal instinct to fear cruel power still existed in her. That instinct had died long, long before I'd ever been chained by Vitus.

I tilted my head. 'Something the matter?'

The air shivered around me at Vitus's glare.

This was a dangerous game I was playing. Poking at the beast enough that he'd forget his purpose, and praying I pulled my hand back quick enough that he didn't snap it off. Because if I stepped too far, it wouldn't just be my life on the line.

His chest expanded with a deep inhale, his golden tunic stretching tight. I loathed the colour.

At last, he held up a hand, twisting it once. The wall behind him shuddered. More Ankurans spilt out, each bearing clay dishes that smelt of spice and meats. The table righted itself, gold-webbing knitting the wood together in time to allow the dishes to be laid out. Lids were whisked away, revealing steaming plates of food. Gravy-braised meats and flatbreads. Charred vegetables and sauces.

'You will eat,' Vitus said, his voice regaining some of its steady authority as he sat at the opposite end of the table. 'And you will remember your place.'

I glared down at my empty plate. 'My place is far away from here.'

When I made no move to serve myself, an Ankuran heaped my plate high. And damn the gods, it smelt ridiculously good.

'Your *place*, little raven,' Vitus said slowly, 'is at my feet.'

My head snapped up, fingers curling towards my palm. The chains clanked, their golden markings carved into my wrists stinging with my ire. 'My place is by my king's side.'

'I am your king.'

'You are *nothing*,' I snarled, my calm cracking as I attempted to launch myself to my feet. The chains held firm. They'd been wrapped around the back of the chair and my waist before being secured to my wrists after an unfortunate incident the first time Vitus had changed his tactics from beatings to bribery. Well, unfortunately for him, I'd rather enjoyed the splatter of his Ankurans' blood as I'd torn through four of them with a fork and my rage.

'You will watch your tongue, girl, or—'

'Or what?' I fell back with another sharp smile. 'You'll beat me? Force your power into me? Torture me until my father takes down the barrier between the mortal and godly realms?'

My smile grew as I lifted one arm as far as the chains would allow. The gown that'd been forced onto me stopped shy of my wrists, covering the scars upon my skin. Vitus despised imperfections. Even so, bruises snuck their way out.

'You've already tried that,' I said, my smile turning bitter. 'And neither my father nor I have budged.'

Me, because there was only one man I'd kneel at the feet of.

My father, because the god of death had the same pride as all the divine. That, and he held no sense of family. Another common trait amongst gods.

Vitus's wrecked body shuddered with a surge of his power. My own Gift – restrained by both the wards carved into me and by the very precious soul it was keeping tethered to this world – surged in response. My breath hissed through my teeth as the wards glowed brighter, pain cutting into me.

'You will learn your place. Convince Dearil to give in to me.'

'Or what?' I challenged.

He smiled. 'Do not forget who you stayed here to protect.'

A chill ran through me. 'Don't forget that he is the only thing that keeps me bound.'

'The wards keep you bound.' Vitus stared at me, his shadow crawling across the table as the light around us brightened. 'And if they did not, you could not defeat me even with full access to your Gift.'

'I haven't forgotten the pain it caused you.' The chains cut into the raw skin at my wrist, warm blood trickling anew as I grinned, trying not to let the fear show. 'The memory of it graces my dreams every night.'

'Pain is not death.'

'No,' I agreed, 'but it can become something far worse.'

Vitus regarded me for a long moment before turning. 'You.'

A woman scampered forward, her head bowed and shoulders curled inwards. Through strings of brown hair, I glimpsed blue eyes. A mortal.

Anger twisted. Over the past weeks, mortals had been a rare sight, but they'd been there. Traitors to their own kind, who'd prostrated themselves so low before the divine that they'd forgotten how to stand. There'd even been a few I recognised. Soldiers who'd made my cruelty seem a lovely dream. Nobility who'd encouraged King Kane's tyranny. There'd even been General Tizan – the man who'd taken the heads of the unit I'd captained in my days of serving the Naruzian army. A man whom one of my closest friends, Deana, held a personal grudge against.

'Yes, my lord,' the woman spoke, her voice a dried leaf brushing over bark. All it'd take would be a gust of wind to blow her away.

'Tell me where the false king resides.'

I stiffened.

'He's currently in Perryth.'

'And the two others we have been keeping an eye on?'

'Deana Riker is with the false king. Jaxon Bladditch remains in Alluvite, overseeing matters there.'

Later, I might worry about what sort of mischief the half-god might be getting into while he *oversaw* matters, but for now, it took all of me to just breathe through my rage. To steady myself in the chaos of my terror.

Vitus nodded. 'How many mortal forces are stationed near Perryth?'

'A thousand scattered amongst the non-believers, my lord.'

'And how many of those blessed with my divinity?'

I stared at him. He had to be referring to the Ankurans. There was nothing blessed about the husks of bodies that'd once housed souls. Creatures cursed to crave anything containing the life they lost.

'Twenty thousand stationed in Ballaronia, ready to mobilise,' the woman said calmly.

Disgust choked me. She spoke far too easily of sending Vitus's creatures after mortals. 'Traitor,' I hissed, but she didn't turn from her master.

He, however, devoted his full attention to me. 'Do you see, little raven, how easy it would be for me to crush your king? Callum would—'

I lunged. Chains dug into my abdomen, but the fools had left enough slack at the arms for me to reach the table. There were no knives in sight. No forks, either. Vitus wasn't a complete idiot. But the clay dishes … yes, that would do.

Ignoring the sting of heat on my fingers, I smashed the dish over the edge of the table. Hot meats spilt over the floor and my fingers as the clay shattered into sharp pieces. I relished the sting of their scald.

'Foolish child,' Vitus sighed, turning to his Ankurans. 'I told you that you could do nothing to me.'

My wrist twisted, the shard flying. Vitus flicked his fingers. A shimmering barrier emerged around him. I'd learnt two weeks before that nothing I flung at him could penetrate that barrier.

But I hadn't been aiming for him.

The mortal woman who'd so easily told Vitus the numbers choked, her hands flying up to her throat as I sank back into the chair, my waist throbbing with what would surely be a round of fresh bruises. Red spouted between her fingers, painting the golden floor. Her lips opened. No words emerged as she staggered a step towards Vitus before collapsing facedown onto the floor. Her body twitched once, twice, before she stilled.

Vitus slowly turned to me, his features a mask of carefully controlled wrath.

There was nothing controlled about my own fury as I snarled, 'You do not speak his name.'

'Callum is nothing more—'

I grasped another shard, barely registering the pain as it sliced through my palm. This time, it found itself buried deep into the eye of the Ankuran who'd served my food. The creature fell, gold-streaked blood joining the mortal's.

Vitus's restraint fractured. He took a step towards me, power sparking. My leashed Gift pounded against my skin, the wards burning as they fought to keep death from leaking into the air.

I didn't care about the pain. All I cared about was that Vitus dared to threaten Callum.

Callum, who was far more than a king to me. My soul-bonded. The only person my soul had sought, even when I'd been lost in the depths of rage and self-loathing. The very person who'd dragged me out of that darkness, only to almost die by Vitus's hands a month ago. Even now, I could feel the soul-bond between us. Dulled, initially through my own decision, and now from the wards leashing my power, but there.

So long as he lived, I would fight.

'Enough of this,' Vitus said as I reached for the next shard, blood dripping from my hand. It mingled with the spilt meats. 'I will not kill him. Not yet.'

I knew he wouldn't. The wards might provide Vitus with extra security, but we both knew Callum was my true leash. His soul, which I'd nearly lost when he'd been stabbed by Liam, the now-dead prince of Archin, was held in place by my Gift, leeching away most of my power.

The moment Vitus killed Callum would be the moment I lost control. I'd find a way to break the wards, even if it meant losing my hands. But Callum – there was nothing I wouldn't sacrifice to keep him alive.

'You do not speak his name,' I repeated, the calm in my voice a lie.

Vitus shook his head. 'I planned to bring Dearil to join us.' He sighed. 'A pity. I thought you might be more amenable to assisting me in convincing your father this evening after such a miserable few nights in your cell. But it seems you are in no mood for decent conversation.'

'There's nothing decent about you.'

Vitus glanced at the Ankuran woman standing by his side. 'Take her back to her cell. We will try this again tomorrow.'

'Giving in so soon? I never knew a god could be so weak.' I clicked my tongue in mock disappointment. 'My, Alexia must be—'

Vitus snapped. He surged forward, crossing the distance between us in a blink. His hand slammed into my chin, forcing my head to crack against the back of the chair. Gold sparked on his skin before spreading to mine, sending burning agony coursing through my body. My muscles locked up, heart forced into a canter as the pain urged me to submit. Inside, my Gift roiled in protest at the opposing power.

The thing with pain, though, is that it tends to numb when it is delivered too often. Vitus had been very generous with the use of his power in recent weeks.

'Her name does not belong in the mouth of mortal filth,' Vitus spat, his fingers squeezing with crushing force.

I smiled through it all. It was an almost comical switch in roles. 'The filthy part of my blood isn't what comes from the mortals.'

'It is your father's fault that my soul-bonded is dead.' His fingers tightened further. The scent of rose attempting to cover up that of rot saturated the air.

If I was anyone else, I might've pitied him. The goddesses, Kerta and Evania, had told me the tale of Vitus's soul-bonded's death. How the gods had once lived in the mortal realm until their fondness for mortals began to splinter the mortal realm. Dearil created a realm that existed between the mortal one and the world after death, forcing the gods to enter before he erected the barrier between the two. Vitus's half-mortal soul-bonded was forced to stay behind, pregnant with his twin children. Within a handful of years, Alexia and the children had been killed, Vitus powerless to stop it.

But I wasn't anyone else. Cruelty existed in every form within the mortal and godly realms. I'd experienced it countless times. Developed my own brand of it, too.

Perhaps, once, I might've felt a shred of understanding for Vitus, but he'd gone after Callum. And perhaps it made me the same as him, but there was nothing left in me to feel anything but hatred for the god.

Vitus must've seen that hatred in my face. He pushed my head further back until I was forced to meet his eyes. More of his power flowed into me. 'You will pay for his crimes. And when you do, you will scream for—'

He reeled back with a hiss as I tore myself far enough free that I could sink my teeth deep into the skin between his thumb and finger. Rot-filled blood filled my mouth. The agonised power surging through me wrenched out so suddenly, it felt like it tore half my organs out with it. Still, I did not relinquish my hold. Did not turn my stare from Vitus's as he yanked his hand free, flesh breaking.

I grinned, the fetid blood tasting like victory. 'Pathetic. You can't even tolerate a small nip from a mortal.'

Anyone with sense would've cowered before the fury on the god's face. Gold cracks sliced down the walls surrounding us, the summer palace we'd retreated to shuddering with his wrath. A pity for Vitus that I'd had my sense knocked from me years prior.

I laughed as he worked his jaw soundlessly, his rage filling me with the only joy I'd managed to find outside of my memories as his captive. He jerked towards the Ankuran woman who still stood beside me and nodded once in a quick, tight motion.

The Ankuran woman stepped forward. Her fist flew towards my temple. Pain flared, and my laughter chased me into unconsciousness.

Chapter Two

Darkness and damp greeted me upon waking. Groaning, I lifted my head from where it rested upon uneven stone, the faint taste of rot still coating my tongue. Nausea swelled as my head swam with pain. I shifted slowly until I was seated upright in the cramped cell. Any amount of pain was worth it for how easily I'd played Vitus.

It was the fourth time his servants had dragged me to dinner, only for it to end with his rage at me still refusing to convince Dearil to drop the barrier. Not that it would matter, though. Dearil would never risk this realm for me.

'You must be careful, child.'

I stiffened at the gravelly voice. Dragging myself over damp stone, I rested my back against the wall, staring out through bars at the faint hints of candlelight beyond. Water dripped on my hand. I didn't bother moving it. 'I don't need your advice.'

'Vitus is not one of your mortal enemies. He is far more cunning. Ruthless. He has had years to plan this. More than—'

'He's a god,' I cut in, picking at a notch in the ground with my thumb. Pain throbbed through my wrists, golden light pulsating from the wards carved there. I picked harder.

There was a pause, filled only by that incessant dripping and the scratching of my nail. 'Yes, child. You must—'

'Gods are all about control.' I cut him off again and shifted, the golden skirts uncomfortably sodden with sweat and water. Closing my eyes, I tipped my head back. The faint impression of the soul-bond pushed at me. I reached for it, but it eluded me, as it had done ever since Vitus had carved the wards into me.

I hated myself for blocking Callum out during the initial days. Not for all of it – he didn't need to sense the pain of Vitus's beatings – but the in-between. The moments where I could've reached for him, whispered my love to him even if he never heard it.

Gods, I'd been a fool. Not just with that, but before, too. When I'd refused to tell Callum out loud that I loved him, for fear of losing him.

'Explain,' Dearil commanded.

I sighed. 'Give even the slightest hint that gods don't have control, and they crumble.'

Another silence. I smiled into the darkness. Hopefully Dearil was pondering whether those words might relate to him.

Chains clanked. Unlike me, who was generously granted freedom from the metal cuffs once I'd been dumped into my cell, Dearil was never free of his. Where wards stifled the Gifts of mortals and halflings, they only muted that of gods. But the chains he wore were the only things keeping him from accessing his power. A power that was perhaps the only thing in existence that could keep Vitus in check.

'An out-of-control god is more dangerous than anything in creation,' Dearil said at last. 'As you should well know.'

I huffed, the air tickling the tip of my nose. 'What a surprise – more cryptic nonsense.'

'Do you know how the barrier between realms is brought down?'

I frowned. 'You have to bring it down.'

'Correct.' A tendril of ice wove under my gown at the chill in Dearil's voice. 'But there are two ways that it can fall. If I make the decision myself, or if Vitus kills death.'

'Then he should kill you so I can have some peace,' I said flippantly, even as terror struck my core. The barrier falling meant more than ending the separation between the mortal and godly realms. It meant Vitus reclaiming his full power. It meant the death of the mortal realm, all to serve his vendetta against mortals from the loss of his soul-bonded.

My friends lived in this realm. Callum lived in it. It couldn't fall.

'It is not as simple as that.'

I sighed, relief softening the sound. Of course it wasn't. *Simple* and *gods* didn't belong in the same sentence.

'I am not Death. I am merely its host. If Vitus kills me, the power over the barrier goes to the next candidate.'

'Fantastic.' I didn't have to ask who the next candidate would be. There was only one that I knew of that bore the misfortune of Dearil's blood. The mere thought of inheriting all that power turned my blood to ice. 'Then he should do that instead.'

'Why do you think he has not?'

'Beats me.'

'Because you are unpredictable.' I drew my knees to my chest, scowling at the shadows as Dearil continued. 'I have existed for centuries, Vitus by my side. He knows me as I know him. But you, daughter, are not one of us. You are a risk. One that could destroy the realm before he has a chance to.'

Not one of us. Neither mortal nor god. Something that did not belong.

But I'd begun to belong, with Callum, before Vitus had ripped that away from me.

'Then he should kill us both and be done with it.'

Dearil sighed. Another victory against the gods – exasperating my unflappable father. 'He cannot do that, child. There is a small chance that Death will not find another suitable host. A small one, but one, nonetheless. Vitus does not wish for his own death. He would not threaten the balance of the realms.'

'Fine. Then we're back to him killing you. He seems to think I'm inferior to him.' My hair tickled my knees as I rested my cheek on them. 'I'm sure he could convince himself that I'll submit to him if he put his mind to it.'

'He does not like unpredictability. Does not like things that go outside his expectations. There is nothing about you that fits, child. And once he has his way, he will eradicate all that does not belong.'

My frown deepened until my cheek, sporting a bruise from the Ankuran, throbbed. It seemed we'd upgraded from absentee father to flat out disparaging. 'Thanks.'

'It does not have to be an insult.' If Dearil had any concern about the irregular patrols of Ankurans overhearing our conversation, he didn't show it. Perhaps because Vitus was already aware of all he spoke of. 'The gods have fitted together for years. We have grown lax in our patterns, and Vitus has used that against us. You can use that against him.' His tone sharpened. 'But not if you force his hand too early. He does not want to kill you, but if you push too far, he will.'

There were plenty of people I'd pushed through my life. Madame Tussant, the adoptive mother who'd sold me to King Kane, the king who'd used my sister's life to force me to do his bidding. Generals and soldiers who'd tried to bend me to their will.

Most of them were dead now.

'You must find a way to—'

'I'm tired,' I interrupted. Gods were always good at telling me what I *must do*. Most of those with power were.

Another soft exhale that might've been a sigh sounded from the next cell over as I opened my eyes, staring at the shapes the sparse candlelight made in the corridor beyond. It didn't dare break through the sanctity of my cell's shadows. I was glad for it – for the darkness and all it hid.

'We must speak of what is to come.'

'You mean in the same way you warned me that Cassie would die?' I snapped, unable to keep my rage from rising. Once, that had been all I was – rage and ruination. Even more so after my little sister had died to allow Vitus to enter the mortal realm. A death that had ended with Dearil bound.

'I cannot predict most deaths.'

'But you knew about hers, didn't you?' I opened and closed my fists, an old ache of grief stabbing anew. Cassie had been the world to me. I'd lost her – and lost myself – before Callum found me again. And then I'd lost him, without ever telling him I loved him. At least, not out loud. 'You said it yourself. That there was always a price to be paid when I prevented a soul from heading for the Gates.'

More silence, this one filled with heaviness. An admittance that, even if he hadn't known precisely what happened, he'd known that Cassie wouldn't last long in this world after I'd bound her soul to her body when she was little more than a toddler.

'And Callum?' I asked, ignoring the lurch in my chest at the memory of his lifeless body. Of the blood and the sense of the bond between us fraying. 'What price will he pay for his soul being kept here?'

'It was never Cassandra's price to pay,' Dearil said, voice too gentle. 'And it will not be Callum's price, either.'

This time, when I said, 'I'm tired,' I wasn't lying. Of course it was my price to pay. I should've been used to it now. To bearing the responsibility of any I so selfishly loved.

But for Callum – for Deana, Jaxon and the others who'd shown me kindness when I'd shown nothing but cruelty – I would pay that price, and pay it gladly, provided it didn't take them away from me.

I might not care to save any kingdoms, but for them, I would fight. That was what I desired. Their happiness. Their safety. If I could achieve that, then it didn't matter what my end was.

First, though, I needed to find a way out of this cell. And once that was done, I'd have to find a way to destroy Vitus for good.

It took hours for my discomfort to give way to fatigue. By the time it did, it wasn't the warmth of memories that found me, nor the dark nightmares.

It was a set of gates that rose high above me, shadows and lights battling upon their surface. The gates were pulled closed, thousands of lights gathered before them. The comforting scent of smoke and jasmine that curled around me and soothed away my worries. The tiny lights hummed in unison, rushing for me as they sung to the power in my veins. Several brushed against my skin, echoes of voices accompanying their touch. Others hung further back, their light more hesitant.

Holding out my hand, I allowed two lights to settle on my palm. They nestled there like children seeking shelter in their mother's arms, frenetic movements stilling. Images flickered before me – a child with blond hair that fell across his eyes, and an adolescent whose scowl was belied by the kindness in her eyes.

Every one of the lights were souls.

I exhaled. It was the third time I'd been dragged to the Gates that existed before the Light and Dark that awaited mortals at their deaths in the past weeks. With Dearil chained to the mortal realm, it seemed the godly realm had given up on him, latching onto my own divine blood since I'd visited the Gates and helped Cassie pass to the Light. Each time, the souls waiting had been countless, clamouring in the space before the Gates after being neglected by Dearil for so long.

The first time, I'd convinced myself it was a dream, until I'd awakened and Dearil had calmly stated, 'You were summoned by the Gates.'

Even the wards Vitus had carved into me weren't strong enough to overcome the will of the realms and the need to maintain balance in everything. As Dearil explained it, the chains he wore were unnatural – abhorrences that should never have been created. Wards, however, came from an ancient language that had existed before the gods themselves. They could restrain, but they could not go against the will of the realms. It was why they failed to properly contain gods. To wipe away a god's power was to upset the balance. So, when the Gates summoned, I obeyed.

Maintain the balance, the air seemed to hum around me, the Gates pulsing beckoningly. *Allow the dead to rest.*

I turned back to the souls as their shapes shifted. The child turned pale, his throat bloodied. The adolescent held a hand to her abdomen, red spilling between her fingers. She whimpered, eyes filling with tears as she stared down at the bloodied memory of her death. The boy clung to her leg. He stared up at me with wide eyes, seemingly unaware of the wound at his throat.

Ignorance was a kindness that many dead didn't get.

'I didn't want to die,' the girl whispered, her voice barely audible, even in the quiet. The other lights around us buzzed with more energy, their movements bordering on angry. She peeled her fingers away from her wound, revealing a deep gash. At the edges, gold corrupted her flesh. 'I was just trying to save my brother.'

They sought comfort, but I did not know how to give it. I was a child of war, bred of violence and hatred. None of Dearil's calm had been passed down to me.

Sorrow clogged my throat as the boy pushed himself closer to the girl's leg. I didn't have to ask to know he was the brother she spoke of. It was clear in the flaxen hue of their hair, the roundness of their cheeks. Innocent victims of a war that the mortal realm had done little to instigate.

I might not know words of comfort to give them, but I could lend them my rage. One day, I would make sure Vitus felt every piece of the pain these souls went through.

'Come,' I said, trying to turn my sharpness into something softer as I crouched before the child to hold out a hand. More souls pushed closer, tangling in my hair and perching upon my shoulders. Their pleas rang in my ears, each more pitiful than the last.

The boy flinched away from me. The girl met my eyes, tears still dripping down her faintly glowing cheeks. After a moment's hesitation, she nodded, nudging him forward.

His hand was warm where he slipped it into mine. It shook. My Gift hummed as I straightened. I held my hand out to the girl next. She had to be no older than fourteen. A child herself.

'You, too.'

'I didn't want to die,' she whispered again, staring at my fingers as though I might lunge to choke her. 'But they were trying to hurt Myril.'

Myril squeezed my hand tighter. I studied the girl. The curve of her shoulders, the tears that wouldn't stop falling. The way she'd only look at Myril for a few seconds before looking away.

It wasn't her own death she was reluctant to accept, I realised. It was his. Her failure to protect him.

This, at least, was something I understood, far more than

empty comforts. I knew that guilt. Had battled it for months, and nearly lost myself to it.

I wouldn't let this soul lose herself over it, too.

'The blame doesn't lie with you,' I said, and she startled at the anger in my voice. I made no attempt to soften it. Sometimes, anger was what was needed. 'Hate those who came after you. Hate the realm for not allowing you the time you both deserve. You can even hate me for being the one to send you on. But don't hate yourself.'

She still hesitated. 'I let them into the house. They looked like our parents, and I let them in.'

My chest tightened.

It was a unique cruelty of Vitus's to use loved ones as his Ankurans. To send them into villages and cities, allowing relief to quickly change to terror as those same loved ones were slaughtered.

'Did you run, leaving Myril behind?' I asked.

The girl jerked. 'Of course not!'

'Did you push him to your parents to give yourself time to escape?'

Anger sparked. 'I would never.'

'Did you take a knife and cut him down yourself?'

Her form became more corporeal. 'No!'

'Then how are you to blame?'

She frowned. 'I could've done more. I could've—'

'You did all you could. You were brave when most wouldn't be. Now you need to be brave again. You need to let go of that guilt so both you and Myril can move on.' It felt strange speaking the words – giving advice that I struggled to accept myself. But in my past visits to the Gates, I'd seen the souls that hadn't passed through, refusing the Gates' call. Seen them so twisted with guilt that they couldn't abandon the mortal realm.

The next time I'd returned, those souls weren't there. They

couldn't have passed through the Gates – not without Dearil or myself to allow them entry. They had simply vanished, gone from this realm and all others.

It was a fate I wouldn't allow for the girl.

'Come,' I tried once more, extending my hand towards her. The scent of jasmine and smoke grew stronger. 'It's time for you to go.' I glanced down at Myril, then at all the lights swarming me. The words were wrong in my mouth, the burden too heavy, but I'd bear it for now. One day, Dearil could retake his mantle and be what the souls deserved. For now, they'd have to put up with me. 'All of you.'

This time, the girl placed her hand in mine. As soon as she did, she squeezed it tight.

'What waits for us?' She turned towards the Gates as I willed them to open. They responded immediately, cracking open. Light and shadows stretched towards us, ice and heat mingling in the air.

I hesitated. I could've lied. Could've told her what she wanted to hear – that it would be a smooth passing. That they'd find happiness in the Light. But I didn't know the answer, and I'd never been the sort to soothe with gentle falsities.

'I don't know,' I said, and she began to deflate. 'But I do know that whatever is beyond, you'll be going there with Myril.'

As if on cue, Myril launched forward, wrapping his arms around the girl.

Their death wounds flickered, then started to fade. 'Don't leave me,' he said, words muffled as he pressed his face into her side.

The girl closed her eyes, grief mingling with resolve as she rested her hand atop his head. 'Never.' When she opened them, determination shone there. 'I'm ready.'

I lifted a hand towards the Gates. Some souls were already gathered there, passing through. Most headed for the Light. Some were dragged into the Dark. Others lingered. Those who were merely uncertain or waiting for loved ones' arrival might last till the next time the Gates summoned me. Those who refused the Gates' call entirely would disappear, crumbling into nothing.

I had no doubt about where the two before me were headed.

I relinquished my hold of the girl, allowing her to move towards the Gates. The Light seemed to grow brighter at their approach.

Before they could step past the threshold, I called out, 'Before you go, can I ask one favour?' The girl nodded. 'Your name.'

'Lilly,' she said, and I engraved that name into my memory alongside Myril's. I protected no kingdom, the mortals who waited for me few.

But the dead had always been my burden, and I would keep the names of those Vitus had killed. The names he would pay for one day.

I smiled. 'Good luck, Lilly.'

There was a ghost of a smile. A movement of her lips that might've been a thank you. And then, she and Myril were gone.

Chapter Three

The scent of jasmine and smoke followed me into consciousness, opening my eyes to whatever awaited. Not much had changed since I'd been dragged into fulfilling my duties. My skin was still gritty, my mouth bitter with the taste of blood. Bruises throbbed. And I was still locked in a musty cell with constant dripping to keep me company.

But the woman was new. She stood on the other side of the bars to my cell, leaning forward as she peered down at me, head tilted.

'Who are you?' she asked as I staggered to my feet, back pressed to the wall.

I remained silent and considered my surroundings. A bare floor. No bed – the rusted metal frame that'd once been here had been removed after I'd managed to slam an Ankuran's head against its edge enough times that their head had turned into a bloodied pulp. The cell bars. Nothing that would be of use if this woman was a danger. From the way my Gift stretched towards my fingers, the wards searing my skin as it kept it at bay, she was.

'Well?' she asked, impatience creasing her brow. Her voice was deep, rich with a melodic accent I'd never encountered before. Despite its beauty, it raked uncomfortably over my skin.

'Kailey,' I said, borrowing the name of one of the guards at Callum's palace.

Her eyes, shot through with strands of yellow, narrowed. 'Lies are my domain. You would do well not to use them against me.'

I shrugged, the movement rustling the stained gown. 'I see no reason to provide you with my name when you haven't provided me with yours.'

The yellow streaks in her eyes intensified. 'Impudent mortal.'

That haughty tone was instantly recognisable. I'd only ever heard gods speak with that sort of arrogance. Smiling, I tilted my head, surveying her with the same cold curiosity she had with me. Dark hair knotted at the nape of her neck. Pale skin and a crooked nose.

None of it meant anything. This goddess wasn't tied to the mortal realm as Vitus had ensured of Dearil. She must only have minutes left to remain before her essence was dragged back.

The eyes were the only clue as to who she might be. They were enough.

'You're Jaxon's...' I trailed off, struggling to find a word to use. *Mother* was accurate, but she was also the woman partially responsible for the death of Jaxon's soul-bonded. I doubted he felt any familial attachment to the woman. 'Blood.'

The goddess, Tarina, lifted her chin, her eyes slitting further. 'Where is that boy?' She peered past me as though he may be hiding in the cracks within the stone. 'It's far past time he overcame his rebellious stage.'

'You killed his husband. I don't think—'

'You,' Tarina snapped, her finger jutting through the bars. I stared at it, debating whether snapping it off would be worth whatever horror the goddess might bring down on me. Tarina ruled over Illusions and trickery. There was no telling what darkness she'd conjure from my mind if displeased. 'You have not told me who you are.' She paused. 'Or *what* you are.'

The dampness from the wall sent a shiver through me, but I hid it from her eyes, standing taller. 'I'm—'

'Enough, Tarina,' Dearil rumbled.

Tarina flinched. I smiled. Problems with my father or not, I'd side with him over the creature before me any day.

Regaining her composure with impressive speed, Tarina lifted a hand. 'Fine.' She glanced towards Dearil's cell. 'But I came to talk to you. I cannot let this ... *thing* listen in.'

'Tarina.' There was warning in that word. Warning and an exhausted disappointment.

'You are frightfully dull.' She twisted her wrist, yellow threads tangling on the fingers of her mortal host. The skin cracked beneath their touch, the strength of her power too much for the human body. I swallowed my cry as a strip of flesh peeled clean away from bone on her left hand.

Whoever that mortal was, they were loyal to Vitus. I didn't have it in me to waste pity on them.

'You must not—'

Tarina flicked her hand. The yellow sped towards me, too fast to avoid. It slammed into my chest. A strange tingling raced over my body. I made no noise. Showed no sign of fear.

'Do not fret, Dearil,' Tarina said calmly as she disappeared from my view, shoes clicking against stone. 'She will not die. I have merely sent her into sleep. I even Gifted her with the chance to dream one of my Illusions. She should be grateful.'

Yellow flickered in the edge of my vision. With each blink, it grew, until all I could see was that colour – far brasher than that which Jaxon wielded, and harsher in the way it stung at my skin. Tarina said something, but her voice was faraway sounding, as though she was several cells down. I staggered forward, my body heavy, my breaths shallowing.

Don't submit, I ordered myself, even as a weight that had no presence except in my bones pulled me to the ground. *Don't sleep. Listen in and use what you can to your advantage. Don't—*

I blinked, lifting a hand to shield my eyes from the stinging sunlight. Its warmth danced over my skin, chasing away the chill that'd embedded itself into my bones from the cells. It took my eyes some time to adjust. Darkness had become a dear companion to me, and it was reluctant to let me go.

Grass bent under my feet. I walked on legs unused to movement, small cramps rioting through them. I smiled at the pain. Smiled at the breeze tickling my skin and the rolling field in front of me.

Freedom. The word rolled through me, filled with delicate hope and long-held desire. I stepped forward again. Let myself tip my head back and bask under the glow of an open sky. Let myself picture an eternity in blissful solitude.

Wrong. The word clanged through me. My head snapped up, the world around me wavering as yellow light fractured the grass and spilt from the sky. Solitude wasn't the freedom I desired. There was something – some*one* – missing.

The Illusion Tarina must have sent me into began to splinter.

Callum. That was the only peace I'd ever choose.

No sooner had I thought it than something in me pulled tight. There was a heartbeat of stillness, the breeze dying, the fracturing of the world halting. Then I was wrenched forward, the world flying by. Green shifted to yellow, so bright it made me wish for darkness. The colour consumed me, grasping at my limbs and begging me to submit. Before it could succeed, there was a different pull. A different colour. Silver and shadows, entwined so tightly that only a complete severing could untangle them.

The Divine

The colours curled around me, cradling me in their hold. Shadows played upon my skin. I smiled. I knew these shadows. Knew that, wherever they led, I wanted to go. It was easy to allow them to take me. To guide me through spinning worlds crafted by Tarina's trickery.

They pulled me straight into chaos.

Screams slammed into me. Some, mortal. Others, not. Smoke and blood filled my nose, the stench chokingly thick. I staggered to my feet, my gown tangling around my legs. A dark blur lunged towards my side. Wheeling around, I swung a fist. It sailed through gold-corrupted flesh, the Ankuran flying past me without so much as a blink.

Heart hammering, I stared down at myself. I could make out the gown and the wards on my wrists. The bruises were faded but there, darkening spots of my skin. Even the faint stench of damp and mould clung to me. But there was something off. A haze to the edge of my body. The faintest impression of the rocky ground through my outstretched arm.

Another of Tarina's tricks, I guessed, lowering my arm as I stared at the anarchy I'd landed in.

Mortals and Ankurans clashed, swords ripping through chests and gold-cracked teeth through throats. The fountain in the middle spurted water tainted by red and gold. An Ankuran fell back into it as a sword was thrust through his chest, water spattering stone.

A mortal man stumbled to my left as three Ankurans lunged at him at once. His sword wavered, terror turning him pale. Even so, he managed to slash the throat of the first Ankuran. The next ducked his blow, turning into him and wrapping its hand around his throat.

The man choked, sword clattering to the ground. He clawed at the creature. It smiled, gold flaring in its eyes as it squeezed. Blood sprayed through the air. The third Ankuran launched itself at the man's legs as his eyes dulled. More joined, their gold-cracked fingers tearing into flesh.

I turned away before I could see the first piece of flesh pass an Ankuran's lips. Everywhere I looked, however, was a new gruesome scene. Fatiguing mortals attempting to beat back the Ankurans. The fallen torn into bloody shreds. Ankurans with bloodstained lips grinning with a god's delight.

Another Ankuran neared me. I swung at it. Again, my hand travelled straight through. Horror was a noose around my neck, choking me. This might only be an Illusion, but I could smell the blood. Hear the screams. See the dying before me. It all seemed so painfully real.

And there was nothing I could do to stop it.

A woman fell in front of me, armour clinking as she slammed into the ground. Her sword clattered away, stopping at my feet.

'Damned creatures don't stop,' she spat. An Ankuran man fell upon her. She kicked upwards, sending him reeling back as she staggered to her feet. Short brown hair clung to her skin, soaked through with sweat and blood. She was young. Nineteen, perhaps. Young, and familiar.

'Kailey?' I said, taking a step forward. The palace guard twisted herself away from the blow of an Ankuran before wrapping her arm around its neck. With a savage twist, she snapped the creature's neck and let it drop to the floor.

She'd become far more ruthless in the month since I'd seen her.

'Kailey! Sword!' another familiar voice cried, a freckled hand reaching through my body to snatch up the sword on the floor and toss it to her. Another palace guard, Corin, stepped through me, thrusting his own gold-stained sword through the chest of an Ankuran. His chest heaved with exertion as he stared down their foes.

'There's too many,' Kailey said as she backed away from an

The Divine

Ankuran who was so far gone that its flesh was peeling off in golden flecks. 'This is far more than what we faced at Derium.'

'We're in Archin now.' Steel rang as Corin parried a blow from a mortal donning golden armour. The man snarled, thrusting at a gap in Corin's armour, who met the blow with impressive ease before returning it with far more success. The man died quietly. 'Closer to the enemy. Makes—'

'Down!' Kailey cried, turning and throwing herself at Corin. She slammed into his side, taking them both down as a mountainous Ankuran swung an axe through the space where Corin's head had been moments before. Kailey rolled off Corin. The Ankuran grinned down at them. He raised the axe, Kailey lifting a sword that would do little but crumple once the axe hit it.

I lurched forward, already cursing the futility of it. This Illusion no longer seemed like one. Not when there were faces I knew in it. Faces I'd fail to save. My hand sailed through the axe, then through the Ankuran. He briefly halted, a shudder running through his decaying body. The gold in his eyes pulsed before his hands tightened on the axe.

I threw myself in front of Kailey and Corin, willing my body into tangibility. Nothing.

The man shifted, his muscles rippling as the axe began its arc. Before it could complete its fall, a blade punched through his chest. Kailey inhaled sharply behind me, rot-scented blood splattering. The Ankuran blinked, the gold pulsing three times before it vanished.

The sword tore free. The Ankuran collapsed at my feet. I exhaled. Illusion or not, Kailey and Corin were alive. I looked to their saviour. Saw his golden hair first, matted with red and gold blood. His proud stance, the ease with which he swung the sword through another Ankuran who dared to lunge at his exposed side. The scar that curled across one side of his lips. All familiar. All *mine*.

My heart stopped. Stopped, started, then sped up as the sounds and stench of battle faded into hazy background. It didn't matter that this might all be Tarina's conjuring. All that mattered was *him*.

I stumbled a step forward as Callum turned his emerald eyes on the two on the ground behind me.

'Pick up your sword,' he said, his blood-speckled smile as brilliantly wicked as I'd remembered. 'We have some more killing to do.'

Chapter Four

Kailey and Corin scrambled to their feet, snapping to attention. Callum turned, surveying the mess of bodies around them. Ankurans blocked most of the streets that twisted away from the square, the buildings stretching their shadows across the fallen. There were no signs of civilians. No signs of other life, either; birds had long since flown from the town.

Three Ankurans raced for Callum, teeth bared and a hatred in their eyes that belonged to their puppet master. They fell to his blade. My body warmed at the sight. He'd always been beautiful, but with a blade, he turned into something far more divine than any god could be.

Gods, I'd missed him. The thought sent a pang of hurt through my chest. This was perhaps the cruellest component of the Illusion. Seeing Callum, knowing I couldn't speak to or touch him. That, if something were to happen, I'd be forced simply to watch.

A fourth approached from one side. Callum didn't bother turning. A knife sailed through the air, slamming into the base of the Ankuran's neck. It fell soundlessly, gold pooling beneath Callum's boots.

It shouldn't have been possible for anyone to saunter through a battlefield, yet the yellow-eyed man who approached did just that as he yanked the knife free of the Ankuran, his nose wrinkling. 'You could've killed that one yourself, Cal.'

Callum didn't glance in Jaxon's direction. 'You seemed bored. I thought I'd give you something to do.'

'I'd rather be bored than covered in filth,' Jaxon muttered, even as he spun and sliced the knife across the throat of a golden-eyed woman. She choked on her blood as she fell.

'Any signs?' Callum asked.

Jaxon shook his head, shoving his knife away and withdrawing a curved sword. Kailey and Corin launched back into the fray, the Ankurans beginning to keep a wary distance from Callum. 'Nothing.'

Callum fell silent. To any other, he might've seemed calm, his eyes scanning the Ankurans. But I knew him well enough to recognise the blanching of his knuckles and the tightness at his jaw. He was a few moments away from losing it. 'And Deana?'

'Checking the buildings, just in case, but it seems unlikely.' Jaxon hesitated before saying, 'I hate to say it, but maybe it's time we return to Naruzia. We could regroup, find—'

'No.' Even the Ankurans seemed to pause at the chill in Callum's voice. Shadows lashed across his skin, violently wiping away a cut upon his left cheek. 'We continue on.'

Jaxon sighed, flicking his fingers towards where an Ankuran lunged at an older man with greying hair. Yellow, a paler shade to Tarina's garish power, slammed into the Ankuran. Its eyes filmed over. It spun, launching itself onto the back of another of its kind, fingers tearing through flesh. 'Cal, I don't think—'

'My kingdom is at war,' Callum said coldly. 'My people are too scared to go out onto the streets. Terrified to allow their own children into their houses, in case they turn out to be Ankurans. Brayden is handling rule of the kingdom fine for the time being.'

I wrinkled my nose at the mention of the only survivor of the Archin royal family, Prince Brayden. He had the skills of a decent ruler, but his personality left much to be desired. 'Retreat isn't an option. If we only defend, we will end up crumbling.'

'You can honestly tell me how quickly we've attacked Archin has been about protecting your kingdom?'

A muscle twitched in Callum's jaw. 'We can't rely on defence alone against Vitus.'

'That's not an answer.' Jaxon eyed some nearby Ankurans, who eyed him back. 'You know I'm the first one to volunteer for recklessness. But your people are exhausted. *You're* exhausted.' He gestured at the dark shadows under Callum's eyes. I frowned at the sight of them, wishing I could scold him for not looking after himself. 'When was the last time you slept?'

'You're being uncharacteristically serious.'

Jaxon grinned, a sight that would've looked out of place on most faces amongst all the death. But Jaxon was the same breed as Callum and I – the sort that relished in violence. 'Thank y—'

'It's grating.' Callum scanned the battle again, seeming to pause on each mortal fighting, checking that they weren't in danger of dying. A true ruler in a way I could never imagine myself being. Seeming satisfied, he glanced back to Jaxon, some of his hardness softening. My breath caught at the rawness there. The pain. 'I can't go back to Naruzia without her.'

Jaxon held his stare for several moments before letting out a dramatic sigh, raking bloodied fingers through his dark hair. 'Well, if the king has given a command, then I suppose I should obey.' His grin grew. 'Let's see how many of these bastards we can take down.'

Callum reached for him. 'Wait. We need to—'

But Jaxon was already gone, launching himself at the Ankurans with a vicious delight that sent even the mindless creatures into a state of panic. Callum sighed, adjusted his grip on his sword, and followed.

I drifted after them, longing filling me. I missed this. Missed fighting by Callum's side. Missed admiring the cruel elegance of his blade and the way the Ankurans toppled before him. Missed the beauty of his triumph. Missed him.

My throat tightened, my fingers curling inwards. For a moment, I hated Tarina far more than I did Vitus.

Callum spun, slicing off the head of an Ankuran woman and catching a child by the throat. More Ankurans spilt from the street, strangely silent except for occasional death gurgles. None spoke with Vitus's voice, or called for Callum. These were nothing more than hollow husks, empty of the god that had created them.

More Ankurans spilt from the streets. They attacked most with hunger-driven eagerness, desiring the life the mortals possessed. With Callum and Jaxon, though, they held back. Their attacks were reserved, their movements restrained. They attacked to harm, not to kill. Even in this Illusion, it was like they knew that Callum was a chain that Vitus desperately needed.

'Enough,' I whispered, fingers digging into my palm. My Gift pressed to my skin, uncomfortably strong, a response to my hatred of being forced to stand idly by in this cruel Illusion. My eyes closed, but the sounds of battle raged on, the stench of death suffocatingly thick. And Callum's presence, real or not, burned itself in my mind. Even without looking, I could sense each of his movements. Feel his rage-fuelled triumph as he cut Ankuran after Ankuran down, uncaring that they might be holding back. Feel the longing that matched mine for intensity.

It hurt.

My eyes sprang open. Fury poured through me, more distinct than it had been. It wasn't enough that Vitus had harmed Callum to capture me. Tarina had to remind me of what I'd lost. And in that, she'd used creatures I despised to threaten Callum.

The Divine

I refused to allow anything to harm Callum, real or not.

My Gift surged, beating against my skin. There was a distant smell of something burning, sharpness circling my wrists, but it was far away, and my Gift was as angry as I was. Gold pulsed beneath the Ankurans' skin. Several faltered, falling to mortal blades. The rest regained their focus, seeming to push against their enemies with renewed strength.

I stared at Callum. Etched the image of him – gold-splattered, vicious and utterly breathtaking – into my mind. My Gift pulsed once more, more urgent this time. Pain lanced through my bones, starting at my wrists and surging upwards. It was nothing against the satisfaction of the silver that sparked on my flesh. It began as tiny pinpricks, like little stars scattered over my skin. Those pinpricks grew, then rose, leaping in crackling lines of power to the bloodied stone.

The power was nothing like it had been. Before, where it could form a wall to take down enemies, it created little more than a ripple that flowed under the feet of those who fought, the vast majority of my power used up by keeping Callum's soul bound. But in this Illusion, it was enough.

The silver found the first Ankuran. It wasted no time, leaping from the ground to swallow it whole. Another pulse of pain rang through my wrists. I ignored it. Ignored everything except Callum. He thrust his sword through the chest of a man, twisting out of the way of a spear aimed at his arm. An Ankuran sliced a sword towards his legs.

Kill it, I willed, and my Gift obeyed. Death was always a willing companion.

The sword clattered to the ground as Callum turned. Gold flared brighter in the remaining Ankurans, veins pressing against fragile skin and eyes flooding with the garish hue.

Another fell to my Gift, silvery ash stolen by the wind. A third crumbled, then a fourth. My Gift hummed with satisfaction. This was what it was designed for. What I was designed for.

I'd missed this almost as much as I had Callum.

The mortal soldiers stared as more Ankurans disappeared, falling to my power with gratifying ease. Those closest to Callum disappeared. It was painfully slow, my Gift only managing to end one at a time, but the death was relentless. Some leftover instinct sent three turning, ready to run.

They died next. There would be no escaping. Not in this Illusion, and not once I freed myself from Vitus's control. They belonged to Vitus, and so there was only one ending.

Again and again, I killed, each death sending a new thrum of pleasure through me. Ash mixed with the blood beneath my feet, forming a thick sludge of death. Rot and blood mingled with the scent of jasmine and smoke, the former beginning to diminish until there was no more for my Gift to grasp hold of.

Seeming to purr in contentment, the silver recoiled, flowing directly into me. Pain still burned at my wrists. I smiled at it. At the death that surrounded me. The soldiers stared around, wide-eyed at the absence of enemies. Jaxon stepped back from the mess on the ground, his brow knitted. And Callum stared at where the Ankurans no longer stood, frozen.

'Soon,' I whispered, taking a step towards him. My chest tightened. 'I'll find you soon.' I lifted my hand, readying myself for the pain as my fingers passed through the Illusion.

Only, they didn't. Warm skin met my touch. Callum's head jerked up, his attention swinging around. I blinked as my eyes met his, the green startlingly clear. 'Chiara?'

My heart faltered at the sound of my name on his lips. 'Cal—'

The world wavered around me, grey, red and gold merging into a tangled mess. Callum's eyes widened. His hand lifted, reaching for me as sharp pain dug through my wrists. I reached back. Any thoughts of Illusions were gone, replaced with the intense desire to cling to him. We were matched in our desperation, his fingers brushing my wrist as though he meant to yank me to him.

And then he was gone, the colours around replaced by darkness and dripping. I inhaled sharply, my pulse hammering and the stench of a battle lingering in my nose. My cheek pressed to stone, damp gathering on my skin from where the water dripped next to my eye.

Tarina's Illusion had broken just as I'd begun to fall for it. I pressed my eyes shut, grief and longing choking me. My dress seemed heavier than it had been, as though it'd soaked up all that I was feeling. All the hopelessness I'd supressed over the weeks as Vitus's captive surged.

A sharp pang of pain opened my eyes. I shifted upright, shifting everything to the side as I glanced down. Golden light shone from my wrists, forcing the colouring through the shadows and onto the stone wall. The wards had been activated. Summoned by the Gift I must've called upon while trapped in the Illusion. The pain faded, shifting from a burning to a deep ache.

Colour caught my eye. Frowning, I twisted my arm, inspecting the wards. Most of it was unchanged, an unsightly shackle around my wrist. Most, that is, except for the spot Callum's thumb had brushed in the Illusion. In that spot, the colour was changed. Shifted into something that I couldn't make sense of.

A single thread of silver, cracking through the gold.

Chapter Five

I spent the next two nights in isolated peace, the passing of time marked only by the burnout of candles. The light would flicker then disappear, leaving me shrouded in shadows, before an Ankuran would rush by with a replacement. I suspected Vitus feared leaving Dearil in darkness, even bound in chains as he was.

As the candles were changed for the third time, I rose to my feet, stretching out the numerous knots that'd collected in my body. I'd torn the golden gown the night the thread of silver appeared, the skirts strangely smelling of blood and smoke. The material sat in a crushed heap to one side. It reeked, but bearing the smell was worth using it as a makeshift pillow.

'Vitus,' I said, throat dry from disuse. The sparse amount of food and water that had been thrown in the night before did little to ease the pang of thirst. 'How do I kill him?'

Shifting sounded. 'You know the answer to that.'

I frowned. 'Kerta and Evania said it can be done with a weapon capable of killing a god, or if the balance between powers is shifted.'

'That is correct.' Dearil sounded worn out, his voice raspier

The Divine

than my own. He'd been trapped by Vitus for significantly longer than I had.

I'd been hoping for a better answer. 'If you were free from the chains, you could deal with him.'

'I cannot.'

Frustration swelled. I stalked to the cell bars, wrapping my hands around their icy surface. 'You will not, you mean.'

'No, child.' Weariness laced the breath he released. It was a surprisingly mortal sound. 'I cannot.'

My hands tightened, then released. Dearil was many things – aloof. A lover of giving cryptic, useless advice. But I'd never known him to be a liar. Turning, I sunk into a crouch, resting my back to the bars. 'Is the effect of the chains permanent?'

'No.'

The wards burned as my Gift sparked, reflecting my irritation. 'Explain.'

'The balance has shifted. It must rectify.'

The burning increased, pinpricks of pain shooting up my arms. The silver thread glowed brightly, my Gift beating uselessly against its restraints. Gritting my teeth, I shoved my Gift down. Damned gods and their balance. 'Then shouldn't you and Vitus have the same level of power? If he's distracted, yours should overpower—'

'I do not have the same power as him. Not anymore.'

Dragging a hand through my hair, I gritted out, 'That makes no sense. You've told me plenty of times that the realms need balance between opposing forces. Life and Death to cancel each other out, all that nonsense. But now you're saying that balance doesn't exist?'

'The balance is righting itself.'

'Gods, it's like speaking to an echo,' I muttered. 'Fine. Then the god-killer is the only way to end him.'

'He keeps the knife with him. You will not get to it as you are.'

I glanced down at the wards. Dearil was, unfortunately, right. I hadn't managed against Vitus with my full power, and now my Gift was restrained. Not only that, but I'd been stuck in a cramped cell for the better part of a month. My body wasn't as strong as I'd like it.

'How do I break through wards?' I ran my fingers across one of them, the gold shuddering under my touch. The silver thread seemed to brighten, as though rising to meet me.

'A mortal need merely cut through them or burn them free.'

I smiled grimly, steeling myself as I dug my nail into the delicate skin of the underside of my wrist. The marks were deep, so I'd have to make sure to gouge even deeper. This wasn't the first time I'd asked Dearil of the wards, but it was the first time he'd given me a straight answer.

'But you are not mortal, daughter.'

My smile faded. Of course it wasn't that easy. 'I'm not a god, either.'

'You possess divine blood. The wards come from the ancient language of the realms and are built of a similar entity to a god's power. They cannot disrupt the balance. They are not enough to bind a god's power, but they do merge with the force of it. The markings run far deeper than flesh. Cutting through them will do nothing. Precise marks must be carved to counteract them, and they must be done with a blade that is more powerful than the god that cast them. Either that, or you must be more powerful than Vitus yourself.'

I frowned. 'So, I can't use my Gift because I'm half mortal, and I can't remove the wards because I'm half god?'

Dearil didn't answer. I cursed, slamming my fist into one of the cell bars. It rattled with the ferocity of my anger. My Gift crackled in my veins, begging me to shove it against the wards until my body failed.

'You must be patient. Bide your time and find the right opportunity. Do not rush into plans that will fail.'

'I don't have time,' I bit out, glaring at the opposite end of my cell.

'You carry divinity. You have thousands of years.'

My fingers curled into fists. 'I don't care what I have! *Callum* doesn't have that time.'

'It is a hard thing, to love one whose mortality is their greatest enemy.'

I laughed, the sound cracking. In the midst of my swirling Gift, an invisible line seemed to pull taut with my grief. I tried to grasp onto it, just as I'd nearly done every day since I'd realised that shutting Callum out of my pain was no longer my choice, but Vitus's. If I did, I might've been able to speak to Callum through the bond that connected us across the realm.

But the wards stopped me, forming a wall where the bond should be.

Swallowing the pain and allowing anger to take its place, I twisted in the direction of Dearil's cell. 'What do you know about love?'

'Too much,' Deril said. 'All the gods do.'

Bitterness choked me. 'Lies.'

'I do not lie, child, even if you wish I did. Love is the most dangerous existence for a god. We fear it like we fear nothing else. Yet we cannot escape it, no more than you can.'

I inhaled, closing my eyes and resting my head on the cell bars. He wasn't wrong. I'd fought against how I felt for Callum from the moment I first met him. And, in the end, I hadn't been able to flee anything. It was that which had led me here. Yet I didn't regret it. Didn't regret him.

'Why do you fear it?' I asked, still not fully believing Dearil.

'Because the divine are meant to be fixed points of time. Beings who are meant to stagnate while the realms progress. Entities that will one day become irrelevant, who will be replaced, just as we replaced the ancients who preceded us millennia ago.'

I shuddered at the thought of the years they'd lived. Of enduring year after year. Watching mortals die and the realm blossom and wither in cycles. And then I thought of an aeon with Callum. Of being by his side through it all.

If that were a possibility, it wouldn't be so terrible.

Dearil continued. 'Love and hate are perhaps the only two things in existence that can change a god. For some, it shifts us towards a sentimentality that we should not possess.' I thought of Evania, goddess of peace, whose haughty aloofness softened when she was with her soul-bonded. 'For others, it corrupts.'

'Like Vitus,' I guessed.

'Correct.'

'And which are you?' I asked. 'What has love done to you?'

'Once, it created my blindness and led to my fall from the throne of the gods.' I nodded. I knew the basics – how Vitus had plotted with the other gods and goddesses to entrap Dearil within the godly realm when he had slipped through a crack in the barrier between the realms. He'd spent years confined before being dragged to the mortal realm, only to find himself as a captive here. 'And it will lead to far worse in the future.'

I scoffed. 'I thought Kyrah was the one responsible for divination.'

'I do not need eyes in the future to understand what it may bring.'

'It sounds like it's a convenient excuse for gods to do whatever they wish,' I muttered, rubbing my hands over my arms as the chill of the air wormed its way deeper.

'Perhaps.'

'Not *perhaps*.' I looked as far as I could down the corridor and saw nothing but the candlelight flickering over stone. 'Look at what Vitus is doing, all because a few mortals killed his soul-bonded centuries ago. That can't be anything more than an excuse to grasp for power.'

Dearil sighed. I frowned, irritated at the sound of it. He had no right to pretend any sort of paternal disappointment in me. 'What would you do, child, if Vitus was to kill your soul-bonded?'

I froze. The words fell far harder than any blow Vitus had given me. An image flashed through my mind. Callum, eyes open and staring at nothing. Dead from a wound inflicted upon him by Liam at Vitus's orders. His soul, desperate to escape my grasp so I could save my power and get to safety.

My Gift rumbled where it was caged.

'Callum will not die.' My voice did not sound like my own. It was fury and hatred, ruination and violence. It was a promise and threat knotted together. The very air seemed to shiver at the sound of it.

Dearil did not acknowledge my words. 'Would you be content to leave this realm unharmed if they were the ones to end him?'

My fury faltered.

I'd never try to destroy the realm as it was now. This was Callum's realm. His kingdom, and his people. To harm it was to harm him. But if Naruzia turned on him? Without Callum here, Naruzia would not be my kingdom. This realm would not be mine to protect. And I knew just how capable I was of destruction.

'I'm not Vitus,' I said quietly, uncertain even to my own ears.

'Perhaps not yet.'

I almost laughed as a surprising hurt twisted inside. I'd never thought of Dearil as family, but that he thought I was capable of becoming Vitus struck hard.

Footsteps sounded, and I rose to my feet, damp clinging to the back of my legs. 'Don't worry. Even if I end up like him, my power's nothing compared to that of the gods. I'm sure I'd be long gone before I could ever do anything to destroy this realm.'

'Child, that is not—'

'What will it be this time?' I cut in as I swung around, smiling at the Ankuran woman who'd stopped in front of my cell. The creature stared back, unblinking. 'A beating? Vitus testing his power on me?'

'Vitus wishes for your presence,' the Ankuran rasped, as four more stepped up beside her, each bearing clubs in case I misbehaved. A fifth hoisted up chains.

'Fantastic,' I said brightly, holding my arms out with an obedience that would've put any properly sentient creature on edge. The Ankurans didn't possess the instincts to be nervous, though. 'I've been finding the company down here rather dreary. We should—'

'Dearil is to come,' the woman intoned. A sixth Ankuran walked by, no weaponry in sight. It seemed Dearil was more placid than I.

I frowned. Vitus's ploys had been predictable so far – force me to a meal with him. Try threats and bribery to coerce my cooperation, even when I pointed out that Dearil wouldn't listen to me. The meal ending abruptly when I did something Dearil would later condemn as being reckless, with a lecture on how I should be careful of Vitus's wrath.

'Why?'

'Vitus has commanded it.'

I sighed, stepping back as the door swung open. 'Yes, but *why*?'

'Because he has.'

Lifting my eyes towards the ceiling, I allowed the Ankuran to snap the chains over my wrists. Their cold weight cut into my skin. 'How informative.'

There was a pause, and then a different voice spoke from the mouth of the Ankuran woman. A voice of ancient malice, of festering resentment.

'Because, little raven, my patience has run thin. Dearil will lower the barrier tonight, or you will die.'

Chapter Six

The dining hall had grown even more golden since the last time I'd been in it. Where the pillars and ceiling had before been fractured by strands of gold, they were now consumed by it. The wooden table was burnished, curling patterns of light that matched the walls carving through it. Even the city outside the window was painted in a garish glow as the sun dipped in the sky.

The Ankurans didn't bother chaining me to the chair this time, only leaving my wrists bound. The chain between the manacles was short, preventing free movement but doing little to restrain me.

In a room with two gods, I was simply the flea that might become a nuisance. Nothing more.

I sat, tense and ready, as Dearil took the seat between me and where Vitus usually sat. Dark chains were wrapped around his body, manacles attached to his wrist. They seemed to hold him like a python, squeezing his body tight while leaving him barely enough room to move his arms, his legs unbound so the Ankurans didn't have to do more than shove or prod him to get him moving.

Unlike my own chains, their purpose wasn't to steal movement. It was to steal his power.

The hair at the back of my neck stood up, the chains' wrongness radiating through the room. Dearil sat straight-backed as though we truly were at a polite evening meal. His chains gave him enough leeway to fold his hands upon his lap.

Dearil will lower the barrier tonight, or you will die.

The words sent ice raking down my spine. If Vitus killed me, it wouldn't just be me that would die. Callum would, too. I needed to find a way to survive the night, no matter the cost.

'Calm yourself,' Dearil said as I glared at the empty chair across from me. 'Your anger will not serve you tonight.'

My glare swung over to the god. The silver of his eyes glowed as he met my glower. 'Maybe if you'd been a little angrier earlier on, Vitus never would've stepped foot in the mortal realm.'

'I have been angry,' he said, maintaining his perfect composure. 'Many times.'

I let out a harsh laugh. 'When?'

'I've felt the betrayal of the gods, just as you have felt betrayal.'

'Anger is useless if you don't do something with it. And you did nothing but remain quietly in your cell, letting Vitus do as he pleased. You could've acted, even if you were confined in the godly realm. Instead, you waited, and now we're here.'

Dearil tilted his head. His hair had grown longer, the black waves tangled where they almost reached his shoulders. Mine likely looked the same, if a little longer. 'Is that what you believe?'

I looked away, finding I couldn't bear to find the similarities between us anymore. There were plenty of them. It was a mockery of how different we were. Dearil was composed serenity. I was wild wrath. 'It's the truth.'

'I have done a great many things I should not have because of my anger.' Dearil stared down at his clasped hands. 'Centuries ago, I destroyed a city for desecrating the names of the gods.'

The Divine

A shudder ran through me as I whipped back to Dearil. 'You ... what?'

He lifted his gaze to mine. 'I was newly created. Young, and fresh to the power granted to me as king of gods. I have learnt since that there are things I must not meddle in.'

My mouth dried. Destroying a city was something I'd expected of Vitus, but Dearil? I'd always assumed killing was beneath him, despite his title as god of death.

But perhaps we weren't as different as I'd thought.

Shaking away the horror, I eyed the Ankurans around us before saying softly, 'I'm not you. And I plan to use this anger however I can to get myself free.'

Dearil studied me for a long moment before dipping his chin in acknowledgement. The Ankurans stood rigidly around, not making a sound. 'I understand.' He looked towards the doors, a line appearing between his brows. 'I sense the time nears for me to leave.'

I shifted, the topic change taking me by surprise. 'What?'

He turned back to me, leaning close and lowering his voice. 'Remember, Chiara. You are my child, but you are as much your mother's.'

Shock ran through me. Dearil so rarely used my name. It was always *child* or, on rare occasions, *daughter*, as though the words were a barrier he'd built between us. To hear it now alongside a mention of my mother – a mortal woman I'd never known and had no care to know – was jarring. 'What do you mean? And why are you leaving?' I narrowed my eyes. 'Have you been pretending to be captured for the damned balance again? Because I swear to the gods, if you were, I will personally see to it that your—'

'I cannot defeat him as I am, and you cannot defeat him as you are,' Dearil interrupted, 'But balance must be maintained.'

'You're making no sense!'

His silver eyes intensified. 'You will pay the price for keeping

Callum's soul bound before the end. I am sorry for that, my daughter. I cannot spare you what is to come.'

I grasped his wrist, squeezing tight. 'Explain properly, you cryptic bastard!'

Dearil smiled, and my grip faltered. 'Know that what I have done has not solely been for the balance. I am afraid I could not stop myself from caring for—'

The doors slammed open. Dearil straightened, his chains clinking. His smile vanished, replaced by his earlier calm as he inclined his head towards Vitus. 'Old friend. It is good to see you.'

I stilled as Vitus stepped into the room. There was something different about him. The gold ruination of Kane's body had worsened significantly, strips of flesh peeling away and attempting to replenish itself in a gruesome cycle. Gold light poured out of every fracture in the body as he stormed forward, ignoring the chair laid out for him. The Ankurans shuddered, seeming to sense their master's rage.

This was not the capricious god I'd encountered over the past month, who only showed signs of cracking when I poked him just right. This was a god on brink of wrathful destruction. Something had happened, and it didn't bode well for me and Dearil.

'You,' Vitus snarled, his hand wrapping in the collar of Dearil's shirt as he hauled him from his chair. A knife sat at his waist, the only weapon he carried. It hummed with the same insidious intent as Dearil's chains. Dearil didn't make a sound, not even as Vitus shoved him to the ground. The chains rattled. 'Have you interfered with my plans?'

Dearil rose to his feet, his arms bound at awkward distances to his body. 'I know not of what you speak.'

'Perryth,' Vitus spat. 'The mortals should have died, yet it was my creations that fell. What have you done?'

'I have done nothing,' Dearil said. 'You have bound me here, Vitus. You have made certain my interference could not be felt.'

The Divine

Gold crackled through the air. An Ankuran fell soundlessly to the ground, fissures slicing neatly through her limbs as Vitus's power grew too great. I clenched my teeth, my bones aching with the brush of Vitus's power against my skin. 'Explain why it was your power I sensed there through the Ankuran I sent to investigate.'

Dearil frowned. 'I do not understand.'

'Two days ago!' Vitus roared, spittle flying in the air.

Shock jolted through me. I glanced down, staring at the thread of silver in one of the wards. A thread that'd appeared after a very realistic Illusion. One from which I'd emerged with startling amounts of pain, carrying the stench of smoke and blood. And in that Illusion, I'd destroyed Ankurans with a power that might very well mirror the essence of my father's.

An Illusion that might not have been an Illusion at all.

The soul-bond. I'd seen silver twisted with shadows. The very same tether that had once dragged me from the Gates and to the godly realm. Had I been drawn free from the Illusion by it? Seen everything by my connection to it? I stared at the wards. If it had been my soul there instead of my physical body, perhaps the wards hadn't been as effective.

The explanation didn't sit quite right, but I didn't focus on it. It would've been impossible to, because of the wrench in my chest as I realised the truth.

Callum had been in front of me. Truly in front of me, and I'd squandered my chance to speak to him.

'I did nothing,' Dearil repeated, maintaining his calm.

Vitus's hand cracked across Dearil's cheek, the ring on his finger slicing into flesh. Silver-threaded blood flowed.

'You lie,' Vitus snarled, raising his hand again. Dearil didn't flinch. 'But I will not stand for your meddling. Not this time.'

A laugh burst out of me. Vitus's hand dropped and Dearil shot a look at me, disbelief in both of their expressions as I quieted.

Vitus had harmed Callum. Captured me. Forced us to be separated. But we still found ways to undermine him.

Straightening, I met Vitus's furious gaze with a saccharine smile. 'Apologies. I was just enjoying the fact that the pathetic mortals you look down on have beaten you yet again.'

Vitus let go of Dearil and tore towards me. I kept my smile as he wrenched me out of my chair. Kept it as he threw me across the ground, my elbow banging painfully against marble. 'Did you know the false king had fooled my spies? That he and Tarina's whelp were not where the mortal woman had claimed?'

I struggled to my feet. An Ankuran reached for me but I twisted, slamming my elbow into his throat. The Ankuran man staggered back, then stepped forward again. 'Call off your dogs, Vitus, or you'll be losing more Ankurans tonight.'

Vitus whitened with fury. 'You dare order—'

The Ankuran brushed his fingers over my shoulder. It was as far as he got before I turned, grasping the sides of his head in my hands and shoving his face into the knee I jerked upwards. Molten blood spattered, but I wasn't done. Spinning, I slung the short chains between the two manacles over his head and dropped myself to the floor, forcing my knee into his back. He fell with me.

The crack of his neck echoed gloriously.

'I warned you,' I said as I shoved his body away before rising to my feet. 'What will it be? I've been rather bored, so if you're keen to diminish your supply of bodies...' I trailed off, raising my brows in silent challenge.

Vitus's lips pressed into a thin line. His fingers flexed at his side before he lifted a hand, halting the Ankurans who'd begun to shuffle towards me. Some semblance of composure emerged. 'Sit. We will discuss what has happened, and then we will discuss the lowering of the barrier.'

Dearil complied. I hesitated before doing the same.

The Divine

Attacking now was foolhardy. I would sit and listen. Bide my time and wait for my moment to strike.

Calmer now, Vitus turned to one of the Ankurans. 'Fetch the mortal woman who fed me the false information. She will have to pay for her negligence.'

The Ankuran bowed stiffly before ambling towards the doors.

Disgust slid through me. It had only been three days since our last encounter, yet he'd already forgotten how it had ended. 'She's dead.'

Vitus tilted his head, his fingers steepling before him. 'I had forgotten.' He looked at the Ankuran again. 'Find another mortal. One of those we have been keeping fresh.'

The Ankuran disappeared. I stared after it, the gold on the wall rippling with its exit.

'Your false king is a fool if he believes he can defeat me.'

I tore my attention away from the wall, looking at Vitus. 'Callum isn't the false one.'

Vitus laughed. 'Mortals believe themselves capable of ruling, yet they have bowed at the feet of any greater being for millennia, kings or not. They are inferior. Fit for propping up the feet of divinity and little else.' He flicked his eyes over me. 'Why, even you would be better suited to ruling than that boy.'

I stiffened. There was nothing in me suited to ruling. The only loyalty I'd ever shown was to those I loved. For them, I would burn kingdoms. But Callum was different. He could've taken the throne and led the kingdom further into tyranny than his father had. Instead, he'd searched for a way to protect his kingdom while I'd only been looking for vengeance for my sister.

My hands fisted. 'There is no being in existence more worthy of the throne than Callum.'

Vitus narrowed his eyes. 'Your king will die the moment I am done with you. And I am very close to being done.'

My heart thudded, but I smiled. 'What, no more attempts to

bring me over to your side?' I gestured towards Dearil, who was watching me with an unreadable expression. 'You even brought my dear father to join us. Wouldn't now be the perfect time for me to convince him to lower the barrier?'

'He will lower the barrier tonight,' Vitus said, tension threading through his voice. 'Or he will watch his daughter die.'

I considered him. The urgency was strange. Dearil seemed to think Vitus would be content to wait as long as needed to get his revenge, yet there was a new urgency to Vitus that hadn't been there before. It couldn't just have been the destruction of the Ankurans in Perryth. Ankurans were replaceable.

I studied him. Understanding dawned as another strip of flesh peeled away, floating to the ground before disintegrating. 'Your mortal host is about to crumble, isn't it?'

Vitus's jaw tightened.

I laughed. 'It *is*. Your time's running out, and once Kane's body can't hold you, you'll be forced to go back to the godly realm.'

'*Silence*,' Vitus snapped, the word ringing through the room. The golden walls shuddered. 'I have come to the realisation that I have been treating you as a reasonable creature, rather than the feral animal you are. Animals cannot be reasoned with. I am not bargaining with you.'

'Careful, Vitus,' I said, leaning forward and grinning. 'Feral beasts have a tendency to bite.'

Before he could snarl something back at me, the door behind him opened, the Ankuran from before dragging in a bound woman. She shook violently, her chest rising and falling in gasps as she was shoved to the floor by Vitus's chair. Vitus smiled, twisting to grasp a handful of the woman's hair. She cried out, eyes screwing shut as he dragged her closer.

I tensed. 'What are you doing?'

'A mortal has defied me, and so a mortal must pay.'

The woman whimpered. Bruises ringed her neck and ran along

her bare arms, some faded and others fresher. 'She had nothing to do with the information reported.'

'All mortals are the same.'

'You could've used your Ankurans to gather information.' My fists pushed into my knees.

'A waste of power.'

A useful piece of information I tucked away for later. Vitus had controlled his Ankurans before. I was fairly certain he'd wipe all mortals from this realm and only use his creatures if it were possible. It was likely he'd raised too many Ankurans, and his power was spread too thin to waste.

'What purpose does killing her serve?' I asked.

'Purpose? Gods have no need of such things.' Vitus rested his hand atop her head, the woman cowering beneath. Even from where I was sitting, I could smell the filth on her.

'Gods must have reason behind all they do, Vitus.' Dearil spoke to the god, but he didn't look away from me. 'Otherwise it will—'

'Upset the balance,' Vitus sneered. 'So you have said, countless times before.'

'I speak only the truth.'

'Fine.' Vitus glanced between Dearil and I before rising from his chair and coming to stand behind the woman. Tears rolled down her cheeks as he smoothed a hand down the side of her head.

Her eyes swung around desperately. She flinched as she spied the Ankurans and paled at the sight of Dearil. Her gaze landed on me last, and it stuck. Our eyes met. Hers were brown and muddied with terror. I didn't want to know what she saw in mine. Whether the silver marked me as the same as the divine beings around her – something to be revered or feared, but never seen as equal.

There must've been some trace of mortality in my face, though, because she lifted her bound hands towards me. 'H-help,' she whispered, leaning forward as though she might crawl towards me. 'Please. I-I don't want to—'

I flinched at the crack of her neck. It was a sound I'd heard so many times before. But with her eyes locked on mine, and her hands lifted towards me, it seemed sharper. As though it were an accusation directed solely at me.

Vitus let go of her, and she collapsed to the ground. Warmth gathered in my body at her death. He raised his hand, golden light streaming down to envelop her as he smiled. 'I needed to replace the Ankuran who was so cruelly killed this evening.' He held my glower for a heartbeat before turning to Dearil. 'Is that reason enough for you?'

I trembled with rage as Dearil sighed but nodded. That death – it hadn't even been about me. Not really. Every piece of this – everything I'd endured – was because of *them*. Because Vitus despised Dearil. That woman's life meant nothing but an indirect taunt at my father. My life was the same.

The warmth in my body shuddered. This was what mortals were to gods. Inconsequential pieces to be toyed with and discarded. I forced myself to watch as the woman rose unsteadily to her feet, her head swinging back into place and golden specks appearing in her eyes. I forced myself to memorise her features, placing them alongside the souls I'd encountered at the Gates.

I could not let her become inconsequential to me.

'Kneel,' Vitus instructed, focus still on Dearil. The newly born Ankuran did so, her expression slack as tears dried upon her cheeks. He rested his hand atop her head. This time, she didn't tremble. 'Tell me, *old friend*, will you lower the barrier, or will your daughter be the next to die?'

With Vitus's focus solely on Dearil, I glanced around the table in front of me. No knives or forks again. No plates, either. Nothing but the gold-burnished wood.

'I will not lower the barrier.'

'Then you will let your daughter die?'

Tipping my head back, I surveyed the chandelier that dripped its gold and crystals in a show of wealth. The candles were too high to reach, and the flames they held too pitiful. There was nothing that held enough of an edge.

'I will not lower the barrier.'

A heavy sigh, laden with disappointment. 'I see.'

Footsteps sounded, the overpowering scent of roses washing over me. Choking on the smell, I straightened, glaring defiantly at where Vitus loomed over me. He looked to Dearil as he slammed the back of his hand into my cheek. Sharp pain lanced. I swallowed my cry, letting blood coat my tongue from the newly opened cut on the inside of my cheek. I righted myself, spitting a mouthful of blood at Vitus's feet.

He still did not look at me.

'I will beat her until she dies.'

Dearil did not look at me, either. 'I will not do it.'

Another blow, this one into my gut. My back slammed into the chair. It rocked back, caught and righted by Vitus as I gasped for breath. Desiccated body or not, the god could pack a punch.

'I will take her apart piece by piece, and make you watch.'

'I will not do it.'

The third blow caught me under the chin. My teeth clicked together, and I barely muffled the cry of pain. More blood coated my tongue.

'I will—'

'*Gods*, Vitus,' I said before twisting to spit a mouthful of blood on the ground. When I turned back to him, smiling a bloodied grin, his nose wrinkled. 'You've tried this all before. That desperate that you're going to try again?'

His hand clenched as he raised it again. His golden eyes finally met mine. 'Desperation is for mortals.'

I nodded with all the solemnity I could muster. 'I see. So that's why you're throwing every last attempt you have at—'

This time when his fist slammed into my mouth, the blow almost felt good.

Vitus didn't bother to catch the chair as it fell back. I reached for him, fingers fumbling in his clothes. They slid to his side, right near where the insidious knife sat. I latched on there, gritting my teeth as Vitus sighed. He didn't look at me as he grasped a handful of my hair, wrenching my head back. Pain tore through my scalp, but I continued to cling on.

'Stubborn mortal,' Vitus spat, yanking harder. A thread of his power lashed out at me and my back arched with pain.

Breaths shuddered through me. I reached further, fingers digging into the cloth of his tunic. A few strands of hair tore entirely out. *Hold on*, I ordered myself even as the pain of his power ratcheted up. Spots of light appeared in my vision. I stretched my arm out. *Just a little further*.

My fingers brushed the cold ivory of a knife hilt just as Vitus managed to throw me away in an almighty heave. I didn't manage to catch myself before I fell. My shoulder took the brunt of the fall, a sharp pain digging through me. Vitus's shadow fell over me. His face was twisted with wrath, his attention fully on me. Gold spilt through the cracks in his skin, and my Gift shivered at the sight.

Yet, despite the sight of the god's fury, I could feel nothing but deep satisfaction beneath the thrum of my heart.

'I will—'

'Your Majesty,' a timid voice called from the doorway. We all glanced over. A mortal child, skin-kneed and pale-faced, stood quivering, his head bowed and his shoulders curled. 'One-one of the women h-have been—'

'Spit it out.'

The child flinched. His fingers curled into his rags. 'One of the women have been possessed by Tarina. She wants to speak to you.'

Vitus glanced down at me, anger carving lines through his crumbling brow. 'Fine. I shall see what she requires, and then we shall finish this.'

I smiled sweetly up at him, ignoring what felt to be a loose tooth. 'I look forward to it.'

The doors had barely clicked shut before Dearil turned on me. 'I warned you to be careful, child. You should have listened.'

Wincing, I forced myself up on an elbow, my bound wrists twisting awkwardly to one side. An ache ran through my jaw. 'How nice of you to be so concerned about me, Father.' Blood dripped from my nose. I let it splatter onto the torn remains of the gown as I staggered to my feet. Several Ankurans watched me. 'Can't have your only daughter show defiance at her own death, can you?'

'You will not die.'

I raised my brows, turning to Dearil as I swiped the back of my hand across my lips. Red smeared across my skin. 'Oh? And how do you propose to stop that from happening? You won't lower the barrier.'

'I will not.'

A strange mix of relief and disappointment filled me. I had no desire to sentence the realm to the full might of Vitus's depravity, but it would've been nice if Dearil showed even a hint of hesitation. But then, our relationship had never extended far past apathy.

Dropping my hands in front of me, I shrugged. 'There you have it. Vitus wants me dead. He'll try to succeed before the end of the night.'

'You will not die.'

Sighing, I met Dearil's silver gaze. 'You can't have it both ways. The barrier falls, or I die.'

'That is not the only end.'

'Steady. You almost sound like you care.' I shook my hands a few times, moving the manacles as close as to the base of my hands as I could.

'I care.'

'Good try, but you need to learn to fake some emotion before I believe that.' I inspected the wards, frowning. Their gold seemed muted.

'And you? Will you let him kill you? Will that be enough to satisfy your anger?'

I looked up. 'Of course not.' I twisted my wrist, flicking a knife into my hand and angled my body so the Ankurans couldn't see it. Even as I shook from the adrenaline and fear that had swallowed me with every moment that had passed since Vitus had thrown me to the ground, I grinned.

Gods were rarely as clever as they thought they were. It was a dangerous trait when combined with how often they underestimated mortals.

My hand thrummed with the blade's power. A blade that I had managed to rip free of Vitus's scabbard just before he had thrown me to the ground. It had conveniently fallen into my hands as I'd tried to catch myself on Vitus's clothes.

The silver in Dearil's eyes burned bright with recognition of the only blade Vitus would bother keeping on his person. The god-killer. 'I plan to free myself, and then bring Vitus down.'

Chapter Seven

Dearil rocked back, his chains rattling. It was satisfying to see him so shocked. 'How?'

'Not everything needs to rely on divine power.' The knife sparked with patterns of colours – silver and gold, rose and red. Others, too, caught in its swirling depths. A labyrinth of the gods' power, all trapped in a single piece of steel. 'Mortals have their own tricks.'

Dearil rose, moving to my side with a grace I could never have managed. He stared down at the knife, then looked to me. 'It mut be Tarina's boy who taught you to steal.' A faint smile curved his lips. 'I am glad he has found himself less lonely in recent years.'

'You know Jaxon well?'

'Of course. It is he I trusted with delivering you to the mortal realm.'

I frowned, a barrage of questions attempting to launch themselves at Dearil. I held them back. Now was not the time, especially with the way the Ankurans were staring at where Dearil was now standing by me, his back further blocking me from sight. Flipping the knife, I turned my hand so that the underside of my wrist was exposed. The thread of silver seemed to have grown thicker. 'If I cut through the wards with this, can I use my Gift?'

Dearil launched forward, moving swiftly to catch my hand in his. His touch was gentler than I'd expected from the god. 'You must not.'

'I must,' I snapped, trying to pull myself free. His fingers tightened. 'You might be content to wile away your time here, but I have people waiting for me.'

And I refused to die here before I'd had a chance to tell Callum I loved him in person.

'That is not what I mean.' Dearil stared down sternly, his eyes pulsing with silver as I struggled to pull myself away from him. 'That knife is a danger to all that is divine. It is not as simple as cutting your flesh. If you do this wrong, you could damage far more than your skin.'

'I don't care what I damage if—'

'I will do it.'

I stilled. 'Why?'

'I have no wish for you to needlessly hurt yourself, and wards on divine flesh can only be broken by exact markings. Ones that counteract those already there while maintaining balance.'

I hesitated before giving a shallow nod, glancing then at an Ankuran who'd shuffled a step closer. 'Be quick.'

Dearil's expression was grim as he took the knife from me. With anyone else, it would have been an amusing sight, seeing him manoeuvre it with the chains not allowing his hands to move more than a hand or two away from his body, yet he managed to make his movements borderline elegant.

He gently pulled my wrist forward. I shifted, disliking how close he had to stand. 'This shall hurt. You must not make a noise, or Vitus will hear through his Ankurans.'

'Just do it,' I said, bracing myself against the back of my chair as I pressed my lips together.

Dearil was right. It did hurt. I sucked in a breath at the first cut. It was shallow, far shallower than the ones Vitus had made, yet I could've sworn my flesh was being sliced free from my bones. Air hissed between my teeth. Dearil paused, his brows drawing together as he looked up at me. 'I do not think—'

'I said *do it*,' I spat out through gritted teeth.

An observer would've almost thought it was him who was being sliced by the god-killer with the expression on his face. If not for the pain, I would've laughed. He wouldn't bring down the barrier for me, but he pretended fatherly concern at pain.

Of course he does, I thought as my body burned with the next mark, one that curved away from the first in the ancient warding patterns I didn't understand. Gods so rarely felt pain. It must be unpleasant for him to witness.

At the third cut, my Gift recoiled violently inside me. I bit down on my lip until I tasted blood. Foreign energy skittered through me – a power that felt like Vitus's, another made of flames and violence, a third of renewal and growth. More tangled amongst them. They twisted in my veins, seeking to hunt down my Gift, to drive it into submission. One, though, dragged my Gift forward, stirring it into a frenzy. One that was the calm to the wildness of my own. Dearil's power.

All this from tiny slices, the godly powers imbued in the knife rioting with my own. I couldn't wait to see what it did when it drove through Vitus's flesh.

Blood trickled down my wrist, gathering uncomfortably under the manacle. The knife lifted, then pricked a new spot, ready for the fourth marking.

The doors banged open. Dearil pulled away from me, sliding the knife into the tattered waistband of his trousers. I turned my wrist over, steadying my shallow breathing. Blood soaked through my skirts.

'What are you doing over there?' Vitus demanded as he strode into the room before he waved his hand. 'Never mind. Sit back down.'

Dearil briefly met my eyes before heading for his chair. Pinpricks of ice scuttled over my skin. Vitus's rage had all but disappeared, replaced by a vicious gleam of satisfaction in his golden features.

Whatever Tarina had wanted to discuss seemed to have pleased him greatly.

My Gift, weakened from the cuts of the god-killer, curled deeper inside me. The power of the wards was still a restraint, though they felt lesser than they had been. More a blanket rather than an ocean to suffocate me.

And through that blanket, a bond of shadows and silver tugged at me.

'It seems you have learnt some bad habits from the mortals,' Vitus said, smiling as he strode to Dearil's side and leant against the table's edge. My heart thudded as I waited for Vitus to spot the knife hilt sticking up at Dearil's side, but his attention seemed to be solely on watching for a reaction.

Dearil clasped his hands. 'I do not know of what you speak.'

'Your lies.' Vitus leant in, his shadow falling over Dearil's form. When Dearil looked up, the silver of his eyes seemed to lessen under the brilliance of Vitus's golden form. 'About the barrier.'

I almost missed Dearil's stiffening. 'I have not lied.'

'Come, now.' Vitus clapped Dearil on the shoulder. Even I could feel the wave of power rolling off him, digging into my flesh and slicing at my bones. I hated to think what Dearil felt. 'We are old friends, are we not? It is time for the truth. How can the barrier to the godly realm fall?'

The Divine

'Death must die, or I must choose to bring it down.'

'That is what you say. What you have always insisted on.' Vitus leant inwards, and I had to strain to hear. 'Yet Tarina said you used to tell her differently. That, before she turned on you and tricked you into the cell I had prepared, you said it was *your* death that was needed.'

Pain flashed through Dearil's eyes. He twisted his head away from Vitus. 'Tarina lies.'

Vitus laughed as he straightened. 'She is known for her trickery. Why, she has spent years keeping this truth from me. She kept your secret for centuries. Your conversation with her must have gone poorly.'

'You know it did. You were the one who sent her to convince me to lower the barrier.'

'Poor Tarina. She truly thought you would listen. That you would choose her – choose the gods – over the mortals. How hurt she must have been when you chose those filthy creatures over her. Hurt enough to betray you again.' Vitus's expression turned ugly. 'She is a fool. You have always been a traitor to our kind, even when you ruled over us.'

Dearil's shoulders sagged. I maintained my quiet, carefully reaching inside for my Gift. I didn't dare try to draw it out. Not yet. The moment I did, Vitus would sense something was off. One mistake, and I'd lose whatever chance I might have.

'I was a poor king.' My father looked up. 'But you do not have to be. You can rule—'

'I shall rule as I see fit!' Vitus roared, his voice sending reverberations through the chair I sat upon. More gold spindled over his skin. There was barely any mortal-coloured flesh to be seen. 'I will give you one last chance, Dearil. I want you to watch your precious mortals burn. To live centuries in suffering. But I will give you up if it means I avenge Alexia. Bring down the barrier, or you will die.'

Something twisted in my chest. Something that felt an awful lot like fear.

I closed my eyes, inhaling deeply as I gently coaxed my Gift upwards. It was slow to come to me, and the wards were too heavy to grasp at much. But it was there. It was ready.

'You do not answer,' Vitus said as I opened my eyes once more, watching carefully for any chance to attack. He wasn't paying much attention to me, but I could feel the stab of golden Ankuran eyes upon me. I'd have to make sure to deal with them quickly. 'You fooled us well over the centuries, pretending that your death was not the key to our liberation. That the barrier was more complicated than that. Some might believe it your nobility, protecting the mortals from the fall of the barrier by hiding the truth.'

He stared at Dearil, his expression unfathomable. 'Yet I know better. You were afraid. Afraid to die, and afraid that the next to take up Death's summons'—his eyes flicked to me, lips curling upwards—'would not be up to the task of taking your place. I must give you credit for that. You were correct.'

'Vitus,' Dearil warned. His voice was low. Quiet and cold. He sounded almost like me moments before I killed. Deadly fury ready to ignite. 'You do not have to do this.'

Vitus sighed. 'Your refusal to speak the truth wears on me. It is far past time we ended this.'

'This vengeance will not grant you peace,' Dearil warned.

Vitus smiled. 'Perhaps. Perhaps not.' His hand shot forward, fingers curling around Dearil's throat. 'But you will not be here to see it.'

Dearil didn't reach for the god-killer. He sat there, stoic, as Vitus's fingers dug in. Gold crackled over Dearil's skin, his shoulders tightening with what must have been agony.

Come on, I urged him silently, my fingers curling into fists. *Take the god-killer. End him.*

Dearil's eyes flicked to the side. His lips curled upwards into a faint smile. My heart thudded, throat tightening. Why did he do nothing?

I must leave soon, he'd said. A chill crawled through me. Was this what he'd meant? But it made no sense. There was no balance maintained with his death. The barrier would fall, and mortals would die.

I gritted my teeth. *Damn it all*, I thought. He was a pitiful father, but he was perhaps the only being who stood in the way of Vitus's reign of terror. I couldn't sit by and watch.

Cold sweat beaded on the back of my neck. I ignored it, fear shoved aside as I lunged to my feet. I threw myself at the knife at Dearil's side. The Ankurans startled, the closest one too slow to catch me. My fingers stretched, focus entirely on the god-killer.

Gold-streaked fingers curled around it before I could grasp hold. I slammed into Dearil, sending us both crashing down as Vitus strolled a few paces away.

'This is what you were after?' he asked, idly flicking the blade through the air. I jumped to my feet, my Gift beginning to spark at my fingers. The wards burned against my skin and Vitus smiled. 'You thought I would not notice its absence? I sensed the moment you had taken it. Foolish halfling.'

Dearil rose beside me. 'Enough. It is time for you to end this.'

I whirled, eyes wide. 'You can't be serious. You're giving up, just like that?'

Dearil smiled. 'This was always to be the end. I must leave for the balance to be maintained.'

'You make no sense!'

'You will understand one day. Two cannot exist where there should only be one. The realms have held on for long enough. Any longer, and they might begin to splinter.'

I shook my head, hands fisting as I spun back to Vitus. I'd had enough of Dearil and his cryptic words. If he intended to die, so be it. It didn't mean I had to stand by and watch the barrier fall. Didn't have to accept the prison of inheriting Death's will, either. The moment Vitus was distracted by Dearil, I'd attack with the measly power I had grasped hold of. Vitus still didn't seem to sense my Gift poking through the cracks in the wards. I could use that to my advantage.

'I agree, old friend.' Vitus's expression was a twisted grin. 'It is the end.'

Dearil bowed his head. I readied myself, sensing my opportunity was coming. 'Do it.'

Vitus started forward, then stopped. Smiled. 'Ah. No, I changed my mind.'

'You should not. This is the way it must end.'

'No,' Vitus said slowly, his eyes flicking to Dearil. 'This is the way you want it to end. I know your secret now, though, and I have an eternity to wait before ending this realm. But you – you have not yet suffered nearly enough to die. Not when your child stands, perfectly alive and well, while mine are long gone – my Alexia, dead.' His smile grew. 'Yes, this is much more fitting. You will learn what it is to watch your family die, and I will wait until a vessel capable of holding your power emerges. And it will, whether it be tomorrow or in a few centuries. Only then, when you are crushed and your mind fractured, will you be allowed the escape of death.'

Dearil jerked. The chains groaned again, tiny silver cracks glowing across their surfaces. 'Vitus, *do not do this*.'

'I believe I spoke the same to you the day you erected the barrier. You ignored me then. I will ignore you now.'

Dearil stumbled forward a step, the silver spreading as colours flashed over the chains. It was as though the chains were finally remembering what they held – not just any god, but the one who had once ruled over them all. The true king of gods.

Vitus flicked his wrist. Golden light flashed, sent the god-killer sailing through the air. More light crackled, guiding its path with deadly accuracy as the air sang with its violent flight. But it wasn't Dearil it was heading towards. It was me.

I twisted, throwing myself to the side. The blade halted, gold pulsing around it, before spinning and following my path. My heart sped up as I spun, ducking its path. Again, it faltered before shooting for me once more. My hip hit the table as I barely dodged its next slice, my chains nearly looping around the wood. I yanked my wrists closer to me, backing away a step as my skin prickled with icy sweat. Vitus smiled all the while. An Ankuran stepped behind me, holding me in place. Another boxed me in from the other side.

Desperation surged. My Gift crackled, but it did nothing except leak silver onto my fingers. It was too weak. *I* was too weak.

A flea amongst gods, about to be crushed.

No, I thought desperately as the blade hovered almost tauntingly, seeming to prolong my final moments of suffering. There was no escape, though. No avoiding the next cut of it.

I'm sorry, I said silently as I yanked down the walls of the bond between Callum and me. I needed to say what I hadn't in person. Needed him to know before I was unable to keep his soul in the mortal realm any longer. *I love you.*

There was a jolt of shock from the other side of the bond, then a burst of sharp, acrid fear. *Chiara, where—*

I shut the bond down again. He didn't have to feel this final blow. I glared defiantly, kicking back at the Ankuran as the knife shot forward. The Ankuran didn't let go, and all I could do was brace myself as the tip angled for my chest. Brace myself for death and whatever awaited me afterwards.

I closed my eyes. Let myself remember Callum. Deana. Jaxon. Cassie. All those who'd loved me when I'd believed myself undeserving of it. Those who deserved better than what this realm had given them.

Something thudded, a wet, meaty sound that jerked my eyes open. A shadow stood in front of me, chains clanking as they staggered back a step. The Ankurans let go, having no reason to keep me bound. Not when the knife had found a target.

But it was not my chest the blade had sunk into.

Dearil fell to his knees before me, the god-killer embedded in his chest.

Chapter Eight

'No,' I breathed, cold washing over me. My Gift crackled, the realm shuddering its shock alongside me. I dropped to my knees in front of Dearil. Silver-streaked blood coated my hands where I pressed them around the knife. It dripped onto the chain between my manacles, staining it. 'No, why did you—'

Dearil covered my hands with his, ceasing my trembling. He smiled, unconcerned by the blood leaking from the corner of his lips. Unconcerned that he was going to die bound in chains, barely able to even hold my hands as he did. 'My time ... has come.'

I shook my head. 'It hasn't. You're a god. The god of death. You can't just—'

He lifted a bloodied hand. His smile faltered for only a moment as his chains pulled tight, yanking his hand to a stop halfway to my cheek. His eyes were dying stars amidst the golden light of Vitus's power. 'My daughter.' His body spasmed. A choked sound left me as flickers of light – rose, red, yellow, gold and more – coiled around his body and under his skin. The silver flickering on his chains pulsed as he panted, eyes opening once more. 'I did not – want—' Another spasm, this one more violent. Sweat beaded upon his skin. 'To add to your pain.'

I stared at where his blood coated my hands. It was sticky against my skin. Jasmine and smoke filled the air around us. 'I need you alive so I can resent you.' My throat was tight, eyes stinging. Silver crackled over my skin, and I did not know which of us had managed to break the restraints on our power. 'So that I can hate you for not being a father to me. So—'

'You fool,' Vitus interrupted, his hands curling around Dearil's shoulders and wrenching him away from me. I fell backwards as an Ankuran caught my hair, yanking it. Vitus's expression was twisted, rage and hatred filling it. '*She* was meant to die, and you would see the pointlessness of continued defiance. You were meant to live in eternal suffering!'

'Ah.' Dearil coughed as Vitus dragged him to his feet, more blood spattering over them. I wrenched myself free, rising unsteadily to my feet. My heart was caught in a fist, and nothing I did freed it from that pain. 'Old – friend. You ... never did ... understand ... me.'

'Let go of him,' I snarled, blood dripping from my fingers to mar the golden floor.

Vitus's head jerked in my direction. 'You,' he seethed. 'You have overstepped yet again. You have—'

'No,' Dearil rumbled, his hands closing over Vitus's. The chains that held him shook, silver cutting through them. 'Leave ... her.'

Vitus stared at Dearil, then at the chains. His fury heightened. 'You will find a way to live. To experience what I have.' Gold fissures pulsed wildly. 'I will see you corrupted for what you forced onto Alexia. All your morals will crumble, and I will be the one standing tall in the end.'

'I will die regardless,' Dearil said, almost gently. Pain wracked his features, his body caught in its webbing. 'For what ... we once ... were. Let her go.'

For what we once were. Two gods who'd clung to their own ideals over their centuries – Dearil to his balance, and Vitus to his corrupted love and vengeance. Who'd been brothers in every sense but blood.

Dearil was a fool to believe that anything of that still remained in Vitus. That Vitus was anything but hollow, built of bones and blood, who wished to make every god into replicas of himself.

Vitus laughed. I moved.

I slammed into the nearest Ankuran, knocking it into the ground. My chains rattled as I drove its head into the marble three times. Vicious lines of gold splattered. Vitus jerked, swinging towards me.

I didn't let myself feel any sorrow as Dearil faltered, Vitus's hands no longer holding him up. The wards burned, but my Gift burned hotter. It crackled through my veins, rising to my fingers as I aimed myself at Vitus.

They might restrain me, but they could not hold me completely.

'Impossible,' he breathed, and staggered back a step. Not in fear, but shock. 'The wards—'

Something cracked nearby. Vitus and I both swung towards the sound as the ground beneath our feet started to quake. Ankurans toppled like toys shoved by a tantrumy child, their screams filling the air around us. Above, gold wavered in billowing sheets, its power faltering.

The stench of roses battled that of jasmine as Dearil met my eyes. His irises were no longer that of dying stars. They were far brighter. A light that threatened to consume any who dared defy it. There was a second crack, and then another. The wicked chains around him began to writhe as though they were truly alive.

Silver pulsed through them, the fury of the light's movement belying the steadfastness of Dearil's face.

'Do not—' Vitus started, but he was yet again cut off as Dearil's chest rose in a single inhale.

The quaking under our feet stilled. There was an implosion of noise and light, a sudden whirl of silver that stole even the strongest flickers of gold. My breath caught, my body locking up.

Dearil exhaled.

A force slammed into me. The silver exploded outwards, slamming through the room. Dearil said nothing as the silver cut through three Ankurans, turning each of them into silver mist that spread through the room. I lurched forward, sensing my chance as Vitus snarled his fury. I made it a single step before my breath punched out of me, a wall of power surging upwards. Power made not of gold, but of silver – a vertical lake, smoother than any surface I'd encountered. I swung towards Dearil as another link of the chains on him snapped, the metal clanking as it finally fell to the ground.

Vitus screamed, a wordless sound that shattered through the stone above. Rocks and dust fell as I pressed my hands to my ears, pain pouring through me. My lips pressed together as the scream stretched and Dearil straightened, his shoulders squaring and chin lifting.

Even with the knife buried deep, there was no mistaking him with his silver-filled eyes and luminescent skin. Silver shot free of him, slicing through Vitus's scream as though the sound had been something tangible to cut down. This was what divinity was meant to be, I realised. Unbreakable.

'You!' Vitus snarled even as he stumbled back a step, the gold at his hand throbbing as though in pain. 'You should not be capable of this! You—'

Dearil did not even glance his way, instead he was focused

entirely on me. His momentary strength was faltering, blood still dripping from his wound. Yet that power persisted. 'Now is not the time for his death.'

Any sense of fear or awe crumbled under his words. I pressed my hand to the wall, pushing with all my strength. It hummed against my skin. This was nothing like Vitus's power, that forced everything in its path to submit. It was breathtaking. As unwavering as Dearil himself was.

And it was in my way.

'What are you doing?' I bit out, slamming my fist into the wall. It held firm, not even a ripple staining its surface. Silver misted around me, prickling my skin and tangling in my hair. I ignored it.

Dearil dropped to a knee, his hand pressing to the god-killer. His skin shone with the same brightness of his power, even as he paled further. 'You ... cannot. Not ... yet.'

'Damn you,' I snarled, beating my fist into the wall again and again, until my hands ached with pain. The silver only flared brighter. It was a pool of starlight, far more powerful than anything I'd ever conjured. The sort of power that the realm itself seemed to feel, the air growing heavy with its density.

Under its calm, though, there was a hint of something else. A writhing in the air around me, a prodding at my own Gift. It was as though whatever restraints Dearil had slipped over that power, it yanked against, a wildness to it that threatened to break his hold.

Terrifying, I thought, even as I continued to batter against it. The power could remake realms. Destroy them, too, if it chose to rain death down. This was what Dearil was, under his calm façade and the chains that had bound him. Perhaps the only being in existence who could contain such horrifying power.

'I cannot ... hold out ... for long.' Dearil coughed again. 'The barrier will ... fall. My power seeks ... a new ... vessel. It is ...

why I ... could break ... the chains. They cannot hold ... that which has no vessel.'

This time when I slammed my fist against the wall of silver, I could've sworn it splintered. 'He needs to die. You have—'

'You ... are not ... ready.' The brightness of Dearil's eyes flickered, but the wall remained.

'Dearil,' Vitus warned, straightening as Dearil lifted his other hand, now able to extend it fully with the chains gone. 'She will die. What you do is pointless. My vengeance will be—'

Silver crashed into Vitus, flooding from Dearil. There was no trace of roses and rot anymore. Only smoke and jasmine and death.

My earlier thoughts circled in my mind. Beautiful. Terrible. And utterly overwhelming.

The wall in front of me wavered. Light flared, stinging my eyes and consuming the Ankurans around us as Vitus went flying, slamming into the wall opposite. The building shook around us. Dust fell and the windows shattered, glass shards flying into the night beyond.

Now, I thought as the silver barrier flickered. I raced through. I could get the god-killer, drive it through Vitus and—

Silver wrapped around me, tighter than any chains. My body froze, muscles straining. Fury pounded against my skin, the wards glowing their garish colour as my Gift fought to free itself.

'Let me kill him.' I glowered at Dearil. 'Stop protecting him.'

'I protect ... you.' His body trembled as his hands fisted. Silver pooled beneath my feet. The world wavered around me, and panic struck at my core. 'Picture your ... home.'

'Don't you dare,' I seethed, my fingers twitching where they were held. My arm shifted downwards. He was going to do what I had with Callum. He was going to send me away.

But I could feel death gathering in my bones, warming my body. Knew that, if he sent me away, I would lose the only being that shared my blood. A man who might not have been a father but had meant more than I'd realised to me. Might also lose the only chance I'd have at stopping Vitus before the barrier fell.

Come on, I urged my Gift desperately. But it wasn't enough, still tentative to defy the wards. My pulse quickened. I needed to think. Needed to—

'You will be ... better ... than I,' Dearil said, lips curling up in a smile. His fingers sprang open, the silver below leaping up to consume me. 'My daughter.'

'Don't!' I screamed, but the silver was too strong. It swallowed me whole, turning my world into brilliant light. I tried to picture the room I'd just been in, to beg the tear Dearil had opened between the realms to deposit me back there, but it refused. I was caught in its grasp, and it was not mine to command.

The silver shuddered. A shard fell away, revealing blackness beyond. Fear spiked through me. There was something wrong with that darkness. It didn't feel like shadows or a mere absence of light. It felt like ... nothing. An abyss that would pluck at the very fabric of my being until I came apart, disintegrated into the same nothing it was made of.

Instinct warned me that being trapped between the fabric of the realms when Dearil's power failed would be an end far worse than death. Another shard fell, yet it still did not deposit me anywhere. It obeyed Dearil's will – to not allow me to return but allow me the choice of where I'd end up.

He'd sacrificed some of his power to send me away. I hated him for it. Hated that he'd managed to crumble all my years of resentment in this one act, destroying what I thought I had understood about his apathy.

It was easier to believe I had been no one to my own father than to be on the verge of losing someone who might have cared more than I had realised.

The silver shuddered again. For a moment, I thought I almost heard a voice snapping at me to make a decision. A voice that sounded too much like my own.

Home, I thought desperately. That's what Dearil had said. Frantic as more silver splintered, I searched my mind for any memories of home. Of where I wanted to go.

There was only one image I could conjure. The very same one that had saved me in the darkest nights in my cell.

Home, I thought again, the panic ebbing a fraction. It was all the silver needed to recede. I had a heartbeat to gain my bearings – a sky lit only by torches, grass plagued by shadows and a field of gold-veined corpses – before I dropped from where I hung above the ground. I slammed into something, metal clanging as I hit the ground.

'Don't kill me!' my unfortunate landing spot yelled, voice hoarse with terror. He shoved me away, his armour clanking. Gold and red blood painted his breastplate, his skin damp with sweat. He raised his sword high, arms trembling, and body open for attack.

'Godsdammit!' I cursed, rolling out of the way as the blade plunged down. Dirt flung through the air. My manacles dug into my skin, blood still oozing from Dearil's markings. 'Can you—'

'Don't kill me!' the young soldier cried again, the sword swinging in another unpractised arc.

'You're the one swinging at me!' I kicked upwards, my back pressing to damp soil. His breath slammed out of him as I connected with his midsection, driving my heels deep enough that I was fairly certain a rib must've cracked. The soldier fell to his knees. I didn't waste time, diving for the sword he dropped.

I smiled the moment my fingers closed around the hilt. Gods, did it feel good to bear a weapon again. Twisting, I levelled the point at the base of the soldier's throat. He paused mid-scramble, staring up at me with round eyes.

My smile faltered.

This was *not* where I'd intended to land.

'Who are you?' I demanded, my hands awkwardly grasping the hilt. The manacles would have to go soon. 'Who do you fight for?'

He blinked. 'Are … are you a spirit?'

I scoffed. 'Do I look like a spirit to you?'

His brow creased as he looked me over. Torn golden gown, bloodstained wrists with golden markings, manacles. 'Yes?'

'Well, I'm not. Spirits are nothing more than a story.'

Deciding Vitus wouldn't have bothered to leave an idiot like this boy alive to serve him, I lowered the sword, glancing over at the field. Corpses covered the ground, their forms shadowy in the darkness. Faint shimmers of gold clung to a few of them, signs of a fresh battle. A few armoured soldiers milled around, grabbing limbs and dragging bodies into piles.

'What happened here?' I asked, turning back to the soldier.

He scrambled to his feet, snapping to attention. 'I'm afraid I have to detain you, ma'am. We can't have intruders in our camp.'

Irritation spiked. Dearil was dying somewhere. The moment he died, this realm lost its best chance at beating Vitus. And if that happened, that power would end up in a vessel that I wasn't convinced would be able to hold it.

The thought of it – of all that power, coursing through me and confirming that Dearil had really died – sent ice digging through me. I couldn't inherit Dearil's power. I'd never wanted the divinity that had already been forced onto me through my cursed blood.

But I'd landed gods knew where, too far to stop what might come. Knocking out the boy wouldn't do me any good, though. Stabbing the sword into the ground, I lifted my chained hands. 'Fine. Bring me to whoever is in command of your forces.'

The boy reached for the chains, then paused. 'Ma'am, your

wrists.' He motioned to the blood dripping from beneath the metal. 'I should—'

'Gods save me,' I muttered, rattling the chains as I shook my hands once more. 'How did someone as soft as you end up out here?'

Firelight caught the flush on his cheeks as he grasped the middle of the chains gingerly. 'M-ma'am—'

'You shouldn't call a prisoner *ma'am*.'

'But—'

Silver sparked on my skin. The boy flinched back as the wards flashed. My Gift surged, greedy for the gap in the restraints that had formed from Dearil's markings. Still not at full strength, but enough to do harm. Sucking in a breath that failed to do much calming, I called back my Gift. 'I do not have time to deal with you. Take me to whoever is in command.'

He turned, seeming to look around for someone who would have more of an idea of what to do with me than he did. I closed my eyes, trying not to let my anger take hold. I was exhausted, in pain, and struggling not to let grief break through the walls I'd built. There was no telling how violent my Gift might get if I lost my patience. 'What's your name, soldier?'

Instinct must've kicked in at the command in my voice, because the boy immediately replied with, 'Eamon, ma'am.'

'I told—' Shaking my head, I opened my eyes and said, 'Never mind. Eamon, go find someone in charge. Bring them back here.'

Eamon shifted. 'I don't think I should leave, and two of our commanding officers have left to scout a nearby—'

'You have two minutes to bring someone back. Otherwise, I'm going to kill every last soldier I come across.' I let just a hint of my Gift slip through, smiling through the pain of the wards. 'Starting with you.'

Eamon turned and ran off, disappearing into the darkness. I waited until I was sure that he was the only one patrolling the area before exhaling and sinking into a crouch, letting my head drop forward. Everything hurt. My cheek and stomach from Vitus's blows and wrists from the wards. Even my feet stung with tiny cuts from gods knew where.

But I wasn't concerned about that. I was more occupied by the strange sensation inside me. The sense that something was shifting and stretching deep within. My Gift fluctuated with the sensation, burning hot one moment and disappearing the next. Swallowing my fear, I forced myself to my feet and tipped my head back. The wind brushed over my cheeks, sweeping away strands of my hair. Above, the night stretched on in its eternal blackness, only the stars watching over me.

It was here that I allowed my eyes to shut, only for a few moments. Where I allowed tears to well, but not fall. I was free. I would see Callum again.

But the cost of it all…

I sucked in a deep breath, forcing myself to stare at the starlight until my vision blurred. Dearil wasn't dead yet. There was still time. My Gift was too reluctant to emerge to travel through the realms. Unlike Dearil, whose power must've briefly overpowered the wards, I couldn't even fully break free of the restraints upon my wrists.

I knew it was futile. Knew Dearil was already lost to me and to the realms. Yet I couldn't stop clinging to the vague hope that he might survive. That I wouldn't have to bear another burden because of the blood he'd cursed me with, and I wouldn't have to lose yet another person who might have meant more to me than I'd realised.

He'd been a terrible father, but he was still my father. And that last glimpse of him… I shook my head, but the image didn't disappear. The smile. The softness in his eyes. The affection finally breaking through his voice as he'd called me his daughter.

I should have been allowed to resent him until the end. It would have made everything far easier.

'Stop with that nonsense, soldier.'

I straightened at the voice.

'But I'm telling the truth, Commander!' Eamon pleaded. 'There's a spirit. She appeared in rags and chains, and she used a strange power! My ma always told me that—'

'Superstitions have no place on the battlefield. And people don't appear from thin air.' I pressed my hands to my chest at the familiar female voice. A fresh round of emotions swelled. I swallowed them back, turning to find a blonde woman with soft features and hard eyes storming my way, dragging Eamon behind. 'Spirits do not—' She stopped, her eyes widening. Her hand dropped from Eamon's arm. 'Chiara?'

I smiled weakly, a rush of exhaustion passing through me. 'Deana. It's been a while.'

Deana staggered forward a step, then another, and then she was flying at me. I braced myself as she wrapped her arms around in a tight embrace. 'Oh, gods. Gods, Chiara, is it really you?' She lifted her head and pulled back, hands coming to either side of my face. Shadows played across her features, but they did little to hide the shock and relief in her expression as her eyes filled with tears. 'Gods, it really is! But how? What happened? Are you all right?' She shook her head. 'No, of course you're not. You're—'

'Excuse me, Commander,' Eamon said, lifting a hand as one might with a tutor. 'But did you call her Chiara?'

Deana pulled away long enough to flash a brilliant smile at Eamon. His eyes widened as though he'd never seen my friend make such an expression before. 'This is Chiara Halnea.'

'Ch-Chiara Halnea?' Eamon paled further. He swayed on his feet, then abruptly fell to his knees, his forehead pressing to dirt. 'Gods forgive me. I didn't know that you were her. I pointed my sword at you! The king – he'll take my head for this. He told us we were to treat you as queen—'

'He did *what*?' I glanced at Deana, my brows creasing. 'Tell me he didn't.'

She shrugged, her fingers still curling around my arm as though she was afraid I might vanish if she let me go.

Eamon continued his babbling. 'Gods, have mercy on—'

'If you're going to ask for mercy, don't bother turning to the gods,' I said, and Eamon flinched. Shifting my attention back to Deana, I demanded, 'Where is he?'

'He and Jaxon went to scout to the west. There were rumours of Ankurans gathering a few kilometres past the campsite.' She gestured behind her, where I could vaguely make out shapes that must've been tents between flickering campfires. 'He's been – well, it's good that you're here. We should—'

She broke off, stumbling as an almighty crack sounded. The ground beneath us trembled, shouts rising as torches fell from where they'd been positioned. Eamon yelped, pressing his hands flat to the ground while I crouched low, my chains dragging in the dirt.

'What's happening?' Deana shouted as more thunderous cracks came. She crouched alongside me, her hand steadying on my shoulder as a knife flickered into existence in her hand. The traces of her Gift from Kerta disappeared in smoky tendrils of red.

'Above!' Eamon cried, pointing upwards.

My heart beat hard against my ribcage as I tipped my head back. Before, the sky had been a blanket of black pricked through with silver.

Now, the silver reigned. It coated the sky in fluid luminescence, rippling with the violence of a sea about to rise into monstrous heights. The shouts fell silent as others noticed the same. Around us, the air seemed to thicken, smoke and jasmine chokingly thick. Thicker even than it had been when Dearil had unleashed himself on Vitus.

'My gods,' Deana whispered, her fingers digging into me. 'This—'

That thing that I'd felt before – the shifting inside – jolted. My breath hitched as my Gift rolled with the same intensity as the sky above. Silver flared in my vision, even brighter than the sky above. 'Deana, I think—'

My words finished in a gasp as what felt like lightning slammed into me. I was vaguely aware of my feet lifting from the ground, of Deana calling my name and Eamon crying something out, but it was all distant, like an echo that couldn't quite penetrate my mind. My back arched as my veins seemed to fill with molten metal, power surging through me and battering into my Gift.

My Gift quivered, uncertain whether to flee or embrace the intruder, my mind pulled into pieces and reassembled as the sensation of lightning flowed through me again and again. I was a vessel too small to contain what came, a lake ill-equipped to fit the ocean. It was an agony far above that of the wards. An ecstasy more complete than my Gift. It was both wrong and right – a piece that did and did not fit.

One final pulse shot through my body, and then the silver vanished from my vision, my body sagging against the soft earth. I panted, blinking away the remaining silver as the sky above pulsed three times with the same incandescence. Then, all at once, the silver splintered and fell in giant shards. Someone screamed nearby and Deana curled over me protectively, but there was no need. The silver dissipated, drifting off in weaving strands of light before fading into nothing.

Silence filled the air.

'What was that?' Deana breathed, rolling off me and leaning back to inspect the now-normal sky.

I wondered if she sensed the same as I did – the irrevocable shift in the realm. The absence of an entity who'd dominated myths and legends. The destruction of the force that had protected us for centuries.

'That,' I said slowly, pushing myself to my feet and brushing myself off, 'Was the destruction of our last line of defence.'

'You can't mean—'

'I do,' I said grimly. 'Dearil is dead. The barrier between our realms has fallen.'

And that meant Vitus was one step closer to destroying us all.

Chapter Nine

Deana pushed herself to her feet, dirt clinging to her trousers as she stretched a hand to me. Golden blood clung to her skin. 'We should find Callum and Jaxon.'

I took her hand gratefully, my muscles twinging in protest as I rose. My skin prickled uncomfortably, still feeling the effects of whatever had happened when the barrier fell. Soldiers rose in the distance, picking themselves up from between the Ankuran bodies.

A deep chill settled over me as I stared into the darkness of the killing field. A darkness that seemed to shift under my gaze, coalescing in places and lightening in others. Grasping the sword I'd dug into the ground, I tore it free. 'Deana, get those soldiers to fall back.'

She stilled next to me. 'Is something wrong?'

I frowned. 'I'm not sure. It just looks … strange.' I couldn't put the chill of wrongness into words. The sense that some of the creatures that existed on the other side of the barrier had wasted no time in crossing over.

Deana hesitated for only a moment before nodding and

swinging to Eamon. 'Run to the camp and send one of our fastest riders west. Tell His Majesty that—'

Death came quickly, but it did not come silently. A soldier, too far away to discern any of his features, screamed, body rising several centimetres above the ground as his back arched. Messy darkness exploded through his chest, his body jerking before being flung to one side. He slammed into two others, taking them down.

'*Go*,' Deana snapped, as the knife she'd held shifted into a sword, red light glowing. Eamon didn't need to be told a third time. He spun, racing for the campsite as Deana turned to the field. 'Men! Retreat to the—'

A second soldier cried out, darkness shifting around him and wrapping around his throat. This one was closer to us, and closer to the torch light. Close enough that I glimpsed limbs too thin and long to be human, and a shadowed body that moved in jerky movements. The creature turned. Twin pricks of white light glowed like eyes, a slash of the same light crossing from one side of a head-shaped shadow. The slash stretched wide as the shadowed fingers curled around the man tightened. He choked. Something cracked beneath those dark fingers, and the man fell silent.

'Jaxon told us about these,' Deana breathed, the torchlight emphasising her stark paleness. She had a mind suited to strategy over impulsivity; she knew not to leap in to fight before she'd gathered stock of the situation. 'Shadow wraiths. Creatures of Akmad's.'

I narrowed my eyes, trying to discern what was darkness and what was the wraiths. All I could see were nervous soldiers swinging around, trying to seek out their enemies. A shadow moved and a soldier screamed as they were struck. 'Did he say how to kill them?'

A woman swung. Her sword passed through the wraith before her, the creature dissipating like smoke.

'The heart.' Deana tapped her chest. 'It has to be precise.'

I considered the creatures, then nodded. 'Then I'll make sure it is.'

Deana's hand shot out as I took a step forward. I glanced back at her, brows raised at the frown she wore. 'Callum will be back soon. We should wait. You're injured, chained and clearly exhausted. You should—'

'Join in the fight so I can get some rest quicker?'

Her lips pressed into a thin line. 'I forgot how aggravatingly similar you could be to Callum when it came to stubbornness.'

'It's part of my charm.'

'Chiara, let me handle this.' There was a note of pleading in her voice. 'Go find Callum. Let him know you're safe. Gods, I don't think he'd survive if you returned only for something—'

'Deana,' I interrupted her, but gently, and her expression bore a conflict of emotions. 'I want nothing more than to go to Callum. But we have enemies right in front of us. Enemies you know I can help fight. What do you think will happen if I go to Callum now?'

She frowned. 'You'd likely both run straight back into danger.'

'Exactly.' The wind caught in my hair, tossing it back from my face. I inhaled, letting the coolness of it settle within me and placate the strange sensation still pushing at my skin. A large part of me yearned to do exactly what Deana had suggested – to find Callum now. To let him wrap me in his arms and pull me close. But these shadow creatures were partially my responsibility. It had been me Vitus had tried to kill. Me whose life Dearil had saved at the cost of his own. I was a barely restrained vessel of rage and sorrow, with the perfect targets laid out before me.

Besides, I was itching for a fight.

Deana sighed. 'Fine. But if you get injured, I'm telling Callum this was all your idea.'

The Divine

'That's fine.' I strengthened my grip on the sword and began to stride forward, dirt clinging to my bare feet. 'It's not me who should be worried this night.'

Deana sighed again but followed, the hill sharply descending into the flatness of the field. The shadows were still wary, flickering in and out between soldiers who'd pressed their backs together, swords pointed at the darkness.

I reached for my Gift, but hesitated moments before tearing it out. It sat oddly in my veins. It wasn't the restraint of the wards that felt wrong, though. It was something else.

Sword it was, then.

'Hold your positions!' Deana called, her voice turning authoritative as several soldiers cowered at our shadows falling upon the ground. Only a few more torches remained standing. The rest had been knocked over when the barrier fell. 'Don't break ranks, or—'

A muffled sob sounded to the left. A soldier with flaxen hair and terrified eyes sliced wildly at shadows before launching herself towards the hill Deana and I had come from. Her armour clanked, hair flapping in the wind.

'Helen, stop!' a soldier I recognised as Corin shouted. He reached out a hand but didn't move away from the rest.

The darkness shifted then reassembled, forming the unnaturally elongated form of a wraith. The slash upon its face curved upwards as it slashed down with black-clawed hands, aiming for Helen's exposed back.

My sword found it first. I stabbed the blade upwards, driving it directly through the centre of the creature's chest. It jerked, black liquid spraying through the air. An unearthly wail pierced the air as it writhed upon my blade, attempting to pull itself free. I twisted the sword deeper. The wraith froze, then shuddered. Splinters of light ran through its form, its wail dying as the darkness crumbled into pieces.

Stalking forward, I grasped Helen by the arm, shoving her towards the group of soldiers. 'Next time your commander speaks, you obey. Understand?'

She sniffled, trembling as she stared up at me as though I were far more monstrous than the wraiths. She likely wasn't wrong. When she still didn't move towards the other soldiers, I yanked her along with me, pushing her at Corin.

'Keep her by your side,' I snapped, turning to Deana.

'L-lady Chiara?' Corin stammered as he pulled Helen into the centre of their ranks. 'But how? His Majesty said—'

His words were cut off as an eerie moan began in the darkness around us. A torch flickered, then sputtered out, then another, then another, until the field was shrouded in black.

'I don't think they liked you killing one of their own,' Deana muttered as we turned, our backs to the soldiers and blades raised.

'No,' I agreed. Before, it had seemed like they were almost curious in their kills. Wary, too, as though they'd been pushed through the barrier and been unlucky enough to find themselves amid Ankuran corpses. But I'd just marked us as an enemy, and they weren't curious anymore.

Kicking away a corpse in front of me, I closed my eyes and calmed my breathing. My sight would only serve to play tricks on me now. Better to trust my other senses.

Air shifted to my right. My eyes flew open as I sliced my sword in an arc. It sailed with lethal intent, jerking in my grasp as it ran into something semi-solid. A tremble ran down the blade's length, and then a disembodied laugh echoed around as the resistance vanished. I caught myself before the sword could find one of the soldiers behind me.

A sharp scream sounded. I whirled, chains rattling as the scream faded into a whimper. The darkness was too thick to make anything out. I tipped my head back, finding no sign of the starlit night above. It was as though we'd plunged into a pool of ink.

'Who's hurt?' Deana called, her voice further away than I'd expected.

'Annalise, Commander,' Corin called back, his voice firm despite the fear in it.

'Is she conscious?'

The sound of shuffling bodies, then, 'No.'

Deana swore. Red flashed in the depths of shadows, allowing me another glimpse of her pale features as her sword shifted into two knives. 'It's going to be difficult to aim for their chests when we can't see them.'

'If we stab the shadows enough times, we'll get lucky.'

A chuckle rippled through the dark as something shifted nearby. Praying it wasn't a foolish soldier trying to escape our prison of darkness, I lunged.

'That seems a solid plan for you,' Deana said as my sword met the same resistance as before. This time, it held firm for longer before disappearing. A sign I'd been closer at getting its heart, perhaps. 'But us ordinary soldiers would be dead before we managed to kill one of them.'

I frowned. She was right. Stabbing blindly would leave the soldiers open for attack. Several were already breathing heavily enough to wake the dead, and the few steady lunges I heard upon the ground weren't met with the same wail I'd elicited from the wraith before. 'Then I'll have to resort to something a little more powerful than a sword.'

Keeping my sword raised high, I shoved past the frantic beat of my heart, the cold sweat upon my skin, and reached inside for my Gift, waited for it to leap to my skin with its usual vicious joy.

But what I found surging through me didn't leap. It slammed through me, battering against my skin like a monster begging to be let out. Smoke and jasmine filled my nostrils, my body burning with the fury of the power. I stumbled back a step as it shoved at both my restraint and the wards. It was feral. Far more so than my Gift had been in the months I'd almost lost control after Cassie's death.

Another laugh came, raking sharp claws through me. I didn't think it came from the shadow wraiths. No, that sound had echoed in my own head, wilder and more unmanageable than anything I had encountered before.

Fear wrapped around me. It was too much. Too wild. Even with the half-crumbled wards, instinct warned me that the amount that'd slip out would be uncontrolled. I might end up killing everyone here along with the wraiths.

But if I did nothing, they would die anyway. I could sense the wraiths malicious eagerness. Felt slippery fingers slide over my skin before vanishing, as though playing. Letting us know they had us right where they wanted us, and we had nowhere to run.

I let go of my Gift, and it sunk back, rumbling deep in my blood with its annoyance. A shudder ran through me. No, my Gift definitely wasn't an option right now. Not when I couldn't control it.

The echo of laughter cut off. A voice sharper than any blade I'd wielded sliced through my mind as it whispered, *I will never be yours to control.*

I almost faltered. That voice ... the press of the Gift against my skin, so *hungry* ... it was nothing like the Gift I remembered.

'Chiara?' Deana called. She must've managed a lucky stab, because there was a shriek of pain and wrath before splinters of light cracked through the dark. For a moment, the wraiths were illuminated around us. At least three dozen, all with their white eyes fixed on the band of soldiers who stood in defiance of their fear. They circled us, trapping us in. 'Your Gift might come in handy right about now.'

'Dammit,' I muttered as the light fell away, thrusting forward and sending my sword through the chest of a wraith. This time, the wraiths were smart. One shoved me away, sending me staggering back as I fought to keep my hold on the sword, the rest wrapping sinewy bodies around the dying one as light spilt from its form. 'I don't think my Gift is a good idea.'

'Why not?'

Behind, there was another flash of light, a soldier crying out in triumph. Again, the darkness flooded back in far quicker than we could take any down. A sharp crack ricocheted between the space.

I stepped forward, my breathing too loud in my own ears, and nearly tripped over an Ankuran corpse. Stumbling, my foot slammed down into its chest, rotted flesh and brittle bones cracking beneath my weight. Nausea swelled at the wetness that seeped between my toes as I pulled myself free.

'If you're after a quick death, then it'll come in handy.' Someone yelled in pain, and my fingers tightened. A thud quickly followed. 'But I'd rather try to get us all out of here alive.'

I could almost feel Deana's questions prodding at me, but she'd always been the most level-headed of my friends. She knew to save her questions. 'Right. Then—' She cut off, crying out. I only had a moment to hear the sound of a body flying before she crashed into me, sending us both toppling to the floor. A body collapsed beneath us, and my stomach roiled.

'Commander?' one of the soldiers called, worry lacing her voice. 'Are you—'

'*Focus*, Abigail,' Deana snapped. Her hair tickled my cheek as she rolled off me with a groan, forcing herself to her feet. I rose with her.

Something crunched nearby, and Deana flinched, her elbow knocking into my arm. I grasped hold of her, my chains rattling. Dark had a way of making even the bravest of soldiers vulnerable. Leaning in, I whispered, 'They're picking us off.'

There'd been three distinct sounds of swift death so far. The thud of a body falling. The crack of a neck snapping. And just now, the crunching of bones that should never be crushed.

'I know,' she whispered back. 'Do we fight our way out?'

I shoved Deana to the side as something whistled through the air. A woman screamed in agony. 'Do you think the wraiths would just let us go?'

'Not all of us,' Deana said. 'But you and I might manage it.'

It was the easiest solution. The wraiths were rather light on their attacks on us, as though they sensed Deana and I were as likely to cut them down as they were us. But we couldn't move through the darkness they'd brought with them with all the soldiers. The wraiths would simply move with us. If Deana and I were to punch through, however, we could make it out of their shadowed cage.

There was no telling how easy it would be to break back through, though. And there was every chance everyone inside would die before we could.

Once, I wouldn't have hesitated. There was no question between the lives of strangers and my own, particularly with Callum's life entangled with mine. But that was the problem. Before, I hadn't had Callum. Before, these had only been strangers.

Now, they were his people.

I sighed. 'We're not going to do that, are we?'

'No,' Deana said, a hint of a sigh in her voice. 'We're not.'

'Then I suppose our plan will have to be stabbing until we hit something vital.'

'Remind me to never put you in charge of strategy.'

I smiled into the darkness. Something shifted ahead. Letting instinct drive me, I thrust my sword forward. A wraith wailed, its eyes flashing brightly enough to illuminate me in its ghostly glow. Gritting my teeth, I twisted the sword. Before the creature could crumble, a second wraith barrelled to my side. I twisted, sacrificing my sword to avoid its claws. The air whispered past me, darkness falling as the injured wraith took my sword with it.

Another caught me by the shoulder. I swallowed my cry, staggering to the side. There was another Ankuran underfoot, and I fell backwards, barely avoiding my head knocking against the ground. I needed to end this soon. My strength was rapidly draining.

I struggled up, my hand squishing into something I didn't want to think about. Before I could make it to my feet, another force slammed into my chest. My breath left me, my back colliding with the ground. I lifted my chained hands, but there was nothing to grasp hold of, the shadowy force disintegrating every time my fingers tried to catch hold of it.

Let me out, my Gift seemed to hiss, pressing against my skin. Golden light flared at my wrists, momentarily spearing the darkness. More shadows gathered, covering their glow as pain burned up my arms. *Let me show you what destruction I can bring.*

But Deana was too close, and there were soldiers around.

No, I snarled, but this was not the usual force of my Gift, and it seemed to snarl right back at me.

The shadow pushed down harder, and I could almost feel my bones groaning under its weight. My Gift writhed. All it needed was for me to lose my iron grip on it, and it'd free itself. My heart thudded. I tried to suck in a breath, but the air refused to enter. Aching pain shot through my chest and ribs. Something sharp pricked at my skin.

My Gift shuddered. I didn't think it was my fear that did it.

It was ecstasy. Anticipation for the moment it broke my grasp.

And, godsdamn it all, I was a heartbeat away from letting it go. It slipped from my hold, the pain increasing in my arms as the partially severed wards attempted to turn the power into a trickle. Silver sparked. One of the wraiths shrieked as my Gift found it.

Before my power could truly free itself, the weight on top of me disappeared, a wail tracking its flight through the air. I rolled, gasping for air. My Gift roiled in fury, bucking against my hold as I shoved it down again.

The cries of the soldiers began to die off, one by one, replaced by cheers as blackness split with the milky light of the moon. The shadow wraith's screams took the place of the soldiers. I blinked, staggering to my feet as a creature stumbled to the ground, a familiar dark-haired soldier driving a sword through its chest.

Kailey straightened, wiping black blood from her face. Our eyes met. Her mouth fell open. 'Chiara?'

But I was already turning, my heart thumping as creatures died around me. My Gift, which had only moments ago been so unruly, curled through me, warmth filling me. I knew this sensation. Knew the way my very soul seemed to shiver in anticipation. The way my eyes seemed to know just where to look.

Straight at Callum.

Chapter Ten

Callum was already staring at me when I finally found him amidst the chaos, sword in one hand and armour splattered with black. The wraiths were gone around us, but it wouldn't have mattered even if any had lingered. Nothing else mattered except him. His lips parted, then formed my name. I couldn't hear him speak, but I could see everything. The shock. The relief. The release of a month of pain and longing. All matched with the shuddering release in myself as I gazed at my soul-bonded.

I was running before my mind caught up, shoving my exhaustion away. I leapt over bodies and wound through where reinforcements made their way to the injured and dead. The stench of death lingering in the air didn't matter. Nothing did as Callum staggered forward a step, then another, and then raced to meet me. My feet caught on an Ankuran corpse and I fell to my knees, the impact stinging, but it didn't matter because he was there, and his hands were pressed to my cheeks, and his voice was whispering my name again and again like a prayer.

The realm faded to just the two of us as Callum pressed his

forehead to mine, his cheeks wet. 'Is it really you? This isn't some strange hallucination?'

I curled my hands around his wrists, his pulse frantic under my touch. *Home*, my body sang. This was what I'd pictured when Dearil had sent me through the fabric of the realm. Not a place, but a person.

'It really is,' I whispered back. My fingers dug in hard enough that it must've hurt, but Callum didn't pull away. If anything, he only pulled me closer, our breaths mingling in an air that should've only belonged to the death that had just been wrought, yet had become far more significant.

'Chiara, I—'

'I love you,' I interrupted.

Callum stilled, then pulled away a fraction. My fingers tightened their grip. 'What was that?'

I gazed up at him. Traced the features I'd clung to in my cell. There was the scar crossing his lips. The strands of shadows that wove through his eyes. The tousle of his golden hair and the slight upwards turn of his nose. 'I love you, Callum.' The words shuddered through me, coming to life after being contained for too long. Words I should've spoken aloud long before.

Callum blinked. 'I didn't quite catch that. Could you repeat it—'

I dug my nails into his wrist. 'You've heard it twice. Be satisfied with that.'

His smile flickered in and out of existence as he ran his eyes over me, pausing on the bruises I was sure were forming on my cheek from Vitus's blow, then the deep stain upon the ruined gown from Dearil, before settling upon the manacles on my wrist. There was enough light from nearby soldiers – soldiers I could *feel* gawking – that I was sure he saw the blood drying there. The chafing at my wrists, and the wards new and old.

'What—'

The Divine

'Later,' I said softly, leaning forward and resting my head on his shoulder. 'I'll tell you later. Just ... let me be here with you.'

Callum's hesitation was in the tension of his shoulders, but he lifted his arms, one wrapping around my waist and the other around my back. His breath tickled my cheek.

'You're really here?' he asked again.

I shifted, peering up at him through blood-matted hair, and raised my brows. A crescent moon hung as his backdrop, casting a pearlescent glow on the world. 'Would you prefer me not to be?'

'*No*.' The word snapped out of him with so much vehemence that a passing soldier startled, their sword thudding to the earth. Callum's fingers curled in my hair as he stared down at me. 'Gods, *no*, Chiara. I want you here, always.'

I almost answered that I always would be but stopped myself. We'd each made promises we couldn't keep in the past. Callum had promised to save my sister but had chosen me instead. And I'd promised to save myself over him should things go wrong when facing Vitus, but that had felt impossible. I wouldn't mar our reunion by another vow I might not keep.

I would do anything for Callum, even if it cost me everything.

'I missed you,' I said instead. 'So much.'

Callum smiled crookedly. His thumb brushed over my cheek, wiping away wetness that might've been from tears or blood. 'I'm never letting you go again.' He leant forward, his lips pressing to my forehead.

I breathed in his scent. Melted into his touch. 'That would be impractical.'

'I'm a king. Kings do all sorts of impractical things.'

I raised my brows, pulling back from him. 'Like what?'

'Like this.' He shifted his hand, curling it around the nape of my neck as his other arm drew me close. His lips found mine – gentle at first. Sweet and tender, like he was probing to see if I was really all right. Patient, as he'd always been with me.

But I'd never been the patient kind.

I drew him to me, falling into his kiss with the desire of a starving woman. That was enough to convince Callum. His grip tightened, his kiss deepened. Became more desperate, as though I was the very essence that gave him life. His armour was cold, but his hands were warm where they pressed, sending my skin tingling with desire.

My Gift thrummed more powerfully than it ever had before as I pressed upwards, seeking more. Needing more. It sang the rightness of this. Of me and him. Of us.

But my Gift was rising too high, pressing on the wards and sending stings of pain through me. I pulled away, and Callum's sigh of disappointment coasted over my skin. 'My Gift is … wrong.' Angry. Sharp. Hungry.

My pulse quickened, cold sweat prickling my skin.

'We can figure that out later,' Callum said, and all I needed was his voice to wash away the unease. 'All that matters is that you're here. Safe.'

He was right.

I pulled him to me this time, my fingers pressing greedily into his skin as our lips met again. Before he could deepen the kiss, though, someone coughed. I froze, remembering myself, then began to pull away. Callum held me tight, our lips millimetres apart.

'We're in the middle of your soldiers,' I whispered, eyes closed as our breaths synchronised. 'Not to mention the corpses.'

'I told you,' he whispered back, 'Kings do all sorts of impractical things.'

Callum began to draw me back to him, and I didn't have it in me to resist. Not when every part of me wanted this. Wanted him.

Another cough, followed by, 'Your Majesty?'

This time, I opened my eyes. Callum sighed, his breath grazing my skin. Any sense of cold had disappeared, my body flushed with need. 'Ignore them.'

Gods, I wanted to, but the interruption had forced reality back onto me. I wrapped my hand around Callum's mouth when he attempted to lean in again, keeping it there as I rose to my feet. 'Tend to your duties, Your Majesty.'

His lips pressed to my palm, sending a new shudder of desire through me.

No, I reminded myself sternly. There were things that needed to be discussed, and I knew the moment I let myself fall back into Callum's arms, I would be absorbed so completely by him it would be some time before I could drag myself back to doing what I needed to.

Keeping my hand in place, I glanced over at the soldier who'd approached us. She was a tall woman with a broad set of shoulders and blonde hair cut close to her scalp. There was something familiar about her features, though I was certain I'd never seen her before. 'I'd recommend speaking now, or you might not have a chance to.'

The woman eyed me. For a moment, I thought she might refuse or demand respect from me, the stranger before her, but she nodded once. 'We've dealt with the creatures. No more were spotted, but Commander Deana has called for all soldiers to pull back to the camp for the night. Should I gather any of the commanding officers for a meeting?'

I glanced around. For soldiers who had been given a command, they were doing an awful lot of gawping. My attention shifted to Callum, who was looking all too pleased where he knelt by my side, not seeming at all obliged to answer. I pulled my hand away and lowered my voice. 'A king shouldn't be kneeling next to me.'

He smiled. 'You are the only being in existence I would kneel for.'

Heat prickled my cheeks even as I glowered down at him. 'Callum.'

His smile grew, and I began to regret being the one to pull away. 'If my captain commands it, then I must obey.'

'Gods,' I muttered, turning away and praying the shadows would hide the darkening of my cheeks. The woman stared at us curiously, as did most of the surrounding soldiers. I could see Deana with Kailey some distance away, inspecting darkened spots of grounds where the wraiths had died.

Callum's hand rested on the small of my back as he stood beside me, seeming disinclined to let there be any distance between us. 'This is General Jade. She's been in charge of organising scouting teams to go ahead of us.'

Jade smiled at me, crumbling some of the hardness in her features, and that sense of familiarity niggled at me again. 'I'm—'

'Captain Chiara Halnea.' Jade crossed an arm over her chest, bowing low. 'It's an honour to meet you.'

I stared down at her bent head before turning to Callum, bemused. He grinned in response. 'What have you been saying about me?' I narrowed my eyes. 'I heard something interesting earlier from a soldier. Something about treating me like a queen?'

He raised his free hand in protest. 'This has nothing to do with what I said. Jade volunteered to accompany us rather than leading her own squadron like the other generals. Apparently, she knows of you.'

Frowning, I turned back to her. I was still certain I hadn't met her, but the familiarity gnawed at me as she straightened. It was in the humour in her eyes and the smile she wore. A smile that was exactly like—

'Ada!' I said, naming the woman who'd been my second-in-command when I'd captained as part of the Naruzian army.

Jade's smile grew. Black blood spattered her cheek but, like Callum and I, she seemed unbothered by it. It was a mark of a

The Divine

woman who'd seen her share of battles. 'My niece. She spoke highly of the girl-captain who led her unit to victory when they should've been met with death.'

Shame twisted, and Callum's fingers pressed more firmly to my side. He'd always been good at sensing when I needed steadying. Ada's death had come after I'd let my anger slip, killing the son of a high-ranking noble. My entire unit's beheading was the price General Tizan had wrought from me. 'I'm sorry for your loss.'

'I can see what you're thinking,' Jade said, sorrow mingling with gentle admonishment. 'But you'd do her pride in you an injustice by taking the guilt of her death as your own.'

I swallowed, then nodded.

Callum, again intuiting that I didn't have the words to respond, shifted forward. 'There will be no meeting tonight, General. Tell the other commanding officers to check on their subordinates. Make sure everyone is accounted for and set up a watch in groups of at least three. The fires are to be kept bright for the entirety of the night.'

Jade snapped to attention. 'Yes, Your Majesty.'

She began to turn, and Callum called, 'And send someone to find that lazy bastard. He wasn't riding too far behind me. He managed to miss the entirety of that fight – if he expects to continue along with us, he is to be at the strategy tent in an hour.' He glanced at me, frowned, then amended, 'Make that two.'

I didn't need to ask who that *lazy bastard* was. There was only one man I knew who was capable of sleeping through the barrier falling and unearthly creatures wreaking havoc. Jaxon Bladditch, egotistical criminal and my closest friend. I narrowed my eyes at Callum, then said to Jade, 'Tell him to be there in fifteen minutes.'

'Two—'

'*Fifteen minutes*,' I snapped, glowering at Callum. Jade, hiding a smile, bowed and hurried away. 'We need to meet with him and Deana as soon as possible.'

Callum frowned, stepping back to examine me. 'What you need is to be treated for your wounds and rest.'

I raised my brows. 'And resting was what you had in mind?'

Callum smirked back, and rolling my eyes, I turned my back on him and began the stride up the hill towards the campsite, my legs aching with each stop. 'Come on, King. We have a war to plan.'

Chapter Eleven

'This is a compromise.'

I scowled down at Callum, who was currently in the process of cleaning my feet with a damp cloth, his brows drawn together as though it was the most difficult task he'd ever encountered. 'I said I'd do it myself.'

Callum pulled the cloth away from me as I snatched for it, water dripping onto the floor of the tent. With its high top, chairs bearing plush cushions, and a table spread with carefully kept maps, the tent was a far cry from the cramped spaces I'd lived in during my days as a captain. The lantern lights chased away all but a sparse few shadows, woody incense drifting through the space. A strategy tent for a king. From the wrinkle on Callum's nose as we'd entered, he also found the luxury ostentatious for an army at war.

'I'm not an invalid,' I snapped even as I settled back in the chair, rubbing my wrists. Callum had demanded we find someone to remove the manacles first – a man Gifted by Adwin who could control the minerals in the metal.

'I never said you were.'

'Then stop treating me like one.'

'I'm not,' Callum said calmly, dipping the cloth back into the water before wringing it. 'I'm treating you like a queen.'

The word thudded through me. I stared down at Callum's head as he inspected the cuts on my feet. *Queen.* Was that what he wanted me to be if we survived this?

My Gift bucked as though in protest, and that cruel voice from earlier whispered, *You could never be anything of the sort.*

I flinched at it. Less in fear that I might be losing my sanity if I was hearing voices, and more because it was right.

'Callum, I—'

'This had better be important. I was halfway through a rather pleasant dream,' a sleepy voice drawled, accompanied by Deana's muttered, 'Stop making a scene and go in.'

Callum set down the cloth, rising to his feet. He shifted forward, his fingers brushing over my shoulder. 'Nice of you to join us when we were fighting for our lives.'

I heard the shrug in Jaxon's tone as he said, 'You did fine on your own.'

'What was the point of you insisting on coming along if all you're going to do is complain about the mud and avoid half of the fights?' Deana asked, slamming herself into the seat opposite me. Despite her irritation, there was a softness in her eyes as she looked over my shoulder at Jaxon. 'You even went to the trouble of leaving a decoy in the palace. Might as well have stayed behind yourself.'

'And risk my pretty face being injured by Ankurans sent to the capital because Vitus decides I'm a threat as a halfling?' Jaxon's smile tightened. 'I paid quite a high price a few centuries ago for him to consider me subdued, and I'm afraid I'm too stingy to allow that price to go to waste.'

'You're risking your pretty face being injured now.'

'Don't lie, darling,' Jaxon said, and my lips kicked upwards at the familiarity of this scene as Callum settled next to me, his fingers twining with my own. 'You like this pretty face.'

Deana's cheeks pinkened. She turned away from Jaxon to smile brightly at me. 'Please deal with him. He's been insufferable lately.'

Footsteps sounded, and Jaxon rounded the chairs. 'Who are you talking—' He stopped short as his yellow eyes caught on mine. 'Chiara?' Before I could say anything, he glanced between Callum and Deana with suspicion. 'Is this another of Callum's hallucinations?'

'If it was my hallucination, would you be seeing her?' Callum replied drily, though his fingers tightened on mine as though he feared I might disappear.

Jaxon shrugged. 'Stranger things have happened.'

'No, Jaxon,' Callum said with a sigh. 'This isn't a hallucination.' He raked his free hand through his hair, pulling it back from his face. He'd freshened up as much as a clean cloth and a handful of minutes allowed, the black blood gone from his features. 'There was a battle not long ago, in Perryth. I ... saw you. Or I thought I did, but...' He trailed off.

I thought of that moment at the end of what I'd assumed to be an Illusion where my eyes had caught on Callum's. Maybe he had truly seen me. I squeezed his hand tighter.

'Stop hogging her, Cal,' Jaxon said.

Callum frowned, reluctantly relinquishing his grip of me only long enough for Jaxon to sweep me into a hug. I relaxed into it for a moment before elbowing him in the side.

Stepping back, Jaxon grinned. 'I see a month hasn't lessened your gentle nature.'

'I see a month hasn't made you any more bearable,' I retorted.

'You three are the only ones I've come across who think my presence is anything short of captivating.'

'I doubt that,' Deana muttered, standing to haul Jaxon over to a chair. She forced him down, her hand lingering on his shoulder before she sat herself beside him. Jaxon shifted, his body tilted fractionally towards hers.

Well, *that* had certainly changed. Last I'd seen them, the two had been pretending to despise each other – a job they did poorly with the way they'd begun to conveniently appear from the same direction every morning, tired yet pleased-looking.

There'd be time to tease Deana about it later. First, I needed to fill them in.

'Dearil's dead,' I announced.

Deana and Callum turned grim-faced. Jaxon froze, his skin paling. 'What?'

Callum reclaimed my hand, his thumb brushing over the back of it in silent reassurance. I inhaled and closed my eyes. Everything had been a rush – Dearil shoving me through the realm, reuniting with Deana, the barrier falling and the ensuing fight. Callum.

Now, though, grief for a god I barely knew jabbed through my relief at our reunion. I swallowed, a knot forming in my throat. Dearil was gone. He might not have been family like Cassie had been, but he was … someone. A god who perhaps hadn't been as cold as I'd thought. And he'd died to save me.

'Dearil,' I repeated, opening my eyes. 'He's dead. Vitus killed him.'

Jaxon exhaled, dragging a hand over his face. When his hand fell, his eyes were glassy. It seemed he knew Dearil better than I'd thought. Deana reached over, laying her hand on top of his. 'I see.' He glanced at the tent flap behind me, a cold wind blowing through. 'The barrier?'

'Don't tell me you actually slept through the quaking earth and that silver light,' Callum said.

A flash of a smile appeared on Jaxon's face, though it stretched thin. 'Just as you have your talents, I have mine. Sleeping happens to be one of them.'

'It fell,' I confirmed, and the power in me rumbled as though in agreement. 'We were attacked by shadow wraiths.'

Jaxon shuddered. 'Nasty creatures.'

Deana leant forward, her brows drawing together. 'Are you all right, Chiara?' Her gaze dropped to the markings at my wrists. 'You spent a month—'

'Tell me what's been happening in Naruzia,' I said quickly.

Callum's voice warmed the bond between us. He used it so naturally, as though we'd been conversing in our minds our entire lives. *We'll be talking about that month later.*

My lips pressed together. *We will not.*

Callum sighed.

Deana settled back into her chair. 'The attacks by the Ankurans have increased. Callum ordered the smaller towns to be evacuated and moved into Alluvite. Most mortals are now aware it's not an infection but a god, but we've kept the extent of Vitus's plans from them.'

Callum tapped his finger against my palm as Deana continued talking, explaining how half the forces were left in Alluvite while the rest were separated to invade Archin – where we currently were, apparently. I glanced at him, raising my eyebrows in silent question.

We need to talk, Captain. You should know better than to keep everything to yourself.

I frowned as Jaxon started to ask Deana questions about the shadow wraiths. *I don't keep everything to myself.*

There was a thrum of exasperation through the bond. I shifted, trying not to let my own frown deepen. *I haven't been able to speak to you for a month, Chiara.*

The words stabbed through me. *Vitus blocked the bond with wards.*

From the moment I first reached you down it?

Silence stretched down the bond.

Another sigh from Callum as his finger began to sweep across the back of my hand. *Are you all right?*

I almost answered yes. Almost snapped at him that everything was fine.

But it would be a lie, and I had no wish to lie to him.

Besides, despite my protests, he was right. Keeping everything to myself had almost ruined me in the past. I couldn't let it do the same to me now.

I don't know. I stared down at where his hand held mine. *The captivity was nothing new, and he didn't stick with trying to coerce Dearil by hurting me for long. He seemed to realise I wouldn't cave. But … it wasn't like before.*

Before, when I'd been owned by my cruel adoptive mother and later King Kane, it'd been all I'd known in life. Suffering was a fact of existence, just like breathing, rage, sadness – and the numbness I'd often retreated into.

But with Vitus, I'd known there was something better out there. And that – the loss of it, of Callum – was far worse than any physical pain could be.

Callum's thumb swept slowly. *And Dearil?*

I exhaled. *He was a stranger to me.*

He was, Callum agreed, *and he was also your father.*

Can you call a god who was absent most of my life a father?

Depends. *Do you want him to be?*

I hesitated. *I don't—*

'Don't you know it's rude to hold a private conversation around others?' Jaxon said, rapping his knuckles against my head.

I narrowed my eyes up at where he'd crossed the room to loom over me. 'I'd say it's equally rude to interrupt.'

Before Jaxon could retort, Callum leant forward, drawing all of

The Divine

our attention without having to say a word. 'How much do you know about wards?'

Jaxon tilted his head, leaning back on his heels as he slipped his hands into his pockets. 'Enough to have placed wards around this camp to prevent unexpected visitors at night.' He grinned, pulling a carved piece of stone from his trouser pocket. 'Plus, our own personal protection, of course.'

That explained why I'd ended up so far from Callum when I'd travelled through the realm's fabric. Callum gently lifted my hand, exposing the golden lines around them. The silver strand had thickened, and the markings Dearil had made glowed with the same light. 'Do you know how to undo these?'

I'd filled Callum in on the wards during our walk to the camp. He'd grown silent for some time after that, and the shadows in his eyes warned that his quiet rage was not yet spent. Jaxon bent, inspecting the lines. Redness marked my skin underneath, the brush of air enough to sting the chafing.

After some time, Jaxon shook his head and straightened. 'Afraid not. Wards against realm travel are the simplest of markings. These are far more complex and carved into a surface less malleable than dirt. Wards to hold back the sort of power Chiara has would need an expert hand to fix.'

'Kerta, then?' I suggested. The goddess of war had been friendly enough upon our meeting – more so than her haughty soul-bonded, Evania. She was also firmly against Vitus.

Pushing back strands of dark hair from his brow, Jaxon shook his head again. 'Kerta was never interested in wards. Evania's too flighty to learn them properly. And those silver markings – they're not like any wards I've ever seen.'

Frowning, I pulled my wrist back to myself and held it so that the lantern light fell upon the marks. The silver seemed to shift as I turned my wrist. 'Surely gods keep tomes. Wouldn't there be one about wards?'

'There is,' Jaxon agreed, 'but Dearil and Vitus use wards differently to the rest. To the other gods, they're tools. But Dearil is – was – the oldest amongst the gods, and Vitus second. To them, the wards were a language that died with the ancients who came before them. I don't think Dearil was copying down a ward to counteract Vitus's. I think he created a brand-new one using what he knew.'

I dropped my hand into my lap. 'Would cutting off my hand work?'

'You are not cutting off your hand,' Callum said, weary exasperation in his voice.

One side of Jaxon's lips lifted. 'Always with the extremes. But, no. Maybe it would've worked if you'd done it straight away, but you've had the wards for too long. Their power would've melded with your power and blood by now.'

'Fantastic.' My fingers curled into a fist. 'So, we're going to go against Vitus with my Gift practically useless.' It hadn't felt quite useless before. Foreign, yes. Dangerous. But not useless.

'Maybe,' Jaxon said. I looked at him, something in his tone reminiscent of the way he spoke when he was trying to pull off one of his scams. He merely shrugged before turning to Deana. 'It's late. We should leave these two be and plan our next steps this morning.'

Deana rose with a fatigued sigh. 'I never thought I'd live to see a day where you're the responsible one.'

'I'm always responsible when it comes to ensuring you and I have time to—'

'Never mind.' She grasped him by his elbow, ignoring the too-pleased grin he gave her. Her expression softened into a smile as she looked at me. 'It's good to have you back, Chiara.'

I returned her smile. 'It's good to be back.' And, despite all that had led to me coming here, despite the very real possibility we would all die soon, I meant it.

I had never known contentment was possible in the middle of an army campsite.

Yet here I was, wrapped in Callum's arms with his fingers toying with my damp strands of hair, as contented as I could be in the circumstances. Light from the iron brazier in the centre of his tent cast a soft glow across us, shadows not daring to disturb our reunion. It had taken some time to scrub a month's worth of dirt and blood from my skin, but with help from Deana, I managed. Once I'd slipped on a fresh tunic and trousers, lent to me by Kailey, Callum had whisked me away before I'd had a chance to talk any more to the others.

Not that I'd minded, of course. The thought of talking to anyone other than Callum tonight had been overwhelming.

Sighing, I nestled further into his protective hold, my cheek resting on his bare chest. The comfort of his heartbeat was more of a lullaby than even the sweetest of voices could be.

'You're certain this is really happening?' Callum asked for at least the fifth time that evening.

I looked up at him. Strands of shadows from his own Gift's mark wove through the brilliant green of his eyes. No matter how perfectly I had tried to preserve those eyes in my memory, their beauty still snatched my breath away. Reaching up, I pressed my hand to his cheek. 'I refuse to believe otherwise.'

Twisting, Callum pressed his lips to my palm before shifting them to the delicate underside of my wrist. Tingles spread from where he kissed, lasting far longer than his touch did. 'Thank you.'

I shifted, reaching up to run my fingers through his hair. 'For what?'

'For coming back to me.'

'Always.' The bond between us filled me with a warmth I

couldn't put into words. I didn't know which of us it came from. It didn't matter. All that mattered was that we were together again. Smiling up at him, I tugged at the end of his golden hair. It had grown since I'd last touched it. 'You need a haircut.'

'I was rather busy, Captain.'

I lifted an eyebrow. 'Too busy to spend a handful of minutes trimming it?'

'Yes.' He caught my hand, lacing his fingers through mine. 'Particularly when the only two who wouldn't be too terrified to cut it are Deana and Jaxon.'

It was clear why Jaxon wasn't an option, but... 'Deana could've done it.'

The scar on his face curled upwards along with his lips. 'Have you seen Deana's attempts to cut hair before?'

'Can't say I have.'

Callum's grin grew. 'Let's just say there was a good month of experimenting with as many head coverings as she could find.'

I laughed at the image, and Callum's expression softened. Propping myself up on my elbow, I narrowed my eyes at him. 'What is it?'

'That sound.' He twirled my hair around his finger, tugging it gently. 'I didn't think it was possible to miss something this much.'

'Oh?' I leant down, curling my hand around his shoulder. He studied me with intense scrutiny, as though he were engraving every moment in his memory. 'You just missed my laugh?'

He curled his hand around the back of my neck. Even if I'd wanted to, I wouldn't have been able to resist his downward pull. As it was, resisting was the last thing on my mind.

Callum's lips found mine. The kiss lingered, and I let myself be consumed by it. Nothing mattered except for him.

When he pulled away, his lips twitched at my sigh of disappointment. 'Of course not. I missed you, Captain.' His fingers trailing down to trace circles on the back of my shoulder as I settled back down. My skin warmed with every movement. 'Every second you were gone, I missed you.'

Closing my eyes, I let the steady thumping of his heart peel away some of my anxiety. Callum was here. He was alive. I was with him. 'You shouldn't have come for me.'

The circles paused. Callum shifted and I sat up, curling a blanket around my bare shoulders as he frowned. 'What?'

'You should have stayed in Naruzia,' I said, twisting the corner of the fabric. The material creased in violent lines. 'You're the king. Your kingdom's hope. You can't—'

'I will always come for you, Chiara,' Callum interrupted, sitting up with me. He cupped my face in his hand, calluses from years of sword-training a familiar comfort to my skin. 'No matter what happens. No matter where you are or who I might be to others. *You* are what matters to me.' I opened my mouth, but he wasn't finished. 'And don't tell me you wouldn't do the same.'

My mouth closed. He was right. I would never let who I was meant to be or what I was meant to do stop me from coming for him if he was in danger.

Even so, the thought of what he had been heading towards sent anxiety spiralling through me. I let him guide my head to his shoulder, his arm curling around my waist. 'I love you, Callum. Enough to destroy me if something happens to you. Enough to destroy everything in this realm, too.'

'Say it again,' he whispered.

'That I'll destroy—'

Callum pulled back enough to flick my nose. I grinned. 'No. The first part.'

'I love you.'

'Again.'

'I love you.'

'Again.'

There was no choice but to do as my king commanded. I said it as he drew me to him. As he breathed my name back, devotion embedded in his voice. As he made up for all those hours we'd spent apart. I said it until it became a prayer. A hope that this love might be enough. That the coming war wouldn't take him from me.

And there, in the safety of Callum's hold, I allowed myself to believe that that might be true.

The shouts of soldiers beckoned me from where I'd been stalking the edges of the campsite, scouring the landscape around for all possible angles of attack. Inbria, which sat towards the middle of Archin, had become a wasteland of barren fields and abandoned homes, the once thriving farming community now housing little more than ghosts. Deana told me that morning that most of the towns in Archin were like that, emptied of people since the massacre Vitus had led a few months prior. The larger towns and cities were worse, plenty of the corpses of the too young, elderly or decrepit left to rot in the sun, deemed as useless as Ankurans.

Dust on the ground was easily unsettled by the slightest of movements as I made my way to the raucous noise. The patrols Callum had set around the perimeter of the campsite, a sprawling mass of tents and soldiers that constituted at least two thousand men, were doing an adequate job, checking every shadow and crack for signs of danger. Despite the edge of tension in the air, they held their heads high and didn't cower at sudden moves or sounds.

Callum had, reluctantly, disappeared with General Jade some time in the morning. He'd suggested I come with him to discuss a missive they'd received from General Jakob in the east a few days prior. I declined. My responsibility was Vitus. It was best I didn't

The Divine

meddle in things that were designed for royals and commanding officers to take charge of.

The twisting pathways between tents opened up into a wide space, bodies packed together. I hovered in the shadows, watching as money exchanged hands between grinning soldiers at the back. There was a meaty thud from somewhere in the middle of the pack, then a collection of roars of victory and cries of defeat. Curious, I stepped forward, trying to peer through the cracks of the crowd. There were too many, though, and their excitement was too great to make way for me.

There was a frenetic edge to the excitement. A thread of tension they were trying to shake off. There were two ways soldiers tended to relieve themselves between battles. One was rarely done in such a public display, shared breaths and heated touches staying in the shadows.

The other involved fists and violence. Unluckily for this crowd, I had a good amount of tension of my own I needed to rid myself of.

'Who's next?' Jaxon's voice emerged from the centre with its usual brazenness.

There was a heartbeat of silence, and then a soldier a few bodies in front of me raised their hand. 'I'll go!'

Cheers rippled around me as Kailey, dressed in a grey cotton shirt and trousers, walked forward. The crowd split, forming a corridor that led directly to a grinning Jaxon and a sheepish man sprawled out on the floor, sword at his side. As Kailey reached the centre, the man rose to his feet and joined the crowd, several soldiers giving him sympathetic claps on his back.

'I'll bet you two silver she lasts three moves,' a man with a thick beard of red muttered, coins appearing in his hands.

'My captain's much better than any of the rest,' a woman next to him whispered back, drawing out two silvers. 'I'll bet she'll last five.'

It seemed Kailey had been promoted since I'd met her in Naruzia. A smart move from Callum – she was well liked and had a steady head on her shoulders. Leaning forward, I asked, 'What's happening?'

The man startled, knocking into the soldier in front of him. He stared at me. 'When did you get here?'

I ignored the question, looking to the woman. 'Well?'

She grinned, her front teeth crooked. 'Lord Jaxon has been training us every morning. The longest anyone 'cept the commander and His Majesty has lasted against him's been twelve moves – that was General Jade.'

I raised my brows. 'Let me guess – a percentage of all the bets made against his opponent goes to him?'

'That's right.'

It seemed *Lord* Jaxon hadn't lost his scamming ways since he'd left Naruzia. Back there, he'd run a lucrative fighting pit, The Den, and made a good deal of money off painting me as weak only for me to win every fight.

The sun beating down on the back of my neck, I watched the crowd's reactions as they gasped, cried their delight and moaned their defeat.

'Six moves!' someone called from near the front. The man who'd bet on three groaned, dropping the silver into the woman's hands.

'How much of a cut does Jaxon take?' I asked.

'Thirty per cent.'

'And does he lose anything if his opponent were to win?'

'He's sworn to repay all the cuts he's taken for the day if that were to happen. Keeps plenty willing to fight him.' The woman laughed, shaking her head. 'But there's no way that anyone—'

'If you want to earn your money back, bet as much as you can on his next opponent,' I advised the pair.

The woman frowned. 'That seems a good way to lose all my money.'

'Next!' Jaxon called.

I grinned at the woman. 'The only way you'll lose money is if you bet he's going to win.'

Their shocked gazes followed me as I forced myself through the crowd, dodging elbows and shoving through bodies. It wasn't the first time I'd had to do so. The places Jaxon and I had frequented in the Naruzian slums were far more packed, and the people there were liable to dig a knife into another's side for trying to move past them. In contrast, the sweaty bodies and sideways looks were pleasant.

I caught another glimpse of the arena that the crowd formed. Dirt had been smoothed, the rocks and sticks that littered other parts of the campsite absent. Unlike Jaxon's fighting pit in Naruzia, this ground wasn't stained with crimson. Instead, the only mark of his fallen opponents were small scuffs in the ground.

I reached for the bond between Callum and me. *How necessary is Jaxon's pride to your plans for war?*

There was a startled burst of amusement rippling down the bond, and then, *I'd say a solid blow to it would be more helpful than harmful.*

I grinned. *I'll take that as permission, then.*

Not that you need my permission in the first place, Callum said, somewhat delicately, *But what have I just given permission for?*

Nothing too important. Just a little gambling. I tucked away flyaway strands of my hair and rolled up the cuffs of my tunic, bouncing slightly in anticipation. Gods, it had been some time since I'd had a good fight without my life being in imminent danger. *Apparently, our friend has been running a version of a fighting pit in your camp.*

There was a pause, then, *Your friend, Captain. He's mostly just been a problem for me. Explains why he's been so shifty every time Deana finds him with a group of soldiers.*

Don't worry. I'll make sure he's punished.

I will prepare my Gift for healing Jaxon once you're done, then, Callum said, laughter echoing after his words.

'I'll challen—' the woman in front of me broke off with a grunt as my elbow found her side.

'I'll go next,' I called, finally breaking through the bodies.

Jaxon's grin faltered, the practice sword he held drooping. 'On second thought, five challengers is enough. We can call it a day and—'

'Oh, we couldn't possibly do that,' I cut in with my own grin. Tilting my head upwards, I raised a hand to cover my eyes from the sun. 'We've still got a good few hours before the daylight runs out. Why not use that time to entertain?'

Jaxon shifted, his eyes narrowing. 'I'm afraid I'm quite fatigued.'

'Yet you were fine a moment ago.' Spinning with the showmanship Jaxon himself had taught me, I called out, 'What do we think? One more fight?'

There was a rippling of murmurs, and then a grinning Kailey called out, 'One more!'

The two I'd spoken to before echoed her call, and it spread, the words jumping from person to person until the crowd was yelling their approval, grins splitting their faces. A hooked-nosed man at the front smiled, turning to his companion and flashing a golden coin. The companion shook his head, hands up as he tried to back away.

I stepped forward. 'What are you betting?'

The man startled, his head swinging towards me. 'Me?'

'You,' I echoed. 'What are you betting?'

His cheeks flushed. He glanced to Jaxon, then back to me. 'Ah ... nothing, miss.'

The Divine

'Go on,' I said, trying to emulate a placating tone. 'I won't be offended.'

Rubbing the back of his neck, he folded his fingers around the gold. 'I was just...'

'One gold that you'd be defeated within one strike,' the woman he'd offered the bet to said, eager to cause trouble for her friend.

I raised my brows. The few who recognised my face were smiling with sharp delight. 'And you refused that bet? Seems a good deal to me. All I'd have to do is last two or more strikes and you'd win.'

It was the woman's turn to shift, her army-standard clothes rustling with her movement. 'It's just...' She coughed, looking to her friend. He shrugged, apathetic to her plight. 'Well, you're not exactly built as a fighter, are you?'

I looked down at myself. A more discerning eye might've seen the scars and recognised some as being from blades, or looked at my eyes and had the sense to be unnerved by their silver colouring. But most would see, as Vitus had, a short woman, bruises darkening several spots of her skin. Thinner than I'd have liked after a month of captivity.

Weak, they must've thought. Another of the fresh recruits, maybe.

It was time to show them otherwise. The soldiers needed to know to stay out of my way on the battlefield, and they needed to understand without Callum ordering everyone to treat me as a leader.

I wasn't a leader. I was a nightmare turned into their ally.

'Then will you make a bet with me?'

Jaxon sighed. I ignored him, watching the woman.

Her brows bunched. 'A bet?'

I nodded. 'I last five strikes, and you give me a gold piece. I win, and you give me two.' The male soldier choked on a laugh.

I didn't mind. It'd make my victory all the sweeter. Glancing at him, I smiled. 'You can bet too.'

The two nodded, eager to snap up the winnings that'd never make it to their hands. Even if I lost, any coin would have to come from Callum – I held none of my own. And I knew I wouldn't lose.

Turning, I grinned at a resigned-looking Jaxon. 'I hear you'll lose all your cuts from today if someone wins against you.'

He folded his arms, looking rather put out by my interference. 'That's because I was meant to win all the matches.'

'Giving up already?'

Jaxon perked up. 'Can I?'

'Of course not.'

His shoulders slumped. 'Do I get to take a cut of your winnings? I taught you how to scam people like that, after all.'

'Of course not.'

A few of the soldiers who'd caught Jaxon's words glanced at each other, confusion carving lines into their brows. Jaxon sighed. 'Most people spend time *talking* to their friends after being apart, not leaving them hideously bruised.'

'Most friends don't spend the first two months trying to cheat the other out of their winnings,' I replied. 'Don't think I've forgotten how light my last few pays were at The Den.'

A grin appeared at the mention of his cheating ways, Jaxon looking entirely unrepentant. 'If you allowed yourself to be cheated, then you're fair game.'

'If you allow yourself to be beaten, then you're fair game,' I mimicked with an equally amused grin. 'Enough avoiding. I'm here to fight.'

Try not to kill him, Callum added. *Deana's a pain when she's in a bad mood.*

I scoffed as Jaxon narrowed his eyes, clicking his tongue in disapproval at my silent conversation. *Focus on Jade, Your Majesty.*

I'm sure the general has far more important things to talk to you about than a little sparring match.

Nothing's more important than watching Jaxon get his arse handed to him.

'Are we fighting or am I to endure another five minutes of you wearing that disgustingly affectionate smile on your face?' Jaxon drawled as though he hadn't been trying to avoid the fight moments before.

That affectionate smile sharpened once more. 'I hope you won't regret that comment. Ready?'

Any trace of casualness disappeared from Jaxon's demeanour. Despite his fondness for moving like he was eternally on the search for somewhere to recline, he was far from lazy. His affected insouciance only served as a sharpening tool for his cunning. The sword lifted, the dulled steel angling at my throat. 'You've been away for a month. I've been training for most of that time.'

I laced my fingers together before pushing them outwards, my muscles aching sweetly at the stretch. 'Then this defeat will be particularly bitter.' I eyed his sword. 'Where's mine?'

Jaxon shrugged. 'I have to make this fair somehow.'

The daggers Callum had made sure to give me that morning were pressed to my side, but I didn't grab them. If I was to win, I wanted my victory to be complete. I lifted my hand in silent summons, our shadows stretching over the circle around us. A hush fell.

Jaxon didn't hesitate. He thrust forward, his sword angling for my chest with a blow powerful enough it might've cracked a few ribs if it connected. I twisted, the air shifting as the blade moved past me. Spinning, I aimed my fist for his exposed side. Jaxon was no fresh recruit, though. He was a halfling with three centuries of experience. His elbow slammed down, knocking aside my fist.

'That's one blow,' I called. Someone muttered their dismay in the crowd.

I stepped back, opening my arms in invitation for Jaxon to swing again. This time, he arced his sword through the air. It cut for my neck. I ducked, but the sword followed me down, Jaxon's expert hand adjusting its movement. Rather than try to avoid it again, I lunged forward. Jaxon cried out, his feet in danger of entangling as he narrowly avoided being taken down by my tackle. It would be easy to pursue him – to kick out his knees or slam a fist under his jaw.

But it had been a while since I'd sparred, and I wanted to stretch this out a little while longer.

Again, I stepped back. 'Two.'

'You've got slower,' Jaxon taunted, circling me with excited anticipation in his eyes as he watched for my next blow.

'And you've got sloppy.' I feinted forward, driving my fist towards his stomach. He lifted the blade, the flat of it blocking any blows. Instead of trying to continue or retreating, I lunged to the right. Jaxon whirled with me, but I was too close, my hand closing on his wrist. It was time to end this.

Tightening my fist, I drove it upwards, angling it to sink into Jaxon's gut with a blow that'd surely leave him doubled over and vulnerable.

Yes, the power in me rumbled. *End it.*

I inhaled sharply as my Gift rose, paying little heed to my attempts to shove it back.

No, I corrected myself. Not my Gift. This was something … different. The same thing that smothered the bond between Callum and me. A power that followed no command of mine.

Don't, I warned, trying to wrangle a hold on it as the wards began to glow golden. *Don't you—*

I am not yours to control, it said, and it sounded like wrath given voice.

Silver flashed and pain flared with the wards. My pulse

quickened. I tried to stop the blow, but it was too late, my muscles were slow to respond to my commands.

Jaxon cried out as my fist connected. Something crunched under my blow, the sword clattering to the ground as he flew backwards. Silver flared. The brightness of it stung my eyes almost as much as the wards that burned their marks into my skin. Jaxon crashed into the closest soldiers, sending them toppling.

And the Gift – that damned voice that seemed to have sprouted from whatever this power was – it *laughed*. Laughed with vicious abandon.

Wide eyes fixed on me. The crowd moved back as I stepped forward, my throat tightening. Light played upon the ground, silver overtaking the sun for its brightness. My vision tinged with its colouring as Jaxon groaned, rolling onto his side. He pressed a trembling fist into the ground, attempting to rise. He managed to get only a few centimetres up before he collapsed back, his face white with pain.

Fear wrapped around me. I hadn't meant to do that. Hadn't meant for any of that power to slip through. And this – what I was seeing before me – was just a strand of it. The barest hint of what the wards had allowed out.

I will not be contained, the power whispered, its voice ice on a winter's day. *And I will never submit.*

I didn't answer. I couldn't. It would be nice to think the voice was insanity. But I knew better. Knew that that sort of malice couldn't merely be a figment of my imagination.

The Gift had changed, and it had become something terrifying.

Those Jaxon had knocked over rose to their feet. One's expression was twisted with pain, arm clutched to their chest.

'Lady Chiara?' Kailey called, glancing between Jaxon and me. She moved to take a step forward. 'Should I—'

'Don't!' I said sharply, holding up my hand. Silver crackled in the air around us. More soldiers shifted away, fear turning them tense.

They should be scared. That silver could kill them in an instant – a dangerous enough thing when I was in control.

I wasn't in control now.

'I'm glad I didn't give you a sword,' Jaxon said, managing to rise this time with another's help. 'Or I—'

'I need to go,' I said abruptly. With that, I turned on my heel and stalked away, sparks of silver marking the path of my cowardice.

Chapter Twelve

'Did that tree do something to offend you?'
Pressing my lips together, I didn't answer Callum as I flung my fifth dagger at the lone tree I'd found some distance away from the camp. It landed a perfectly spaced centimetre from the other four, a straight line wrapping around the girth of the trunk.

'Or are you trying to see how many daggers you'll need to rid Archin of one of its few remaining trees?'

The next thud was particularly vicious. 'You came because you heard what happened.'

'No,' Callum corrected, passing a dagger over my shoulder as my hand fell to my empty scabbards. I took it, my fingers brushing his. 'I came because I felt your fear down the bond and have now discovered you taking your anger out on an innocent tree.'

'I'm not angry.' The blade Callum had given me buried itself in the hilt of another, the pair quivering violently. 'Why would I be angry? Jaxon didn't do anything wrong.'

'You weren't angry at him.' Another blade appeared. A splinter of bark fell away from the tree. 'You were angry at yourself.'

My hand dropped to my side. The skin at my wrists still ached, and my hands stung with blisters from the number of times I'd thrown the daggers only to yank them out. My time in the cells had softened my body in ways that unsettled me almost as much as the wards. 'I used my Gift. I didn't mean to, but ... it broke free.'

'Like you used to worry about after Cassie died?'

I shook my head. Back then, I'd drunk myself into a state where my Gift was suffocated. Any lack of control over it then had been because I had no handle on my own emotions. 'That's the thing. I was enjoying myself. It was a friendly match, and there was no threat to my life. But then this power sprang forth, and it was so *violent*. Not hateful – not like how Vitus's power feels – but it wanted blood. Wanted death. And it felt so natural.' Tipping my head back, I stared at the leaves above, the filtered sunlight doing little to warm my cheeks. 'I couldn't rein it in.' I paused, then added, 'I don't think this power is mine, Callum. I think ... I think it belonged to him. To Dearil. It doesn't obey me.'

Callum's arm wrapped around my waist. I relaxed into his hold, my back pressing to his chest. 'You'll find a way to manage it.'

'It spoke to me, Callum. Just like you speak down the bond. And it was so ... so *hateful*. So furious.' I shuddered at the memory of it. 'It told me I could never control it.'

He didn't falter at the possibility that I might be going insane. 'You'll find a way to, Captain.'

'I might not.' Not when it was so out of place in my body, far too large for me to contain.

'You will,' he said, completely confident. 'Because you always manage the impossible.'

Tilting my head further back, I frowned up at him. Callum

smiled back down, his scar lifting with the curve of his lips. 'Having that much faith in a person is dangerous.'

'Aren't gods meant to love that sort of faith?'

Huffing out a breath, I went to pull away. 'Halfling. Not a god.'

Callum laughed, the sound curling through me as he tightened his hold. 'Such a temperamental goddess you are.'

'Such an obnoxious king you are,' I said, flicking his chin and wriggling out of his hold as he bent to kiss me. Despite my foul mood, the sheer disappointment on his face had me grinning. 'Did you only come to check on me?'

'Mostly,' he said. 'But we're also meeting General Jade and the three captains present to discuss the next steps. If you need more time, though, I can tell them to get lost.'

'Callum,' I sighed. 'You can't tell your commanding officers to get lost when we need to plan for war.'

'I most certainly can.' His smile turned sharp. 'In fact, I did a rather wonderful job of it back in Naruzia when Lord Ayden suggested I *settle down and find myself a wife*.'

I raised my brows. 'You *told* him to get lost?'

Callum shrugged. 'I dangled him from a window at the top of the palace until he regained his reason.'

I wasn't sure what reason anyone would gain when threatened with death. I smothered a smile as I sighed. 'Callum.'

'And I told him he should consider himself lucky that you weren't there.'

My grin broke through. I strode past him before he could see it. He was right. I would've done much worse than merely threaten bodily harm. 'We should go.'

His hand caught mine, reassuring in its firm grip. 'Do we have to?'

I gave him an exasperated look over my shoulder, regretting it the moment I turned around. The sinking sun set a haziness upon him, blurring the strands of his golden hair and turning his eyes brighter than they usually seemed. The sight of him was enough to snatch my breath away. To coax me into finding somewhere to hide away in with him and only him.

'The barrier's fallen. We've already wasted a day.'

His fingers tightened, then relaxed, head dipping. 'I know. And I know we should go, but ... the moment we step into that tent, we're heading into a war that we might not win.'

'You were already heading into a war,' I pointed out, turning fully and stepping towards him.

'No, I wasn't. I was heading to *you*.' He brushed hair behind my ear, his touch leaving trails of warmth upon my skin. 'But I have you now. And this war – Vitus must have his full power, or at least be gathering it. Other gods will side with him. And the price of it – gods, I might lose every person I'm meant to protect.' He closed his eyes, the golden light doing little to lessen the shadows in his face. 'There's a whole kingdom of people who depend on me. If we lose – if those people suffer – it'll all be on me. This meeting is going to inevitably lead some of my soldiers to their death.'

This was the price of ruling, I realised. Taking each of the lives – and all their deaths – onto his shoulders. Yet, unlike me, Callum didn't run from that responsibility. He shouldered it. Struggled under it. But he never turned his back.

Shame tightened my chest. 'You are a good man, Callum. A good king. Whatever decision you make, it'll be the right one.'

'And if that decision leads everyone to their death?'

'Then death was the only way this was ever going to end up.'

'Now who's the one with blind faith?'

'It's not blind. I see you. See the sort of man you are. And this meeting – I'll be at your side through all of it.' Just as he'd always been by mine, even when I thought I didn't want it.'

The fear didn't disappear from Callum's eyes. His shoulders didn't relax, and he didn't lose the undercurrent of tension. But he nodded, then held out his hand. 'Then let's go plan ourselves a war against the gods.'

'You saved me a few gold pieces,' Jaxon announced, throwing himself onto a chair with surprising alacrity for someone so recently injured. He wore no shirt, bandages wrapped around his midsection. 'The soldiers all pitied me enough that none of them made me pay up.' He flashed a grin, but it was edged with pain. 'I should be thanking you.'

Deana hit the backside of his head. 'If you hadn't been encouraging bad habits amongst the soldiers, this would never have happened.'

Jaxon grinned with immense satisfaction as Deana leant towards him, unfurling the edge of the bandage to inspect the redness mottling his side. Her fingers trailed over his skin, and his grin grew. 'This is fun. The band back together.'

Kailey walked into the tent, bowing low to Callum before hurrying to an empty seat at the far end of the table to where we were positioned, as was proper of her ranking. Another was already seated, alternating his glare between me and Jaxon as though he couldn't decide who was more worthy of his disdain.

General Olisker, a squint-faced man who I'd only had the displeasure of meeting once before, sniffed. 'This is war planning, boy. It's not *fun*.'

I wondered how much his face would screw up if he learnt how many centuries the *boy* had lived.

Jaxon rolled his eyes, sighing exaggeratedly. 'Of course not. You wouldn't know fun if it hit you in your dull face.' The halfling leant back in his chair, pushing it back until it was at a sharp angle. He tended to do that – take something perfectly safe and push it to see how far it would go, until he, or someone else, got hurt. 'Let's see. A war against gods. The possibility of spilling blood. A triumphant story about the mortals rising against the gods.' His dimples flashed as he tipped that chair back further and further until I was sure it would topple. 'Fun.'

Olisker twisted, his extravagant coat filling up much of the space on his chair. 'Your Majesty, it is not proper for commoners to be seated at such a position of honour.'

Callum lifted a hand. A message boy by the name of Aaron stepped forward, pitcher of wine and cup already in hand. He began to pour the crimson liquid, but Callum took both from him, sending the boy scampering back into the shadows with a wave of his hand. 'I didn't seat Jaxon anywhere. You saw it – he seated himself.'

The older man's skin turned ruddy under his beard. 'Your Majesty, it was a stretch to allow that man entrance into our strategy tent under the pretence of him being a lord, but the *woman* cannot be allowed entry.'

My fingers itched to reach for my knives. Callum grasped my hand, squeezing lightly. *Let me try handle this one, Captain. If I fail, then you're welcome to turn my tent red.*

It would be easier to just cut him into shape.

The corner of Callum's lips twitched, the movement so small only I seemed to notice it. *Unfortunately, I have need of Olisker's links to the nobility. It's difficult enough fighting a war with gods. I'd rather not add a civil war on top of that.*

I blew out a breath, settling back into my chair. I didn't bother voicing what I was sure Callum had considered himself countless times – that he could use his sword to instil fear into everyone under his command. It was how his father had ruled.

But Callum had never been his father, no matter how hard Kane had tried to force him to be.

Taking a long draw of wine, Callum said, 'I asked Chiara to be here.'

'Your Majesty, this is highly improper and—'

'Say that first part again.'

The blustering general blinked. 'Y-Your Majesty?'

Callum nodded, his smile slow and sharp. His fingers curled around mine, holding tight. 'Exactly.'

Olisker shifted in his seat under Callum's hard stare, looking far more uncertain than he had moments before. I didn't blame him. Most with sense would falter under those sharp eyes. I only smiled. 'I don't understand what you are saying, Your Majesty. I was talking about the—'

'I am saying,' Callum interrupted, leaning forward a fraction in his chair. Olisker leant back in his. 'That I am king. Tell me, Olisker, do you believe a king should not be allowed to select the members of a war council?'

Olisker threaded his fingers together. Jaxon watched with intense interest, his eyes darting between the pair, while Deana sighed, adjusting her weapons. 'That isn't what I'm saying. I—'

'Because I know my father did. In fact, I believe he *only* allowed those he chose onto his council. No one else was allowed a say.' Callum's smile sharpened. 'Do you respect me less than my father, General?'

I almost felt sorry for the general as he sank into his seat, the creases in his skin deepening with his frown. 'No, Your Majesty. I do not.'

'Good.' Callum tapped his finger against the arm of his chair. Every rhythmic crack of nail to wood sent Olisker flinching. I only smiled more. This was the man I loved. Someone capable of using only words to bring an arrogant noble to heel. 'Because while I am not my father, I will not let disrespect slide.' The tapping paused. 'Especially when it comes to Chiara.'

Olisker's lips pressed together. He looked down at his knotted-together hands, saying nothing. The message was clear. He would obey because Callum had commanded it, but the respect would never truly extend to me.

A crease of displeasure appeared between Callum's brows. I squeezed his hand lightly. *Can I try something?*

You never need my permission. His eyes slid to me, narrowing in consideration. *Though if we can limit the bloodshed, that would be appreciated.*

Choosing to ignore that last part, I folded one leg over the other, smiling in what I hoped was a friendly way at Olisker. From his scowl, he didn't take it as such. 'Is it my common blood or my accomplishments you don't respect?'

'Does it matter?' he sneered, any trace of politeness vanishing from his voice.

I didn't mind. I'd been spoken to in far worse ways by men far more powerful than he. Very few still lived. 'Fine. I can't change my blood, but I've captained units in the army since I was fourteen. I've also faced our enemy and survived multiple times. I might be the very best shot you have for surviving the next year.'

From the curl of his top lip, he didn't agree. 'They likely didn't see any need in keeping you alive. That doesn't make you anything special.'

'I never said I was special.' I leant back in my chair, trying not to reach for my knives. 'I'm only pointing out that I'm as worthy of being here as you.'

A vein bulged in Olisker's forehead. His hands fisted, one slamming onto the table and rattling Callum's cup. Callum caught it before it could spill its red liquid across the wood. 'Listen here, little girl—'

That was all it took to shatter any pretence at civility. The derision in his tone – the utter *condescension* after all the things I had survived and all the horrors I'd suffered – I'd had enough. Enough of his attitude, so haughty when his uniform was pristine, his hands untouched by hardship. He was soft. Weak.

And yet he looked at me like I was the one worth nothing.

Before anyone could stop me, I'd whipped out a knife and sent it flying across the room. Olisker yelped, throwing himself to the side. A thud sounded as the knife sank into the back of his chair, the hilt quivering.

Forcing my fingers to loosen where they still clutched Callum, I said, 'Call me whatever names you want. But don't you ever refer to me as *little*. Not when you're the one who's fallen to my feet.'

Olisker rose slowly, his face was pale with rage but his hands trembled with fear. He brushed himself off, glancing at Callum as though he expected Callum to berate me. Callum maintained his composure, the only sense of his fond exasperation echoing down the bond.

I shrugged at the sidelong glance he gave me as Olisker straightened his vest, ripping the knife free of his chair. He hurriedly placed it on the table when I glared. I reached for the bond, trying to force repentance into my tone as I said, *Whoops*.

Wry amusement came back at me. *He's not even meeting your eyes now.*

Callum was right. Despite the clear anger, it seemed I'd scared Olisker enough that he seemed to look everywhere but at me. *Seems I'm no good at being civil.*

I never said you had to try for civility, Callum said down the bond, traces of amusement warming me. *That's my approach. I know to expect violence when it comes to you.*

Somehow, the way he said it didn't make it feel like such a bad thing.

Deana coughed, drawing my attention. She'd lifted her fist to her mouth, but I still caught the corner of her lips twitching upwards as she watched Callum and me.

'This world won't survive the two of you, between Callum's apparent *civility* and your...' She trailed off, waving her hand in the direction of my knife. 'It was bad enough when you were at each other's throats. But working together? You're menaces to this realm.'

Callum reached for a fresh cup, ignoring my attempts to take it off him. He poured water into one, anticipating my preference. I ignored Olisker's irritated huff at a king serving a commoner. 'Menaces are what this realm needs right now. And we need the generals to obey us. If this is how we achieve it, so be it.'

I took the cup, swallowing a mouthful before placing it down. 'If we're at each other's throats, we'll never survive this war.'

Deana raised her brows. She leant in, lowering her voice as she glanced to Olisker. 'And this'll stop him hating you?'

I smiled sweetly. 'Absolutely not. But he'll think twice before questioning my place here again.'

The tent flap rustled, and General Jade appeared, dusk bringing its hazy hues behind her. She stopped short as she stared at the scene – Jaxon grinning, Deana sitting back with an expression of resignation, and Callum calmly taking a drink of his wine, while Olisker squirmed in his seat. She blinked, then took a seat, taking it all in stride.

A man followed behind her, a limp sending his tall form leaning to the right. He stepped carefully around, planting himself firmly beside Kailey who watched in rapt awe. The two exchanged quiet words, the man motioning towards me once. Kailey leant in, whispered something, and he straightened, turning to stare at me in the same awe that she did.

'Violet?' Callum asked.

'Sent her out with one of the scouting groups earlier,' Jade replied, sitting next to Deana and ignoring the general whose unrelenting glare I could feel digging into my skin. The moment I looked at him, however, he looked away. 'Henri was coming in when she left, so I brought him along with me.'

The Divine

The man next to Kailey crossed an arm over his chest and bowed as much as his seated position allowed. 'Your Majesty.'

'You may rise.' Callum turned to the map spread between us. 'You captained a unit in the west, Henri?'

Henri nodded. 'There are a thousand men over there. General Elijah is leading them. We were making good progress, but the other night there was some ... disruption. A silver light, and—'

'The barrier between the realms fell,' Callum supplied, as easily as one might discuss their morning meal.

Henri blanched. 'Is that why half my men took their own lives?'

A thud turned everyone's attention to Jaxon. He'd sprung to his feet, his chair toppling behind him and fists pressing to the table. He fixed narrowed eyes on Henri. 'Explain.'

'There was the silver light, but another came after. Those closest to the source took their blades and shoved them through their chests or sliced their own throats.' Grief left its dark stain in his eyes. 'My sister was amongst them. Friends, too. People who had no reason to do anything of the sort.'

'Were they smiling?' Jaxon asked, urgency threading through his words.

Henri nodded, his eyes pressing shut. Even Olisker seemed affected enough to remain quiet. 'Most of them. A few screamed, but ... yes. They were smiling.'

Jaxon slammed his fist into the table, rattling the cups there. He said nothing, his lips pressed into a thin line as he whirled and dragged a hand through his hair. His body was taut with tension. Deana rose, placing her hand on his arm, and whispered something to him. There was a moment of apprehension, and then all the fight rushed out of him. He nodded before turning and sitting back down beside her.

'You know what caused this,' I guessed, having suspicions of my own.

'Tarina,' Jaxon said, the ice in his voice carrying fear as much as fury. 'She used to play these sorts of games with other halflings before they died. She'd create elaborate Illusions to draw people into. Her favourites would live in those Illusions forever. Those she disliked would believe themselves to be greeting an old friend or hugging a loved one as they killed themselves.'

Callum was quiet for several long moments before he asked, 'How powerful is Tarina compared to the other gods?'

'Not as strong as Vitus and Dearil. Likely around Kerta's level, if I had to guess.' Jaxon stared at the tent entrance as though he could see her coming for us through the darkness beyond. 'But she'll be angry now. And given she can't blame Vitus, she'll be blaming Chiara instead.'

'Angry?' I asked. 'Why?'

'Because Dearil's dead.' Jaxon frowned. 'Tarina's always had an obsession with Dearil. She wanted him in her grasp, and she must have thought Vitus was about to give it to her.'

'Why is she taking it out on the mortals?'

'She is as indifferent to mortals as any other god – except for perhaps Dearil and Kerta – but think of her as a child who's had her newest plaything snatched from her.' Jaxon shrugged. 'She's throwing a tantrum – one guided by Vitus's wish to ruin the mortal realm. Essentially, she's both angry and bored. She's taking it out on the old toys she has, not caring which of them she smashes in the process. And you, Chiara, will likely be the next best replacement she can think of to take out that anger on.'

I shuddered at the thought of the goddess treating mortals as toys, taking their lives with little more than a flick of her fingers because she was *bored*. 'But—'

Footsteps rushed towards the tent. We all turned, hands falling to our respective weapons as the soldiers Callum had posted outside snapped, 'You can't go in, sir. If you— Sir!'

The tent flap was shoved open, a stern-faced man breathing heavily as he slammed to a stop before us. Corin, the freckled guard I'd met at the palace, rushed in behind him, his eyes wide as he glanced between everyone. 'I tried to stop him, Your Majesty, but—'

'It's all right,' Callum said. 'You can go.'

Corin nodded and disappeared back outside.

It took me a while to place the man. Soot and blood marred his features, turning tanned skin into a ghastly display of horror. His dark beard was a scraggly mess as he dragged a hand over his face, several cuts lashing the back of his hand. The man stared around at us, one of his eyes milky from the scar cutting over it. He inclined his head towards me, Deana and Jaxon before bowing to Callum.

'Your Majesty,' he rasped, voice sounding as though he hadn't touched water in days. He swayed as he straightened.

Kailey leapt to her feet, pulling out a chair and ushering him to it. He sat heavily.

'General Jakob. You're meant to be pushing forward in the west.' There was no condemnation in Callum's voice, only question. 'You encountered trouble?'

'Aye,' Jakob said grimly. Blood oozed from a wound on his cheek, deep enough it should've had stitches a while ago. 'You could say that.' He took in a breath, and I braced myself for the next round of bad news. 'The thousand men you sent with me are slaughtered.'

Callum stilled. His expression grew blank, but I felt it – every piece of grief and rage that flooded down the bond. Unlike me, he didn't try to stop it. Didn't hide himself from me. He simply gripped my hand harder. 'Get the general a chair at once.'

Kailey leapt up, pushing her own chair towards the general. Aaron rushed off to fetch her a new one, returning moments after Jakob had slumped down. He kept his shoulders straight, but his fatigue, and a pain far deeper than physical agony, were evident in the tightness of his features.

Callum kept his voice firm but not unkind as he said, 'When you're ready, General, make your report.'

Shame forced Jakob's gaze down. I'd only met the man once – at the same time I'd met Olisker. Unlike the latter, he'd left a favourable impression on me. Stern, hard, but fair.

'General Sophia stayed behind, Your Majesty. She – well, I insisted on sending one of the soldiers, and we tried, but they were killed too quickly. She insisted that you didn't lose two generals in one go. I tried to force her to leave, but—' He broke off.

My hand throbbed where Callum held me. He seemed to sense my pain, his fingers starting to slide away. I grabbed him before he could disappear. He'd held me up enough in the past. It was time for me to return the favour. 'If you need rest, General, we can—'

Jakob shook his head. 'No, Your Majesty.' He winced at interrupting a king, but Callum merely nodded at him to continue. 'Sophia's always been a stubborn old woman. The creatures that came at us – there were those Ankurans you told us of. Shadow creatures. Others made of vines that choked any they caught to death.'

'Scythes,' Jaxon supplied, his voice still tense. 'Adwin's creations, given life by Vitus.'

Jakob nodded. 'Fearsome enough enemies. But we were so focused on them that we didn't notice the mortals behind.'

'Mortals?' I asked. There hadn't been many in Vitus's palace – mostly those delivering messages and serving the god. I'd hated every one of them that had done it willingly.

Jakob's expression darkened. 'Led by an old friend of ours. Tizan.'

Deana and I stiffened in unison. We each had our own history with Tizan – me from when he killed my unit, her from when he tried to force her into a marriage she did not want when she was little more than a child.

A red knife flickered into Deana's hand, called by her Gift. 'Tizan's still alive?'

'Aye. Alive and as nasty as ever. He and his men were the ones who cut my men down when we called for a retreat. If Sophia hadn't called for a change in strategy – to ensure at least one of us survived – I'd be dead, too.'

Callum's fingers blanched where he clutched the cup. I reached over, removing it before he could upend the wine over himself. His fingers flexed around empty air. Turning to Jakob, he said, 'Go to the medical tent. I will be there later to heal any wounds.'

I frowned, using the bond to scold Callum. *You need to rest, not use your Gift. Let the non-Gifted healers look after him.*

He glanced over at me, shadows writhing in the emerald of his eyes. *These are my people, Chiara. My responsibility.*

Exhaling, I gave him the smallest nod. I didn't like him using his Gift, especially when the marks of exhaustion were so heavily engraved in his features, but I knew that Callum needed this, just as I so often needed to spar to release my anger. This was how he alleviated the guilt he shouldn't have to bear.

'Your Majesty, I should stay to plan—'

'Rest, General. You have done enough today. I will relay details of our meeting once I think you're adequately healed.' Callum held Jakob's stare for several moments before beckoning over Aaron. 'Take the general to the medical tent. Make sure he receives everything he needs.'

Aaron bowed before ushering Jakob out of the tent, all of us ignoring Jakob's protests that he would be perfectly fine and had absolutely no need of the king's services. Even Olisker failed to protest Callum's decision.

I was the first to break the silence that followed. 'So, we're facing destruction from all sides.'

'My concern is less about the creatures,' Deana said, 'and more about the gods who are responsible for them. We know Vitus is in this realm.'

'It's real, then?' Kailey asked quietly. 'This war – we're to go against the gods?'

The soldiers had all been told we were up against Vitus, but hearing it and seeing the outcome – the destruction of the forces, the tales of creatures that went beyond imagining – was vastly different.

I glanced at Callum. He'd looked tired before. Now, he looked exhausted. His body tense, as though it were the only thing that kept him from crumbling. He'd only just admitted his fear – the people he'd lose because of his decisions as the king. Now, he was faced with that terrible realisation that it was inevitable. I wanted to reach over, to coax him into looking at me and to tell him all the ways this wasn't his doing. But he wasn't just my Callum here. He was the king, and there were too many waiting on him.

He nodded. 'It's real.'

'Oh,' Kailey whispered, the sound so small it was almost swallowed up by the space.

'This is ridiculous, Your Majesty!' Olisker piped up, finally regaining his voice. A pity. I was enjoying its absence. 'Gods are great beings. We cannot defy them.'

Callum stared at the man. 'Then do you suggest we lie in front of them and wait for them to kill us? Because that's what they're here to do, Olisker. Wipe our realm of mortals.'

The man bristled. 'But Vitus is the most divine—'

'Vitus is a cruel bastard who enjoys inflicting suffering on others,' I said, my voice low as the wards stung at my skin. Olisker paled at my expression. At the hatred and rage. The resentment and grief. At the burden of all I'd lost because of Vitus, and all I might lose should he succeed. 'And if you are going to defend him, then you deserve to die alongside him.'

Olisker sank into his chair, still bristling but somewhat subdued. He hadn't bothered to wipe the blood from his nose, and it dripped onto his lap.

Deana turned to Callum. 'We have four separate forces at the moment, not including those back in Alluvite. We can send—'

'No.' Callum shifted forward, studying the map. 'We need to bring the forces together, not separate them further. Send a missive for those to the north and east to head for us. Any injured will head back to Alluvite. Replace them with those who can fight.'

'And you, Your Majesty?' Jade asked. 'It would be best for you to return to Alluvite, too. You can strategise from there, and send your commands through the generals.'

'I can strategise perfectly fine here. We'll create two main forces – one to head off Tizan, and the other to go to the east. It should be enough to delay a full-scale invasion, provided no other gods decide to get involved before then.'

'Absolutely not,' Deana interjected. 'You are the king, Callum. Staying at the front line is not an option for you.'

'I am king,' Callum said calmly, interlacing his fingers. 'Which means these people are my duty. If I'm not willing to risk my life for them, then I don't deserve to be their ruler.'

Jade rubbed her chin. 'Lady Deana is correct, Your Majesty. Your father—'

'Was a tyrant and a coward. I am not him.' There was no room for argument in Callum's voice. 'I will stay.'

'Talk some sense into him, Chiara,' Deana snapped, then glanced at where my finger was tapping the hilt of my dagger as I lost myself to quiet contemplation. She sighed. 'Actually, don't. Your sort of sense is the same as his.'

'He's right, though.' I reached forward, tapping on the map

where Tarina was said to be. 'We already have one goddess joining this war. How long until Vitus emerges? We need to take whatever advantage we have early on.'

'But we don't need the king to do it! Or you, for that matter. If Callum falls, I imagine it'll be you who—'

'We're the best fighters,' I interrupted, not wishing to hear where Deana was going with that. 'Even if my Gift is … misbehaving, I can fight better than most. Callum can, too. Are you really going to take us off the board when it's already clear we're at a massive disadvantage?'

There were a few moments of silence. Olisker reddened, seeming to have something to say, but a sharp glance from me and he kept quiet. From his contributions so far, whatever he had brewing was only going to racket up the tension.

Deana blew out a long breath. 'I guess that means we're staying, then.'

'You should go to—'

'Do not finish that sentence,' Deana warned Callum. 'I'm not leaving you and Chiara here alone. Who knows what the two of you would do?'

Jaxon sighed. 'I suppose hoping we'd all take a few days of rest was wishful thinking.' He rose to his feet, stretching. 'I've had to do more in a handful of months than I've done in a century since meeting all of you.'

Those in the tent who were unaware of Jaxon's halfling nature gave him odd looks. Deana scoffed. 'That's not difficult.' She shifted her attention back to me and Callum. 'If we're going to be heading off to two battles, what's the plan?'

'Once the soldiers gather, we'll separate. You and Jaxon head for Tizan. Chiara and I will head for Tarina, and—'

'No,' Jaxon interrupted, his arms dropping to his side. His face was riddled with a conflict of emotions, rage and fear the most dominant. 'I'll be going for Tarina.'

I narrowed my eyes at him. I was well aware of Jaxon's hatred for his mother, but he was also the sort to avoid any situation he didn't have an upper hand in. It was unlikely that was the case with Tarina. Was it simply revenge he was after? 'Then you and Deana—'

'You should come with me, Chiara,' he said. 'She's a goddess. It might help to have you by my side.'

Callum tensed. 'No.'

Jaxon raised his brow. 'Making decisions for her, are we?'

Callum turned to the occupants of the tent. 'This meeting is at an end. We will meet again tomorrow morning to discuss next steps.'

'Your Majesty, we must decide—'

'Out,' Callum said, voice low as he glared at Olisker. 'Now.'

The generals and captains hurried out of the tent, leaving Jaxon, Deana, Callum and I behind.

'This isn't about making decisions for Chiara,' Callum said, the moment the tent emptied. 'But I'm not going to let you dictate where she goes because you think she'll be useful. Chiara isn't a tool for us to wield. She goes where she wants.'

'And have you asked where it is she wants to go?' Jaxon asked, unbothered by Callum's anger.

'He doesn't need to. I go with him,' I said. I'd been separated from Callum for too long. I wasn't about to let him go now. Especially not with the gods in our realm. The thought of it – of being away from him, and all that could happen in that time – sent chills through me.

Jaxon studied me for a long moment, his expression unreadable. I stared back at him. I knew this wasn't the most logical choice. That Jaxon was right, and my presence might make a difference in a fight against a goddess.

But logic didn't matter when it came to Callum. All that mattered was that I was by his side.

At last, Jaxon shrugged. 'Fine. I'll be taking Deana, then.'

'I never agreed to that!' she protested, twisting towards him.

He smiled back. 'You wouldn't want to leave me alone and unprotected, would you?'

'You'll be going with an army,' Deana said. 'That's far from alone.'

They fell into arguing, though their words held a soft edge that once hadn't been there. It was already clear what the outcome would be. Deana, for all her easy irritation with Jaxon, wouldn't leave him by himself so long as I was there to guard Callum, and vice versa.

Callum reached for me, grasping my hand in his. 'We'll handle Tizan quickly. We can rejoin with them afterwards.'

I raised my brows. 'You seem confident in our win.'

His smile was warmer than the sun at its peak, washing over my skin. 'Of course. I have you, now. Tizan doesn't stand a chance.'

I wanted to believe him. Yet, no matter how much I tried to, I couldn't shake the tendril of unease that curled around my heart. I knew battles and war. Knew how quickly they could be decided, and how others could stretch out. Years of hard-won instinct warned me that this particular war would be short and bloody.

I just wasn't sure whose blood would be spilt before the end.

Chapter Thirteen

Something was dripping. The sound of it yanked me from sleep, my heart stuttering. I tried to even my breathing, but my chest was caught in a vice. Maybe I'd dreamt everything up. Maybe Tarina had visited again and cast me into another Illusion. As though in confirmation, my wrists throbbed with sharp bolts of pain. I'd never escaped at all. I was back in the cell, unable to do anything but serve Vitus's whims. I was alone, at the mercy of a capricious god. I was—

An arm tightened around my waist. Callum's breath tickled the back of my neck, and his scent curled around me. Closing my eyes, I exhaled.

I was safe. I was with Callum.

Even so, my heart refused to calm. Worried I'd wake him, I slipped out of his hold. The shirt he had lent me did little against the cold. I padded over to a blanket, neatly folded in the corner and wrapped it around my shoulders, fingers rubbing at my wrists. We'd talked little after meeting with Olisker, Jade and Henri, both of us exhausted by the day. Callum's exhaustion was different from mine, though; sleep had dragged him under quicker than it had me. Where I'd had little to do but sleep for days at a time, he'd seemed to have no rest at all in the past month.

Making sure not to disturb him, I sat at the side of the bedroll. The darkness was thick, but the glow of my wards washed over his features. A curl of gold rested on his forehead. I brushed it away. His hair was the only thing of that colour I could ever adore.

His hand shot up, curling around my wrist. I startled. His eyes met mine, pupils dilated under the glow of the wards, chest rising and falling with panting breaths.

'You weren't here. You were gone, and'—he blinked, the claws of whatever nightmare had found him slowly unlatching—'I thought I'd lost you again.'

I pressed my hand to his cheek. 'I'm here, Callum.' A breath shuddered through him. His fingers tightened on my wrist as though he were truly afraid that I might drift away were he to let go. 'I'm not going anywhere.'

Slowly, his grasp loosened and he dragged his hand over his face. 'I know, but – I can't feel you with the soul-bond. It's *there*, and I know you're at the end of it, but'—his voice grew hoarse—'it's worse now than it was when Vitus had you. Like there's something else pushing down on the bond.'

Guilt twisted through me. I waited until his eyes met mine. 'It's all right. I'm here. I'm not going to leave you.'

'But you did.'

I froze. 'What?'

He watched me carefully, no sign of the wicked humour I loved in his expression. 'You did leave me. Or you made me leave you.'

My hand dropped. I shifted from the bed as he sat upright, blankets pooling around his bare torso. The vanishing of his touch left my skin cold. 'You're talking about when I sent you through the realm to escape Vitus.'

'I'm talking about when you decided your life was worth less than mine, and you used it as a distraction.'

I folded my arms. 'It was the best choice we had.'

'No,' he said quietly. 'It was the easiest choice.'

The words speared through me. I glanced at where the tent flap fluttered, the sounds outside quietened with the night. 'We shouldn't talk about this tonight. We've only just reunited, we're both exhausted and—'

'We need to do it tonight,' he said, dragging my attention back to him. His jaw was set, his mouth a hard line, but his eyes were cracked through with pain. 'Do you know what my first thought was when you shut down the soul-bond? I thought you'd died.' His voice fractured with grief. 'And that I wouldn't even get a chance to say goodbye.'

My fingers dug into my arms. His words were tiny knives, carving deep into me. 'I made sure nothing came through the soul-bond to stop you panicking over every little bruise I got.'

His fingers flexed. 'Did you not think I'd imagine the worst possible things in that silence?'

My eyes closed, my arms dropping to my side. Callum was like me, forged from pain. Someone whose imaginings of the worst possible things – things he'd endured at the hands of his father, forced to heal himself over and over so that no scars were left on his body – were far worse than most realities could ever be.

'No,' I whispered. 'I didn't think.'

Callum exhaled roughly as I opened my eyes once more. He dragged his fingers through his hair. His hair had grown longer, I realised, and his form was sharper than it had been before. As though, in his desperation to find me, he'd forgotten to care for himself. 'You let yourself believe you were unnecessary.'

'Not unnecessary,' I argued, 'but you're the king, not me. The kingdom needed you. I needed you safe.'

'And *I* needed you.' Callum stepped forward, his shoulders straightening and eyes blazing with a fury I suspected had been building for a month. A fury he'd only allowed himself to feel now that I was here by his side. 'What you did *ruined* me. It was my fault you were there. My fault Vitus ended up with you in his hands.' His eyes dipped, landing on the wards. 'My fault you were hurt. If I'd just ignored the threat Vitus gave and not agreed to meet him by myself—' He stopped, spinning abruptly and stalking to the other side of the tent. His shadow disappeared as darkness surrounded him, too far from the reach of the wards' glow.

'Then Vitus would've found a different way. One that might have ended in far more blood.' The amount of blood spilt that day had been horrifying enough.

'Then we would've paid that price,' Callum said fiercely, turning back to me. 'Gods, the whole city could've been bled dry if it meant you were safe.'

'You don't mean that.'

'I do,' he insisted. I continued staring at him until he sighed, his fists loosening. 'Or maybe I don't. I don't know. But I do know that month without you was torture far worse than anything my father could've conjured.'

'I'm sorry.'

Callum flinched at the words. 'Chiara, I wasn't expecting an apology.'

I smiled. Once, those words had been impossible for me to squeeze out. Apologies were admitting wrongs, and admitting wrongs led to pain. But Callum, who'd come from a childhood as cruel as my own, had apologised with an ease I'd envied. Never carelessly, and never to anyone who didn't deserve one, but he still managed it.

If a king could admit he was wrong, then so could I. 'I wanted to protect you. It was all I could think about in that month – keeping you safe, even if it meant keeping you away from me. And I thought I was managing it. But all I did was hurt you. Hurt both of us.'

He stepped forward, stopping at the boundary of light. 'I love you, Chiara. And the thought that you might disappear from me again – that next time it might be more permanent...'

I closed the distance between us, grasping a handful of his shirt and dragging him down, stopping just shy of our lips touching. 'Then I promise that I will never shut you out again. That I will fight to the very last bit of my strength to stay with you.'

'We don't have a good history with promises, Captain.'

We didn't. One of his had ended with my sister dead, and mine with us separated. 'This is a vow I won't break. But only if you swear the same.'

There was a flicker of hesitation, and then resolve solidified in his expression. 'I do.'

When I kissed him, I did it with all the strength of my determination, and every piece of my love. Of my need for him in a way that had always gone far beyond simple desire. Despite the broken promises that had come before, there was a trust that curled through the bond. A complete faith that I meant what I'd said, just as I fully believed the same of Callum.

Callum pulled away first, and I fought to keep from dragging him back to me. 'Any thoughts on why your Gift is playing up?'

Something crackled in my veins, that same foreign power from before. I shuddered at its touch. 'I think ... I think it might have to do with Dearil's power.'

Callum froze, then tilted his head. 'You said you felt Dearil's power before. Can you explain it to me?'

'Dearil died, which means his power must've found a vessel,

and I suspect that I'm it. The voice seems ... woven, I guess. Like it's a part of that same power.' I shrugged, as though I wasn't terrified of the power in my veins.

Callum's blink was the only sign of shock he gave. Then he grinned. 'If you have Dearil's power, doesn't that make you a god? You outrank me now.'

My shoulders tensed. 'I don't, and I'm not.'

'I think a god of death far outranks—'

'I'm in the mortal lands, which means we obey mortal customs. And I am not the god of death,' I said, more harshly than I meant to. Callum's smile faltered, concern softening his expression. I cursed myself. I was taking out my unease on the last person I wanted to. Shaking my head, I sighed. 'I'm sorry. I'm exhausted. Let's try to get some more sleep.'

'You're still *you*, Chiara. No matter what power is in your veins.'

I looked away from him. 'I know.'

He tucked one of my curls behind my ear, his fingers lingering. I leant into that touch, wishing I could hoard the warmth for all the times I struggled to find anything but cold. 'Do you?'

I prodded at the power sleeping in my veins. It stirred, and I shuddered at the feel of it. Of how it seemed embedded into every part of me. 'Of course,' I lied.

Callum saw through me. He always did. 'I don't think—'

'Sleep,' I said abruptly. 'We both need sleep.'

His concern softened, fingers curling under my chin to tilt my face towards him. 'I love you, no matter what you are. Whatever might lie in your body doesn't change the fact that you're mine.'

Once, I might have snapped at him that I wasn't a possession for him to keep. But he was right. We belonged to each other, irrevocably. 'It's strange to think we might never have met if your father hadn't been such a tyrant, isn't it? Or if Vitus hadn't been involved in manipulating his decisions since we were children.' Even the thought was enough to make me want to grab on tight to Callum and never let him go.

Callum leant in, his forehead pressing to mine and lips pausing tantalisingly close. 'I would have found my way to you, no matter what.'

'What if I'd been raised in the godly realm?' I pointed out. 'You couldn't have found me there.'

He pulled away, grinning at my grumble of protest. 'I would have found a way.'

'But if you hadn't met me, you wouldn't have been reacquainted with Jaxon so—'

'Always so stubborn,' he murmured, then cut off any further protests with another kiss. I closed my eyes, melting into his touch. For a blissful moment, even the power inside me quieted, held at bay by the warmth of Callum's kiss.

Callum pulled away far too quickly. I attempted to tug him back, but he held firm. 'You were the one who said you needed sleep.'

'Sleep can come later.'

'You look exhausted.' He gently manoeuvred me away, forcing me back onto the bed. I scowled up at him, feeling far too much like a small child being put to bed. His lips curved further upwards. 'Sleep, Chiara. There will be plenty of time for this later.'

I didn't voice what I was sure Callum was already well aware of. That there might not be. Not if Vitus won what was to come. 'I don't need sleep.' I smiled up at him with as much innocence as I could muster. It wasn't much. 'I've had plenty of it in...' I trailed off as Callum's expression darkened.

I shouldn't have brought us back to that month.

He sighed. Before I could find some way to wheedle a few more moments from him, he slid his hand over my eyes. It was warm, the calluses more familiar to me than my own. Despite my attempts otherwise, my eyes shut. 'Sleep.'

I reached for him, curling my fingers on his. The dripping still sounded outside, and a spike of fear embedded itself into my chest. I tightened my hold on him, grabbing onto the bond when words failed me. *You'll be going to sleep, too?*

He seemed to understand what I didn't say. The silly fear that I'd wake up, and I truly would be all alone. *I'll be here, Captain. I promise I'm not going anywhere.*

His arm found its way around me again, and I sank into his touch. His breathing evened out far quicker than mine did, though his hold didn't loosen. That sound, accompanied by the steady thrum of his heartbeat against my back, was enough to lull me to sleep.

I didn't know how long I existed in the warm embrace of unconsciousness, Callum's hold keeping nightmares at bay. It might have been a minute or a handful of hours by the time my Gift shifted. I jerked awake, startled by the sudden movement. It was unlike anything I'd experienced, almost as though someone had grasped hold of the power and tried to yank it – and me – away. I pulled back, and the power settled back.

Frowning, I peeked open my eyes to glance at the wards. They hadn't glowed bright as they usually did when I tried to use my Gift. Nothing more than a trick of my mind, then.

Sighing, I pulled the blanket tighter to ward off the chill as I settled back down, nestling into Callum's side. He was still here, just as he had promised. My eyes shut. Morning was a while off, and I sensed I'd need whatever rest I could get.

The yanking came again. Only this time, it was far more vicious – less a child tugging at a mother's skirts, more a clawed monster tearing their prey away from safety. I inhaled sharply as I bolted upright. The Gift surged, rising up like an inferno. It didn't seek to explode, though, and the wards showed no reaction.

The Divine

No, it seemed to want to consume. It spilt over my skin, rolling in waves until my vision was blurred with silver. My pulse quickened. Something was very, very wrong.

'Callum,' I said hoarsely, holding my fingers out in front of me. They were made of nothing but light, no flesh to be seen.

Instantly alert, he lurched upright, grasping my arms. 'What is it? What's wrong?'

I shook my head, pushing my hand up. 'Don't you – my Gift. It's – I don't—' I broke off, frustration swelling as a line of confusion appeared on his brow.

The yanking turned sharp – a beckoning that refused to be ignored. My hand trembled as I sucked in a breath. Callum's touch grew softer, though he didn't seem to loosen his hold at all. My sight blurred further, turning Callum's sharp features into something indiscernible.

It was that which drove the terror in.

'Don't let me go,' I begged, trying desperately to grasp for him with my silvery fingers.

'Chiara?' Callum's voice bounced around as though trapped in a small space. His face swam in and out of view, fear growing starker with each moment. The yanking was more incessant now, like a knife cutting at threads. With each cut, my Gift rose higher, the light shining brighter. 'Chiara, what—'

'Don't let me go,' I begged again, voice cracking. 'Please, Callum.'

'I won't,' he said back, his voice both close and far away.

A pulse of my own power came out of me like a punishment for ignoring the call, sending me flying away from him. I cried out as I slammed into the ground, the pulling strengthening. It wanted me to follow it. To give in.

I wouldn't let it. Scrambling onto my feet, I lunged for Callum as he reached for me. Our fingers brushed. His terror-struck stare met my own as his lips formed a shout I couldn't hear. And then, there was a final yank. One far more brutal than the ones before. One even I couldn't ignore.

A flash of brilliant light. The scent of smoke and jasmine. And, with it, every sense of myself was undone as I was flung between the realms.

Chapter Fourteen

I became loose threads, spinning through the realms with no control over my destination. Colours and scenes flashed by in a dizzying array – a forest of fanged creatures and darkness, waves crashing upon bleached bones, golden trees stretching high into the air as leaves drifted upwards to reconnect to their branches. I tried to reach out, to grasp hold onto anything, but the pulling was too insistent, my defiance destroyed before it'd fully formed.

Waves of heat and ice rolled through me, alternating so quickly that I had no time to adjust. Nausea rose and fell with it, painful bursts of my Gift shuddering through the parts of me that still held together. Snatches of sounds passed me by, but I couldn't make sense of any of them.

As abruptly as it'd started, the movement stopped. I slammed back into existence, staggering forward a step as my muscles struggled to remember how to cooperate. The silver faded, replaced by a familiar space, ending in gates of shadows and light.

Frowning, I glanced around. There were a few lights around, but the souls didn't flock to me as they usually did. Instead, they hung back, buzzing with what seemed to be anticipation. I stepped towards the closest one. Before I could reach out for it, my Gift flared painfully, my muscles locking into place. Gritting my teeth, I attempted to force out another step, but the silver only flared brighter, wrapping around my joints with more forceful restraint than any chains could manage.

Only once I relaxed and turned to the Gates did the pain fade.

My frown deepened. 'Stubborn power,' I muttered, and I could've sworn silver sparked in snide retort.

It seemed I had no choice. Walking forward, I let the pull I'd been caught by since waking in Callum's tent guide me to the Gates. Souls hovered behind me, their usual whispers gone. With each step, the power in me glowed brighter. Stopping before the Gates, I tilted my head back. They were the same as they always were – tall, imposing, and filled with quiet power. But they also seemed different. More synchronised with the silver energy, as though they were a physical manifestation of the power in my veins.

Chiara. My name burst with desperate terror down the bond, Callum gripping it tight. *Chiara, where are you? What—*

I'm all right, I replied, staring up at the Gates. The power surged, yanking against any hold I might have on it. *I'm at the Gates.*

As in the Gates souls go to? There was a heartbeat of silence. *You can't be serious.*

Despite my situation, I smiled. *Oh, I absolutely am.*

You... I didn't need the bond to hear Callum sigh. I imagined he was running his fingers through his hair, his terror turned to exasperation. *You'll give me a heart attack one of these days.*

Guilt needled at me. This might not have been my fault, but it was my divine blood that had dragged me here. *I'm sorry.*

As long as you come back to me safely, I'll forgive you. The bond went quiet, Callum giving me space to focus.

I lifted my hand, then hesitated, fingers hovering shy of touching the surface.

Everything will change. The words rattled through the air, spilling from the Gates and from my own power. They coiled around me, too tight. A strange understanding flooded me. A sense that I knew exactly what would happen when I touched the Gates. When I accepted the summons, and all that came with it.

The role the realms had decided for me. The role Dearil had left behind.

I took a step back. 'I don't want it.'

The power's excitement at finding me shifted, its energy growing and crackling. I shoved it back, turning my back to the Gates and sliding to the ground. The Gates wouldn't let me go, I knew, until I'd accepted what they offered. But I couldn't fill the spot Dearil had left. It was too much, and I had never wanted it.

Drawing my knees to my chest, I set my cheek upon them and closed my eyes. I'd outwait the Gates. Let them find another candidate.

I knew whose soul it was who settled beside me, sitting with the same quiet patience he'd always possessed. The soul had a different feel to the rest. Far stronger, yet hazier at the same time. A lightning bolt whose fate was to disappear, while the insignificant blades of grass stayed.

'This is where you farewelled your sister, is it not?' Dearil's voice was both the same and entirely different to what it had been in life. Still deep, a hint of a rasp to his words. But the edges of it were softer, warmer, as though death had stripped away all the years that had carved into him and left only his core.

A mix of love and pain gathered in my chest as I thought of the last smile my sister had given me before she passed through the Gates. 'It is.'

'Death might be the way of things, but it is a terrible thing, to lose one so young.'

I had no desire to discuss Cassie with him. 'Are you here to tell me I have to accept the role?'

'No.'

I opened my eyes, though I didn't look at Dearil. I studied the souls before me instead. Each bright. Each with their own story. And most, I knew, had been cut down far too soon. 'Are you here to travel through the Gates?'

'Gods do not have a place in the afterlife of mortals.'

'Then where will you go?'

'I do not know.' I glanced over, catching a hint of a smile on Dearil's light-blurred features. 'But I look forward to it.'

'You could be headed straight for a torturous existence.' I trailed a finger over my knee, drawing small circles. 'Or you might cease to exist at all.'

'Then that is to be my fate.'

I blew out a breath. 'You're far too accepting of things.'

'Not at all, my child.' A hand rested upon my head, a gesture of affection I'd never received in Dearil's lifetime. 'I am simply old. Too old. I wish for rest, no matter what form it comes in.'

'And I get to take on all the burden of being what you were?' I asked bitterly.

'This has always been your place, even before my death. It just took the realms some time to realise that.' He laughed, the sound sending souls scampering through the air with delight. 'The power that gods inherited has always been stubborn and slow to change. It was the same when the gods took over from the ancients. The realms' power had no wish to see new rulers at first. It only accepted us once the ancients died, leaving the power no choice.'

A soul flittered closer, alighting on Dearil's shoulder. I looked over at him – at the genuine fondness in his smile as he ran a finger along the glowing orb. 'Why did you do that? Take the knife for me?'

The Divine

The soul nuzzled Dearil's cheek before flying away. He watched it go, a touch of sorrow in his silver eyes. 'I was fading, child. Have been fading for eighteen years. If I did not die now, I would die soon. I would much prefer to die doing something than die for nothing.'

My brows bunched at the sentiment. It sounded like something I might believe. Not Dearil, who'd always put his duty as a god above all else. But perhaps this was who he truly was, beyond his divinity. Someone whose warmth left traces in his eyes as he met my gaze. Whose sternness was easily stripped away to reveal the affection beneath. 'What do you mean by fading?'

'There must always—'

'Be balance.' I lifted my eyes towards the unending white above us. 'I know.'

He chuckled. 'Yes, I suppose you do. It is the same with the role of the gods, and why most gods kill any children – halfling or otherwise – who show signs of too much power. Halflings are always weaker than the fully divine, even if they were to inherit a parent's power. But even the smallest traces of that power can become a threat.' He held out his hand, cupping a soul gently. 'Death can only be contained in one form. You were growing stronger, and the balance was lost. There was too much death for life in the realm. One of us had to die to right the balance before you grew too strong.'

'Then why not let that one be me?' Most of the other gods would've made sure it was that way.

'Because you are my daughter.'

Dearil said it so simply, as though it explained everything. As though parents didn't beat and kill their children every day in the mortal realm. As though some of the gods didn't do far worse. I knew better. Sharing blood didn't stop hatred and violence.

'The power speaks to me. It's not like my Gift. It's cruel. Unpredictable,' I said, not ready to acknowledge what he'd said.

Dearil nodded, as though this was to be expected. 'Then perhaps you should listen to what it is trying to say.'

I scoffed. 'You say that like it's normal to hear the power speak.'

'It is. It spoke to me plenty of times.' There was a smile in his voice that twisted a strange spike of envy through me. It almost sounded like the power had been a friend. If that was the case, then that same power had marked me as an enemy. 'The power is ancient. It has had a form of sentience since before my creation. And now it is your role to manage it.'

My fingers curled. 'So, you die and I'm now the god of death?' I smiled, a twist of my lips that was accompanied by a bitter stab. 'Fantastic. Just what I need.'

'Possessing a god's power does not make one a god.' Dearil watched me carefully, light drifting around him as though drawn to his wavering form. 'The power belongs to a realm before it belongs to gods, and it seeks a vessel. If the vessel is not suitable ... you saw what happened to the king who contained Vitus's power.'

I lifted my hand, watching the silver dance across my palm. 'Even better. I either become a god or I fall to pieces because of the power.'

'You are not at risk of death from your power.'

'But you just said—'

'You are not mortal. But you must master the power my death granted you. If not, you will find that the power masters you.'

That very same power chuckled in my mind. *You will never master me.*

My fingers curled into a fist. The silver wormed its way through the gaps between my fingers. 'And Callum? Kerta and Evania seem to think he'll be the one to inherit Vitus's power if we succeed.'

'Ah.' Another trace of a smile. 'I think your king will be just fine.'

Relief flooded through me, the silver shifting from crackling to gentle undulations over my hands. 'Why?'

'I have met the boy. He is the type who would make the impossible possible for the person he loves. If you ask it of him, I am sure he could conquer Vitus's power.'

I sighed. Vitus wasn't wrong. 'Then I suppose I should try to do the same.'

The words tasted like a lie, but Dearil did not seem to notice. 'You should. And you must do it soon. The gods will take some time to acclimatise to the mortal realm, and their power will be temporarily weakened from the travel between realms. They will wait until their power is at its fullest. But once it is, Vitus's victory will be assured.'

A chill ran through me. Pushing myself to my feet, I turned to regard the Gates. 'What did they bring me here for?'

'To identify their new master.' Dearil pressed his hand to the Gates, and the light and dark shifted. 'A formality required to set the balance once more. It should not be difficult for you, given the Gates already accept you. All you need to do is touch them.'

I hesitated. 'And this means I accept the power?'

'No. This means you accept your role ruling over death. The power, though, has not yet become yours. It is up to you to make sure that happens. You need to learn to listen to it so it may listen to you.'

Nothing was ever easy. Every step I took forward, something new seemed to be added to my shoulders. And this – accepting a role ruling over death – was a burden I didn't think I'd be able to manage. I might've been born with a trace of divinity, but I'd lived a slave. There was nothing in me that knew how to rule.

But I needed to return to my friends. To Callum. Needed to be by their side to plan for the next steps. I had no choice but to accept.

Swallowing, I pressed my hand to the Gates. The power Dearil's death had granted me rolled through me, its strangeness uncomfortable in my veins. The Gates rippled, their light and dark mingling into a whirlpool of varying shades. The souls around me started to whisper, their voices filling the silence with excited tones. Beyond the Gates, I thought I could sense more – the souls who'd not yet found their place between the Dark and the Light, curiously pressing against the Gates at the sense of the new force on the other side.

The whispers grew to a frenzy, a wind that came from no discernible source whipping around me. Dearil smiled as he stepped back. 'Do well, my daughter. Be better than I.'

And then he was gone, and I was in the middle of a maelstrom. Souls flew past me, fragments of pasts accompanying them. A girl, falling into a river as she tried to chase after her big sister. A man sick in bed, chest rattling with a cough as he waited for the family he knew wouldn't come. An elderly woman who opened her door to her daughter, knowing that the woman with golden eyes wasn't truly the one she'd watched die a week before.

So many souls. So many deaths.

But they weren't all terrible.

There was a mother who smiled as she bled out, her newborn babe squalling healthily in her arms. The wizened man whose great-grandchildren crowded around his armchair. A child too young to understand that the golden creatures battering at their door were his end as his pa rocked him to sleep.

The whipping wind stopped, the souls settling down as the Gates cracked open. Unlike before, I could see past the threshold. See souls waiting to be judged, some nervously flickering about and others calmly staying in place. But there was still nothing beyond those souls. Even gods couldn't meddle in what came after death.

The air hummed, the power that sustained the balance satiated. There was no trace of the god who'd been there moments before. I only hoped he'd found the rest he was after.

Another tug came – an insistence that I return to where it had stolen me from. *Back to Callum*, I begged the power. *Please*.

But the realms had rarely respected my wishes in the past. I was yanked from the Gates and sent hurtling through flashes of colours and snatches of sensation. Once again, I had no control. I was simply a puppet, guided by the whims of ancient power.

As quickly as it had snatched me up, the power let me go. There was a single second to catch my breath before it fell away entirely, and I plummeted towards the unknown.

Chapter Fifteen

I slammed into a branch, the wood creaking before it snapped. There was a brief pause in momentum, my breath snatched from me, before I was falling again. The ground rose to meet me, stars laughing at my landing beyond a canopy of leaves. I groaned.

Damned power of the realms. It could at least have placed me on the ground. The air was crisp, sweeping over me and stealing the lingering scent of death's power from my skin. It took several minutes for the throbbing in my head and back to subside. Stones poked into me, twigs uncomfortable beneath me. A few leaves had made the fall alongside me and now rested upon my skin.

Dearil's power roiled beneath my skin. Deciding that to force my aching body up would be too much effort, I lifted my hand, extending it to the night's sky. Leaves shuddered above as I reached for the power, just as I had reached for my Gift countless times before, directing it at a tree to the left of the one I'd landed in.

The breeze stilled. Smoke and jasmine filled the air around me, too thick and too fast, as the power surged for my fingers. I gritted

The Divine

my teeth, trying to grasp hold of the power. *Just the one tree*, I ordered it.

For a heartbeat, I thought it might obey. The rush of power hesitated, silver illuminating the space around me. My fingers were lit in their glow, competing with the stars for brightness.

A harsh laugh shattered my hope. The power's voice seemed to sneer as it said, *You don't give me orders. I am not yours to command.*

Before I could stop it, it launched free, the wards singeing my skin as silver arched through the air. It slammed into the tree I had directed it towards. In moments, the vitality of the plant was gone, trunk withered and brown leaves dropping to the ground. But it did not stop there. It slammed out again as the tree vanished entirely in a cloud of silver ash.

Stop, I shouted in my own mind as I tried to yank it back. It laughed again, the sound oddly familiar as it sliced through the tree behind, and then the next one and the next – until a line of silver ash sliced through the forest around me. Only when it had devoured ten trees did it sink back beneath my skin, its laughter echoing in my mind.

My hand thumped back to the ground, my teeth gritted. If I had used that around people, there was no telling what destruction it might have caused. I closed my eyes, my breaths shuddering through me. This was why I'd never wanted to be a vessel for a god's power.

I wasn't Dearil. I could never hold the calm he did. Destruction and violence was what I'd been raised with. I didn't regret all of it, but now, there was far more at stake than just me if I lost control.

It meant I couldn't trust the power. And if I couldn't trust the power, we had just lost a valuable weapon.

When my breathing settled, I opened my eyes, and found four sword points levelled at my throat.

'Damn the realms,' I muttered. This was becoming too familiar a welcome.

'Who are you?' a woman demanded, shoving her sword closer to me. 'Where did you come from?'

I lifted a finger, pointing at the jagged remains of the branch I'd fallen from. 'Isn't it obvious?'

Someone must've shifted a lantern closer to us, because warm light spilt over the woman's features. She was older, her wiry hair greying. My eyes fell to her uniform. The sigil of Naruzia was emblazoned upon it.

At least the realms had the decency to deposit me in semi-friendly territory.

'Don't get smart with me,' the woman snapped. The three men with her stared down at me with a mix of bemusement and resolve. 'Are you a spy? An assassin? It was a mistake to come here.'

The flicker of the lantern shoved closer, the light stinging my eyes. I winced, lifting a hand to block it. Swords shifted in warning and I dropped my hand, forcing back my instincts. We needed every soldier we had, and injuring these four for doing their jobs wasn't advisable.

Even so, my temper was fraying quickly. I needed to find Callum soon.

'Lady Chiara?' The lantern appeared above my eyes, too bright to see past. 'Is that you?'

'You know her, Eamon?' the woman asked. Her sword eased back.

My eyes adjusted enough that I could make out a pair of brown eyes and youthful features. Eamon, the same soldier I'd encountered when Dearil had shoved me through the realm's fabric, stood over me, eyes wide. 'This is Chiara Halnea, ma'am. You know – His Majesty's...' He trailed off, the lantern light deepening the colour of his flush.

The Divine

'You expect me to believe the future queen just dropped from the sky?' the woman scoffed.

I frowned. What sort of rumours had Callum been spreading that these people believed me to be their future queen?

'She does that sometimes,' Eamon said. Four disbelieving eyes turned his way. He shrugged, the movement jostling the light. 'What? She does.'

'I don't think—'

I'd been at the Gates too long to stay here while they argued over what they did or did not think. Callum would start to get worried soon. I lashed out with a foot, slamming it into the side of the woman's knee. She cried out as she fell – rather dramatically, I thought, given I'd made sure not to break anything. The three others with swords startled. Eamon backed away, leaving us in shadows as I twisted, narrowly avoiding a rather nervous blow from one of them. I reached for a dagger before realising I was still wearing Callum's shirt, much of my skin exposed from it.

No wonder the woman was so reluctant to believe Eamon. I'd dropped out of the sky, had leaves tangled in my hair, and was wearing nightclothes. I'd be sceptical, too.

One of the men raised his sword. 'Surrender. We'll bring you to the main—'

'I think that's quite enough of that.' A dark figure jumped down from a concealed branch, his smile caught by the light as Eamon deemed it safe enough to move forward. 'You might find yourself without a head if our king ever discovers you raised a sword against Lady Chiara.'

The men lowered their swords, faces paling. The woman stayed where she was. 'Then … she is the future queen?'

'Perhaps.' Jaxon leant against a tree, his yellow eyes filled with amusement at the fear on the soldiers' faces as they realised their error. 'But regardless of what she might become, she's definitely not someone you want to piss off.'

The woman turned to me. 'My apologies, Your—'

'It's fine,' I cut her off before she could add on a title that didn't belong to me.

'Continue on your patrol,' Jaxon said, a thread of steel weaving through his words despite the almost lazy smile on his face. 'I'll escort her back.'

The five soldiers hurried off. I was almost insulted by their eagerness to leave.

I folded my arms as I regarded Jaxon. 'You were watching all that?'

He smiled. 'I was.'

'You could've intervened earlier.'

Coming forward, he laced his arm through mine. 'But where would the fun in that be? Besides, I was having a rather glorious dream that you interrupted. There was a—'

'Where's Callum?' I broke in before I could find out what sort of horrendous things Jaxon had dreamt up. Unease still thrummed through me, refusing to settle along with the power that wasn't mine. Everything that had passed with Dearil had happened too fast, and I felt unmoored. Callum had a way of soothing my greatest fears in a way no one else could. 'He's probably out of his mind right now. I should go to him straight away. Explain—'

'Callum's not here, Chiara,' Jaxon said.

An owl flew off a nearby branch as my steps faltered. 'Well, not *here*,' I said, 'but in our tent—'

'He'd be about a five-day ride away right now,' Jaxon said slowly, as though anticipating a violent reaction.

I frowned as we paused in the shadows, the amber glow of campfire flickering from beyond the trees we were hidden behind. Trees which hadn't existed anywhere near where I'd been before. 'That makes no sense. You were at the camp with us. Deana, too.'

'I was. Two weeks ago, when you disappeared.'

Ice swept over me. Two weeks. Fourteen days where the gods

had walked this realm, and I had not. Fourteen days where Callum had been alone. Where we couldn't reach each other through the soul-bond.

Sensing my agitation, power began to crackle, silver flickering over my skin. I couldn't focus on it, though. All I could think about was those two weeks.

'He's fine,' Jaxon rushed to say as the space around us lit up in silver strands that heeded no command of mine. 'Well, he's a mess – I thought he might ride out to face Vitus himself when you went missing – but I explained what must've happened. It was the ascension, correct? Dearil once told me about it. I should've thought to warn you, but'—he shrugged—'there was a lot going on.'

I nodded, barely focusing on his words. Was Callum all right? Had there been any more battles? If anyone had harmed him – if there was even a single cut that hadn't been there before I'd left—

The silver intensified, eager to use my rage to fuel its hunt for life.

'Gods!' Jaxon yelped, taking a step away from me as stinging pain shot through my wrists, the wards unable to contain the divine power. He reached for me, then halted. 'He's fine, Chiara. I promise. He's—'

'Where is he?' I demanded.

We'd only just been reunited, and the realms had torn us apart again. I *hated* the realms for that. The power that governed all that existed. To cruelly bind us with a soul-bond, only to keep us separated. Fury swirled. If Callum died while we were separated, I would find a way to make that ancient power pay for it.

'There was an attack.' The silver brightened. It lapped at the trees, sending three crumbling into ash. 'Not an attack he was involved in! Reports of a god of shadows in Naruzia, while Tizan's army has disappeared. We suspect there's someone in the army feeding information to the enemy, and Tizan was warned we'd be going after him. Deana managed to convince Callum to go with her to Naruzia to check on the damage.'

Some of my terror flickered, but the rage wasn't done yet. Neither was the foreign power. It pushed at my skin, begging to be let loose.

Jaxon continued. 'She practically had to drag him with her, though. Convinced him by saying there were more resources in Alluvite – ones he could utilise to gather information on where you might end up.'

'He's unharmed?'

'As far as I know.' Jaxon eyed me for a moment as the silver subsided, seemingly satisfied by the ring of death it'd created around us. Dead grass crunched under his feet as he stepped forward, gingerly laying a hand on my shoulder.

I eyed him. 'What are you doing?'

'Uh … comforting you?'

I glared. 'Then why does it feel like you're attempting to pet a mountain cat?'

His hand fell away. 'I'd rank you as considerably more dangerous than a mountain cat.'

'Where are we?' I scoured the area. The surrounds were foreign, the trees taller and sparser of leaves than those that grew in Naruzia. A few small animals stared out from their hideaways. 'Archin?'

Jaxon nodded. 'To the east. Unlike Tizan, Tarina hasn't disappeared. We received another report of a unit lost a week ago.' He caught me by the arm as I began walking away. 'Where do you think you're going?'

I stared over my shoulder at him. 'To get a horse.'

'Of course.' His grip firmed as I tried to pull away, silver no longer lacing my skin. 'And why are you getting a horse in the middle of the night?'

'Because Callum's in Naruzia,' I said. 'And I'm here.'

The Divine

Jaxon blinked, his eyes more feline than ever under the combined light of the stars and the glow of the wards at my wrist. 'You're planning on riding to Naruzia in the middle of the night?'

'It's not like I can use my Gift, is it?' I gestured to the wards and then to the deadness around us. 'Dearil's power isn't exactly obedient.'

The power stirred. *You think I would obey you?*

Shut up, I snapped back.

'You're not going to ride to Naruzia.'

I frowned, his words barely reaching me. There was very little space left in my mind for logic. I was too consumed with the power prowling in me, and the distance between Callum and I. A distance I could rectify.

I stared at where he held me. 'Of course I am.'

'No, you're not,' Jaxon said, firmer this time. 'You're going to stay with me. We'll face whatever trap Tarina's laid for the soldiers, and then we'll head back to Naruzia. Together.'

'I'm not going to wait another day to—'

'*Think*, Chiara,' Jaxon snapped, his grip tightening. 'You get a horse and ride out. Then what? Do you know where in Archin we are? Or how to reach Naruzia?'

My cheeks heated. 'I know how to use a map.'

'Fine. You use a map. What next? Vitus has been quiet for the past two weeks, but what if he attacks in the meantime? Or what if one of the other gods rises and sees you by yourself?'

'Then I'll cut them down.'

'With what power?' he asked bluntly. He gestured to the wards. 'You said it yourself. Your Gift is unresponsive, and Dearil's power is uncontrollable. The gods will be building up their own power. At least if you stay with us, you'll have an army at your back. And me – I might not have the power you do, but I have more than Gifted mortals.'

I wrenched free of his hold. 'And what if Callum is hurt? What if he dies while we're apart?'

Jaxon sighed, dragging his hand through his hair. The golden glow of the wards caught the shadows under his eyes. He looked haggard in a way I'd never seen him. 'Have you thought about what will happen if he finds out you've ridden off by yourself?'

I hesitated. In truth, I hadn't really been thinking past needing Callum. It was as much a physical need as anything else, my body uneasy without him by my side. 'I—'

'He'll throw himself into any danger to get to you,' Jaxon said. 'Use your soul-bond, Chiara. Let him know you're safe. That you're unharmed.'

I blinked. The soul-bond. In between my conversation with Dearil and everything since, I'd been so focused on getting to Callum I had forgotten what I had at my disposal.

All it took was the slightest prod of the bond and it flared to life, emotions pouring down in overwhelming waves. Terror, exhaustion, relief. And, under it all, anger.

Chiara? My chest tightened at the sound of Callum's voice, Jaxon turning to inspect trees that had just become immensely interesting.

My fingers flexed. I wished I could reach out, wrap my arms around Callum and draw him close, but he was too far, and my power no longer controllable. *I'm here.*

You said you'd be right back. There was that anger. It hardened his words, turning them into knives that raked over my skin. *You said that, and then you disappeared for two weeks. Two weeks where I didn't know if you were breathing or if you—* He broke off, some of the anger pulling back. The knives of guilt stayed, though. *I'm sorry. I'm not angry, I'm just—*

Worried, I finished for him. Because of me, yet again.

You're safe?

The Divine

I nodded before realising he couldn't see me. *Aside from an unruly power that won't listen to me? Yes. I'm with Jaxon.*

That unruly power seemed to coil tighter where it had tucked itself, as though annoyed I was even speaking of it. It was quieter, though, than it had been before, Callum's voice as much a balm to it as it was to me. *Can you control it enough to come to me?*

My hands clenched. *No.* It was clear Callum was trying not to let his disappointment echo down the bond. Some slipped through all the same. *I can ride out for you, though. Tell me where you are and—*

No. I frowned at the quick refusal, trying not to be hurt by it. Just like with Callum's disappointment, though, some of it must have slipped through. He hurried to continue. *I want you by my side, Captain. Gods, there's nothing I'd like more. But war's here, and I'm not the only one who needs you. If you're with Jaxon, the men would do well to have you at their side. They're headed for Tarina. Stay with them for now.*

Is that an order, Your Majesty? I meant the words to sound teasing. They didn't.

Of course not. You are your own person, Chiara. You can decide what you do and who you will help. If you truly wish to leave them, then do it. I'll handle whatever comes.

I frowned down at my hands as I knotted them together, itching to do exactly that. *But it would help you if I stayed.*

There was a long silence, long enough that I almost thought Callum had gone to sleep. Eventually, a soft, *yes*, came down the bond. Pain was etched into that word, as though admitting that being apart might help win the war was physically painful. *And it would help me to know you have Jaxon to watch your back.*

You'd trust Jaxon?

With my possessions? Absolutely not. With fighting by your side? Yes. He sighed. *And Deana's been fretting almost as much as I have. I think it would be good for her to know you'll keep Jaxon safe.*

I frowned down at my hands. He was right, but it didn't stop the disappointment tightening my chest. *I told you, the power isn't listening to me. I don't know how much help I'll be.*

There was a ripple of amusement. *When have you ever relied on a god's power, Captain?*

Despite myself and the longing to hold Callum rather than just speak to him in my mind, my lips twitched up. I brushed my fingers over one of the knives at my side. *I suppose you're right.*

I usually am.

I laughed out loud, Jaxon startling and shooting me a raised-brows look over his shoulder. Motioning for him to turn back around, I said, *Seems your crown's inflated your ego, Your Majesty.*

It's not ego if it's true. Warmth spread down the bond, mixed in with a longing so deep I felt it in my soul. *The moment I have you back, I'm never letting you go again.*

Is that a promise?

I could picture the exact shape of Callum's wicked smile as he said, *Most definitely.*

'Are you finished yet?' Jaxon called. 'Because I need my beauty rest, which I can't get until I know you're not going to do something harebrained.'

Jaxon's being a nuisance, I said with a roll of my eyes. *I should deal with him.*

Good luck. The bond hummed with Callum's voice. *And come back to me unharmed.*

You, too. I swallowed back the urge to beg him to stay connected to the bond. It felt cold without Callum's presence.

Jaxon seemed to sense our conversation was over, slinging an arm over my shoulder and pulling me to his side. I let him. 'Did Cal convince you to stay?'

I frowned. 'Unfortunately.'

'Excellent. This way you'll be helping me remove my mother's threat. Less chance of harm coming to Cal with Tarina sorted.'

The Divine

I sighed, relenting. He was right. Riding out to Callum now was folly. Reckless in a way that might put more than me in danger. But if we could handle Tarina, that was a danger wiped out. One less threat to Callum and his kingdom.

What I needed could wait. I'd need to trust Callum to stay safe. Deana would guard him with her life, and Naruzia was less dangerous than Archin for the time being. Besides, Callum had always been adept at protecting himself.

The gods are here, my own voice whispered in my head. *Can he protect himself from those?*

My pulse quickened at the thought. At what might happen if Callum fell. At what I might do. But I shoved it away. If what Jaxon said was true, Vitus hadn't yet made his first appearance since the barrier fell. That meant we had to get rid of all the enemies we could before he showed. And I was uniquely positioned to help with that.

This was how I would make sure Callum survived this war. Make sure his kingdom didn't crumble.

If the thought of prolonging that separation sent a stab of pain through my heart, then I'd just have to deal with it.

Jaxon began walking, practically dragging me along with him. 'Oh, and you'll need to make sure to keep Cal far away from sensing any danger you're in. Soul-bonded are often idiots when it comes to each other. You two have a particular fondness for reckless behaviour.'

'We don't have a *fondness*—'

'You were about to ride out at midnight without any real plan.' Jaxon grinned as he manoeuvred me towards the campfire, the hum of voices reaching us. 'Enough of that, though. You took up Dearil's mantle?'

My hands formed fists. 'Unfortunately.'

His grin grew. 'So, you're a god.'

'I'm not a god,' I snapped. 'I only inherited Dearil's powers.'

'I wouldn't be so sure about that.' Jaxon sighed when I continued scowling. 'Do you have to be so stubborn all the time? It's not that bad to be a god. Most would welcome the opportunity.'

I didn't answer. He was wrong. Being a god was perhaps the worst thing I could've become. All the burden that had been Dearil's had become mine. That included the mortal lives he'd looked over, ensuring balance remained so the realms wouldn't fall into ruin.

I'd never been driven to protect more than a select few people. Callum. Cassie. Deana and Jaxon. And perhaps there was room for some softness in me for the palace guards who I'd become friendly with, like Corin and Kailey, but ... a whole realm of people?

I was ill-suited to this job. Ill-suited to anything to do with ruling. Dearil had been right in the cells when he'd pointed out how similar to Vitus I could become. What I might destroy if given the motivation. I was made for blood and violence, not laws and ruling. Not like Callum was.

Staring at the approaching campsite, I prodded at the power in my veins. It crackled back, uneasy under my touch. A bitter smile twisted my lips. Even my own Gift refused to listen to me. No, I decided. Being a god did not suit me at all.

I only hoped the realms – and Callum – wouldn't end up paying the price for my failing.

Chapter Sixteen

My horse did not like me. That was fine. I didn't particularly warm to the coltish beast, either, as it tossed its head for the fifth time in the span of a handful of minutes, veering off the dust-covered road we travelled down. Up ahead, General Jade – who was thankfully in charge of this battalion rather than Jaxon – rode steadily, Captain Henri by her side. She'd accepted my appearance with surprising calm. Henri, on the other hand, had spent most of the past few days sending me a mixture of fearful and awed glances.

'Damned beast,' I muttered, tugging on the reins. The horse gave a final head-toss before returning to the road. I'd tried to convince Jade I was perfectly content to walk, but she'd insisted I use the beast. So that people knew I was in command, she'd explained.

When I'd pointed out I *wasn't* in command, nor did I have any intention of being, she'd merely smiled.

I kept my eyes mainly on the line of soldiers in front of me. Some spoke in low tones, walking together in small groups as the higher-ups rode with the supplies. Others maintained their silence, as subdued as I was by the desolate landscape.

It was hard to see what Archin once might've been. The sun glared down with a vengeance, turning every soldier within eyesight into sweat-soaked messes. The carcasses of once-bountiful trees bent in deference as we passed, their leaves vanished, while shrivelled grass curled around the base of the trunks. It was a vastly different picture of Archin to the one Prince Brayden had painted of his kingdom. He'd spoken of rolling grass and trees that delighted in the sun's warmth.

Now, even the air smelt off. There was no scent of fresh flowers, no baking bread from the empty town we'd passed through not long before. The air was stale, like this entire kingdom had been trapped in a cell, just as I'd been.

Twisting in my saddle, I glanced over my shoulder. Behind the blur of grey buildings that had once been Kerryth, the sky was shifting into hazier shades. Somewhere that way was Naruzia.

My fingers tightened in my reins, teeth clenched. If I spun the horse now and rode back as fast as I could, it'd take me a week, maybe two if I were to encounter anything unpleasant. I could do it. Could abandon this army to their fate and return to Callum's side. The last I'd heard from him, he'd almost reached Alluvite to regroup before heading out again.

It was tempting. The thought of his arms wrapping around me, his words whispered into my ear – gods, I didn't want to resist the urge. Longing wrapped around me, squeezing until I inhaled sharply and turned back to the front.

'You regret agreeing to head east, don't you?' Jaxon appeared at my left, looking miserable under the sun.

'Callum's people need us there,' I replied stiffly. And they did. None of us knew what we'd face upon arrival at where half of Jakob's forces had slashed their own throats. If anyone were able to resist the Illusions of a goddess, it'd be Tarina's son. I might stand a chance, too, if I could wrangle Dearil's power under control.

From the hissed-out insults the power sent back to me every time I so much as reached for it, however, that seemed unlikely.

'Doesn't stop you wanting to go find him.'

I sighed, tipping my head back and closing my eyes. The sting of the sun almost felt good. A distraction from everything that I desperately needed. 'You don't want to leave this behind for Deana?'

'Absolutely,' he said without hesitation.

I lifted my head, a few strands of hair falling over my eyes. Dragging a hand through them, I asked, 'Then why don't you?'

He hesitated, his eyes shifting away from me, before saying, 'Because you're here.'

I raised my brows. 'You don't think I can look after myself?'

'Oh, I know you can. But Deana is with Callum. Can you imagine the pain I'd go through if I returned and told them I'd left you behind?'

My lips curled upwards. 'I'd pay good coin to watch the thrashing Deana would give you.'

Jaxon grinned. 'I'm sure you would.' His smile faded. Two women, each with blonde braids and a similar roundness to their cheeks, rode alongside us. One surreptitiously glanced at Jaxon, blushing, but Jaxon paid her no mind. It seemed Deana had somehow cured him of his tendency to collect and break as many hearts as he could. 'I told you why I'm here. Your turn. Why are we not riding back to Naruzia this instant?' he turned to me and said.

'You were the one who told me not to.'

'Yes, but I'm surprised you listened. You rarely do, especially when it comes to Callum.'

I scraped my thumb nail along the rein. 'If there really is a god there, these people will all die.'

Jaxon shrugged. 'So, they die. It wouldn't be the first time either of us has allowed people to die so we could get what we wanted.'

The blushing soldier paled as she overheard that. She rushed ahead with her friend. I sat quietly with Jaxon's words for some time. He wasn't wrong. I protected my own, but these people – most of them weren't mine. They were strangers. The only ones I knew were Henri, Jade and Eamon, all of whom meant very little to me. I might've felt I owed something to General Jade for Ada, but even she was a stranger, and nothing I owed was worth more than my need to be with Callum.

But… 'These are Callum's people,' I finally said. 'If they die, then he'll find a way to blame himself for those deaths. He takes far too much onto himself already. I won't let these people be an extra burden for him.'

'He's told you he wants you to do this?'

I fell silent, stretching out for Callum.

I scoffed. 'Of course not. The idiot told me to do what I wanted, and damn all the consequences, as long as it made me happy.' I could almost hear Callum's voice warming my skin; felt his hand pressing to my cheek. My next breath shuddered through me, and I had to resist reaching out to him. We both needed to focus on our own tasks. 'And then he'd try to take on the entirety of whatever we faced so that I – and everyone else – didn't have to be endangered by it.'

'And you'd inevitably throw yourself into danger.' Jaxon sighed. 'I'm starting to understand why Deana's always complaining about the two of you.'

My horse began to veer once more. I wasted no time in pulling it back around, the disobedient creature snorting as though amused by its own antics. 'We're not the ones Deana's usually complaining about.'

'It's practically flirting when it's about me.' I hid a grin. He wasn't wrong. 'So, I suppose that settles it. We're going to launch into a battle so that your king doesn't feel sad.'

'That's certainly one way to put it.' I glanced over the trail of heads, the horizon a blur of golden light and dark ground. 'And the sooner we can get this war over with, the sooner Callum and I can be together without worrying about something tearing us apart again.'

'You're turning soft,' Jaxon teased.

Tiring of riding, I tugged on the reins and, pulling my horse to a stop, swung off. My legs ached at the long hours riding as I landed. 'Shut up.' I glanced up at Jaxon, my brows furrowing as he, too, tugged his horse to a halt. 'How did you end up on a horse, anyway?'

He grinned and I could already feel my sigh building. 'Don't you know? My poor knee'—he reached to rub it unconvincingly—'plays up when I walk for too long ever since I rescued our dear king from Archin.'

I stared at him. 'Your knee shouldn't even have been *bruised* after that. Plus, we both know your body's sturdier than most mortals.'

'It's an emotional scar, Chiara.' He clicked his tongue. 'You need to be more empathetic.'

Stepping aside so Jaxon could drop to the ground, I ran my hand down my horse's side. Now that I wasn't riding it, it seemed content to stand still and await its next command. 'You were just telling me I'd turned soft.'

'Did I say it was a bad thing?'

'It was implied.'

'Always imagining thing that aren't—'

'Lady Chiara?' A young woman approached, her dark hair in twin braids. When I turned to her, she snapped an arm across her chest, bowing stiffly.

Jaxon leant into my side, whispering, 'What did you do to that poor girl? She looks terrified.'

Nudging him away, I studied the soldier as she remained bowed. She was young – fifteen at most, though she could've been younger – and possessed rounded features that accentuated her youth, though the muscles in her arms were strong. When she remained bent over, I frowned. 'You can rise.'

The girl snapped up so quickly that one of her braids whacked an unfortunate passer-by. 'Thank you, ma'am.'

'You don't have to…' I sighed at the expectant look in her eyes. 'Never mind. What do you need?'

'Ah… General Jade wished to see you, ma'am.' The girl clasped her hands behind her back, planting her feet firmly apart. 'She says we are to reach the area reported by Captain Henri soon and she wants to know what our next moves should be.'

I frowned. 'She's the general. Shouldn't she be giving me the orders?'

The girl shifted. She glanced at her feet, then back up at me.

Biting back another sigh, I said, 'Tell me. You won't be in trouble for relaying the general's words.'

'Well, ma'am, she said that you'd try to claim you had no role leading, but His Majesty made it perfectly clear, when you went missing, that if anyone were to treat you as anything less than queen, he'd drag them by their'—she blushed, lowering her voice —'balls through Alluvite and—'

Of course he had. I pinched the bridge of my nose. 'All right. That's enough.'

'But Jade's a woman,' Jaxon pointed out unhelpfully. 'What will he do—'

'Go bother someone else,' I gritted out. Jaxon beamed, staying firmly planted by my side. I dragged on the reserves of my patience to stop myself from sending him flying, which wouldn't be good for the soldiers' morale.

The Divine

'General Jade also said you're the best shot we've got at winning this war, and she wants to hear your opinion.'

'All right.' I began to turn, but the girl remained there, still staring at me with awed eyes. I paused. 'Is there something else?'

'Ah ... no, ma'am.' She fidgeted, her hands unclasping then clasping once more. 'Well, there is, but I'm not sure if I should say it. That is, I don't think – well, it's not important, ma'am.'

An unexpected warmth gathered within me at her nervousness. She reminded me of soldiers who'd fought under me in the past – new recruits, fresh to battle, who were eager to impress and tried hard to hide their fear. In my own way, I'd made sure most had survived; made sure they fought in battles where they had a chance of surviving rather than holding them back until they were inevitably thrust into something they'd never win.

It'd been a while since I'd seen such hopeful innocence in anyone's eyes.

'What's your name?'

'Amara, ma'am.'

'You can ask what you want, Amara.' I glanced over my shoulder. We still had at least two hours of sunlight left. Delaying a few minutes wouldn't cause any harm.

'Not ask, ma'am.' Amara's hands came to her front. She fiddled with the hem of her tunic, her cheeks darkening. 'I just – well, I wanted to thank you.'

'Thank me?' It took me a few moments to understand before I nodded. 'Oh, the fight the day the barrier fell? No need to thank me for that. If I didn't fight, those shadow wraiths would've had me, too.'

'Not that.' Amara hesitated. 'Three years ago, there were mass raids of the northern towns.'

I nodded. It'd been a horrific time. The towns close to the Naruzia–Archin border were poorly protected, and the people living there considered dispensable by King Kane. I'd been fighting with the second-last unit I'd captained.

'One of those towns, Undia, was attacked. I lived there with my ma and my little brother. We hid, but they would've found and killed us eventually. But then a Naruzian unit appeared. Your unit, ma'am. You saved us by killing the raiders. Saved me. And I —' She bowed again, her next words coming out in a rush. 'Well, I just wanted to thank you. You were the reason I volunteered for the army. I want to be strong like you, so I can protect my family this time.'

And then she turned and ran, disappearing into the crawl of the soldiers. I blinked, slack-jawed as I stared after her. Jaxon huffed a quiet laugh beside me. 'Seems you've got a fan.'

'She's a fool if she looks up to me,' I muttered, even as heat prickled my cheeks.

I'd hated my time as Captain. I never hated the fighting – that sort of violence was bred in my blood – but I'd despised that it was done at Kane's command. That any killing I'd done was for him. Back then, I'd been a creature of rage and hatred, and little else.

Never once had I considered someone might be thankful for what I did. That the lives I'd saved, even incidentally, might view me as more than the monster I'd decided I was.

Jaxon slung an arm around my shoulders as two soldiers took our horses, leading them onwards. 'Let's go, ma'am.'

I gave him a sidelong glare. 'Don't you start.'

'Whatever you say, ma'am.'

I sighed, even as I twisted back to look for where Amara had disappeared. Perhaps, I mused, there might be more worth protecting in this army than I'd initially thought.

The Divine

When night fell, I took myself as far from the main camp as possible, settling myself under the stars. The wind blew its lullaby, rustling leaves and sending branches waving. Above, wisps of clouds crawled lazily across a canopy of stars, their forms so fine that they failed to block any light. Drawing a knife from my belt, I settled onto my back and reached for the bond. *What's this I hear about punishments if people don't listen to me?*

Callum responded immediately. *I'm not sure what you mean.*

Something about a certain king dragging people around by their balls if they don't obey me.

The sound of his laughter warmed my cheeks, despite the chill of the air. *I figured threats were better than them annoying you.*

I can take care of myself.

Oh, I know you can. I was more worried about the soldiers.

I wouldn't have done anything to them. Or at least, nothing too bad. I flipped my knife into the air, waiting until the last moment to catch it on the way down. *Where are you?*

Almost back at Alluvite. There was a hesitation. I stilled before throwing the knife again, higher this time as I braced myself for whatever he was about to say. *I want to wait there for you, but…*

But your soldiers need you. My palm stung with the impact of the hilt slamming into it. I threw it again.

I need to hunt down Tizan once I have more men. He's becoming a problem.

I frowned at the general's name. It seemed he wasn't done giving me reason to hate him. He'd killed my unit, and now his existence threatened to prolong my time apart from Callum. *Gods, I hate this. It's like the realms are conspiring to keep us apart.*

I'd say the gods play a decent part in that. I closed my eyes, imagining Callum's arm wrapping around my waist, just as he'd done on the blissful two nights we'd been reunited, as he spoke. It only made my longing for him worse. *Speaking of gods, has Jaxon mentioned anything of Kerta or Evania?*

I frowned. Kerta was tolerable, but Evania, goddess of peace, was ... well. Tolerable was the furthest thing from whatever she was. *Only that he doesn't think Evania will get involved with either side.*

Callum's anger was strong and sudden. *Of course not. I don't know why I'd expect otherwise. All the gods seem capable of is either apathy or malice.*

The words twisted something in me. I thought of all the times I'd stood with a corpse at my feet and blood on my hands. The number of times I'd stared at that blood and smiled. The rest of the times when I hadn't deigned to give the dead a second glance.

How many had I killed over my life? Hundreds? Thousands?

And with Dearil's power in me, there was no telling how many more I'd kill before I was finally allowed to rest.

Don't do that.

Callum's voice startled me from my macabre thoughts. *Do what?*

Lower yourself to their level. You're not a god, Chiara. You never could be. From anyone else, the words would've been meant as an insult. But Callum had endured suffering at the hands of gods as much as I had.

I kill people, Callum. And I do it easily.

So do I. Would you count me the same as Vitus?

Anger whipped through me at the suggestion. I no longer wished Callum was with me so that I could hold him. Instead, I wished he was here to throttle. *Why would you even say that?*

Exactly. We've both done awful things. No one can deny that. But you've also done great things. You've fought to keep safe a kingdom you don't care for. You've faced a god for the sake of the people you love. And you enter fights you know you can't win, all to protect others. How many gods can claim the same?

I twisted my fingers around the hilt of my knife. Only here

with Callum could I allow myself a moment of uncertainty. *What if Dearil's power changes me?*

You'd never let another's power twist who you are.

I opened my eyes, staring at the star-bright sky. Wind rustled leaves around, yet it couldn't quite penetrate the warmth Callum's words had pulled me into. *Are you scared?*

Of facing Vitus?

No. Of what might happen if we win. As with Dearil, Vitus's power, should he fall, would need to find a host. There were very few Gifted by Vitus in the mortal realm. I'd only ever encountered two. One was already dead.

The silence was heavy with Callum's consideration. Unlike me, he always weighed words carefully. It had infuriated me when we'd first met, the way he'd dug out all the truths I'd hidden through dismissive remarks. Sometimes, it still infuriated me, yet it was one of many things I loved about him, too. At last, he admitted, *Terrified. I've always hated my Gift.* He had. More than I had mine. *And the thought of the same power that stole your sister and nearly took you away from me in my veins...*

Disgust rolled down the bond, and my hands fisted. I hated that this was our solution. We already faced impossible odds, and the outcome – for Callum to be forced to take something on that he despised so much—

But I don't hate that I have to do it.

My fists loosened. *Why not?*

Because I know it's going to save our kingdom. Our realm. Our realm. As though I ruled it next to him. The idea terrified me as much as the thought of being by his side delighted me. *And I know you'll never let me turn into Vitus.*

You would never, I said hotly.

I know that, too. The disgust shifted into something warmer. *But I also have faith. Faith in you. In Deana. Even in Jaxon, though I'd never tell him. Because I know you all care for this realm in your own way, and you wouldn't let me destroy it.*

Dearil's words at the Gates echoed in my mind. He'd been so sure back then that Callum would find a way to master the power, even with his very mortal body. I understood why. *I don't care about this realm as much as you think I do.*

The pause was a thoughtful one, filled only by the gentle breeze. I focused on the moon. Did Callum stare up at it, too, as we spoke? Or was he tucked away in his tent, trying not to notice my absence beside him?

I don't think that's quite true, he said at last. *But even if it was, I think your reasons for stopping me would be far simpler than that.*

Oh?

I don't think you'd let me destroy the realm because you know it would destroy me. You are my tether, Chiara. And I know you'd never let me cut myself loose.

My cheeks heated. *You give me too much credit.*

I don't think I could ever give you enough. There was another pause, this one tinged with disapproval. *You should be sleeping.*

Says the one who was very quick to respond when I called.

I'll always respond when you call.

I prodded at the power, wishing I could travel to his side. I wanted to see his face. To watch the way his lips must have tipped upwards as he said that. To hold him until we both fell asleep. *I miss you.*

I know.

I huffed. *You're meant to say you miss me, too.*

I didn't think you'd be dense enough for me to need to spell out the obvious. I scowled, folding my arms across my chest as his laugh rippled between us. *Grumpy tonight, aren't we?*

Of course I was. It was a cruel kindness, to be able to talk to him when I couldn't touch him. *I'm in a perfectly fine mood.*

You've never been a talented liar. When I closed my eyes, I could almost feel his fingers brushing my hair out of my face, then sliding over my eyes. *Sleep, Captain.*

And, against every part of me that screamed at me to keep talking, to not let any moment with him slip by, I did.

It took us two more days to find the site we'd been searching for.

'This is...' General Jade trailed off, staring at the scene before us with wide-eyed horror.

There was no word for what it was. Corpses stacked high in front of us, each with wounds at their throats or chests. Blood-drenched ground. Flies buzzing, their happy harmony at the new feast setting my nerves on edge. Some of the corpses were old, limbs stiff and signs of bloating showing where they stuck out from under the fresher bodies. Others were newer, the flies less interested in their remains. Jade pressed a hand to her nose.

It wasn't just mortal remains, either. There were bodies so decayed that they could only have belonged to Ankurans. Creatures made of vines that had withered, leaving only husks behind. A few dark spots upon the ground that could only have belonged to shadow wraiths.

'This is my mother,' Jaxon said grimly. He dropped to a knee, swiping a finger through the pool of blood. When held up to the light, it glimmered with faint traces of yellow. He glanced up, his brow furrowing. 'Tell your soldiers not to step a foot closer.'

'We should bury the dead,' Jade said, her features pale. She stared at the bodies.

Jaxon rose, wiping the blood on his trousers. Jade stepped forward. He grasped her arm, hauling her away. '*Think.* Why are there bodies left behind? And why so many in the same place?' He motioned to the area of corpses – an almost perfect circle. 'This is Tarina's power. She doesn't create creatures like the other gods.

She creates traps. Illusions. You step one foot inside the Illusion she's set up, and you'll be smiling as you slit your own throat.'

Jade's throat worked on a swallow before she nodded once, regaining her usual countenance. 'Then there are no enemies here. We should head around. Press on.'

'Maybe,' Jaxon said. I watched him carefully. His lips pressed into a line, his brow furrowing. Before I could ask what he was thinking, he flashed his usual smile at Jade. 'But a little rest wouldn't go astray, would it?'

She frowned, glancing over the bodies. 'The soldiers would be uneasy staying so close.'

'Give them a few flasks of alcohol to share and they'll be fine. We'll head some distance away, anyway. These bodies stink.' Jaxon grasped Jade's shoulders and turned her to where soldiers milled around, a few peering curiously across at us. There was a faint glimmer to the air between us – an Illusion Jaxon had erected the moment he'd spotted the bodies, keeping the soldiers from acting recklessly at the sight of death. 'Have a few drinks yourself. You need to loosen up.'

Jade looked to me. 'Lady Chiara, we should press on, at least for an hour. Get past this mess.'

I glanced at Jaxon. 'He's right. We'll go on for about ten minutes or so and then rest for the night. Fatigue won't do anyone any good.'

Jade hesitated for only a moment more before nodding. She strode in the direction of the soldiers, passing through Jaxon's barrier and beginning to yell out commands to set up camp as soon as she was past it. I turned to Jaxon, folding my arms. 'Well?'

He shot me an askew glance. 'Well, what?'

'She's gone. Talk.'

Jaxon sighed. He crouched again, inspecting the blood. There was a lot of it – some golden, some green, some red. I only hoped the Illusion had lasted for the mortals until the moment their souls departed. At least then they'd have gone to what awaited with a smile. 'Tarina's powerful, but she's not all-powerful. This number of dead – it's a strong Illusion. Stronger than what she'd usually be able to handle.'

I crouched beside him. The closest corpse was purpling, lips slightly agape and eyes a milky mess. A mortal, from the wolf insignia barely visible upon their tunic. 'So?'

'She could only cast an Illusion this size in close proximity.' Jaxon's gaze lifted, his eyes meeting mine. 'Meaning, Tarina is somewhere nearby.'

Chapter Seventeen

I rocked back on my heels, exhaling roughly.
It shouldn't have come as such a nasty shock. I knew who our enemies were now the barrier had fallen. Knew that our purpose had always been to hunt down Tarina along with the Illusioned traps she'd set. But so far, it'd only been the gods' creatures we'd faced. Even our battle with Vitus had been with him possessing only a fraction of his power.

I'd thought we'd have more time before we faced her. Time for me to leash the unruly power in my veins. It had been a fool's hope. Time had never been on my side.

'Will she attack us?'

'If she thinks it's worth the effort.' Jaxon stood, offering his hand to me. I took it. 'My mother has always been prideful. She will only fight battles she can win – she won't waste her time with fruitless endeavours. A few hundred mortals might not be worth wasting any power on.'

There was a heavy silence as we both stared at the corpses, and then at each other. 'She's not going to leave us alone, is she?'

He sighed, running his fingers through his hair. I wondered if

The Divine

he'd got that hair, thick and dark, from his mother. If he hated it as much as I'd once hated my silver eyes. 'No. She's not.' He glanced over his shoulder to where tents were beginning to rise. 'Because we're not just a few hundred mortals.'

I closed my eyes. This would all be so much easier to deal with if Callum were here. Reaching for the bond was becoming a habit for me, one that Callum reciprocated. But right now, it would only make me miss him more if I spoke to him.

'Who's going to be the one to entice her?' I asked, rubbing at the wards as they continued to burn. 'You, or me?'

'She must hate you by now, for Dearil's death.' Jaxon's lips twisted into a bitter smile. 'But it'll be me she focuses on.'

'Why?'

'Because Mother has always loved to control me. She hates me having connections to anyone but her.' Grief flickered across his face as he rested his hand on his sword hilt in an almost tender motion. 'Unlike the halflings she killed for being too powerful, I'm no threat to her position as goddess.'

He lifted his hand, yellow threading on his fingers. Tiny butterflies danced in the air. 'The realm seeks to maintain balance in divine powers. It's like a scale, tipping in the direction of power. If a halfling possesses too much of it, divine power starts to shift from god to child. For those of us whose power is barely more than a talented, Gifted mortal's'—the butterflies vanished to dust —'well, we're not enough to tip that balance.'

I frowned. 'But your power isn't only slightly above a mortal's.'

Jaxon preened. 'Of course not. But by the time my power made a showing, I was old enough to know to hide it. And I'm not like you – not strong enough to tip those scales violently enough that the realms demand immediate balance. The shift of power is more of a trickling, too small for Tarina to sense it yet.'

'But she will notice, eventually,' I said.

His smile faded. 'Eventually, yes, but not for a long time. I've made sure to never seem a threat to Mother's power. She's far too focused on getting her pitiful, useless son back under her control to suspect me of hiding anything.' His voice turned raspy as his grip firmed on his sword. 'She's been trying to get me back there for two centuries.'

I stared at where his other hand remained on his sword. Two centuries. That must've been the amount of time since he'd first escaped the godly realm and met Garrett, the man he loved. 'That won't happen.'

He nodded, a smile creeping over his face. 'She won't be able to stand up to Dearil's power.'

I winced. I hadn't quite got around to explaining my current dilemma to him. 'About that... I can't exactly use it.'

His smile froze. 'What do you mean?'

I shook my head, frustrated. Lifting my hand, I tried to will the power forward. The silver sliced at my veins, pulling a hiss from me. *Come out*, I ordered.

The surging worsened. The wards at my wrists glowed, their pain scalding as the power seemed to scream a protest in my mind. *Not yours to command!*

As quickly as it had come on, the power vanished back into a slumber. I dropped my hand to my side with a shrug as Jaxon stared, his face quickly paling. 'It's either nothing or it destroys everything nearby.' There'd been dozens of trees that had already felt the brunt of my attempts at using the power. I turned my hand over. 'The wards—'

'Shouldn't completely constrain it.' He shook his head, frustrated. 'Dammit, Chiara, your little visit to the Gates was meant to solve the problem with your Gift!'

My shoulders slumped. 'It doesn't listen to me.'

There was a pause. Jaxon stared at my hands in disbelief. Then, he laughed. It was a sound filled with hollow hopelessness, the edges of it sharp enough to cut off my skin. He shook his head, dragging fingers through his hair. 'Perfect. Absolutely perfect. We're all going to die.'

I clenched my teeth, irritated at the bite in his voice. 'We're here to face Tarina.'

He curled his hand around his sword. 'And how do you propose we do that when you can't even control your damned Gift?'

'If we all face her, we can try to bring her down.'

Jaxon shook his head. 'No. There's no way we're doing that.'

'But that's what we came for! You were on your way here to do exactly that without me.'

His jaw tightened. He shifted, his eyes flicking to the side before back to me. 'I was going to scout out what was happening and see if I should join the fight or not.'

I narrowed my eyes, interpreting his words. 'You were going to see what the odds were, and if they weren't in your favour, you'd leave these men to their fate?'

'They're not my men!' Jaxon snapped. My hands flexed at my side, but I had no right to be angered at his words. Not when I'd told myself the same. 'Callum is the one who sent General Jade and the soldiers to face whatever had killed all the other soldiers out here.' He shook his head. 'I should never have agreed to accompany them. I knew Tarina would be involved. That she might be here. Why did I ever think we stood a chance?' He laughed wretchedly. 'We're all going to die.'

'But we do have a chance!' I protested, unsure when it was that I had become the optimistic one. 'You said it yourself – if we take out Tarina, then Callum will have—'

'Gods, it's always Callum, isn't it?' I startled at the fury in Jaxon's voice. 'Every decision you make is about what will keep *him* alive.'

I stared at him. Jaxon had so rarely spoken a word of anger

towards me. Towards any of us, really. But now – now, it simmered in his eyes as though finally breaking free of the fury that had gripped him for far too long.

Part of me recognised this rage wasn't about me. That it was his grief – a grief that had festered for too long. One that could only come from a broken soul-bond. If another was here, they might've pitied him. Might've spoken soft words and smoothed the sharp edges of his sorrow.

But I was mostly made of sharp edges myself, and I'd never been good at meeting anger with gentleness. My hands curled into fists. I spoke quietly, but the words trembled with my rage. 'That's not fair. You would've sacrificed anything for Garrett. Don't berate me for doing the same.'

'But I would have at least considered the rest of us lowly beings. How many do you think will die while you're trying to protect your king?' He watched my expression, barking a laugh when uncertainty crossed it. 'You haven't even considered it.'

I swallowed my anger. He was right. All I'd been thinking about was Callum. What this victory would do for him. Not the lives that might be lost. I flexed my fingers, settling my breathing before saying quietly, 'You're right. I hadn't.' Jaxon opened his mouth, the wrath in his eyes warning that his next words would be sharp, but I spoke first. 'But even if I had, my answer would be the same. Tarina needs to be stopped. She will kill plenty more if we leave her be.' I held his gaze. 'This changes nothing. We will face Tarina, and we will find a way to win.'

'Do you want to know why I was outside the main camp the night you returned to the mortal realm?'

My brows drew together. 'I assumed you were just going to places you shouldn't be.'

'I was deciding whether to leave.' Jaxon's shoulders were straight, rigid with anger and fear. 'I'd spent nights thinking about it. Questioning whether there was any point in staying, knowing my mother was what the army headed for.'

The air bit at my skin as I asked, 'But you didn't.'

'I didn't, because just like everyone else, I let myself be swept up by you. I stopped questioning this mission. The great Chiara was here, so we had nothing to be afraid of. There was no chance of failing with the power you held.' His smile was sharp. 'Power that you apparently don't have.'

I shook my head. 'I can still fight better than most. I can—'

'You can do nothing against a goddess like Tarina.' Jaxon shook his head. 'If I face her, all I'd be doing is throwing my life back into my mother's hands. We have no chance of winning.' He spun, his boots hitting the earth in angry thuds as he started to storm away.

'You're a coward.'

Jaxon froze. His hands fisted. 'What was that?'

'You. Are. A. Coward.' I enunciated each word, letting them slam into him. 'You're happy to leave this realm to despair because it's easier for you. Because you're too scared to face your own mother.'

Spinning back around, Jaxon cleared the space between us in a handful of steps. His features were barely controlled fury as he stared down at me, his chest rising in a furious breath. 'Damned right I'm too scared. You know why?'

'I—'

But he hadn't been searching for an answer. 'Tarina took everything from me. She stole my freedom. Any chance of a normal life. And then, just when I thought I had both in my grasp, she and Vitus took my soul-bonded.'

Some of my fury wilted. My chest ached as I reached out a hand for his. 'Jaxon, I understand how hard that was, but—'

'No.' He batted away my hand, his hit stinging. 'That's the

thing. You don't understand. Because I'm not as lucky as you, hidden away from the gods' eyes. Not as protected.'

My anger snapped. I slammed my fist into his jaw. Unlike last time, my power didn't rise, but it was done with the full brunt of my anger. Jaxon's head whipped to the side as he staggered a few steps back. His hand lifted, lips pressing into a thin line as he glared defiantly past me.

'Don't you *dare*,' I seethed, 'suggest I was lucky because I didn't have gods after me. Not when mortals are equally as capable of cruelty. Not when *you* were the one who left me at that woman's doorstep.'

There was a flicker of shame in his expression at the mention of my adoptive mother. For a moment, he seemed to deflate. But we were made of the same material – stubborn pride and boundless anger, even if he did usually keep his hidden far better than I did.

'Fine,' he snapped. 'You're not lucky because you were hidden. You're lucky because you've never had to understand the pain having a soul-bond can cause you.'

My fists tightened, nails biting into my palms. 'How can you say that? I watched Callum die, Jaxon. Watched him bleed out and—'

'He came back.' Jaxon said it so quietly I almost missed it.

I blinked. 'What?'

'You got to bring him back.' Jaxon held up a hand, closing it around nothing but air. His expression tightened as though he'd thought he might be able to grasp onto something precious. 'But Garrett was just … gone. I'm not special like you. And I wasn't enough to save him.' He laughed bitterly. 'I would do anything – give up anything – to get even a piece of him back.' There was no trace of insincerity in his eyes.

I thought of those terrible moments when I'd thought Callum

was dead. How time had stretched out, how I'd shattered. How desperately I'd grasped hold of his soul.

What would I have become if I hadn't saved him? Scared of Vitus in the same way Jaxon feared his own mother?

No, I realised. I would have become something far worse.

Jaxon wasn't done. 'It wouldn't matter if I couldn't keep him. I'm beginning to forget him. Forget what his face looks like. What his voice sounds like. And it's like he's dying all over again. So, yes, Chiara. I do think you're lucky.'

My anger wilted. I slumped. If something happened to Callum, I might very well have carved away every piece of me just for another glimpse of him. 'Jaxon—'

He shook his head in a sharp motion. 'I never should have come to face Tarina,' Jaxon said, his voice regaining its firmness. He shoved past me, and I let him. 'And if you do, I hope you're ready to bear the cost of the lives you'll lose.'

Chapter Eighteen

Jaxon disappeared for the entirety of the night. I ignored the questions about his absence, discussing instead next moves with Jade – and Henri, the captain who'd relayed the news about what had happened to the soldiers. By the time I stumbled into my own tent and collapsed on my bedroll, the sun was already peaking above the horizon.

The few hours of sleep I did snatch were fitful, filled with images of Callum lying injured in a place of darkness. Yet, the harder I tried to reach him, the further he'd drift, until he was so enveloped in blackness, I couldn't sense him at all.

When I woke, I rolled onto my side, I stared at where light peeked through my tent flap, intruding on my sanctuary. I closed my eyes, trying to imagine I was in Alluvite, Callum's arm curled around my waist and his breath tickling my neck. That I'd roll over as he blinked awake, his lips curving into that crooked smile he always seemed to save for me.

The imagining only made the hurt of his absence worse.

I reached for the bond, the feel of it an addiction I couldn't rid myself of. *Are you awake?*

The Divine

I am now.

Wincing at the grogginess in his voice, I stared at the light bleeding into my tent. I much preferred sleeping outside, under the blanket of stars. This tent, with all its careful luxury, was uncomfortably far from the tight spaces and ragged bedrolls I'd slept on as Captain. *Jaxon doesn't think we should go after Tarina.*

Just like that, any sense of weariness disappeared from Callum's voice. *You found her?*

We think we found her, I corrected. *She's set up Illusions. Jaxon thinks it means she's close by. He also thinks we don't stand a chance against her if I can't use my power.*

There was a careful pause. *And what do you think?*

I shifted onto my back, the blanket tangling at my waist. Crisp, morning air brushed my skin, urging me to rise for the day. I wasn't quite ready to leave Callum to face the day's trials, though. *I think this might be our only chance to take Tarina down before Vitus plays his hand. And I think leaving those Illusions be will lead to the deaths of too many more who stumble into them. We have to make sure they, at least, are destroyed.*

Quiet approval ran down the bond. I smiled at the brush of it. *Then you know what you have to do.*

Jaxon—

—will come around, Callum finished for me. *You two are too close to let some small disagreement come between you.*

I made a noncommittal sound, shoving off the blankets and yanking tangled curls out of my face.

Don't you have a goddess to catch, Captain? Callum admonished, almost managing to hide his own reluctance.

I could say the same to you.

I'm the king. I can do as I please.

I frowned. Callum joked about it plenty, but I'd been with him for a fair amount of the time since he'd been thrust into the role. Seen the way the lives he was responsible for had piled onto his shoulders, one after the other. Seen the shadows beneath his eyes and how he'd ignored his body's need for sleep in favour of managing his duties.

Callum might be king, but he was far from free to do as he pleased.

You're not to allow yourself to be harmed, Callum said as I sighed, glaring at the peeking of sunlight for intruding on my time with him. *You will win this battle.*

My lips curled upwards. *If my king commands it, then I'll have to make sure to obey.*

And then Callum was gone from his end of the bond, his own duties calling him away from me.

I forced myself to rise, ignoring the aches of exhausted muscles and the grittiness of my eyes. With the circle of corpses not too far away, we couldn't afford to waste time here. Rotting bodies had a way of beckoning all sorts of infections and illnesses. We had few enough soldiers as it was. We couldn't lose any more to such a meaningless death.

'Morning, Lady Chiara!' Amara chirped the moment I set foot outside of my tent. She shoved a cup of the bitter brew I'd become accustomed to in my days of the army into one hand, a roll of parchment under her other arm.

'Not a noblewoman, Amara,' I sighed before taking a sip of the drink.

'But His Majesty ordered everyone to treat you as—'

'Treat me as a fellow soldier. Or an army captain, if you must.'

Amara didn't lose her smile. Jade had assigned her as my personal attendant the previous evening after much debate about whether I needed one. A surprising number of soldiers volunteered to take the role. I'd chosen Amara, who'd been the only one I recognised.

Now, though, the sight of her cheery visage so early in the morning made me regret my choice.

'Any reports from the past hour?' I asked, stomping my boots a few times to shake off the coating of dust from the previous day's travels. Men and women milled around us, many scarfing down food before hurrying to sharpen weapons or maintain armour. There was no telling how long we'd be stopped here, so better to get duties tended to quickly.

'No movement from any direction,' Amara reported, hurrying to keep pace as I strode for Jade's tent. 'We've also kept a careful eye on the bodies as you recommended. Nothing's stirred, and no one's gone close to them.'

I nodded. Good. Ankurans rising from that mess was the last thing we needed. 'And we still haven't heard from the rest of the Naruzian forces?'

Amara shook her head. 'Evan tried to divine their location yesterday, but his Gift's not strong enough. All he got was murky brown colouring in the water.'

Evan was one of Kyrah's Gifted, able to divine the location of small possessions. An army was far from small. I tried not to let the failure stab at me too much. Part of me had been hoping he might catch a glimpse of Callum when he tried his divination. It'd been a fool's hope.

'What about—'

'There you are.' Jaxon appeared from between the tents ahead, sporting a grin and a bruise that wrapped under his jaw. 'I've been looking for you.'

I narrowed my eyes. He showed no signs of the outburst he'd had the day before. If he was going to pretend it never happened, I suppose I could do the same. 'Why?'

He stepped forward, wrapping an arm around my shoulders and dragging me away from Amara. Several drops of hot liquid spattered onto the ground from my cup. Leaning in, he lowered his voice. 'I think I've found her.'

I handed Amara my cup before I upended it over myself. 'You think?'

Jaxon nodded, glancing warily at Amara. Less mistrust, I thought, and more worried about the panic that hearing who'd caused the corpses would bring about. Sighing, I indicated for Amara to stay as I stepped away. I folded my arms. 'Well?'

'Two kilometres north. There's a mass of creatures – mostly Ankurans, but some scythes – Adwin's vine creatures – and shadow wraiths. But they're all acting oddly. Staying in one place instead of moving, which they wouldn't do unless someone powerful was in command.'

'And you found them ... how?'

'Just lucky, I guess.' Jaxon shrugged as he shifted. 'We should attack them as soon as the men are ready. No sense in waiting now.'

I narrowed my eyes at him. 'You seem ... confident. More than you were last night.'

His grin flickered before returning. 'We should at least destroy the creatures there, and the Illusions. They'll be a threat to anyone who gets too close to them. Best to stop future soldiers dying if we can.' He glanced back in the direction he'd come. 'Besides, if we destroy the Illusions, Tarina will undoubtedly show herself. She hates when plans go awry.'

'But you said it was foolish to face her.'

'After some deep reflection I've realised that, for perhaps the first time in my life, I might have been a tiny bit wrong.' Jaxon shifted with a sigh. 'It happens on occasion, and it is rather unsettling to be so close to that woman again.'

I eyed him. 'You're not the type to get unsettled.' No, he was far more likely to run before it got anywhere close to unnerving for him.

'That's because you've never seen me around my mother.' He shuddered, his smile faltering again. He shook off the unease. 'But

I've slept my nerves away. Even if we lose horribly, Tarina likes dramatics. Getting to me during some lowly battle wouldn't quite suit that flair of hers. She'll wait till the time is right. Which means we have the perfect chance to bring her down. Tarina's as arrogant as any god. She'll come once the Illusion falls to see who's dared meddle with her plans.'

I frowned, inspecting his expression for any sign of falsehood. He smiled innocently back. I let it go, deciding exhaustion had been the main aggravator the night before. Exhaustion, and grief. 'Have you informed General Jade?'

Jaxon winced. 'She's a little intimidating.' His arm squeezed harder until I shoved him away. 'That's why I thought you could do it.'

Gods, I'd chosen an idiot as a friend. 'You're several centuries old. I'm sure you'll survive.'

I began walking once more, Jaxon easily matching my pace. He gave me a pleading look. 'But she *likes* you. She hates me.'

'Couldn't imagine why that would be. You only convinced her soldiers to give you a horse to ride – a horse that could've been used for equipment.'

'That's nothing—'

'Not to mention, you've managed to convince half the people here that you're a lord despite very much *not* being one.' I paused, then added, 'And don't think I didn't notice how many extra weapons you seem to have accumulated.'

'Exactly! I'm very likeable if people are willing to give me their things.'

'*Stealing* does not count as them giving it to you,' I said. A woman stepped out of our way, head bowing as we passed her by. 'Maybe we should go ourselves. If Tarina has an Illusion set up again, we can just—'

'No,' Jaxon interrupted firmly. 'The whole army has to be there.'

'Why?'

'If Tarina releases the creatures from her Illusion, they'll attack. We might be stronger than mortals, but we're not invincible. Even you can't kill that many without your Gift. And you need to survive for Vitus.' He turned to inspect the northern horizon. 'This is what the army came for, remember? To shatter the Illusion that's killing people, and capture Tarina if possible. Besides, Illusions aren't easy to bring down. If we're going to try, we'll need every hand available to help.'

I pressed my lips together. I didn't like it, but he was right. It'd be so much easier if I could've gone and handled it by myself. 'Fine. We find Jade, and then, we prepare for battle.'

Jaxon hadn't been exaggerating what he'd seen. I kept low to the ground, peering over the crest in the hill as soldiers quietly waited behind me. Creatures sprawled out on the dust-covered ground. Ankurans with their golden-cracked flesh, shadow wraiths darkening the air around them, and scythes with humanoid forms wrapped in thorned-vines. Each standing eerily still, eyes glazed over.

There was no sign of the goddess, but Dearil's power twisted inside me, rising and falling in nauseating surges. The air seemed to thrum with a force vastly different from my own, not dissimilar to when Tarina had come to the cells to speak to Dearil. But this power – it was far more than it had been.

A chill washed over me. I turned, creeping down the hill to where Jade and Henri stood at the front, fully armoured and grim-faced. Jaxon was seated on the ground, one hand raised over his eyes as he tipped his head back to inspect the sun-soaked sky.

'There's at least four hundred,' I whispered, keeping my voice low.

The Divine

Henri perked up. He was older than me by at least ten years, but he moved with far more of a bounce than I could've mustered. 'We have five hundred and two.'

Jaxon raised his brows and rose to his feet, brushing himself off. 'That's very specific.'

'You need to know how many men you have,' I said, scanning the soldiers before us. This was far more than any number I'd ever led into battle, but the role of commanding would fall to Jade and Henri. I had a different part to play – one that involved a goddess. 'Knowing each man's strengths and weaknesses is how you win a battle.'

I knew very few of these people, though. Jade. Henri. Amara. Eamon. A few others who'd approached me or I'd run into at some point during my time in the army. But too many were mysteries to me, weapons that I had no idea how to wield.

Frowning, I shoved that thought away. I didn't need to know these people. This wasn't my army to command.

'Having greater numbers won't necessarily put us at that much of an advantage,' I said, satisfied that most of the soldiers seemed to at least know how to hold a sword. 'These creatures don't feel pain like us. They don't feel fear. They will attack to kill, no matter what injuries they may bear.'

'Then we go with the strategy.' Jade crouched, pulling out the parchment she'd hastily sketched on earlier. 'Jaxon, you said your mother can't cast two Illusions at once?'

He nodded. 'That's correct. She can cast an Illusion over a space, and it will infect as many minds as are in that space. But the Illusion she must have going with the creatures is already at the limits of her abilities. It shouldn't take much to break it, so we need to be careful. Once one of the creatures dies, it's likely the Illusion on all of them will shatter.'

'You're sure?' I asked, Dearil's power rolling through me. I grasped a mental fist around it, trying to strangle it before it burst free in its unsettled state. It seemed to snap angrily back. 'Because if you're wrong—'

'I was forced to stay by her side for a century, Chiara,' Jaxon said, voice hardening. 'I know what I'm talking about.'

Jade nodded. She tapped a spot of black. 'Then we'll keep the forces split. We won't interfere with her Illusion until we're sure we have the creatures contained.' She glanced at me. 'And then it will be your turn.'

I nodded, careful to keep any sign of nerves from my expression. If the soldiers could stand against a goddess, then I could damned well do the same, power or not.

I glanced to the east, where a blur of dark shapes that had to be one of the two groups of soldiers who'd separated from us stood. If I looked the other way, I would've seen the second group.

'We'll be the decoys once she arrives,' Henri added. 'Get her attention on us and—'

'No.' I glanced up, eyeing the soldiers behind. There was resolve in their eyes, but also terror. We'd chosen this group of four dozen as the ones with more experience. Those who wouldn't balk or flee at the first signs of danger. Even if this plan worked, many of them would die today. 'You and Jade can't come with us.'

Jade's lips thinned. 'I'm the general. I need—'

'To stay alive to give orders.' I glanced over my shoulder at the hill, the creatures hidden from view beyond. 'Jaxon won't be killed. I don't think Tarina would kill me, either – she might hate me, but she serves Vitus. I'm willing to bet he wants me chained rather than dead, to keep that damned balance. But as soon as they identify you or Henri as a leader, you'll be targeted.'

Jade still didn't seem happy when I looked back at her, but she nodded reluctantly. It was a sensible move, and we all knew it.

'Amara.' I beckoned the girl over. She hurried, her armour turning her movements stiff. 'You're to head for the east. Remember the signal for movement. If you—'

'My, what a lovely gathering this is!' a light voice called out, rolling through the air. 'Where was my invitation?'

Ice trickled down my spine. I slowly straightened, heart thudding, as I turned. The air seemed to hum around me. Not with my power, though. With *hers*.

At the top of the hill, a woman stood. Her dark hair spilt down her back in gentle curls, shining with the sun's glow. She took a step forward, her movements graceful, her golden gown completely out of place amongst the armoured soldiers. I tensed, my hand dropping to my dagger.

Jaxon reached out, tapping the back of my hand. I met his eyes. He shook his head, his face pale.

I didn't have to ask why his eyes had widened, or what had caused the trembling in his fingers. I wouldn't even have needed to see the woman's yellow eyes, so like Jaxon's, or the way the air shimmered with a soft glow around her, the very scent of the air changing to become softer, sweeter. A lovely Illusion.

This was Tarina.

A sharp gasp rippled behind me, one of the soldiers calling out a warning. I swung back around, Tarina disappearing and reappearing directly in front of me. I tried to stumble back a step, to pull away from her touch, but she was too strong, her presence overpowering. 'I recognise you.' Her red-painted smile grew edges. 'Dearil's child. What are you doing here?'

She's beautiful. The thought wormed into my mind as Tarina's visage took on an ethereal quality, her skin smoothing and lips becoming fuller. Her lashes lengthened and darkened, and the scent that followed her – something floral and sweet – intensified, becoming almost alluring. I should do whatever she asked of me. A woman like this couldn't be evil. She couldn't—

A sense of wrongness clanged through me. I blinked, and her features returned to normal. Still undeniably lovely, as was characteristic of the divine, but less compelling. I smiled. 'We're out for a picnic.'

A small line appeared on her forehead. Her nails bit in deeper. One broke skin, a bead of blood dripping down my chin. 'How did you do that?'

I frowned. 'Do what?'

'You should answer any question I ask.'

I reached up, grasping Tarina's wrist and yanking it away. She was soft under my grasp. Untouched by the suffering of a mortal life. 'Perhaps I'm not as weak-minded as the divine fools you've been interacting with.'

'What a strange child.' She glanced past me, eyes narrowing at the soldiers behind me. 'My Illusions are not meant to be broken. Not even by some offspring of a god.'

I frowned. That wasn't what Jaxon had said.

She lifted a finger, pointing it somewhere behind. 'You will do well enough. I must check there is no interference to my power.'

I spun, hand falling to my dagger as I lunged for the soldier she'd pointed at. Before I could reach them, the soldier smiled, withdrawing their sword. Metal rang. His eyes took on a yellow sheen. I was too far to stop him as he lifted his sword, holding it to where his armour finished. The soldiers around him stood still, expressions slack.

I whipped my hand forward. My dagger spun through the air just as he began to draw his sword across his throat, red spilling across and under his armour. The tip speared his hand. The soldier screamed, stumbling back as his sword clattered to the ground. He blinked as he fell to his knees, one hand pumping blood, the other clutched to where blood leaked from a thankfully shallow wound at his neck.

The soldiers around him stirred. 'Peyton?' one cried, dropping to the man's side and pressing her hand to his neck. 'What – why?'

The Divine

'Gods,' Jade whispered, her voice hoarse with fear. Henri had stumbled back, too.

'*God*, dear. Only the one of me.' Tarina turned her yellow eyes onto me. 'You are just like your father, no fun at all.' Tarina sighed as I turned, fury lighting my veins with its molten power. 'But it seems my power is fine. It is *you* that is the abhorrence.'

'Why did you come here?' I gritted out. There were no sounds beyond the hill – a good sign. The creatures must still be trapped in her Illusion.

'I came to see what all the fuss is about.' She trailed her finger down my cheek before hooking it under my chin. I didn't pull away. Better her attention remained fixed firmly on me than it wander to the others. 'A pity Vitus prefers knowing where Dearil's power is stored. I would have enjoyed killing you.'

She began to turn. It was the first opportunity I'd had. I yanked two fresh blades out, driving one for her neck and the other at her back. Tarina spun. Her beautiful features no longer remained such, yellow light cracking through as her lips pulled into a sneer. Her hair took on the colour of her power as she slammed a hand out. It connected with my chest before my blades could connect with her. Pain lashed through me, the air punching free of my lungs as I flew backwards, crashing into the soldier I'd flung my dagger into earlier. He cried out at the impact, both of us falling backwards.

Pain lanced through my side, but now wasn't the time to dwell on it. I flipped myself onto my feet. Dearil's power. I needed to find a way to use it, to counteract the ethereal glow that was turning the closest soldiers stiff and complacent.

I will not bow to you, the power hissed in my mind.

Frustration built, and I stretched out for that power, wrapping it in the vice of my own mind. *You will obey.*

I will—

'Oh!' Tarina's sneer disappeared. 'I almost forgot the second thing I came for.' She extended her hand, her palm smooth and free of calluses. 'Come, pet.'

'You're not taking—' I cut off as Jaxon stepped forward. He didn't look at me. Didn't look at anyone as he placed his hand in hers, shoulders stiff but head held high. I stared at his back, anger twisting through me. Beneath it, though, there was something far worse. Hurt. 'Jaxon?'

'Such an obedient boy I have raised,' Tarina said, patting his head like one might do a puppy. 'I asked him to bring me those who would dare raise their swords against me, and here you are.'

'Jaxon?' I called again, taking a step forward and palming my fourth dagger. I only had one more after this. 'Step away from her.'

'Sorry, Chiara. I did tell you she would like the dramatics of taking me.' Jaxon finally glanced over his shoulder. His lips were twisted into his usual smile, but this time, the amusement was at my expense. 'If you'd managed to beat Vitus the first time ... well, that would've been a different ending. But there's no beating him now. I'd rather be on the winning side.'

Rage simmered, and Dearil's power simmered alongside it. For once, it was in agreement with me.

'Coward,' I spat. I couldn't reconcile the smiling man in front of me with the same one I'd laughed with – and occasionally at – over the past months. The man who had fought with me to save Callum, and who had come for me when I'd been captured.

I'd always known Jaxon was two-faced. How had I been so naïve to believe the face he showed me was the real one?

Kill him, the power whispered, its beat timing with my heart. *Kill him, kill him, kill him, kill—*

'You said that last night.' Jaxon slid his hands into his pockets, his smile growing wider. 'If you'd been smarter, you would have remembered that about me when I suggested we come here today.'

He was right. I'd been an idiot. A blind fool who had forgotten all the betrayals that had been carved into my flesh over the years. Trust was a luxury I had never been allowed. Yet I'd taken to it all the same, and all the people who'd followed me here were about to pay the price alongside me. 'Why?' Blood wet the palm that didn't hold a dagger, my nails biting in deep as though I could gouge out the sting of hurt. All it did was drive it deeper. 'Why would you do this?'

'Who can say?' He lifted a hand, his own power crackling along his fingers. For a moment, he simply stared at it, his expression inscrutable, before he looked back at me. 'Maybe I was just bored.'

'Liar,' I seethed. I couldn't allow myself to believe he'd betrayed us over something so trivial.

He winked. 'Always.'

'You'd betray us this easily?' The power squirmed, its silver crackling on my fingers. Tarina's eyes dropped to the incandescence. She gave a dismissive huff, brushing her hair over her shoulder. It only sent my rage higher. 'After everything?'

Jaxon didn't even bother looking at the power. He knew that I couldn't use it, not like I once had. He knew, because I'd trusted him enough to tell him.

Idiot, the power taunted. *So gullible.*

Shut up, I snarled back, and its wicked laughter echoed.

'Is it really betrayal if I wasn't loyal to you in the first place?' The sun illuminated the slyness on his face, far better suited to shadows than here. 'Look, we had a good run. Cal gave me some fancy jewels. I got free run of the city. But I've got a better deal.'

'What deal?' I could barely breathe through the hurt and fury. I searched his face for some sign, *any* sign, that he was trying to lure Tarina into a trap of some sort. I found nothing but vague amusement. 'What could she possibly give you that would be worth betraying us all?'

Tarina laughed, the sound crueller even than that of Vitus. 'Why, the one thing even your precious father could not grant.'

I flicked my eyes between them. Despite the similarities, there were clear differences. The sharpness of their smiles. The hardness of their eyes.

It was a cruel trick, making me think there was anything in Jaxon that might be redeemable. But I wouldn't let myself be fooled now.

'What?' I demanded, then pointed the blade at Tarina when she went to answer. 'Shut it. I want to hear it from him.'

Tarina's cheeks mottled. I didn't care. Not as I looked the liar in his eyes. Not as he tilted his head, his smile dropping and shards of ice piercing through his voice. 'She promised to give me Garrett back.'

I stared. Of anything I thought he might say, that had been the last. And yet, it was perhaps the only thing I couldn't offer. No power I possessed could bring his dead soul-bonded back to life. Not when his soul was already gone. 'Impossible.'

'Not for Mother.' Jaxon let her comb her fingers through his hair like he was some sort of doll. 'She's far more adept with Illusions than I am. She promised me that, when this is all over, she'll cast me into an Illusion so real I won't even know I'm dreaming.' His smile softened. 'I'll have an eternity with Garrett.'

My knife trembled as my fist tightened. Part of me could understand the allure. If Callum died, the temptation of a dream of my life with him would be far more desirable than the reality I'd be forced into.

But Tarina had had a hand in Garrett's death. To go to the person who'd murdered his soul-bonded... Disgust was too weak a word for what I felt.

'You bastard. You'd betray us for an Illusion?' I breathed, stepping forward again. Tarina's fingers curled possessively around his shoulder. 'How long have you been planning this?'

Jaxon's smile didn't falter. 'The night the barrier fell down, Mother visited me. She offered me quite the comfortable life should I go to her. One that doesn't end with me dead.' The yellow of his eyes sharpened and, for a moment, I couldn't tell them apart from Tarina's. 'All I had to do was do as she bid for a few weeks. Report on the mortals' movements. Especially yours.'

'Tizan,' I realised, my fury turning my words scalding in my own mouth. Tarina watched, amused. 'You said it was suspected that there was a traitor who'd leaked the plan to send more after him. That was *you*.'

Jaxon clapped, the sound cutting through the thudding of my heart. 'And she finally understands! A pity you weren't quicker, though. If you'd realised sooner ... well, we wouldn't be in this predicament.'

'I trusted you. *We* trusted you.'

'You can't blame me for you allowing yourself to get too soft.'

He was right. 'Deana will hate you for this.'

If my words impacted Jaxon at all, he didn't show it. 'I warned you, didn't I? I'd give up anything to have even a piece of Garrett back.' He gestured at Tarina. 'Mother's offered me that piece.'

My rage built, coiling through me like a serpent readying to strike. The air stilled, the breeze dying. There was a loud crack, and then absolute silence fell upon us. There were no sounds of soldiers behind. No rustling of fabric or shifting of feet. Not as the wards around my wrists burned and Dearil's power grew along with my fury.

'Mother,' Jaxon said, taking a step back as silver began to spark. 'We should go.'

The power was different this time. It still wasn't my own, but it existed in tandem with my will. It fed on my rage. Fed on the stab of hurt. Jaxon was like family to me. I'd known he could be a coward, but never once had I believed he'd turn his back so fully on me. On Deana, too. I wanted him to regret it.

Kill him, the power began again as it had before. *Kill him, kill him, kill him, kill him, kill, kill, kill.*

Oh, I was going to.

Jaxon grinned, winking. 'I'll be seeing you on the next battlefield.'

I flung my dagger. Before it could reach him, there was a flash of yellow light, and Tarina and Jaxon were gone.

Chapter Nineteen

Jaxon had betrayed us. Not only that, but he'd planned to do it from the night the barrier between realms came down. My anger mounted, until it was nearly at the level it'd been after Cassie's death. The sort of anger that could consume me. Consume everyone else around me, too.

You fool, the power whispered, its anger spitting with as much violence as my own. *This is your fault. You let him get away. You did this. You let him betray you.*

The silver at my fingers sparked brightly. Rage shuddered through me. It wasn't only aimed at Jaxon. The power was right. This was my fault. I knew Jaxon. Knew he was as morally bankrupt as they came, and yet I'd let myself believe he'd fight for the mortals when there would be no real win for him.

Jaxon had never been interested in saving others. He'd enjoyed gold. Luxury. And the one thing we couldn't offer – Garrett.

In the end, he'd chosen the memory of his soul-bonded over us.

How he must have laughed at my naïveté. Beneath my feet,

flickers of silver crawled across the ground. Wherever sprouts of life grew ash took its place, the power greedy.

My idiocy might very well cost Callum this war if I didn't find a way to fix it. Jaxon knew too much. And if he was now working with Tarina, it wouldn't be long before Vitus knew of my failure with my power. The mortal realm would fall because of it.

'Dammit,' I cursed, spinning around and yanking on that stubborn power. There would be time to dwell on my failures later. Time to plan my revenge, too.

The soldiers shook themselves free of Tarina's control, Jade emerging first. She paled as she took in the silver wrapping around me, turning the ground between my feet deadened and cracked.

'Where's Jaxon?' she asked, looking around.

It was precisely the wrong thing to say.

'Not here.' Dearil's power refused to sink under my skin. It had found an out, and it wasn't going to re-enter its cage. I staggered a few steps back as it lashed out at Jade, just barely missing her. The ground next to her feet withered.

'And the goddess?' she asked, edging away.

'Gone,' I bit out. 'And I suspect those creatures she's got waiting for us will be coming very—'

A scream reached us from the east. My head snapped in the direction of the sound. The group of soldiers there – two hundred of them – were moving in strange patterns. Most of them stayed together, but a few broke away, fleeing, before they came to a sudden halt. Metal flashed under the sun, blades driving down. My mouth dried as, one by one, the soldiers dropped, lives ended at their own hand.

'Gods,' Henri whispered. I wrenched my attention away from the group of soldiers, ready to tell everyone not to approach. But Henri wasn't looking to the east. He was looking to the west. To where dozens of soldiers stood.

The Divine

Heart thudding and dread rising, I turned in time to see the blood pool beneath bodies as, just as with those in the east, blades slit throats and plunged through chests. Around me, soldiers gasped and muttered. Someone sobbed. Another fell to their knees, retching. Terror permeated the air, and my heartbeat roared in my ears.

Jaxon had lied about how many fields of Illusions Tarina could make. That lie had just cost us at least fifty soldiers.

How much more had he lied about?

This wasn't the battle they'd been expecting. It was far worse – one conducted within their own minds. Jade took two steps towards the west, sword held tightly. I lunged to grab her, stopping short when silver sparked.

'Stop,' I ordered. 'We're too far, and there's nothing we can do now.'

'But our forces...' she rasped 'if we don't have them, then we'll—'

I pressed my lips together as she broke off. Jade, a general and an experienced soldier, was trembling. She must've encountered plenty of death in her life. Seen throats slit and comrades fall. But this was divine power, and fear had struck her hard.

I opened my mouth to say something to snap her out of it. Before I could, sounds rose from behind the hill. A chill settled over me. The sounds of feet shifting over dirt. Of vines snaking their way towards us. Of creatures, previously held in an Illusion, now set free.

And we'd just lost most of our army.

She looked at me, her expression grim. 'What do we do?'

I took a deep breath. We were outnumbered. Most of us outmatched. The creatures coming from us belonged to the gods, and the soldiers were very much mortal.

But I was not. And I wouldn't let these people die today.

Jaxon thought I was weak. That I couldn't control my power.

Maybe he had a point about the power, but in this – in violence and death – I'd always excelled where others might've balked. Godly power had never come into it. I wouldn't cower from this.

A battlefield was where I reigned.

'Jade, take half the men. Have around fifty approach from the west, and the rest from the east. Stay away from the bodies – there's no telling how long the Illusion will last.' She nodded, signalling to the soldiers. 'Henri, you'll stay back with the other half.'

He frowned. 'You'll need as many fighters as we have.'

'We will, but going all at once will expose our numbers and make it easier for the creatures to attack us. The Ankurans might only be sentient when controlled by Vitus, but I have no idea how intelligent the scythes and shadow wraiths are. You'll wait until you're signalled. Jade's men will box in the creatures. It'll be easier to kill them.'

'And you?' Jade asked. 'Will you be leading one of the first attacks?'

I smiled, turning towards the hill. The creatures would crest it soon. We had to move before they did. 'I'll be attacking head-on.'

'That's madness!' Henri took a step forward, stopping short when the silver crackling under my feet intensified. It was just barely restrained, threatening to break free of my pitiful control as soon as it had enough reason to. 'At least take some men. You need—'

'They'll be in the way.' I held up a hand, watching the silver curl around my fingers, the brightness easily overpowering that of the wards.

Kill, it whispered, its eagerness more alarming than its anger had ever been. *Destroy them all. This is what they deserve. What Jaxon deserves.*

I didn't dare let go of it. Not when it might take down more than the creatures. But I'd fought and survived for years without relying on it. Death was a language that existed far beyond this ancient power, and I'd find a way to bring it to our enemies.

Striding forward, I tore from the ground the knife I'd thrown at Jaxon. Chunks of dirt came with it, several shrivelled weeds scattering, life sucked out of them. I tucked it back into my belt, replacing it with a fresh one. I'd be saving that knife for when I saw Jaxon again.

'Where should I go, Lady Chiara?'

I turned to Amara. She stood, her armour awkward on her as she stared up at me with wide eyes. *So young*, I thought. Too young to be on a battlefield.

It was a strange thought. Once, I would've been the first to throw her in, certain that keeping her back would only harm her in the long run. That our kingdom was destined to forever be at war, and the children within it fated to lose their innocence too young.

Now, though, I wanted to believe that peace might await somewhere after all this.

'Stay with Henri.' I met his eyes, and he nodded, ushering her to where the other soldiers he'd be commanding were standing. Eamon was there, as were more I recognised. All of them were younger, those who didn't have experience upon battlefields.

Taking in a breath, I spun and strode for the hill. I didn't check to see if Jade was in position. She either was, or she wasn't. Delaying any further now would only increase the risks to everyone's lives.

The sun turned the ground a burnished gold as I crested the hill. Silver spun around me, its energy rampant, the wards scalding my skin. Movement halted below. Eyes flicked my way – ones of bright white light emerging from shadowy forms. Dark hollows buried in vines. And eyes of fractured gold, filled with the malice of a god.

None of the creatures spoke. The Ankurans lacked the cruel

smiles of those possessed by Vitus's sentience, their features twisted with mindless hunger, while the wraiths and scythes swayed as though awaiting commands. Obedient dogs, chained to their master's desires.

I lifted my chin. My chains were gone, my will my own. And I had no intention of waiting to bring destruction upon them all. As though sensing my intent, a shadow wraith lurched forward. My eyes locked on it, and I smiled.

I fell upon the creatures, their stillness finally breaking under the unfurling of my violence. The shadow wraith I'd chosen died quickly, my knife sinking deep into its chest. It wailed its agony as it fell, splintering into ash-like shadows that coated the ground. An Ankuran swiped for me, veins bulging under fragile skin. Its throat split easily, rot-scented blood splashing onto the ground as it attacked.

A vine lashed out, aiming for my ankle. Twisting, I stomped down, catching it underfoot as I drove my knife up through the jaw of a second Ankuran. The creature gaped open in silent agony as I ripped the knife free, shoving it into those crowding behind. Fingers grasped for my hair, trying to tug me off balance. I spun with their pull, hand lashing around the throat of a scythe. They died like the shadow wraiths – blade to the heart, a wail of pain, and they then broke into tiny pieces of withered vines.

My heart thrummed in my chest as blood splattered across my skin in violent shades of gold, black and green. Not in fear. In a sense of *rightness*. Of belonging.

Dearil's power flared, hot against my skin, as though it, too, wanted to experience bloodshed. I shoved it back as an Ankuran attempted to send a spear through my side. Catching the shaft, I drove my knee into the wood, splintering it in two. The stinging pain left on my skin vanished as I lunged forward. My knife drove through the Ankuran's throat.

The sun illuminated the fall of each creature, capturing their deaths in beautiful artistry. The fall of their bodies, the spatter of their blood. I cut again and again, barely pausing as yells sounded and boots thundered, bodies slamming into the creatures from the left and right. Steel sang alongside my own as Jade's forces joined the fight. My grin grew, thoughts of Jaxon's betrayal momentarily fading.

A shadow creature broke apart before me, revealing a sweaty-faced Jade. She grinned back, her eyes shining with the same brightness I'd once seen in Ada's. An eagerness to achieve victory, no matter the cost. 'Thought you might be leading us to our deaths.'

I lunged past her, catching an Ankuran in the chest. 'Yet you followed me here anyway.'

'Aye,' she agreed, her movements synchronising with my own. She wasn't the beautiful fighter Callum was, nor did she possess the skill of Jaxon or Deana, but she was good. Better than good. Creatures fell under her blade almost as quickly as they did my own, a few shying away from her expert swings. 'I figured disobeying you would be far more dangerous than fighting these.'

'Not sure if that's a compliment'—I broke off, ducking under a shadow wraith's swing at my head. Pushing myself upwards, I slammed my knife into its chest, its body wavering and then disintegrating—'or an insult.'

'Definitely a compliment.'

I spun as a mortal soldier screamed nearby, and caught a glimpse of red spurting from between the gaps in his armour. Terrified eyes met mine for a moment, and then the soldier was gone, disappearing under a blur of shadows, vines and gold-tipped fingers. Another soldier backed away, faced with a shadow wraith. I lunged forward, slicing through creatures as the soldier tripped over a body, falling backwards with a cry.

The shadow wraith raised one of its bladed arms, the darkness undisturbed by the sun. My breath rasped, sweat trickling down my back as my slashes grew more intense. The arm descended. The soldier flinched.

I launched myself onto the creature's back. Its shadowy form began to turn wispy under my hold.

'No, you don't,' I gritted out, raising my own arm and plunging the blade through its back.

The wraith screamed, body writhing under my hold. Black blood, unnaturally cold, rained over my face. I kept my hold, fearing it'd try to take out its final vengeance on the man trembling before it.

Instead, it stilled. Stilled, and began to laugh.

The laughter crawled over my skin as more creatures joined in, peals of eerie discordance ringing through the air. The clang of steel softened, soldiers backing away. An Ankuran to my right halted, fingers wrapped around the throat of a woman. Her legs kicked uselessly in the air as the Ankuran man turned its golden eyes to me.

'Little raven,' he hissed, and my breath hitched. I knew that voice. Hated that voice. 'Found you.'

'Vitus,' I snarled back, tearing my knife free as the shadow wraith's laughter died, its body falling apart. 'Hiding behind your creatures again?'

'I have no reason to hide from you.' The Ankuran's eyes flicked down to the wards at my wrists. Tracked over the half-complete counter markings. 'You're a halfling with a power that doesn't belong to you. You're of no threat to me.'

I smiled, trying to ignore the pounding of my heart. 'If I'm no threat, then it should be easy for you to face me yourself.'

The Ankuran's head cocked. 'I would concern yourself less with me, and more with *them*.'

A crooked gold-veined finger rose, pointing over my shoulder. I followed the point. Looked past the creatures as they renewed their efforts of fighting, soldiers buckling under their strength.

Past where mortal bodies were beginning to fall, far quicker than before. Up the hill.

There, at the top, Ankurans stood, stretched in a line of golden abhorrence. And forced to kneel before them, faces pale and armour gleaming under the sun, were the soldiers we'd left behind, Amara and Henri in the centre. Henri held his chin high, a cut allowing blood to run down his cheek. Amara tried to do the same. Even at this distance, though, I could see her terror. See how she tried to hold herself upright, even as that terror threatened to crumble her.

'With my full power returning, it is rather easy to move my soldiers through the realm,' Vitus said almost conversationally. 'And when Tarina delivered word of your presence ... well, I had to bring you a surprise.'

'Let them go,' I said, my fingers tightening on the knife. I could run for the hill. Try to cut down as many Ankurans as possible. I wouldn't make it, though. Not with other creatures in the way. 'They're all young. Inexperienced. No threat to you.'

He laughed. My throat dried, my pulse quickening. 'Oh, I think not, little raven. You should not have involved yourself in the affairs of mortals. Let this serve as a reminder of that.'

I lurched forward as horror raced through me. Lifted my hand and tried to grasp onto any semblance of power, to pull at the realm and let myself slip through it so I could reach them in time.

I will not, the power spat. *I am not yours to command*.

Still, I tried, my legs burning as my mouth opened in a scream, any creature who dared get between me and the soldiers falling to my blades. Amara's eyes met mine as the Ankurans, at least two to every mortal soldier, placed their hands on the sides of the mortals' heads. She smiled as those golden fingers tightened. Closed her eyes as I screamed her name, screamed Henri's and Eamon's, just *screamed*.

Cracks sounded, each of them brutally slicing through the

violence below. One by one, the mortals dropped, their heads twisted to the side, eyes open and unseeing.

I staggered to a stop, my throat tight, horror flooding through me along with the warmth of their deaths. All those lives, gone in a moment. Perhaps if Dearil stood where I did, he might have waxed poetic about how it was simply the way things were meant to be. How fighting against death's beckoning was a folly that went against nature itself. Maybe I'd even be able to find some tiny gratitude that their deaths had been quick.

But his power had chosen poorly. I was not Dearil. I did not possess his dignified presence, his grace and calm. And most of all, I couldn't separate myself from the happenings of mortals. Dearil might've been content in the godly realm, but Vitus was in *my* realm. And those mortals – those soldiers – were under my command. There would be no impartiality. No divine aloofness.

Please, I whispered to the power. Let it feel my rage and sorrow. The same rage and sorrow I thought I could feel in its silver depths. *Just this once.*

In response, the power shifted a fraction. Not in submission, but in fragile acquiescence.

The Ankuran's voice rang out. 'See, little raven? This is—'

'Enough.' The word clapped out of me, striking through the cries of those around me. Silence fell. It wasn't the silence of creatures and mortals shocked into quiet. No, this silence was heavy. Unnatural. The deathly quiet of forced stillness.

I turned to the Ankuran housing Vitus. Power swelled around me – mine yet not, Dearil's yet different. It was strength and authority, wildness and rage. Silver cracks appeared underfoot, shooting across the earth. The Ankuran stared, its fingers trembling at its side. Not in rage or fear, but because it *couldn't* move. Not as the weight of death's power pressed down from all angles. The wards were a faraway pain, the power possessing my body. It grasped hold of my rage – over the deaths, over Jaxon's betrayal. Over being separated from Callum yet again. Wrapped itself around the red-hot emotion until it was impossible to tell one from the other.

Kill them, it purred through my mind. There was no malice in the power's will this time. No hatred in its nature. This was what it was made for – to kill. To bring death. *I will use you well. Let me do as I please.*

Yes, I whispered back, and its glee mirrored my own.

Bones cracked as the Ankuran's jaw gaped, gold seeping beneath its skin. Vitus's power – too much of it for the once-mortal form. The creature shuddered under the god's wrath, but he was too far away, his power too diluted here. All he could do was force out a rasping, 'That power does not belong to you.'

The smile that spread across my lips was mine, yet not. An expression borne from the power as much as it was my hatred of him. This was the power's opposite. The life to its death. And Vitus was mine – a reminder of what I could become, if I let myself turn into it. Of what I'd willingly devolve into should Callum die by the end of this.

'You're right.' I crouched, fingers splaying as I pressed them to the cracked earth. My eyes met his and held. 'But for once, we're in accordance.'

Gold flared bright. The silver flared brighter.

It leapt into the sky, far higher than any wall of power I'd been able to summon in the past. Tingling rushed over my skin, a cascade of colour that turned death into something beautiful. The sunlight was blocked out, the world around becoming cast in shades of luminescence so bright it scarred my very soul. There was an explosion of sound – a thousand voices, a million whispers, twining together into a cacophony of souls embedded into the very essence of the power. Those around me lost their form, becoming less corporeal and more bundles of light – bright ones for the mortals, their souls glowing with their life. Dark spots where light should exist for the rest.

Smoke and jasmine curled around me as I closed my eyes.

Let me do as I please, the power seemed to thrum through me. It pushed at my anger. Reminded me of the souls I'd already lost. Of Amara, with her wide eyes and dark braids. Of Henri. Of the others, many nameless in my mind.

Yes, I replied simply.

The silver crashed down.

It slammed into the dark spots first, engulfing them in one massive wave. There were no shrieks of pain. No cries of fury. Only death in its silent glory as it turned the godly creatures into ash. The silver spread, lashing out at where the power had frozen the creatures in place, until the only trace of gold that existed was that of my wrists. Until shadow wraiths, scythes and Ankurans alike were gone, their dark hollowness vanished from my world of silver.

I exhaled. *Good*, I thought, lifting a hand as though to call the power back to me.

I'd forgotten, though, that this power did not belong to me. And it was far from being satiated.

I am not done, it snapped at my attempts to subdue it. *I will never be done.*

A sharp pain tightened at my wrists, my arms throbbing with it. The power lunged away from me, lashing out at the nearest light. My breath hitched. I desperately attempted to grasp hold of it. To wrangle it under control.

But I wasn't enough.

Anger turned to panic as silver coated the nearest bright light – the soul of the man who I'd saved not long before. His soul flickered. The silver brightened, humming. A faint line appeared beneath the light of his soul – a fraying thread.

'No,' I whispered, lurching forward. The light around was too bright to make out any shapes. My feet caught on a body, my knees slamming into earth I had only distantly been aware was there. I didn't stop. I crawled towards that soul, towards that fraying thread. If I could get to it – if I could somehow hold onto it, stop the power that threatened it—

The thread snapped. The soul flickered out of existence.

Ice sank into my bones. I couldn't stop this power. It wasn't going to be Vitus or any other god who killed the army. It was going to be me. My failure to control what had been forced into me. The scent of smoke and jasmine strengthened, stinging at my nose and watering my eyes. I staggered to my feet as the silver lunged again, searching for its next victim. There was no blade that could cut it down. No Gift that could stop it.

Everyone was going to die.

Chiara. My name broke through the silence of death. A strand of shadow stretched through the silver – far darker than the hollowness of the creatures had been, yet somehow more full of life than even the mortal souls.

I knew that voice. Knew it because it was carved into my heart. *Callum.* The silver hesitated around me – not coming back, but not progressing forward, as though it, too, had been waiting to hear his voice.

You're unharmed?

The wards stung my wrists. *I'm fine.*

Why do I feel like you're lying to me?

I pressed my hand to my chest, the sound of his voice sending a stab of longing through me. I didn't just want his voice. I wanted *him*. All of him here with me. But if this was all that was given me, I'd greedily accept it. Especially when his voice seemed to soothe the power as much as it did me. *What about you? Have you been injured? Are you okay?*

There was a long, terrible moment of silence. My throat tightened. The silver began to writhe with energy, twisting as though it was turning its sights on the mortal souls once more. And then, *I'm uninjured.*

I heard what he didn't say. *But you're not okay.*

Of course I'm not okay. I just felt your terror down the bond, Chiara. What's happening?

I closed my eyes. *I didn't mean to let you feel that. I'm sorry.*

Don't ever apologise for something like that. Tell me what's happening.

I killed one of your soldiers. The words spilt down the bond, quicker than I could stop them. The silver power shivered as though delighted by the admittance.

I could almost picture Callum's surprise – the slight widening of his eye, the single blink he'd give in admittance of his shock. *Did they ... do something to you?*

No. I— I swallowed, digging my nails into my palm. I didn't know where my knife had ended up. It must've fallen somewhere, lost in the misty silver curling through the air around me. *I have Dearil's power, Callum. But it ... it isn't mine. There were Ankurans, and they killed your soldiers, and I – I snapped. I thought I could control the power. That it'd take out the creatures and leave the rest.* My hands trembled, and I was suddenly thankful that the power had at least frozen everyone else. Callum was the only one I would willingly bear myself to. *But it won't come back, Callum. I tried, but it killed one of your soldiers, and it's going to kill the rest, and—*

It's all right, Chiara.

It's not! The words shuddered free of me, filled with panicked anger. *This is your army. Your people that I might hurt.*

You are mine. More than any army or any kingdom. You. Even if you killed everyone there, it wouldn't change that. Another pause before he added, *Though I'd rather you didn't if you could help it.*

I pressed my lips together. *Not helping.*

It was only partially the truth. Something that had knotted in

The Divine

my chest began to loosen, and I could've sworn the silver flickered around me.

If it's anything like my Gift, it's reacting because of your emotions. The words were thoughtful. Considering, in the same way that Callum was, no matter what problem came his way.

Of course it is, I replied, a little snappishly. *But I've never been great with handling those, have I?*

You can take control of it, Chiara. You've commanded a king before. This should be easy in comparison.

I narrowed my eyes into the silver mist. *This is a divine power. I'm pretty sure it comes before a king.*

Does it? he asked. There was teasing in his tone, but he was right.

Of course it didn't. Callum came before everything, even the divine. Perhaps especially the divine.

As though sensing my thoughts, he said, *Imagine I'm in front of you.*

I wished he was. I closed my eyes, trying to picture him there. His hands pressing to my cheeks, fingers trailing lazily over my skin as he tucked my hair behind my ear. His lips pressing to my forehead, then trailing lower, finding my mouth. The desire that'd settle over me. The need. How his touch would ground me, anchoring me to reality before I could slip away.

That's it, Callum said. *You're almost there.*

And I was. The power was slipping under my skin, burying itself back in my blood as my anger and panic settled. It unwound itself from my anger, the pain of the wards ebbing. Slowly, I opened my eyes. The world was misty around me, but the sun was beginning to peak through, the blood- and ash-covered ground visible beneath my feet. I exhaled, shoulders relaxing. *I did it.*

I knew you could. Promise me you won't forget that you've saved more lives than you've taken today. His voice was even softer – little more than a tendril of breeze curling through the mist. *Can you handle the rest on your own?*

I narrowed my eyes. *Why do I think you're ignoring something important for me?*

Oh, it's just a little fracas with some Ankurans. I'll be—

I cut the connection short. Of course, Callum would ignore his own safety for me.

I pressed my eyes shut against the harsh stinging of the sun, head bowing. The scent of smoke and jasmine was replaced with that of blood, the thick metallic tang carried by the breeze. I breathed it in. Let it remind me of what I had done. Of what I had saved, too.

I opened my eyes. Stared at where the soldier I'd saved had been cowering before the disappeared Ankuran. All that'd been left behind was his blood-covered sword, silver ash forming a murky mess with the red on its surface. I'd done that. I'd killed him.

For a moment, I envied the woman I'd once been – the one who'd been made of nothing more than sharp edges. The one who wouldn't have thought twice about the lives the power had taken.

But that woman had been miserable. Miserable and unbearably alone.

Even if Callum wasn't by my side, I wasn't alone any longer.

So, I acknowledged the shame and guilt as I knelt on the ground and picked up the sword. It was ill-suited to my frame – too long, and unlike the knives I preferred wielding. Even so, I sheathed it and strapped it to my side as I rose. It would serve as a reminder – not only of what I could do if I wasn't careful, but of what I needed to learn to protect.

The wards gave a small sting as I straightened. The threading of silver had increased, thick enough to cover a quarter of the gold markings. Once, I might've thought that a good thing – the colour of my own Gift breaking through. But there was no telling if it was whatever remained of my Gift doing that to the markings, or if it was the unruly power. A power that I feared far more than any restrictions on my Gift.

Jade staggered to my side, her face pale and hair plastered to her head with sweat. Her hands closed on my shoulders. 'What happened? I was fighting, and then – they're all gone.'

'Yes,' I said quietly, glancing over to the hill, to the bodies that had remained untouched by my power, their armour gleaming uselessly. 'They are.'

There was a heartbeat of silence as Jade shifted her attention in the same direction as mine. Her fingers tightened, then dropped. 'Henri was getting married in winter. And Matthias – the one on the far left – he has two girls, no older than four. Eamon's older brother was injured in the Archin war and was waiting for him to return home. Jemima was going to open her own tailor's shop once this was all over. Amara ... gods, she wasn't even old enough to *know* what she was going to become.' A breath shuddered through Jade. No matter how many battles she'd face, it seemed death had become no easier for her. 'What am I supposed to do? I failed them. How can I face their families?'

There was a time when I wouldn't have understood and urged Jade to forget them. But I remembered Amara's smile. The way she'd thanked me for saving her town. Henri's quiet respect when I'd lived most of my life never expecting such a thing. The small gestures of the other soldiers – their quickness to accept me despite my strangeness, the ones who'd shared food or offered to help with menial tasks.

I might not be able to lead a kingdom, but these people – the soldiers whose lives were risked on the battlefield – were mine. These were the sort I'd grown up with. Who'd saved my life as many times as I'd saved others. I wouldn't do them the discourtesy of burying their deaths.

'The only way you fail them is by turning their sacrifice into something pitiful. You remember their faces. Their names. Remember their smiles and why they were here. And when you next fight, you fight for them.' I clasped Jade's arm. 'We will make sure our enemy pays for their deaths.'

Jade hesitated before nodding slowly. She dragged a hand over her face, fatigue turning her movements sloppy. 'What next?'

I looked around. The remaining soldiers – no more than three hundred – were slowly staggering towards us, the wounded tended to by those who'd fared better. Every set of eyes was glassy, every face pale. Dustings of silver ash coated most cheeks, spatters of black, gold and green splashed across armour.

We might have been the last ones standing, but we had not won this fight. There'd been far too many lost. And Jaxon... Well, I would be finding a way to make him pay for these deaths, too.

'We burn the dead.' Instinct told me that in my sleep, I'd be ushering those dead beyond the Gates, too. With that many gone, our numbers were too low to hope for any success in serious battles if we were to push on. Maybe the power would emerge again, but if it did, there was no telling whether it'd be willing to admit defeat like it had today. 'We return to Naruzia. We regroup. And then, we come back for the gods. We make sure they feel every bit of pain we did today.'

Chapter Twenty

The night came quickly, but sleep came far slower. I stewed in my fury at Jaxon for most of the day as we burned the dead and made sure that none of Tarina's Illusions remained. By the time I collapsed into my bedroll, muscles aching and mind a mess, I was far past the point of exhaustion.

The realms had different plans for me than sleep, though.

I could feel the Gates calling me. They tugged at my soul, begging me to tend to the dead. Smoke and jasmine surrounded me in its embrace. But the dead that awaited me would be the soldiers that had died. Those I'd failed to protect.

Terror stabbed through me as I felt my soul being yanked to the other realm. Instinct had me reaching for something, *anything*, to grab hold of. For a moment, I thought I had a handle on something warm and filled with life. Something overwhelmingly familiar.

Before I could figure out what it was, I was shoved into the space before the Gates.

I kept my eyes shut as long as I could. Souls buzzed along my skin, their warmth more than I deserved. Trickles of voices whispered around me. Some, I thought I might have recognised. Others, I did not. I crouched low, head bending and arms wrapping around my ears to block them out.

'I'm not your god,' I whispered, my voice cracking with the words. 'Go into the Gates yourself.'

The buzzing grew. It was almost frantic, as though it had something to say.

'Go!' I shouted, flinging one arm towards the Gates while keeping my eyes shut. I didn't want to see what wounds they wore. Didn't want to count how many I continued to fail. A tugging in my soul told me the Gates had followed my command, opening so that souls could travel through.

I hated those Gates. Despised that they recognised me as the god of death. Loathed the way their presence yanked at the power festering in me.

'Go,' I said again, softer this time, my voice thick.

There was another hesitant brush of the souls against my skin and then they were gone, each disappearing to their end. A shuddering breath ran through me. I waited for my soul to descend back to my body. I wouldn't cry. Not here, and not in the mortal realm.

Everyone needed my strength, not my weakness.

Seconds ticked by, stretching to minutes. Yet I did not move from the other realm.

Something brushed my arm. It was gentler than the insistent souls had been. Warmer, too. Quiet in a way that settled some of my nerves.

'How long do you intend to keep me waiting, Captain?'

My head shot up so quickly I almost cracked it on Callum's chin. He smiled down at me, his eyes bright with humour and smile soft with warmth. 'How? I don't— How?'

'I was in quite an important meeting when the bond ... well, it was like it pulled me free of my body. One moment, I was in a meeting with General Elijah before he returns to Alluvite, planning our strategy for going after Tizan, the next, I was here.'

My heart stuttered as he flashed another grin. In the strange space before the Gates, there was nothing to distract from his beauty. I studied the features I'd already carved deep into my mind. I must have grabbed the soul-bond when I'd instinctively reached out before, dragging some part of Callum here with me.

The realisation sent a bolt of fear through me. If I'd done it at the wrong time – if Callum had been in the middle of a battle rather than with his general—

Callum stepped forward, his hand cupping my face and smile disappearing. 'Don't do that.'

My brows drew together even as I leant into his warmth. 'Do what?'

'Think about worst possible scenarios. I'm glad I'm here. That I get to see you.' His eyes traced every one of my features as intensely as I did his. Sweeping his thumb across my skin, he shifted closer, barely any space left between our bodies. 'Glad that I get to touch you. To—'

I pulled away, eyes narrowing at the shades of purple and blue on the right side of his face. 'What's that?'

He twisted, attempting to cover the marking. I grasped his chin and turned his face back to me. The bruise was a nasty one, stretching from the corner of his eye and disappearing under his hair. My frown deepened.

'I was hoping you wouldn't notice it.'

'Wouldn't notice it?' He winced as my grip on him tightened. 'I'd have to be blind to not notice that. You were meant to be keeping yourself safe, Callum.'

He covered my hand with his own, his fingers annoyingly warm. 'I'm perfectly safe. Do you see any other marks?'

'I haven't looked yet.'

Callum's smile grew suggestive. 'Would you like to?'

Yes. 'No!' With an irritated huff, I yanked my hand from his and stepped back, putting space back between us. 'Tell me what happened.'

'Just a minor skirmish on our way back out of Alluvite. A few dozen Ankurans ambushed us.'

My disapproval grew. 'Would this be when you were talking to me earlier?'

He tilted his head. 'If I said no, would you be less angry?'

'Idiot.' I hit his shoulder and he stumbled back a step, grinning. It infuriated me. The air around us shifted, as though in eager anticipation as I glowered up at him, strands of silver and shadows breaking up the endless space around. The few remaining souls – those that were too nervous to pass the Gates – hummed. 'Where was Deana in all this?'

'Back in Alluvite.'

I stared, caught between disbelief and anger. 'You left behind your best guard when you're going after Tizan?'

'I left behind one of the few people I trust with leading Alluvite,' he corrected. 'And brought five hundred men with me instead.'

'You need to be more careful,' I scolded.

'And you need to talk to me.' Callum caught my hand, tugging me into him. I held firm against his touch for all of a second before relaxing. His other arm curled around my waist as he stared down at me, the green of his eyes brighter than the freshest of spring grass. 'You're angry at something.'

'Yes. At you.'

'Liar. Being worried isn't the same as being angry.'

I huffed an irritated breath. 'I'm perfectly capable of being two things at once.' He continued to stare at me expectantly, just as he always did. Never prodding or pushing unless I needed it. Just waiting for me to be ready. I broke his stare, resting my head to his chest. He was so real. So solid.

The Divine

I could already feel the heartbreak of letting him go.

'Something happened today,' I admitted. 'Jaxon—' I choked off, his name bitter on my tongue. For a moment, the power surged, the souls around growing frenetic in their buzzing.

Callum, though, didn't flinch. He merely ran his fingers through my hair, waiting until the silver sparking on my skin died down. It never lashed out at him. Perhaps it knew that its touch wouldn't harm him as one of Vitus's Gifted. Or maybe it knew that was the one sin that would force my hand and send me on a search to carve it free from my soul.

Once it vanished, Callum stepped back. He spread his arms when I looked up to him, his brows raising. 'Well?'

I folded my arms, annoyed at how quickly my body had chilled away from him. 'Well, what?'

'Are we going to spar?' He glanced over me. 'You're clearly angry.'

'That has nothing to do with sparring.'

He tilted his head, his gaze knowing. 'But getting some of the anger out with your fists could help you talk about it.'

In spite of everything, a smile crept onto my face. I shook out my hands, grinning up at him. He grinned back. 'Don't expect me to go easy on you because your pretty face is bruised.'

'When have I ever wanted you to go easy on me?' he replied, his hands already loosely fisting. He raised them, challenge bright in his expression. 'Don't keep me waiting.'

'Never.' I launched myself forward, excitement thrumming in my blood. I'd missed this as much as I'd missed his touch. The challenge in his eyes. The taunt in his voice. The not knowing which of us would come out triumphant.

I spared no mercy as I sent my fist driving for his already bruised cheek. Callum twisted, swinging his elbow up to deflect my blow. I spun with it, hair flying as I sent my foot flying back. It connected with Callum's midsection, his grunt broadening my grin.

We were at the Gates. This should have been my realm. My domain.

Yet Callum kept up with me with astonishing ease.

Every jab I sent his way was met with one of his own. When I grasped a handful of his tunic, yanking him towards me as I drove my knee up, he caught my arm and twisted me the other way. When his foot lashed out in what would have been a painful blow at my knee, I whirled past it before sending my own foot driving at his torso.

He danced out of the way, a delighted laugh leaving his lips. I laughed with him, the sound equally savage. We were two weapons – two monsters who had become so much more than what we were supposed to be. And we were perfectly suited in our savagery.

'You are brilliant,' Callum said as he ducked under a jab, managing to connect one of his own with my shoulder. The pain only sent further delight through me, a reminder that this was real. *He* was real, and he was mine. 'Absolutely brilliant.'

'And you're a shameless flirt.' I dropped to the ground, rolling to avoid a sweep of his leg. Popping up on the other side of him, I grasped a handful of his tunic, yanking him off balance. I hooked my foot on his ankle, pulling hard enough that he slammed to the formless ground below. His chest rose in pants, sweat beading upon his skin as I fell with him, driving my knee into his chest.

'You're extraordinary when you're like this.' He reached up, tugging on one of my curls.

I frowned. 'Like what?'

'Being *you*.' Before I could celebrate any victory, he grasped his own handful of my tunic. With a savage jerk, he rolled us both, straddling either side of my body with his legs. His grin was the most beautiful sight I had ever seen, the scar curling up one side of his face lifting with how bright it was. 'Completely, unforgivingly yourself.'

I jerked my knee up. Callum slammed his leg over the top of it. In response, I drove my head up, connecting with his forehead. Grunting, he fell backwards, holding his forehead. My own gave a sympathetic throb. 'Like I said, a shameless flirt.' I lunged forward, driving my forearm into his throat. He fell back. I grinned, my nose nearly brushing his, our shared panting mingling between us. 'Lucky for you, I happen to have a soft spot for flirts.'

'And I have a soft spot for brutal women.' He yanked me down, closing the distance between us. His lips crushed to mine, both of us equal in our desperate hunger. I gripped his tunic, my tangled hair a curtain around us, as he curled an arm around my waist. For a moment, the war didn't matter. That we were between realms didn't matter. All that mattered was *him*.

And then his arm was tightening further, our kiss breaking as he flipped me onto my back. He grinned in beautiful triumph. 'I win.'

'Cheat,' I muttered, trying and failing to hold back my own smile. 'Sorry to say, but I don't think that'd work on any of the gods.'

Callum laughed as he got to his feet, holding his hand out to me. 'I don't know. I reckon I could sway Vitus with that move.'

My nose wrinkled at the thought. 'Don't put that picture in my head.'

I was rewarded with another laugh before Callum grew sombre. He sat down, tugging me down beside him. As though sensing the need for privacy, the nosy souls around us started to drift away, taking their silvery light with them. 'So? You going to tell me what happened?'

I frowned down at my feet, as bare as they were where my

body was currently sleeping in the mortal realm. Any joy I'd felt from that fight faded. 'Jaxon betrayed us.'

Callum jerked beside me. 'Explain.'

At the sound of the icy wrath in his voice, I reached across, lacing my fingers with his. I didn't look up, though. Didn't want to see whether the extent of his rage mirrored my own. If his heartbreak was the same. 'He sold us out to Tarina. Went with her, too, all because she's promised him a life stuck in an Illusion with Garrett.'

Silence stretched for some time, Callum merely holding onto me. Finally, just as I thought I might break, he said, 'Gods, Chiara. No wonder you're angry.'

I closed my eyes. Just like always, he seemed to know that asking too many questions now might break me. I'd share it with him in time. Right now, though, the hurt was too raw. The disbelief too fresh. My power might be contained here, but if my anger rose and I went back to the mortal realm, there was no telling what might happen.

'Someone's going to need to tell Deana.' I swallowed, my heart already aching for her. 'It'll be like telling her Jaxon chose Garrett over her.'

'Not even Garrett. I think she could understand if it was the real thing, but for Jaxon to betray her for an Illusion?' Callum gripped my hand tighter. 'Jaxon had better pray he never sees her again.'

'Will you tell her?'

Callum winced. 'As much as I wish to take that burden off of you, Deana stayed in Alluvite when I headed out for Tizan.'

I stiffened. 'Why?'

'It was the best choice. I promise you, I considered all options, but I needed someone I trusted back at the palace. Deana was the only person I had.'

The Divine

Exhaling, I decided I didn't have it in me to argue with him tonight. Not with the hurt of Jaxon's betrayal so fresh.

I studied the way our fingers interlaced so tightly, almost like they'd been stitched together. 'Do you think…' I exhaled, a strand of my hair fluttering with the force of it. 'Jaxon said I couldn't understand what it is to lose my soul-bonded. If you lost me, what do you think you would choose if given an option?'

Callum stiffened at the mention of losing me. I glanced up at him. His jaw was rigid, his features tense. Even so, there was clear thoughtfulness in his eyes as he considered the question rather than brushing it off. 'I'd like to think I'd choose to fight for those who live.' He sighed. 'But I don't know. The thought of losing you … that month without you destroyed me. If there was no chance of getting you back, I don't know what I might do for even one last glimpse.'

I nodded. I'd thought the very same.

'It doesn't mean you have to forgive him, though.' Callum met my eyes. 'Hate him as much as you need to. Be angry. Be whatever you need to be.'

'I don't hate him,' I admitted, leaning my head on his shoulder. Jaxon was my closest friend. One of the few who had withstood me and not run away. I didn't think I knew how to hate him. Rage, though, was far easier to hold onto. 'But he's going to be down a few important body parts the next time we meet.'

Callum's laugh wrapped around me, warmer than any blanket could be. 'That's my girl.' He rested his cheek atop my head, curling his arm around me and bringing me closer to his side. I shut my eyes, letting the steady sound of his breathing soothe away any fear, any anger or sorrow. Let myself just be in his presence for however long we had left.

The silence that fell was not uncomfortable. It was warm. Solid. The sort of quiet that promised safety. It was exactly what I needed. Exactly what we both needed.

And so we stayed, wrapped in our cocoon of silence in front of the Gates, waiting for reality to drag us out of the protection of each other's company. It didn't take long, the Gates wavered and the souls turned hazy. But it was slow to come. Slow enough to allow Callum to press his lips to mine once more. The kiss was long. Lingering. Sweet.

Enough so that, when I slammed back into my body and opened my eyes to the world, the day seemed perhaps a little less harsh than it might have before.

The journey back to Naruzia was a long one. Of the three hundred who'd survived, fifty were injured seriously enough that they were unable to easily be moved. After shifting to a safer spot in one of the ruined Archinian towns, we made the decision to leave the majority of forces behind for a few extra days to recuperate. I didn't have the luxury of time to wait with them. Neither did Jade, whose position as General made her invaluable in future battles. Leaving a veteran soldier in charge, we took a small force of forty to head for Alluvite. The landscape was endless dirt and withered grass, the sun unrelenting in its heat. We passed through three towns north of the Archin-Naruzia border. Each was as silent as the last.

By the time we passed through the outskirts of Naruzia and the small city of Alarnis came into view, everyone seemed desperate to lay eyes on another mortal face. We'd ridden hard during the day, desperate to leave Archin behind, and stars were beginning to emerge. The first hint of moonbeams only deepened shadows across the land. I narrowed my eyes at the city, struggling to spot the gleam of lantern lights in the windows of buildings or hear hints of nighttime happenings that should've been starting to make their way to us.

The Divine

'We should stop here,' I murmured to Jade, who rode next to me. 'Morale's low enough already.'

She looked towards the city, her shoulders slumping as she understood what I was saying. 'Eamon's brother lived in Alarnis. Henri's sister and niece, too.'

'At least they don't have to hear of each other's deaths.' It was a hollow comfort.

As wounds were checked and a meal was started, Jade and I selected five of the more level-headed amongst the soldiers to approach the city with us. Alarnis had once been a bustling hub of street stalls and performers, well known for putting on performances that even nobility would travel to see. In my early days in the army, we'd fought a battle nearby against Archinian soldiers. My captain of the time, Leila, had ordered us all to take a night of respite within the city's confines.

I hadn't known what *respite* was meant to be at that stage. So, I'd walked through the streets, heavily cloaked, my hood drawn low. There'd been plenty of beckoning hands, the performers unusually unfazed by my glares. Fire-eaters had waved flaming sticks high in the sky, spinning the fire through the air with easy elegance. Women wrapped in silks with bells on their ankles and wrists had danced between it all, offering bright smiles to any who flashed a coin their way, and slipped fingers into unprotected pockets. Even amongst the despondency that had been King Kane's rule, the people of Alarnis had managed to find a way to smile. To prosper, even.

Now, as we walked through it, it was as much a city of the dead as any of the places in Archin had been.

'This doesn't look good,' Matthias, an older man of fifty with a solid frame and a smattering of freckles, whispered as we passed empty buildings.

Doors were cracked open, revealing only shadowy glimpses of the interiors of what had once been lively households. Glass shards sprinkled the streets, the windows that they had once been a part of now jagged, gaping holes. Inside, the barest glimpses of knocked-over candles and rotting plates of food were visible. Weeds clung to the ground, stretching straggly stems towards the abandoned homes. Clothes scattered over cobblestones, often lying next to belongings that had been littered in nearly every direction, as though a force had torn items from homes and strewn them with a carelessness that bordered on anarchy.

The streets, once only quiet in the few hours that passed in the time where the day drifted over to the next one, were now only filled by the haunting wail of the wind.

'Maybe there are some survivors,' a soldier by the name of Sadie suggested. 'If we—'

'I don't think there's any survivors,' I cut in, and they all fell silent, darkness falling upon each expression. Jade shot me an admonishing look. I ignored it. There was no point stretching out hope where there was none to be had.

'Should we check the houses?' Jade asked as we slowed, eyeing a small townhouse with a door that remained only as splinters. It swung on its hinges every time the wind whipped past, emitting a creak that echoed plaintively across the stone of the streets. A pair of boots, their size suggesting they belonged to a man, lay in the street.

I shifted, my grip tightening on my sword. There were some things, I knew, that were not made to be empty. This city was one of them.

I looked at the five soldiers, frowning at their pale features. They were on edge as it was, and I didn't think I was going to find anything good in the house. 'I'll go. Stay out here. Check the nearby streets.'

Jade obeyed, ushering the others away. I approached the townhouse, pushing on the ruins of the front door. It swung open.

The Divine

It was impossible to see far past the threshold. Shadows swept over the floor. A rotten smell emanated from inside.

My grip switched to my knives, their familiarity more of a comfort in the dark. I edged my way down a narrow hall, entering a small room. A dark shape lay in the corner – a cot, I thought it might've been, an armchair placed next to it. It was difficult to make much more out in the darkness.

Wood creaked underfoot. My boot connected with something soft. I sheathed my knife, fingers curling around a small cloth doll. Its fabric was rougher in some spot where small hands might have clutched it repeatedly over a period of months, hair tacky with something that flaked away onto my fingertips. I stepped towards a shard of moonlight illuminating the dim space. It fell upon my fingers, capturing red in its pearly hues.

Blood. That was blood on my fingertips, coating the doll's hair and clothes.

A chill settled over me. Slowly, I turned to the armchair and cot. Waited for my eyes to adjust enough that I could tell that the shapes were not as they should be, the top of the armchair bulging. I stepped forward. Tucked the doll into a pocket, its arms hanging limply out. Took a breath and forced my legs to continue crossing the distance between myself and that chair.

The armchair was occupied, a woman splayed on top of it. One arm was flung over the side, the other down the front, long hair tangled around a face I was glad I couldn't quite make out, particularly with the darkness staining it and her throat. And underneath … underneath the woman's body, tucked away as though she might shield them from the evil that had descended here, were two shapes. Bodies that were unfairly, cruelly small.

I was selfishly thankful for the darkness shielding the cause of their deaths from me.

It took some time for me to leave, my chest tight. There was no sign of the owner of the boots I'd stepped over outside, the crispness of the air breaking through the stench of decay. It wasn't hard to guess where their owner had ended up. He must've been deemed *useful* by Vitus, his body taken to become an Ankuran.

Unlike in the towns we'd passed through, though, the children and woman had been left behind. Vitus was becoming picky. The thought that he was now able to be, no longer relying on sheer numbers to overwhelm the mortals, sent a shudder of unease through me.

'Well?' Jade asked as she rounded the corner, moonlight turning her already whitened face paler. 'Anything to report?'

I brushed my fingers over the doll's head. 'Keep the soldiers away from the city. We've got a fair distance to travel yet.'

Jade's lips flattened. She nodded her grim understanding. 'And the rest of the houses?'

I hesitated. A large part of me wanted to agree that we should search them. To give in to the warmth of hope. The problem with that warmth, though, was that the cold was far starker afterwards.

I was used to that cold. The soldiers were not. I started to turn. 'Take them back. I'll search Alarni alone.'

'It'll take far too long. Besides, you've been working far harder than most of us. You need to—'

A pealing bell rang through the air. It wasn't the discordant clangs of an alarm, but the sprinkling of chimes scattered through the wind. A sound most might consider soft. Lovely. The epitome of a peaceful beckoning.

I felt anything but peaceful as I whipped back to Jade. 'Where are the others?'

'Resting around the corner.' Jade motioned towards the darkened street she'd come from.

'Good.' Palming the knife I'd slipped away in the house, I shifted in front of her, keeping my voice low. 'Go to them. Stay quiet and get out.'

'But—'

The Divine

'That's an order, General.' I cut her a look, letting her see the immovability of my expression as the scent of fresh roses bloomed around us. The air heated with warning of the coming power. 'Go.'

Jade was technically ranked higher than me. She was a general. I'd held no post since I'd left the army. But she snapped to attention, nodded and turned, her steps light upon the stone.

I waited until I could no longer hear her before I flipped one of my knives in the air, catching it by the hilt as it fell. 'If you were going to hide, you shouldn't have made such a noise with your arrival.'

The air shimmered around me, the moonlight shifting to a pale pink that lit the street with the same brightness a sun might. The scent of roses intensified, far fresher than that which trailed Vitus. 'Your decorum is disgraceful, child.'

I smiled, making sure the curve of my lips held an edge. 'You finally showed up. I was wondering when you'd deign to grace this realm with your presence.'

The woman who stepped into the light was nothing short of breathtaking. Her hair, long, and as pale as the moon above, fell over her shoulders like silken sheets, her rose-coloured dress sweeping just above the dirtied ground. The air itself seemed to worship her feet as she glided towards me. 'Is that disgrace what passes for mortal manners?'

I met her eyes, flipping the knife once again. It flew high this time, seeming to cut through strands of moonlight before falling back to my hand. 'Would you like me to greet you without my manners, Evania?' Another flip. 'Those sorts of greetings tend to sting.'

The goddess of peace eyed my knife, a wrinkle appearing upon her upturned nose. 'You were not this rude when we first met.'

'Because when we first met, you hadn't abandoned the mortal

realm long enough for Vitus and his friends to do *this*'—I swept the knife around, gesturing to the emptied buildings around us—'to my realm.'

She didn't bother following my gesture. My teeth clenched tighter, anger rolling through me. It wasn't as sharp as it had been with Jaxon's betrayal, but it wasn't far off. I had very little patience for gods. 'Gods must not interfere in the happenings of mortals.'

I stepped forward. Unlike Evania, I was very much grounded and filled with the opposite of *peaceful* emotions. 'Then you should've dragged Vitus back to your little realm, and made sure *no* gods interfere.'

'You do not understand the way of things.' She lifted her chin higher. If it went any further, she might find herself looking at the sky. 'You are nothing more than a halfling.'

'And you are nothing more than a coward.'

Rose sparks flew in the air, Evania's eyes brightening with the first emergence of her wrath. Despite her title, the haughty goddess was far from a calm creature. 'Do not insult me, girl. I will not tolerate—'

'Where's your far better half?' I interrupted, brushing by her and crushing the budding flowers that had begun to bloom underfoot. A small tingle of energy skittered over my skin from her power. 'If I have to interact with any of you divine fools, I'd rather it be her.'

'Kerta does not obey the whims of those with mortal taint.'

I spun. 'Why are you here, Evania?'

Her lips flattened. She looked away. 'I have a message to deliver.'

'So, you don't obey me, but you'll act as a messenger?' I smirked. 'Good to see gods have standards.'

Evania's cheeks flushed. 'If you must act this way, then I shall not grant you the message.'

The Divine

I tapped the flat of my blade against my thigh, raising my brows. 'All right.'

Her pale hair began to take on an ethereal glow as her flush deepened. 'I will leave. I am not bluffing.'

My smirk grew. For a moment, I saw Cassie standing in front of me, her little arms crossed, her cheeks reddened with all the frustrations a child could hold as she threatened to never talk to me again after I told her it was bedtime. Her brows had always held the same scrunch to it Evania's now did, filled with the naïve obstinacy of one who refused to learn that not all their whims would be met.

But where Cassie's temper tantrums involved stomped feet and pudgy fists, Evania's involved far more power. If not for the soldiers who might still be in the city confines, I might've tested her further. A wounded pride was a mild punishment for all her divine apathy to the deaths that'd plagued our realm.

I didn't want to risk any lives except my own, though. So, with practised patience, I sighed and said, 'Fine. Apologies, great divine one. Please bestow upon me your godly message.'

'You are starting to sound like that meddlesome boy.' Evania glanced behind me. 'Where is Tarina's whelp?'

Any trace of amusement vanished. 'He'll be finding himself a home in the Dark once I find him.'

Evania's hair swayed with a breeze that didn't touch me. 'He allowed his cowardice to win out.'

'The message,' I said curtly.

'You are to remove yourself from this war. Your body is a vessel for divine power. You must not—'

'Who is this coming from?' I interrupted, anger beginning to flicker inside.

'All of those who remain as they should.'

'As they should?' I laughed even as I flung my knife, anger and a power that didn't belong to me sending the point cracking through stone. Dust rose as the grey crumbled on a wall behind Evania, who stared at me with disapproving eyes. 'You mean the ones who've failed to do anything to stop this unfolding.'

'We prepared you as well as we could. Gave you the knowledge to defeat Vitus when you were still a simple halfling, and—'

'You sent me into a shitshow knowing full well I would be unlikely to claim any sort of victory.' The knife still in my possession trembled with my anger. 'I watched Callum *die* because the power I had was nothing compared to his. Do you know what it feels like to have your soul-bond snap?'

Evania paled.

I smiled again, my cheeks aching from the expression. The humourless, cold thing was all I could wear to keep from crumbling. 'Of course you don't, because you and Kerta stay far, far away from danger. You let those with mortal blood pay the price of all your godly arrogance. If I'd been unable to bind Callum's soul to his body, I would've gladly followed him into what awaited. But instead, *I* sacrificed my power. I sacrificed my freedom. I lost my father to gain that freedom back, and just when I had Callum back, the damned realm tore us apart again.'

'That is not—'

'So, no,' I cut in, not caring to hear what she had to say. 'I will not *remove myself* from this war. I will spill my blood and give my life for this realm. For these people. For Callum. And if that makes me a terrible member of the divine, so be it. A terrible god is not such a bad thing to be.'

'You must listen. You are new to the power – a power you have failed to claim. If you continue on, you will bring chaos to all the gods.'

I prodded at that very power, just to see how it felt in Evania's presence. It shuddered awake, its icy voice slicing through me in seconds. *Destroy her, kill her, end her, ruin her—*

I turned my attention away from it before I could give in to its desires. The power was still as unruly as it had been when I'd first inherited it. But I was beginning to understand some of its desires. Its hatred of anything that sought to order it around.

'Let me guess – instead, I'm meant to step back and use the mortals as playing pieces, just as you did with me? Let them die in my place? No great loss if they're wiped off the board, right?'

Her gown shimmered as she stared back at me coolly. 'It is what it means to hold a god's power. You may be too weak to be a true god, but you are far from mortal. You must—'

'Enough,' I said, and my voice filled with the same power it had when I'd spoken the word to Vitus. One that threatened the snapping of restraint on that power she mentioned. Evania must've sensed its coming because she stilled, her rose power fading. I reached into my pocket and stalked forward, shoving what I had there into her hand. 'Take this. A remnant of one of your *playing pieces*.'

Evania looked at the doll I'd handed her, tilting her head. 'Why do you give me this?'

'To remind you that not everyone gets the eternity that gods do.' I curled her fingers around it when she tried to drop it onto the floor. 'This belonged to a child. A child killed by creatures you gods created.'

'We maintain distance from mortals and their wars. It is the way of things,' she said.

I shook my head, disgusted. 'How many years have you lived?'

Evania blinked slowly, rather like a cat that had been confronted by a mouse. 'Millenia.'

'And how many wrongs have you committed?'

'Gods commit no—'

'Plenty, I'm sure. That child never had the chance to make those choices. Never had the chance to decide what she'd live for.

All because the gods deemed her worthless.' I stared at Evania, voice hard as I asked, 'Is it really the innocent who're worthless?'

Evania was a prideful creature, vain and arrogant, but she wasn't made of the same irrationality as Vitus. Buried somewhere inside – somewhere deep, deep down – there had to be a piece of her that was untainted by the years. A part of her that had once looked at the mortal realm and revelled in the peace her presence could bring. Her haughty anger subsided, replaced by something softer. Something uncertain. 'Vitus betraying the ancient laws does not excuse us to do the same.'

'I'll pass that onto the children I help pass the Gates.' My voice was laced with bitterness. 'I'm sure that'll ease their passing as they cry for the life they couldn't have. A life they might've been able to grasp hold of if the gods hadn't abandoned them to a war that your king created.'

Evania looked up. For a moment, her eyes did not seem those of a god. They were soft. Vulnerable. Almost human. 'It is the way it has always been. There must be the divine, and there must be the mortal. Never together.'

'Then perhaps it is time for that to change.' I looked down to where my skin pressed to hers – one set of fingers ridged with scars, the other perfectly smooth. Both, however, carried flakes of the child's dried blood. 'Doing nothing doesn't make you better than Vitus, Evania. At least Vitus knows what he fights for. But you – when all you do is watch, you stand for nothing.'

'We cannot interfere,' Evania insisted. 'We must stay impartial.'

I pulled my hand away, turning my back to her and striding into darkness. 'Then stay away. But I will not let this realm die.'

I made it six steps away before Evania called out, 'How old?'

Pausing, I glanced over my shoulder. She was staring down at the doll now cupped between her hands like it was a delicate bud, one wrong touch away from crumbling. 'I didn't get a good look, but … three, maybe four, at most.'

'So young, even for a mortal.'

I didn't think Evania was aware she'd spoken. 'Many of the dead will be.'

'We cannot interfere,' she muttered once more. The air around her began to shift, rose spilling from her skin as the realm's fabric warped. The scent of roses began to fade as the rose curled around her, ready to pull her through the realms to wherever she was travelling to.

Before it could block her completely from my view, her fingers tightened around the toy, pulling it to her chest. Her head bowed and her eyes closed, a glistening tear falling from her lashes. A goddess crying for a mortal child.

But the tears had come too late. The child was dead. The mortal realm was perishing. And the only gods we might've had on our side had abandoned us to our fate.

Chapter Twenty-One

I didn't sleep that night. Instead, I headed off alone, finding a space where only buildings and bodies existed. Shadows crawled along the ground, the moonlight shy in the abandoned alleyway. There was no warmth of death around. Any souls that had existed in this place had long fled the mortal realm.

It made it the perfect place for me to practise.

Loosening a breath, I lifted my hand, palm facing the sky. *Come on*, I urged the power embedded in my veins. *Come and play.*

My heart beat three times in the silence. Then, in a violent surge, my hand lit up with silver. The power thrummed under my skin, less sinister and more like a disobedient soldier ready to throw a fit. I scowled down at my hand. The silver sparked brighter. It kissed the night air, spitting up at the stars above.

Gritting my teeth, I pointed my hand towards a nearby building. A vine curled up the side, a few leaves clinging stubbornly to its length. *Destroy that*, I ordered.

The silver sparked again. *I do not obey you.*

So you've said. I squared my shoulders, feeling only slightly ridiculous as I glared at the silver. *But you're in my body. My blood. And you will do as I command.*

The power seemed to sneer back at me. *Never.*

Do it. I flexed my fingers, forcing all of my will – my anger and hatred of the burden this power had given me – at the pest.

In response, it flared. I started to smile, victory carrying a sweet taste.

The power must have tasted it, too, and found it foul. It exploded outwards. Light flared, stretching for the sky and stinging my eyes. I cried out, stumbling back as the wards burned my skin, their golden lost to the silver. Pressing my hand to my eyes, I waited until the light had faded before opening them again, ignoring the blur of tears.

The power had done as I'd asked. It had taken the vine, turning it to silvery ash.

It had also stolen every other sign of life in this corner of Alarnis. The weeds shooting through cracks in the cobblestones. The small potted plant left abandoned at a windowsill. Even the leaves that must have fallen from the vine that had scattered further along the street.

The silver vanished, leaving my skin cold and my eyes still sore from its tantrum.

The message was clear.

The power had no desire to play, and it still refused to obey.

Sighing, I let my hand drop and trudged back to camp, trying not to focus on how the only weapon we had was all but useless in my hands.

We didn't stop near any other towns or cities on our way back to Alluvite. The soldiers who'd entered with Jade and I spoke little of what we'd found in the city, but the rest seemed to sense the unease twisting around us. Everyone's fatigue diminished under the weight of what we'd encountered, even the horses seemed to travel with renewed speed back to Naruzia's capital.

Every night, I practised with my power. Every night, it either surged out in a violent tantrum, or it refused to show at all.

By the time we reached Alluvite's outskirts, I was sweat- and dust-soaked, my limbs heavy with exhaustion and my mind filled with fury over the goddesses' apathy, and wrath at Jaxon's betrayal. I tugged on my horse's reins, guiding it to a stop as the open road narrowed into the shadowed alleys of the outer streets of the city. There were several groans of relief behind as soldiers dismounted, aching muscles relieved of the aggravation of hard riding.

My boots thudded onto stone, relief at having ground under my feet rather than a horse flooding me. I stretched my arms overhead, a breeze turning my sweat-soaked garments cold. We had passed some sentries some way back, one sent ahead to warn the palace of our imminent arrival. Other than that, there had been no sign of life.

Jade appeared at my side. Unlike me, she was a talented horsewoman, riding with an ease I envied. She stared at the city, the white monument of the palace looming high in the centre. The wisps of clouds in the sky did little to stop sunlight from gleaming off the structure. The brightness of it had long turned the streets below into a darkened maze, the contrast deepening the shadows that clung to every twist and turn.

'I was going to send those well enough to go straight to the outer barracks or their homes,' Jade said, pushing up her long sleeves to her elbows, 'but I don't think that's a good idea.'

I stared into the darkness ahead. The outskirts belonged to the commoners – those with little money but plenty of ruthlessness. Slums that the smarter nobility knew to fear for the quick fingers and silver tongues that owned the area. Jaxon had been the greatest of them – a king amongst criminals, lording over them all with his easy smiles and quick cruelty. How quickly their king had abandoned them to their fate.

But perhaps the people had abandoned him first. There was no sign of movement. No sounds or curious eyes watching us from dark corners. Only silence and stillness. I nodded grimly. 'We should head for the palace. There'll be someone in command there.'

If Alluvite hasn't fallen like the rest of Naruzia, I thought but didn't voice. The words formed a sticky web of dread inside me, collecting my thoughts and twisting them into dark what-ifs. My skin grew icy. This was Callum's city. Callum's people. The place he'd returned to. If it had fallen, that might mean—

I shook those thoughts away before they could tear into me. I'd spoken to him that morning in brief, hurried words as we both headed out for the day. He wasn't in Alluvite anymore. He was safe.

'Let's go,' I said before I could fall any further into the trap of my thoughts. We walked quickly, the injured recovered enough that they could manage on their own. Every turn we made, I'd find myself hoping to find a familiar sight – a child pickpocket darting forward in an attempt to claim our belongings, the scent of meat roasting at a nearby marketplace. Gods, even the sounds of a drunken brawl would've been appreciated.

But there were only our footsteps echoing around us, even as we crossed from the slums into the merchant-occupied streets, and then into the widened roads and vast gardens belonging to the nobility.

'You don't think…' Jade trailed off, glancing over her shoulder at the others before twisting back and lowering her voice. 'Could we have already lost?'

I touched my knives, checking they were all ready to be withdrawn at a moment's notice. 'I don't think so. The air smells too … musty. Not like the other towns.' In those, the air had smelt of rot and blood.

Jade curled her fingers around her sword, her expression unconvinced. 'Maybe we should send the men back. You and I can—'

Steps echoed down the street, cutting her off. I spun, almost flinging my knives at the chest of the newcomer before I recognised her. Tension seeped out of me as a woman built of muscle and self-assurance lifted a hand in greeting. 'Lady Chiara.' Commander Lena, the woman responsible for training and managing the city guard, bowed low before me. 'I received word that a silver-eyed woman approached the palace.'

I eyed the top of her shorn head. 'This is a rather different greeting to when we first met.'

She straightened, her expression unapologetic. 'I believed you a threat to His Majesty then.'

I smiled, recalling how she'd eyed me suspiciously when Deana had dragged me to the palace a month after I'd sworn to kill Callum. What a fool I had been. 'Is Deana in the palace?'

Lena nodded. 'She will be able to explain everything to you.'

A strange mix of eagerness and reluctance filled me. Part of me couldn't wait to see Deana. The rest dreaded having to tell her about what Jaxon had done. Still, a meeting was inevitable. I needed to sort out my men first. 'We have some wounded amongst us. Is there an infirmary set up anywhere?'

Lena nodded, glancing at Jade. 'You remember the way?'

'Assuming it hasn't moved in the past month, yes.'

'Not moved,' Lena said grimly. 'Only expanded.'

Jade motioned at the soldiers to follow her towards the palace, pausing briefly at my side to say, 'I'll go with them. Make sure everyone settles in all right.' She nodded to the commander. 'Good to see you're still alive, Lena.'

'Likewise,' the commander said, a hint of a smile appearing on

The Divine

her stern features. Jade took the arm of one of the injured before heading for the palace.

'The city seems empty,' I said as Lena tilted her head in indication that we should also begin walking. 'Has Alluvite been attacked?'

She sighed. 'Not as badly as the rest of Naruzia, but there's been some small attacks. Mostly in the unprotected parts. We've shifted all we could into the palace and set up a makeshift infirmary there. The rest are at or near the barracks on the outskirts. Easier to defend that way.'

I nodded. 'How many dead?'

'From the city? Only two hundred. We burned the bodies straight away.' Broken glass crunched underfoot as we turned a corner. The stench of blood only seemed to increase. 'From Naruzia? Thousands that we know of. Most of the towns were wiped out before we could be of help. Alarni—'

'I saw,' I said quietly.

'There've been a few who have managed to make it to Alluvite. We managed to evacuate Garcella in time, and the closest towns were able to make it here. But we're spread too thin, and our enemy replenishes itself in a way we can't. We're managing here so far, but if our frontlines break and the full force of the enemy enters Naruzia…'

She didn't need to finish. I'd seen Archin. The absence of life. That was what awaited Naruzia should we fail.

'Would you like to wash up?' Lena asked, giving me a quick once over. I was aware of the mess I looked – my hair a mess of knots that'd take a great deal of pain to untangle, my face dirt-covered, shadows curving under my eyes. 'Your rooms were ordered to be kept free. I can—'

I shook my head. 'Take me to Deana.'

The palace grounds were swarming with far more people than I'd ever seen there. The gardens, once maintained with strict standards, crawled past the confines of the soil, crushed beneath quick feet with little care for the presence of greenery. Any spare space was filled with a makeshift tent, families huddled beneath the cloth. Children stared out at me with haunted eyes and grim expressions, clutching their parents' hands. Others were by themselves – small groups of grubby-faced kids who startled whenever someone came too close.

'Some feel uncomfortable in the palace,' Lena murmured, stepping aside to let a woman carrying a tower of blankets through. 'They're unconvinced His Majesty isn't responsible for our kingdom's current state.'

I couldn't blame them. The king most had known for their whole lives had been a tyrant whose cruelty was felt in the far reaches of the kingdom. Callum might've worked hard to reverse the scars Kane left behind, but he'd been king for less than a year, most of which he'd been occupied with the gods. They hadn't yet had the chance to get to know him outside of his father's legacy.

I sidestepped a pack of kids who clung to bread with desperate hands. 'What are food stores like?'

'Struggling. We've taken what we can from buildings, but we're getting nothing from the farms and towns who used to supply to Alluvite. There's too many mouths to feed. We're rationing as much as we can, but we have a month, maybe two, before food runs out.'

One month. The timeline before this all needed to be over and done with.

We walked up the pale steps that led to the palace's entrance. Guards stood by, eyes scanning over the crowds for trouble. They offered a brief nod to Lena before turning back to their duty. 'Numbers of those who can fight?'

'We've got around a thousand in the immediate area. Another

four at the barracks. No clue how many are left scattered across the realm.'

Dismal numbers. The sort that had no chance of success.

Even the stairways were packed, bodies moving up and down at rapid rates. They stepped to the side, though, as Lena led me up a familiar path, a few exchanging quiet words with her. We passed rooms with open doors, bedding placed as closely as it could be. If illness were to break out, it'd spread with a dangerous eagerness. There was another set of doors, and the hallway emptied out, save for two guards quietly bickering by a set of closed doors.

'It's the only area we've kept sealed off,' Lena explained. 'We needed somewhere where we could discuss more sensitive information without worrying about prying ears.'

'Deana's idea?' I guessed.

'Surprisingly, no. Prince Brayden's, before he headed to the western towns to provide support to those trying to flee.'

I raised my brows, surprised. It seemed the arrogant Archinian prince had matured somewhat since I'd last seen him.

We turned another corner. I recognised the hall, its stark white turned dark by shadows. It was the very same place where I'd briefly encountered Lena for the first time. The same place where I'd fought with Callum, hated him, and later realised it wasn't hate I felt at all. My gaze was tugged further down to two more sets of doors. One that led into chambers I'd been given. The other led to Callum's.

It would've been easy to lose myself to a fantasy. To walk past the guards and open those doors, imagining I'd find Callum there. But I knew I wouldn't. He was out fighting a war, and I needed to join him as soon as I could.

'Lady Chiara!' a familiar carrot-haired guard called, breaking away from his argument with his companion and straightening with a grin that was a fraction dimmer than it'd been last time I'd seen him. 'Thank the gods you're okay.'

'The gods have nothing to do with it,' I said as I stopped in front of Corin. He'd lost some of his lanky awkwardness, the sword at his side sitting more comfortably.

An elbow dug into his side as Kailey swept into a bow. 'You're meant to bow, Corin.'

'You're not,' I said as I turned to Kailey. 'Though I'd love to know why you think you should.'

'Lord Jaxon said to,' Corin explained. 'He said you were very particular about how you're treated, and we should make sure to get it right if we don't want to get on your bad side.' He shuddered. 'I *really* don't want to be on your bad side.'

My hands curled into fists, smile tightening. 'I'd advise you to disregard anything that bastard's told you.'

Kailey frowned. Her uniform – a black tunic and fitted trousers – suited her. It also made her seem far more mature than she should be at her young age. 'That's what I thought, but His Majesty agreed that we were to bow to you.'

'I'd disregard everything *that* bastard's told you, too,' I said, with far more affection than how I'd spoken of Jaxon.

'I don't think we can do that.' Corin glanced at Kailey, leant in and lowered his voice to ask her, 'Can we?'

'Of course not,' she snapped, shoving his shoulder. 'Get back into position.'

'But His Majesty said we should obey any command Her Ladyship gives us, so shouldn't we obey this one?'

Kailey turned round eyes to Lena. 'Please, commander. I beg of you. Find someone else to put him under.'

Lena patted her on the shoulder, warmth crinkling the corner of her eyes. It was perhaps the first genuinely fond smile I'd seen her give. 'It'll do you some good. Consider it an introduction to leadership.'

'I'm not that bad!' Corin protested as he straightened, tugging where his tunic had moved into an askew position.

The Divine

'You're worse than bad. You're insufferable.'

The door behind them cracked open, warm light spilling through the shadows. The scent of woodsy incense drifted out, too, covering the stench of dried sweat I could smell on my skin. Deana stood, pinching her brow as she glared at Corin and Kailey. 'How about we say you're both insufferable and call it a day?' She looked past the two, smiling at Lena, before her focus shifted to me.

There was a moment's falter – a blink, then a brilliant beam that chased away the fatigue on her face. I resigned myself to my fate as she lunged, wrapping her arms around me.

'You're here!' she cried.

'Unfortunately for my ribs.' I returned her embrace. 'You're all right?'

'Other than being worked to the bone? Just fine.' She pulled back, grasping my hand in hers and yanking me towards the open door to Callum's study. I followed obediently behind as Corin and Kailey fell back into their quiet bickering, Lena turning to leave.

The room was almost exactly as I remembered it. Callum's desk, window behind allowing light to flow in. A long chaise complete with a table in front of it, empty of the food it usually held. A stack of papers primed to fall. But there was no king to occupy it, turning the vast space into something hollow.

I yearned to reach for the bond, but I had no idea what Callum was doing now. Interrupting him in battle could be disastrous.

I walked towards the desk, skimming my fingers over its surface. Deana had done a good job keeping it orderly, but it was missing the perfect neatness Callum often maintained. My wandering fingers paused on a small pile of papers. Unlike the documents Deana must've been working on, these ones were crumpled, the fold down each of them so worn they must've been folded and unfolded countless times. Picking up the top one, I skimmed my eyes over the familiar messy scrawl. *Archin raiders dead. Unit headed south.*

'He took the rest with him,' Deana said quietly as she perched on the edge of the desk, careful not to disturb the pile of missives.

'I should've told him to throw them out.' Despite my words, I smiled, warmth gathering in my chest. I'd discovered the missives I'd sent to King Kane as a captain in the army nearly two months ago. Callum claimed he'd pilfered whichever ones he could, wanting to hoard my words. That had been back when he knew little more of me than the glimpses he stole in passing, and I knew him only as the prince who seemed to take after his father in all the worst ways.

'If that man could hoard every sound you made, I think he would.' Deana lifted the next missive. She lifted her gaze from the paper, raising her brows. 'How … perfunctory.'

I shrugged, slipping the missive I held into my pocket. Callum had some of these with him. Maybe having one of my own would act like a tether, encouraging fate to send us back to each other. 'If I'd known every missive would be kept like this, I might've been more flowery in my language.'

'No, you wouldn't have.' She placed the missive back down, folding her arms. 'Tell me what I've missed.'

I recounted my journey – what transpired in the godly realm, being deposited back in the mortal one, encountering Jaxon and all that had followed. Deana didn't speak as I spoke. She simply listened, nodding every so often. When it came time to speak of Jaxon's betrayal, however, I hesitated.

Deana picked up on my falter. Her brows drew together. 'What is it?'

'It's…' Again, I hesitated. I'd been responsible for plenty of pain before. I'd killed and tortured. Harmed those who didn't deserve it.

But I'd never had to knowingly break someone's heart.

Despite my every intention otherwise, I must have let some of my trepidation slip down the bond. In an instant, Callum was there, his concern icy pinpricks. *What is it?*

Shifting my gaze away from Deana's increasingly worried one, I rested my hand on my knife's hilt. *I'm in Alluvite.*

It took him only a moment to understand. *Ah. With Deana?*

Yes. Deana leant back, exhaling as she waited for me to speak. Her impatience was marked in the tapping of her finger, yet she didn't say anything, knowing me well enough to recognise I needed some time. *What do I say to make it hurt less?*

Callum's sigh was so real I almost felt it grazing my skin. *I don't think there's anything you can say to make it easier to bear. This is going to hurt her.*

I shifted the knife, loosening it in its scabbard. *I hate this. Why would he do this, Callum? Why would he hurt her so badly?* I'd been cycling through the same thoughts for days, now. There was Garrett, of course. The promise of the Illusion.

Yet I still couldn't piece it all together. Not that he had betrayed us. But that he'd done it so quickly. So emotionlessly.

I don't know. But we'll find him once this is over. We'll make him tell us why he turned on us.

It doesn't help Deana now, I said, turning my gaze back to her. She was watching me carefully, her brows pinched further.

It doesn't, Callum agreed. *But you're with her. You'll make sure she comes out of this okay.*

It was that – his complete faith in me – that had me inhaling and squaring my shoulders. Before I could speak, though, Deana did, her voice cracking in the middle. 'It's Jaxon, isn't it?'

I flinched. 'How did you know?'

She motioned around the room. 'He's not here, and I know him. He pretends otherwise, but he's as much your protector as I am Callum's. He wouldn't abandon you without a reason.'

Her words cut deep. She thought Jaxon had been injured or

killed. Perhaps that would have been kinder than the truth. I closed my eyes. Inhaled again. Steadied myself and opened my eyes once more.

'Is he injured?' she asked, her hands opening and closing on empty air. 'Dead?'

'No. *Gods*, no.'

'Then *what?*' Her voice broke on the second word.

The daylight was deceptively gentle where it crawled through the window, the breeze light enough that it didn't carry the stench of death in from outside. Despite the war that brewed, the room was strangely peaceful.

All it took was a handful of words to shatter that peace.

'Jaxon betrayed us.'

Deana blinked. She opened her mouth, then shut it. Shook her head. 'No.'

My throat tightened. I tried to soften my voice as Callum might have done as I reached between us, grasping her hand in mine. 'Yes.'

She yanked away, lurching to her feet. '*No*, Chiara. No, he wouldn't. He wouldn't.' She blinked again, more rapidly this time. I rose with her. 'He wouldn't, would he?'

I wanted to agree with her. But I'd seen it. All the soldiers who had died because of his choice. How he'd so easily walked to his mother's side. 'He chose Tarina over us.'

'He would never do that. He cares for this kingdom, even if he'd never admit it. Cares for us. For me.'

I shifted. 'He sold us out to her. Left us to die to her Illusions.'

'Why?' she demanded.

'Because he was scared. He was weak, and too afraid to stand against her.'

Deana shook her head again, blonde hair flying in angry flicks. 'He hates his mother! She killed Garrett.'

'I know.'

'You don't! He told me how much he loathed her. He said he'd see her dead if he could.' She trembled. There was nothing of the formidable commander in Deana right now. She was just a woman whose heart had been shattered as she stared at me, waiting for me to give her an answer I couldn't give. 'He loved Garrett more than anything in this world. More than me, I think. He would *never*—'

'She promised to give him an Illusioned life with Garrett.'

It was perhaps the only reason that could have broken through Deana's adamant denial.

It cracked something deep inside me to see Deana crumble. It was her eyes, first – the way the blue blurred with tears. Then her lips, pressing together as she fought against what must have been a heart-wrenching sob. She staggered forward a step. I caught her, holding her upright. Her fingers squeezed my forearms as she said in a whisper, 'Oh.'

I didn't know how to comfort her. I could only hold her up as her knees weakened. 'I don't fully understand it myself.'

'I don't – but—' She broke off, seeming unable to find the words she needed. She pulled herself upright. 'An Illusion with Garrett? You're sure?'

I wished I didn't have to nod.

'I knew, you know,' Deana said, her voice quiet enough that I barely heard her. 'That if Garrett were alive, he'd choose him over me. They're soul-bonded.' She looked back to me. 'And I've seen how intensely soul-bonded love.' She smiled, her expression tinged with bitterness. 'There were nights when I hated myself, just a little, for being relieved Garrett wasn't here. Selfish, isn't it?'

'Love always is,' I said quietly.

'I'm mortal. I'll likely never have a soul-bonded. But Jaxon – I thought Jaxon was my equivalent.' Her focus dropped to where her hands wrapped together, the skin white from how tightly she grasped them. 'And you're saying he chose a memory over me? What else did she offer him?'

I opened my mouth. Closed it. Shook my head helplessly. 'That was all he said. That she offered him an Illusion of Garrett.'

Some of the pain in her expression faltered. 'An Illusion? That's it?'

'Did there need to be anything else, if it was Garrett?'

She frowned. 'It doesn't make any sense.'

I shrugged, helpless against the mixture of grief and anger in her eyes. 'Betrayal often doesn't.'

'That's not what I mean. I mean...' She trailed off, her brows knitting further together, her expression growing stony. 'Tell me everything.'

So I did. I told her of the fight Jaxon and I had had. How he seemed perfectly calm the next day. His lies, and the deaths it had led to.

At that, some of Deana's stony silence faltered. 'You're saying he knowingly led others to their death?'

I nodded. 'It seems that way. Tarina knew exactly when we were coming.'

Deana shook her head. The grief and heartbreak rapidly disappearing, replaced by confusion. 'That also doesn't make any sense.'

'I know it's hard to believe, but—'

'*No*, Chiara. Jaxon is ... well, he's a coward, and he always has been, but he's not a bad person.' She straightened her shoulders, her stoniness turning to resolve. 'He wouldn't sacrifice that many people without a reason.'

I tensed at the spark in her eye. Hope could be a wonderful thing. It could also be the final blade to destroy a person. 'His reason was fear. You've seen him whenever his mother is brought up.'

Deana nodded, the spark brightening. 'I have. He's scared of her, yes, but more than that – he loathes her. Hates her as much as you hate Vitus.'

Even the sound of the god's name was enough to send claws of fury digging into me. 'This isn't the same.'

'Isn't it?' she asked, her voice quietening. She stepped forward, taking my hand in hers. Hers shook, and I realised that hope in her eyes was far more fragile than I'd thought. Yet she chose to trust in it. To trust in him. 'Vitus almost had Callum killed in front of you. If he'd succeeded and then offered you Callum back, would you have taken that offer?'

I hesitated. The thought of Callum dead, of the soul-bond gone … gods, I'd give almost anything to have him back. At last, I said, 'I don't know.'

It was honest, brutal truth.

Deana accepted it as such. 'What if you knew what he offered was nothing but a lie? A fake?'

'No.' I all but spat out the word. Perhaps I would sell my very soul to have Callum back, but if it wasn't the real him, I'd be doing nothing but betraying everything he was. I could never do that.

'Exactly.' Deana raised her chin, letting go of my hand. 'Jaxon would never abandon us – abandon me – for a fake.'

'Deana…' I trailed off, not wanting to finish my thought. To warn her that this trust of hers was ultimately the same as shoving a knife between her own ribs.

She heard the unsaid words all the same.

'No,' she said, quiet but strong. 'Jaxon's a two-faced bastard at the best of times. But he loves me. I have to believe that. Have to believe that I'm worth more to him than a memory. That—' She choked up, looking away as her eyes grew glassy. 'That he didn't betray me. He wouldn't.'

I grappled for the right words. Part of me wanted to smash that hope, here and now, before it sprouted into a vine she found herself hung by. The rest of me, though, wanted her to be right. But all those people killed ... Tarina showing up and taking Jaxon willingly—

Deana smiled as though she were the one reassuring me. 'You have every reason to doubt him. But I believe there's a reason for what he did. So, please – even if you don't trust him, trust me.'

I shifted, my hands opening and closing on empty air. I could take down countless monsters, but figuring out the right thing to do was beyond my capabilities. 'I know you want him to not have betrayed us. Gods, I hope you're right. But if he did—'

'Then I'll execute him myself.' Her smile sweetened. 'After he suffers, of course.'

I studied her expression for several long moments before blowing out a brief sigh and nodding. 'This might turn out horribly for all of us, but I do trust you. If we get our hands on him, I'll follow your lead.'

'Thank you. And don't worry – he's still going to suffer plenty for lying to us.' Her smile dropped. 'Do you think ... he's okay?'

Given I still wasn't as convinced as her as to his motives, I wasn't particularly worried about Jaxon's wellbeing. Deana, though, was another matter, so I forced a smile and nodded. 'Of course. You know Jaxon – he manages to weasel himself out of any scrape he gets into.'

She smiled again, but it was far more fragile than before. 'I know Jaxon,' she echoed, her hands balling at her sides. She inhaled raggedly. 'I need a distraction, or I'll start thinking about all the trouble he's getting into, and then I'll have to start thinking of all the ways he's going to be punished for making me worry.' She turned to the door. 'I'll show you the new layout of the palace.'

I rose to my feet, muscles aching anew after being given torturously brief respite, and followed her out into the corridor.

We turned left, heading to where I knew the corridor ended in a servant's entrance. Deana waved Corin and Kailey off when they tried to trail us. 'Stay here. Chiara and I will do a fine enough job of protecting ourselves.'

The two guards hesitated before nodding, falling back into position.

Deana sighed. 'I'm beginning to understand why Callum was always so desperate to avoid being trailed by his guards. It's stifling.' She grimaced, fishing a key out of her trouser pocket and inserting it into the lock of an inconspicuous door. 'I suspect that's why he left the command that I was to have guards at all times – to make me understand how he felt.'

'Or he was worried about leaving you unprotected when you're in command of a palace with so many strangers in its halls.' Lantern light flickered up the walls of the stairwell, casting shadows of varying shapes along it. The wooden stair rail was cool under my fingers as I made my way down to where two more guards waited at the bottom. 'Knowing him, it was probably both.'

'Definitely,' Deana agreed, inserting a different key into the door at the bottom. Muffled voices came from the other side.

I tensed in preparation for the busyness as the door swung open, revealing what had once been a meeting chamber filled with men and women rushing about, hair tied back and arms filled with medical supplies. None spared more than a cursory nod at us.

'The storage room for the infirmary,' Deana explained, gesturing to where stacks of fresh linen and bandages occupied a table laid out to the left. On the opposite side, a man with greying hair bent over vials of various coloured liquids, inspecting each with a careful eye before plucking one to hand to the awaiting woman. Unlike Callum, all the healers here would have to rely on far more mundane methods than a Gift.

Thoughts of healing turned my mind back to the only direction it ever seemed to want to go – Callum. 'Is Callum … all right? Unharmed?'

'Haven't you been talking to him using your bond?'

I frowned. 'I have, but…' I shrugged. Most of our conversations had been about the war and Jaxon. Every time I asked Callum, he merely said he was doing as well as he could in the circumstance. 'He doesn't want to worry me.'

We waited for an influx of medical staff to clear the room. Four guards joined in the chaos, offering their arms to carry supplies. 'He's alive.'

'That's not what I asked.'

She exhaled, running her fingers through her hair. The blonde strands settled over the shoulders of her black tunic, a far cry from the gowns she preferred to wear. 'Is he physically unharmed? Other than a few bruises and cuts, yes.' Her hand dropped as she looked over at me, her expression gentle. 'But he had to watch you disappear again, Chiara. He was helpless to stop it, and … like I said, he was a mess the two weeks where he had no idea whether you were alive or not.'

My stomach clenched. 'I didn't want to leave.'

'He knew, but after everything with Vitus – gods, he barely slept. Barely ate during that month. If not for his desperation to find you, I think he would've been content to waste away into nothing. He almost returned to that state when you disappeared again. And then, on top of it all, he watched his people die.' We shifted back as two women rushed by, muttering hurried apologies as they snatched up a fresh blanket folded on the ground next to Deana. 'So, is he all right? I'd say about as much as you are.'

I rubbed my wrists where the wards were turning silver. 'I only had you two to worry about. Nothing else.'

'Did you?' Deana's gaze was a physical force pushing at the

side of my head. 'You lost people, too. Over two hundred of your men.'

'That's different. I was only stepping in to lead them. I'm not like Callum. Not made for commanding anything but the battlefield.'

'Then why do you carry that?' Deana motioned towards the sword at my side – the one I'd kept from the man I had killed when I had lost control on the battlefield.

I wrapped my fingers around the hilt. 'Because it was my fault he died.'

'People die on the battlefield all the time, and not always from an enemy's blade. You're experienced enough in battle to know that his death was what paid for the lives of everyone else.'

Logically, I did know that. And I would pay that price willingly, if it came again. It didn't mean I could ignore what I'd done, though.

Deana continued. 'And the little toy you told me you gave Evania? You can't tell me you knew you were going to run into a goddess.'

Renewed sorrow rose as I remembered that doll. The blood soaking it, the body of the child it belonged to. 'Because no child should have their life taken from them like that. I wanted a reminder of what would happen if we fail.'

Deana smiled. 'That's part of what being a leader is. Not just taking commands but seeing the people as your own. And I think you do that, Chiara, though you try to pretend otherwise.'

My frown deepened. I'd spent so long in quiet apathy to Naruzia, ready to sacrifice everything to keep my sister safe. Then, I'd lost her, and I'd found myself drowning in hatred for this kingdom. But now ... now, I knew some of the people here. Knew there was good that stretched past those I loved. Knew there were children, weaker than I'd been and with no one to defend them.

It didn't make me worthy of the power in me, though. Didn't make me worthy of becoming their leader, like Callum was.

'They wouldn't accept me,' I said. 'I've done too many things. People know me from my time as Captain – from what I did. The butcher of Naruzia.'

Deana tilted her head, her smile growing secretive. 'Come with me.'

Leading the way, Deana refused to answer any of my questions as we wove through the healers and through a set of double doors that didn't emit so much as a squeak. Cool air hit my face as we stepped through, accompanied by the sharp sting of medical solutions. Wooden beds lined each wall, a small space between each for healers to go to the bedside of patients. Most of the beds were filled, their occupants unconscious.

'We've had to keep these beds for the most serious injuries,' Deana explained as we passed by the bed of a man with a stump where an arm once was. 'When Callum was here, the beds were cleared relatively quickly, but now...' She trailed off, smiling sadly. 'The healers do what they can.'

I spotted one bed, the sheet pulled high, a human form beneath. A man was hunched over beside the bed, clutching desperately to a pale hand draping out from under the sheet. Warmth filtered through the room – not from the air, but from the death that threatened many who were here.

'There's a separate wing for illness.' Deana stopped at the foot of a bed at the end of a row. A girl was curled up on her side, curls plastered to her head with sweat. Her head was wrapped in linen bandages. Dark red coloured the top of them. 'The system's working so far, but it won't forever.'

The little girl shivered, caught in the clutches of pain. The blood-soaked doll flashed in my mind. 'What happened to her?'

'Her older brother came back from Archin.' Deana met my eyes, the shadows under her eyes growing more pronounced.

'Allie's too young to have spotted the changes in him. She opened the door to him and'—she lowered her voice, leading me away from the girl's bedside—'her mother managed to make it here before succumbing to her injuries. She saved Allie, but Allie's all that survived from her family.'

My heart squeezed for the child. If she awoke, she'd face guilt that should never have been hers to bear. The sort of guilt that'd plague her for the rest of her life. 'Are many in here from Ankuran attacks?'

'Some. Others from the mortals fighting for Vitus, or the other creatures. Quite a few are from the army, but most are those who were simply trying to live.'

My hands clenched. The power rumbled awake. Deana looked down, brows rising as the golden wards began to pulse. I inhaled, waiting until some of my rage abated before scanning the room once more.

There were too many injuries. Too many beds with covered bodies. All because of Vitus's vengeance, the callousness of his followers and the indifference of the other gods. There was nothing natural about this. Nothing right.

Seeming to sense I was on the verge of losing my grip on my rage, Deana tugged me across the room. 'I want you to meet someone.'

She stopped before a man a handful of years older than her with a head of flaxen curls and a freckle under his right eye. He didn't look up from where he was carefully wrapping a wound, and Deana didn't order him to stop. He meticulously curled the bandage around a limp arm, tucking the end in with practised precision before straightening. A sword hung at his side, seeming out of place at a healer's hip.

'Noah,' Deana finally said, drawing the man's attention.

Noah's smile was bright despite the sweat dotting his brow and shadows under his eyes. A scar slashed above his grey collar.

'Commander Deana. I didn't think you'd be doing rounds today.'

'Something unexpected came up.' She gripped my shoulder, yanking me in front of her. I glared back at her and she grinned. 'I have someone I want you to meet. This is—'

'Captain Chiara,' Noah interrupted, his smile widening. 'I'd bow, but...' He gestured around at the tight space we were crammed in.

'I met Noah just before we left for Archin,' Deana explained, ignoring my attempts to pull away from her. 'He's relatively new to being a healer – he was a—'

'Scout,' I finished, recognising the man. I kept my hands away from my knives, even as my fingers itched to grab them. 'You were in one of my first units.'

'At the battle that earnt you your title.'

My lips pressed into a thin line. There was only one title a soldier like him would be referring to. Butcher of Naruzia.

My expression must have revealed more than I meant to, because Noah's smile vanished. 'That title was a disgrace after what you did for us. We'd all be dead if not for you.'

I said nothing. His words weren't wrong, but they settled uncomfortably upon me.

Those years had been a nightmare for me. One I'd allowed to twist me until I didn't have to think about anyone or anything but my sister. The gratitude, so similar to Amara's, both settled uncomfortably and warmed me. I didn't know how I was meant to respond.

'We would've died that day if anyone else had led us,' Noah said. 'All of us in your unit would've. We were young and new to war, or old enough that we should've been long retired, and that ambush...' He trailed off, words failing him as surely as they failed me.

The ambush had been brutal, Archinians surrounding us on all sides. That day was one of the first times I truly recognised what my Gift could do. The havoc and death it could wreak on the world.

I lost half of my soldiers that day.

The Archinians lost all of theirs.

'I was one of the first to be struck down.' Noah gestured at his scarred throat, his smile gone. Even without it, there were markings of kindness in his features that I'd never held in my own. 'I knew I was going to die that day.'

He paused, his eyes far away as he recalled that feeling. I knew it too well – the helplessness and the desperation. The wondering whether it would be better – easier – to give it all up in a moment. 'But then you appeared. The girl leader we'd scoffed at. And gods, were you a sight to behold.'

It wasn't the shadowy claws of fear that sunk into Noah's expression, but a shining sort of awe. The sort of awe that I had never believed would be given to me, deserved by me, for the things I had done. It made part of me cower away, terrified that I couldn't live up to it. It made the rest of me stand up straighter.

Uncomfortable or not, I didn't hate it.

'I don't know that I would've even realised I was saving you,' I said honestly.

Noah shrugged. 'I don't know about that. It would've been easier for you to leave me to die and focus on the bigger threats. Even if you didn't mean to save me, I'm still alive because of you.' He crossed his arm across his chest, bowing his head. 'If you ever need anything I can provide, come find me. I owe you my life.'

An arm looped through mine before I could summon a response. 'I'm back!' Deana announced. 'And I'll be stealing Chiara now.'

I clearly had no say in the matter as she dragged me from the room. As soon as we'd found our way back through the infirmary storeroom and into the quiet servants' passageways, I turned to her and folded my arms. 'Did that have to happen in the middle of the infirmary?'

She looked back at me, smiling with all the perfect sincerity of a master spy. 'It just happened to be where Noah works.'

'You could've suggested we go somewhere quiet for what should've been a *private* conversation.' I shook my head before beginning to climb the stairs, taking them two at the time. 'Don't try to tell me you didn't plan for all that attention.'

Deana's footsteps echoed behind mine. 'Anyone who actually knows you respects you and—'

'I highly doubt that's the case. Vitus certainly doesn't.'

'Fine. Everyone who hasn't managed to piss you off respects you, but your reputation with those who haven't met you is … it's not amazing. Not as bad as Callum's was before he became king, but that's mostly because Kane tried to keep information about you limited.' We entered the corridors that led to Callum's study. Deana quickened to walk beside me. 'A little attention when you're being praised as being a saviour will do wonders for your reputation.'

'I don't need a good reputation.'

Deana swung around me, planting herself in my way and folding her arms. 'Yes, you do. Because when we win this war, the kingdom's going to be in ruins. They'll need a queen they can trust.'

I forced myself to not look away. 'I'm not a good person, Deana. I can't be what these people need.'

'Incorrect. You're not a *nice* person. You're cruel, and often rather mean. Oh, and you have an unusual love for violence and blood. You're impulsive and need a good deal of sense knocked into you most of the time. Not to mention—'

'I get the picture,' I interrupted, flushing. 'As I said – I'm not a good choice for queen.'

Deana sighed, a hint of exasperation winding through the

The Divine

sound. 'Wrong again. You're not just a good choice. You're the only choice.'

'Callum can rule alone. I'll...' I trailed off, searching for something to finish that sentence. If we managed to win this impossible war, Callum would be king. And I ... I would have to find a place in a world of peace.

'I didn't mean you're the only choice because Callum wouldn't have anyone else.' Deana reached for me, gripping my arm as though she intended to shake her words into me. 'I mean you're the only choice *because* you have a cruel side. Because you know how to be tough when the time calls for it, and you don't put up with bullshit. Because, at the end of the day, you are good in your own way to those you decide to protect. This realm is already in ruins. Who knows what state it'll be in by the time this is all over. We don't need nice. We need *you*.'

The power in me rose its head, sparking under my skin. For a moment, I almost grasped hold of it. As though it heard Deana's words, and it felt itself summoned by them. Or it might just have felt the small sense of desire in me. The ambition that was beginning to take root amongst the doubt. That maybe I could do something other than killing.

Deana opened her mouth, about to say something that was certain to only cause further inner conflict. Footsteps pounded down the corridor. Her mouth snapped shut, eyes meeting mine as we frowned in quiet confusion.

Corin swung around the corner so fast he almost slammed into one of the white walls. His chest rose and fell in rapid breaths as he caught sight of us. 'Lady Deana! Lady Chiara! There's a—' He paused, holding up a hand as he gulped down air. I waited with quickly fraying patience. 'A guest. Or not a guest, I suppose. A ... returnee? A resident? Maybe—'

Kailey appeared at Corin's side, her hand slapping the backside of his head. Corin grunted, rubbing where she'd hit and shooting her an affronted look. She ignored it, straightening as she turned her full attention to me and Deana. 'He's trying to tell you someone has asked to see you in His Majesty's study.'

Deana's frown severed, turned all the more frightening by the shadows around us. 'You let someone into the king's study?'

Kailey cringed. 'Ah … not exactly. He just … well…'

Corin jumped in as Kailey fumbled with what to say. 'He climbed through the window, ma'am!'

Deana and I exchanged a look, equal parts confusion and suspicion in Deana's eyes. I was leaning fully towards the suspicion.

'*Who* climbed through the window, soldier?' Deana snapped when Corin stared at us in expectant silence.

He startled, blushing so deeply his freckles disappeared. 'Right! It's—'

I didn't hear the rest of what he said. Not when a familiar lanky figure appeared around the corner, hands tucked into his pockets, posture casual. Deana stiffened. I reached for my dagger.

Jaxon leant against the wall and grinned. 'Did you miss me?'

Chapter Twenty-Two

I ripped out my dagger, but Deana was faster. Red mist twisted in her hands, forming a sword. She lunged for Jaxon, swinging for his neck. He yelped, stumbling away from her blow. The edge slammed into the white walls. Dust puffed into the air, white stone crumbling to the ground.

'Wait! We should talk—' Jaxon broke off as Deana swung her sword again. These weren't the elegant, subtle moves I'd seen her use previously. These were wild, the worry she'd tried to hide since I'd revealed his betrayal manifested as violence.

'Should we help her, Lady Chiara?' Corin whispered as he edged towards me, his hand falling to his sword. I pulled his hand away before he could draw it.

'Deana gets to draw his blood first. If she allows it, I'll be the next in line.' I gave him a warning glare. 'If you even think about butting in, then—'

'No helping. Got it.' His head bounced in frantic nods. Kailey also dropped her hand away from her sword, though she lurched every time Deana swung.

Neither of the guards would've stood a chance, though. Deana was far more skilled than they, and Jaxon had years of experience they'd never be able to obtain with their mortal lifespans. I tossed my dagger, my anger subsiding into amusement as Jaxon stumbled away from Deana's blows, barely missing her drawing blood.

'Draw your sword,' she snapped, thrusting forward.

Jaxon dove to the side, slamming into the stone ground before clambering to his feet. He glanced at me, gaze beseeching. I smiled and tossed the dagger again.

Deana stalked forward. 'Your sword. Get it out.'

'I don't have my sword!' Jaxon protested, backing away from her and towards me. It seemed I was the lesser threat in this situation. 'I left it in Cal's study.'

Catching my dagger, I jabbed the point into the small of his back when he came close enough. Not hard enough to draw blood. Just a reminder that he'd made the folly of entering this castle when he knew who resided here, and there would be no escape.

'Liar.' Deana's sword shifted, shrinking into a knife. She launched herself at Jaxon. This time, he didn't twist away fast enough to avoid her fist slamming into his cheek. He fell hard, landing on his shoulder. Deana fell with him, shoving her arm into his neck as the knife crumbled into red mist. Her fist slammed down again. 'You're such a *liar*. You've Illusioned it or hidden it somewhere. Everything you say is a godsdamned lie!'

'Deana, I can—'

'Do you know how worried I've been?' Her fist fell again. Something cracked and red spattered. 'You lied to everyone, and disappeared with Tarina, and all I could do was wait for you to come back!'

'De—'

'You're a bastard!' she screamed, punching Jaxon again. He

didn't lift his hands to block it. Didn't twist to get out from under her.

I glanced to Kailey and Corin, who were watching the scene with wide eyes. Despite them both being a couple of years older than me, there was something innocent about their aghast expressions. One would think they'd never seen someone try to kill another they loved before.

Deciding I should be the responsible one and protect their naïveté, I tilted my head in the direction they came. Both hurried to obey my silent order.

'Why did you leave?' Jaxon's eyes were dark as Deana hit him again, the crack echoing. 'This is war. You could've been executed for being a traitor if someone else found you. I'd be left here, and —' She cut off, her blows pausing. Her knuckles were swollen, bloodstained.

I watched her. Saw the pain in her features, far more wretched than any Jaxon was showing.

Jaxon's brow creased. His hand lifted, fingers brushing Deana's cheek. 'De—'

She slapped his hand away. 'Don't touch me.'

Jaxon closed his eyes, a sad sigh escaping him. 'I'm not a traitor.'

Deana laughed, the sound broken. 'You think I don't know that?'

Jaxon's eyes snapped open. 'What? You ... knew?'

'Of course I did.'

'But'—he blinked, blood trickling from his lip—'why did you attack me, then?'

'Idiot,' Deana said, her voice choked as tears darkened her lashes. She fisted his tunic, hands shaking. 'Because you threw yourself into danger without bothering to tell me. Without bothering to tell anyone, and you thought you could just waltz back in like everything was fine and—' She broke off, a choked sob escaping her. 'What if Tarina had caught on? What if she'd killed you? You'd have left me alone, just like Garrett left you. Did you bother considering that?'

Pain clouded Jaxon's eyes. I didn't know whether it was the mention of Garrett, or the sight of Deana in such pain. 'I ... you're right. I didn't think.'

Deana's laugh was bitter, her fists dropping to either side of his head. 'You think that excuses it?'

Jaxon withered under her glare. 'It's been a long time since someone's cared enough about me to worry.'

Sighing, I extended a morsel of generosity by saying, 'Maybe we should hear him out.'

Her fingers curled where they pressed to the stone. 'Fine.'

Jaxon started to smile, relief filling his expression.

'But I'm still furious with him.'

The smile withered.

'Be as angry as you want.' I walked over to the wall, leaning against it as I watched the pair. Suspicion hadn't completely left me, but I trusted Deana. Trusted in my ability to cut him down should his words end in deceit, too.

There was a pause, and then Deana rose to her feet. She didn't look at Jaxon but at me, her eyes filled with unshed tears. Her arm wrapped around her waist.

Jaxon deserved a few more blows for making her cry.

He met my eyes as he struggled to stand. I raised my brows. 'Well? Are you going to tell us what you learnt while you pretended to play traitor?'

'Did you know this whole time, too?' he asked.

'Only when you appeared just now.' I ran my eyes over him – the lavish vest he wore atop a silken shirt, its sleeves hideously loose on his arms. The golden embroidery on the vest was the sort of garishness only gods and corrupt nobility could enjoy. 'Even you're not fool enough to appear before us as a traitor and expect to leave alive.'

A part of me had been suspicious since he'd betrayed us, too. His outburst of anger and how quickly he'd turned – Jaxon could be a coward, and he was terrified of Tarina, but I'd also seen his hatred of her. She'd killed his soul-bonded. It wasn't something he could forgive, even if it meant turning his back on his cowardice.

I brushed my fingers over my dagger as I watched him. 'Speaking of leaving alive, how are you here?' I glanced over him again. There was no sign of any serious injury aside from the fresh bruises Deana had given him. 'I can't imagine your mother let you go so easily.'

'You try mustering an Illusion of a thousand-strong army to the east to drag her away from her constant watch and call it easy,' he said. His eyes were duller than they had been when I'd last seen him, as though the Gift that coloured his eyes had been drained. 'Not to mention it had to fool the goddess of Illusions. I'd bet she's stomping her feet right now realising she went on a fool's errand.'

'I can't imagine she'd bother lifting a finger to kill mortals if she already had you.' I pictured the cruel goddess with her immaculate gown and pristine skin.

'Vitus ordered her through one of his Ankurans to see to it personally. Something about pests interfering with his plans.'

I raised my brows. 'And she left you behind?'

'Of course.' His grin grew. 'After all, I'm the only one of her offspring weak enough to not kill at birth. Why would she worry about leaving me with only a handful of Ankurans? It likely never occurred to her that I might Illusion a version of myself to trick the mindless creatures, just like she never thought I might be behind the mortal army mysteriously appearing. Without Vitus inhabiting the Ankurans, they're no better than moving lumps of clay.' He winced.

'Though I almost regret it – the ride back here was awful. Tarina's somehow got herself three horses, and every one of them is a monster. Do you know how many times the one I took tried to bite me?'

I silently applauded the horse for having good taste. 'You think she'll just leave you alone, now that you've tricked her?' Not to mention stolen a horse from her. Only Jaxon would be brazen enough to steal from the gods.

Jaxon scoffed. 'Of course not. Trickery and Illusions are meant to be her thing. She'll try to kill me if she figures out I was the one who left the Illusions for her to find. Lucky the Illusions will seem to disappear like Akmad's shadow wraiths the moment she tries to interact with them.'

I nodded my approval. 'Planting seeds of suspicion between the gods?'

'Pride's an easy thing to manipulate, particularly when it comes to that between the gods. It won't do much, though. Tarina hates dirtying her hands, and she hates interacting with most of the other gods.'

'You're lucky she was as easy to trick as you thought,' I said. 'If she'd caught on—'

'Then I'd be dead. A shame for everyone, I'm sure.' Deana turned towards him. His gaze softened as he looked at her. 'De—'

She held out her palm to him, stalling his words as she turned to me. 'I can't – I need a minute before I slit his throat. Handle him. And if he lies again, end him.'

Then she was storming off towards the infirmary, her hair bouncing angrily with each step. Jaxon stared after her, his expression torn between bewilderment and longing, before he looked at me. 'I don't understand. Would she prefer me to be a traitor?'

'Idiot,' I sighed, walking over to him. 'Of course not. But you lied to her and willingly put yourself in harm's way. Not to mention you're yet to show us any proof of what you say. Did you think she'd get over that with just a few blows?'

Jaxon stared at me. I almost pitied him – it seemed we shared the same ignorance when it came to any sort of relationship. I patted him on the shoulder. 'We should go to Callum's study and talk. And I stand by what Deana said – if there's any hint you lied, you're dead.'

His attention shifted back in the direction Deana had disappeared. There was a moment's hesitation as he seemed to fight the desire to chase after her before he nodded once. 'All right. Lead the way.'

I took a step forward, then paused. My fingers curled, my fist flying too fast for Jaxon to react. There was a satisfying *crack* as the bones of his nose crunched under my blow. He cried out, red spattering both our boots as he staggered away from me, glaring balefully over cupped hands.

'That,' I said coldly, 'was for all the soldiers who died because of your choice.'

'They all would've been killed by Tarina if I hadn't intervened! When I found her, she was planning to trap the whole campsite in an Illusion while they all slept. Only you and I would've survived that. The only way was to convince her it'd be more fun for you all to witness my betrayal.'

'I know.' I strode down the corridor, trusting Jaxon to follow. 'And that's the only reason why you still breathe.'

Jaxon glared at me as he tilted his head, one hand pinching his nose gingerly. I glared back.

'You didn't need to punch *that* hard.'

You should have punched harder, Callum said as I relayed Jaxon's words to him. He'd checked in on me not long before, and neither of us was willing to let go of the bond yet.

'You should've told me your plan.' My eyes narrowed further as blood dripped, soaking into the rug. I leant forward in Callum's chair. 'I'll do a whole lot worse if you get any blood on Callum's furniture. *Or* if you fail to convince me that you're telling the whole truth once Deana returns.'

Tell him I'll do a whole lot worse, regardless.

I rolled my eyes. *Deana and I don't need you to step in.*

I'm really only stepping in for Jaxon's sake, he said. *You might be holding back now, but who knows when one of you will snap? I'm sure Jaxon would much prefer punishment at my hands.*

'Callum wants to know if you'd prefer to be punished by him or by Deana and I.'

Jaxon winced. 'Is neither an option?'

'No.'

'Then him. Definitely him.' He stretched his legs out on the chaise, his head tipping over the end of it. 'Speaking of which, where is Cal?'

'Talking to me.'

Jaxon shot me an annoyed look. I shot him one back. 'I asked *where* he is, not what he's doing. I can tell by that irritating smile on your lips he's speaking to you.'

I brushed my fingers over the corner of my lips. He was right. I was smiling. 'Does it matter?'

Huffing, Jaxon pinched his nose tighter as blood started to bubble once more. 'One little lie and now you're treating me like an outsider?'

'Your lie wasn't little.' I shifted, drawing one of my legs up onto the chair and reaching for the missive I'd placed in my pocket earlier, fiddling with it. 'Callum's not here.'

'Clearly.' Jaxon rolled onto his side and propped his head up. 'So where is he?'

'He's—' *Where are you?*

In Puria. Near the border of Archin.

'—towards Archin. General Tizan's made an appearance.'

Jaxon's face grew cold, the sun coming through the window doing little to combat the ice in his voice as he asked, 'The man who was almost Deana's betrothed?'

I nodded, letting go of the missive and shifting to my dagger. Withdrawing it, I spun it in a circle on the desk. 'Callum will be dragging him back alive if he can.'

'I'm surprised you didn't ride straight for him the moment you returned.'

I pressed a finger to the flat of the blade, stopping its circles. It was in need of a good polish and sharpening, my reflection nowhere to be found in its surface. 'There's more than one battle that needs to be fought. I'd be of more use here.'

'Liar.'

My head snapped up, irritation prickling. 'What's that supposed to mean?'

The blood flow had slowed enough that Jaxon could lower his hand without endangering Callum's furniture and further injury at my hand. Even so, his voice was thick. 'It means you've never been focused on where you'll be of use. You go after what you want, and you don't hesitate to do it.'

I returned to spinning the blade, the hilt scraping lightly over wood. My lips pressed together.

He's right, Callum piped up. At the irritation that might have sparked, he added, *I know you, Captain. Something as trivial as a war wouldn't be enough to stop you from coming to me. So why haven't you ridden out?*

I frowned down at the blade. *Do you want me to?*

Of course I do, but I also think Alluvite needs you. And don't avoid the question.

Callum was right. Everything in me yearned to be at his side.

To fight with him. 'The realm seems so desperate to keep us apart.' I watched light play over the blade. 'Every time we're together, something terrible happens. But this time, the stakes are higher. There's gods out there – gods who have taken notice of Callum and I.'

'You're scared Callum will die because you decide to seek him out,' Jaxon guessed.

Chiara, Callum said, his voice the brush of the lightest of breezes. *I'm not so fragile as to crumble.*

It sounded so silly when they said it like that, yet I couldn't shake that soul-deep dread. The one that warned that this war was not going to end without casualties – the sort of casualties that would ruin me. 'I'm not *scared*. But—'

'But you're scared.' My head snapped up, eyes narrowing. Jaxon was uncowed by my anger. 'And maybe you're right to be. Soul-bonded might be decided by the ancient power of the realms, but that same power seems determined to make them end badly.' He let his hand drop from his nose, the blood all but stemmed. 'Love like that burns too bright to last forever.'

'Kerta and Evania are fine,' I pointed out. 'Maybe the realms only hate me and Callum.'

'I'm sure they do, given how desperate you are to ignore the power they gave you.'

Speaking of which, have you got a handle on it yet?

I scowled, wrapping a hand around my left wrist to hide the silver-streaked wards. 'We're not talking about that.' *The same goes for you, too. That conversation can wait until after I've finished dealing with this one.*

Jaxon sighed, swinging his legs around the side of the chaise and straightening. His face carried the same weariness as Deana's and my own, as though he too had found sleep hard to steal. It was little wonder given who he'd been around. 'Kerta and Evania are an exception. I lost Garrett, as you know. Vitus lost Alexia –

and look how that's turning out...' He hesitated, opening his mouth then closing it.

I leant forward, propping my elbow on the desk and my chin atop it. 'Whatever you're not saying, say it. I'm not in the mood for more secrets.'

He winced. 'Well, there's also Dearil. His soul-bond ended ... badly.'

'He was betrayed, wasn't he?' Vitus hadn't wasted any opportunity to throw it in Dearil's face when we were in the cells. It was one of the few things that could get a reaction from the impassive god.

'Yes. By—'

The doors swung open. Jaxon jumped to his feet the moment Deana walked into the room, his hands clasped before him like a soldier about to get a scolding. 'Deana, I can—'

She walked straight past him, not even bothering to look at him until she'd come to stand beside me. I looked up at her, brows raising in silent question. All she needed to do was press her lips together, her jaw rigid, to tell me how she was feeling about everything.

'You're speaking to Callum?' she asked.

I frowned. Was I really that obvious? 'Yes.'

'Tell him there was an attack to the west. Not a big one – it only took out three units. Lena just came to me with the report.'

I closed my eyes, hesitating for a moment before relaying the information. There was a beat of silence, yet even Callum couldn't manage to hide the spike of fury and sorrow that shuddered down the bond between us. *Only three units is three too many.*

We'll find a way to stop Vitus, I vowed. *No matter what.*

Another stretch of silence before Callum said, *Of course we will.*

For once, though, his words weren't an unshakeable promise. Every life lost, every moment the gods remained corrupting our realm, he drowned himself in more responsibility. More guilt.

I was terrified of the day when I couldn't pull him out of it.

Callum—

Later, he promised. *We'll talk of this and your power later. But best to deal with Jaxon first.*

As though hearing our words, Deana asked, 'Has *he* said anything yet?'

The he in question shot me a pleading look. I ignored it. 'I suggested he wait until you return.'

Deana nodded sharply before finally turning to Jaxon. She folded her arms. 'Explain.'

Jaxon sat down again, his back straight and hands still clasped. 'As I said, I did what I thought was best in the situation. When Tarina visited me the night the barrier fell—'

'So, you weren't just held back from the fight by being a slower rider than Callum. You were just lying – again.'

At the sharpness in her voice, he looked down, shame coating his features. 'I was. She offered me a spot at her side. And she promised me Garrett.'

Deana flinched at Garrett's name. I spoke so that she didn't have to. 'You didn't think to tell anyone?' Another flash of shame as Jaxon met my eyes. He didn't answer. I tapped a finger on my dagger's blade, the sharp ring tap of it ringing through the room. 'You considered her offer, didn't you?'

'Tarina promised me safety. She even offered—' He broke off, his gaze finding the ground once more. I was beginning to think Deana hadn't punched him enough earlier, if he was this reticent with information.

Deana shifted. 'If you're not going to speak, I'm leaving.'

Jaxon lurched. 'No! No, I will. It's just ... she did offer me Garrett. An Illusion of him that I could live out my years in. She knew I was forgetting him. Must have overheard me talking to Kerta years ago and knew how tempting it was. I wasn't really considering it, but ... but I couldn't dismiss it straight away.' His eyes closed, his expression pained. 'She's never offered me that before. Any connections with others went against everything she wanted. And then she offered to not touch those I loved. I couldn't just ignore it.'

'Why didn't you take the offer?' Deana asked. The sharpness had ebbed a fraction, though her words were still aimed to cut. 'If what you've said of Tarina is true, you would've been able to live in the life you wanted, never knowing better.'

'You did say you'd give up anything for a piece of Garrett.' I didn't think Jaxon had been lying when he'd told me that.

He smiled sadly. 'I would. But I know better than to think an Illusion would be him. It wouldn't be real. And it wouldn't have —' He broke off, looking up to meet Deana's gaze.

'Have what?'

'Other people,' he finished lamely.

I raised my brows. Gone was the smooth talker I knew from the slums, who could sweet-talk even the most reluctant of partners into bed. This Jaxon was vulnerable. Scared of losing the woman he loved.

Callum's voice grumbled down the bond. *Gods, he's worse than you were when it came to admitting your feelings.*

Shut it, or I'll stop relaying what's happening to you.

Callum laughed. *As you wish, Captain.*

'Fine. Then why did you end up accepting?'

'When Chiara found me and Jade, we found our way to where Tarina had decimated the army. She found me again the night before we were set to face her. Threatened to wipe out the soldiers in the night if I didn't agree to her bargain.'

'She practically did, anyway,' I pointed out. 'Two hundred died.'

'And all five hundred would have, if Tarina had struck before the soldiers were prepared.'

I dipped my head in acknowledgement, remembering how

easily the soldiers had been overwhelmed. The way their blood had spilt so quickly, their own weapons sliding through their throats as they became entrapped in the Illusion. I might have survived it. Jaxon likely would have. But we wouldn't have been able to act fast enough to save everyone.

Jaxon was quiet for a while, his eyes shifting around the room as though he wasn't sure what or who to look at. Only when Deana shifted, her impatience written in her scowl, did he speak. 'She was curious about Chiara,' he said. 'Angry about Dearil's death, too. She began to ask questions. About why your Gift was so powerful. How you could break through her Illusions. Who your mother was. So, I told her I'd bring the army to her. That she could have her fun, I'd go with her, and she'd stop asking questions about you.'

'Why?' I pressed, a cord of dread coiling in my stomach. A sense that I didn't truly want to know the answer to my question. 'Why does it matter if she asks those things? I've already had Vitus focused on me – I'm not sure Tarina would be any worse.'

'She would be far worse,' Jaxon said grimly. 'Now Dearil's dead, Vitus won't kill you if he can help it. Not if there's a chance the realm's power can't find a new vessel and the balance of gods isn't maintained. But Tarina – if she knew the truth about who you are, she'd stop at nothing to end your life.'

'What truth?' I snapped, patience wearing thin. 'All the gods know by now whose daughter I am.'

'They know your father, but only Dearil knew who your mother was.' Jaxon tensed as he met my eyes, as though he anticipated and accepted the blow that would come. 'Dearil's soul-bonded. The one who betrayed him.' There was a beat of silence – just enough time for Dearil's power to buzz in anticipation, and for every muscle to tense in preparation. 'Tarina.'

Chapter Twenty-Three

There was a clamour of noise. Deana began arguing with Jaxon, who leapt to his feet and defended himself. The noise from outside seemed louder, the buzz of voices in the grounds below slamming into me. Meanwhile, I just sat there. Blinked. Tried to remember how to breathe. How to exist.

It didn't make sense. It couldn't. Tarina was the goddess of Illusions and trickery. I had no such Gifts. And if I was her daughter – hers, and Dearil's – that would mean I didn't carry a drop of mortal blood in my body. That I was and always had been the very creature I hated.

Breathe, Chiara, Callum said, his voice the only calm I could find around me.

I'm breathing, I said even as my chest burned from the too-shallow gasps that were all I could manage to get down.

This doesn't change anything. You are still you.

I shook my head. *But if Tarina's my mother – I'm one of them, Callum.* Disgust filled me, thick and putrid. *Not just forced into the role, but actually one of them. I—*

You are mine, Captain. No matter what blood runs in your veins.

His voice was sharp. Fierce. Unforgiving. *You could be part beast and I would still love you. So don't you dare think yourself anything less than brilliant.*

But my mother—

My father was a tyrant. Gods, he was your enslaver. The man who tortured you. Do you think less of me because I share his blood?

My response was instant and angry. *Of course not!* If anything, I thought all the more of him for it. All the more of his strength in refusing to be what his father might have made him.

Exactly. This changes nothing.

I swallowed at the certainty in his words, wishing I could believe them.

The sharpness of Deana's tone cut through our conversation. 'She can't be a god. That doesn't make sense.' She crossed over to Jaxon, planting herself in front of him. 'If she was Tarina's daughter, how could she have lived in the mortal realm? Gods couldn't exist here without possessing a mortal body. Not to mention you seem to think Tarina has no idea who Chiara is.'

'She doesn't.' Jaxon shifted under Deana's attention. 'If she did, Chaira would've been killed as a babe.'

'What?' I interlaced my fingers, then untangled them, reaching for my dagger instead. It wasn't what – or who – I wanted to grab hold of, the familiar comfort it'd once offered doing little compared to the calm Callum's physical presence might've brought. 'Do gods not give birth like mortals?'

Jaxon's eyes found mine, Callum's amusement rippling as Jaxon said, 'That's what you're asking?'

'It's a reasonable question.' Deana slumped down beside Jaxon, her hair falling over her shoulders. She scrutinised me as though she suspected she could find the level of my divinity written across my skin. 'You're already talking nonsense, but if gods are like mortals, then it switches from nonsense to impossibility.'

'It is the truth,' Jaxon insisted. 'Why would I lie about this?'

Deana glowered. 'I don't know. Why do you lie about every second thing you say?'

'That's—'

'—fair,' I finished for him. 'Now explain. How does any of this make sense?'

'A loophole.' Jaxon stretched his legs out, planting them on the table in front of him. Deana's glower switched to them and he hurriedly placed them back down. 'Dearil knew Tarina was to give birth. He asked me to take Chiara before she could suck in her first breath. I was in the mortal realm with Chiara before she did so, so she was of this realm. A technicality in the barrier that Dearil exploited.'

A barrier he had made. Had he prepared for the possibility of a child, even all those centuries ago?

My eyes slid to the unguarded exit. I could leave now. Run, while they were all distracted. Even as I thought it, I knew I wouldn't. My feet were firmly rooted to the ground, and the wall was all that kept me from crumbling. I wasn't sure I could take one step, much less flee.

I'm with you, Callum whispered, and my breathing settled once more. *Whether you stay or run, I'll be with you.*

'If Tarina had given birth, surely she'd want to find her daughter?' Deana asked.

Jaxon barked out a bitter laugh, pushing himself up from the chair and beginning to pace. I watched his long strides, the movements almost angry as he walked the length of the room. 'Sure. She'd want to find her, and then she'd want to kill her.' His eyes swept over to me. 'Tarina is a jealous, vengeful goddess. She loved Dearil as much as she hated him, and the thought of someone, even her own child, taking up any of his attention, even if he despised her so thoroughly, was unthinkable. Especially when you might be the one to unsettle the balance and lead to Dearil's death, or even her own.'

'She was right, in a way,' I said, turning my wrist over so I could stare at the silver on the underside. Silver that had appeared before Dearil had done anything to the wards. Not because of the soul-bond or anything faulty with Vitus's markings, but because wards were never meant to fully contain gods.

'Dearil told me that one of us had to die. That I was too strong, and the balance needed to right.' I ran my nail over the silver, fighting the urge to scratch until I could dig the divinity from my blood. 'How can Tarina not know about me?'

His lips twitched into a smile that held nothing but coldness. 'Dearil wasn't there at the birth. He couldn't be. He was locked up, though that never stopped Tarina from tormenting him. He sent me with Kerta. I took you while Tarina was half comatose from the ordeal of childbirth. When she awoke, Kerta told her that the babe didn't make it. Of course, Tarina scoured the godly realm to make sure of that, but she never thought to search the mortal realm. She'd had enough children before who had died, though you were the only one I know of born to two gods. Halflings struggle to survive from the moment they're conceived, our bodies often too weak to hold the power in our blood. So, when she couldn't find you, she never questioned it.'

Kerta knew? Callum asked, ice seeping into his voice. I echoed his question.

Jaxon's pacing paused. 'I think she only recently connected you to the babe I took. Evania suspected you had some of Tarina's blood in you, but she seems to believe your mother was a distant descendant of one of Tarina's weaker halfling offspring who'd survived Tarina's tendency to cull any child who posed a threat.'

'They never thought to question more about who my mother might be?'

'Vitus used to bring all sorts to Dearil's cell. Any halflings or descendants of halflings who'd managed to find their way into the godly realm. Most were killed to taunt him, but it wasn't out of the realm of possibility that Vitus might've left one of them in Dearil's cell in an attempt to make Dearil form a connection with them before killing them. The gods who knew of you assumed that was what had happened.' He shrugged. 'Gods are callous by nature. They rarely care about things outside their immediate surroundings. Particularly halflings and mortals.'

I rubbed harder at the silver. Callous by nature. I couldn't deny that I held that same callousness. That the faces of all those I'd killed over the years often grew hazy until they became unrecognisable blurs. I'd assumed it was simply because of the sheer number I'd killed, but perhaps it was my true nature – to see mortals as nothing more than playthings.

That's not true, Callum said, his voice sharp. *You remembered the soldiers who died under your command. You told me yourself of your second, Ada. Of Caden and the others who'd followed you as Captain.*

Who'd fallen under my leadership, I corrected.

His sigh was heavy with exasperation. *Who would've fallen far sooner if they hadn't had you to lead them. And you never let yourself forget Cassie.*

My rubbing paused. He was right.

None of them were playthings. They were people. People who'd been far better than I in all the ways that mattered.

Deana crossed her arms, a stubborn set to her jaw. 'She's not Gifted by Tarina.'

Shadows stretched through the room, the sun beginning to fade from the sky. For a moment, I let myself be embraced by them. Let myself hope I could fade into obscurity, away from all Jaxon suggested. But Jaxon flicked his eyes upwards, a small orb of Illusioned light appearing where his eyes fell. The room was set in stark light, catching the droplets of Jaxon's blood on the rug.

My eyes fixed on them. That'd have to be cleaned before Callum returned.

'Isn't she?'

I forced my eyes away from the blood spatters to look at Jaxon. Lifting my hand, I gestured at the wards with my dagger, the blade passing dangerously close to skin. 'Clearly not. My Gift is death. I can't weave Illusions.'

'Illusions aren't all there are to Tarina's Gifted. There's storytellers, too.'

Callum had once told me his mother possessed that Gift. 'I don't tell stories.'

And you never have? Callum asked.

I... I trailed off. There had been a time I'd told stories. Stories about the happenings of gods. Stories that'd seemed to spin themselves with truths about the gods I should never have known. Cassie loved those tales, begging me for them whenever she had the opportunity.

Ice skittered over my skin, my breaths shallowing. They were just stories. Stories I hadn't told since my sister died.

I voiced this, and Jaxon nodded. 'That makes sense. Your Gift was bound by tethering Cassie's soul. And when it was supressed, Tarina's power showed.'

'I'm tethering Callum's soul now,' I pointed out.

Jaxon gestured at my wrists. 'The wards. They can't completely seal away a god's power, but they can diminish it. Even when you're binding Callum's soul, the Gift you inherited from Dearil is still the stronger of the two, and the one you consciously reach. So, when the wards started to break'—he pointed at the silver lines running through the almost faded gold—'it was death's power that came out first. The wards aren't completely broken, though, and whatever remains of them keeps the traces of our dear mother's power you have subdued.'

'Dearil carved wards to oppose—'

'Dearil did nothing of the sort.'

My lips flattened. 'You lied about him crafting his own wards.'

'Not exactly. I ... misconstrued.' Jaxon flashed a smile he likely meant to wriggle himself out from my glare. He failed. 'Dearil can craft wards, but no wards can undo what has been done. Wards are for limiting access to divine power. For a halfling, that's cutting off any contact with their Gift. For a god, its funnelling down the amount they can access. They don't do the reverse. Dearil simply made you believe you did.'

I rose, turning and striding to the window. The city stretched outside, a dark mass of buildings and shadows, absent of the people who'd once filled those streets. The sky was a muddled mix of blue and pink as the sun sunk towards the horizon. Soon, night would fall, and those in the palace would sink into nightmare-riddled sleep. 'Why?'

'Because you're as stubborn as they come, and you wouldn't be able to break the hold of the wards fully if he simply told you you could.'

'I would've found a way.'

'No, you wouldn't have. The power of gods relies on two things – innate ability and confidence. You have the innate ability. Plenty of it, from what I've seen.'

I flashed a glare over my shoulder. 'Are you trying to say I lack confidence?'

'I'm trying to say that you hate the gods. You'd refuse to believe that you could overcome the wards with your own power because you're smart enough to know that being able to break the wards of your own volition links you irrevocably to the divine. Even now, you're failing to break through when it should've been easy with the power in you. And—'

My mind was already spinning a different direction. 'If this is true, then you're my brother.' The words broke through whatever Jaxon had been about to say. Silence followed them. I turned, resting against the windowsill as my eyes landed on him. He'd frozen where he stood, saying nothing. 'Aren't you?'

'I am,' he said, slowly easing himself back onto the chaise. From the drumming of his fingers upon his leg, he wouldn't last long there.

'And you knew this whole time?'

Deana walked to the doors, leaning against them as though to prevent anyone from bursting in on us. Callum was quiet, but I could feel him down the bond, his presence the only balm to the swirl of emotions I was battling through. Jaxon's drumming quickened. 'I did.'

'Why didn't you say anything until now?' I meant the words as a genuine question, but they sliced out as an accusation.

Jaxon flinched. He ran his fingers through his hair – black hair, as dark and thick as my own – then stopped, hand falling back to his knee. 'You were in a bad place when we met, Chiara. What do you think you'd have done if I'd announced I was your brother?'

'Killed you,' I answered. 'Which you might've deserved given all the lies since.'

Jaxon smiled, but it didn't reach his eyes. 'I deserved it for far more than that.'

I didn't think he meant anything he'd done to me. The guilt he carried belonged to the husband he'd lost. 'And what about after that? We're friends, Jaxon. You made sure of that.'

'It was very difficult to do,' he said drily. 'Do you know how many times you threatened my life in the first two weeks of meeting?'

'Not that often.'

'Forty-seven times. That's more than three times a day.'

Deana grinned her approval.

Only forty-seven? Callum asked. *I'm disappointed, Captain.*

I wasn't in the best place back then. I'm sure I could manage more if I tried today, I replied, before shrugging at Jaxon, a smile creeping up my face for the first time since we'd begun the conversation. 'You tried to scam me at least thirty times. I'd say we're even.'

'I was risking my life just to be around you,' he huffed, his own smile growing more sincere as he sank back, folding his arms. 'You were only risking your money.'

'And my sanity.' I raised my brows. 'So? Why not tell me once we got closer?'

'Partially because Dearil ordered me not to. He was concerned any involvement with me might've brought Tarina's attention down on you. Dearil was good to me, in a way the other gods didn't care to be to halflings. I spent many of the years after Garrett next to his cell. But he can also be *scary*.'

I thought of the stern-faced god with his calm eyes and even temperament, and scoffed. 'There's nothing scary about him.'

'That's because you're of the same breed as him!' Jaxon protested.

'I am *not*,' I snapped. 'Dearil's distant, and composed, and I'm … well. You know what I am.'

'I am *well* aware of what you are.' Jaxon touched his crooked nose gingerly.

I smiled. 'I hope it sets like that.'

'You're—'

Deana groaned. 'Gods, how did we all miss you two were siblings? With the amount of bickering you do, it should've been obvious way sooner.' She held up her hand when Jaxon went to speak. 'Let's stick to what we *need* to know, not go off on another tangent. Dearil told you not to speak to Chiara about it, but we both know you're as good at following rules as Chiara is. So, what else?'

Jaxon's smile faltered. 'I was … scared. I know what I am. And I know who you lost. Your real family.'

My own smile faded, a pain that would never go away

striking my chest. I swallowed past the knot in my throat. Cassie wasn't my sister by blood, but Jaxon was right – she was my real family.

Yet Jaxon had been the first to reach a hand out to me when I'd been drowning in grief. He'd laughed and smiled when I'd snarled and threatened. Spoke truths most would've been terrified to say.

I sighed. I'd always heard family could be tedious, and this was no different. 'I suppose I could accept you as my brother.'

'I'm glad. I'd already begun thinking up the trouble we'll be able to cause. It would've been embarrassing if you'd rejected me.' Despite the flippancy of his words, he visibly relaxed at my acceptance.

Gods help us all, Callum muttered. Deana echoed the same, and I grinned.

'We could've caused trouble before I knew you were my brother.' I tilted my head, then amended, '*Have* caused trouble before.'

'But now we have justification for it.'

My brow creased. 'We need justification?'

'Well, *you* don't. You're a g—' He took in the unease in my features, and amended to, 'The soul-bonded to the king. You'll be able to get away with anything. But I was little more than a poor civilian, trying to make a living semi-honest—' I raised my brows. '*Dishonestly*. Now I'm the brother to the future queen. Who'd dare lock me up?'

I shifted. *Queen* was preferable to *god*, but I still wasn't sure it fit right.

'I'm beginning to think you should've kept your relationship to yourself, Jaxon,' Deana muttered. He grinned. Before he could start up again, she continued. 'You still haven't told us exactly what you've achieved by betraying us for your mother.'

'I didn't *betray* you. I—'

'—led our soldiers into a battle we had no hope of winning,' I finished, a spark of anger reigniting.

Jaxon shifted down the chaise to be as far from me as possible. 'But you did win! Because I encouraged you.'

I gaped at him. 'How did you encourage me?'

'I gave you reason to be angry enough to fight! I heard you used your power on the battlefield, didn't I?'

We don't need Jaxon, do we? I asked Callum, fingers itching to grasp my blade.

He laughed. *He's your brother. Deal with him how you want.*

'You gave me reason to want to track you down to kill you!'

'I—'

'Jaxon,' Deana warned. 'Get on with it. Before I make good on Chiara's threat.'

'Fine.' A grin that promised trouble appeared on his face. 'I stole the chains of the gods.'

Deana and I stared, Jaxon's words settling into the quiet. I spoke first. 'As in ... the chains that Vitus used to bind Dearil? Those ones?'

He nodded, as self-satisfied as a bird who'd collected the shiniest object they could find. 'They've been reforged with Vitus's power after Dearil broke them, so they're not as strong and can be moved around far easier than when they'd had full power, but they work fine enough.'

Ask him how, Callum said. I did as he asked.

'It was disappointingly easy. After all, who'd suspect that the pitiful halfling who'd followed his mother home would be up to no good?'

'Anyone who knows you?' Deana suggested.

'Well, the gods have never bothered to know me.' Jaxon sounded too proud of that. 'They had it locked in a room. The lock was decent enough, I suppose, but it didn't take too long to work around.'

'And why did you bother with the chains? Information would've been more useful,' I said.

'Because, Chiara,' Jaxon said, leaning forward, 'of all the gods siding with Vitus, there are only two who truly care about the destruction of this realm – Vitus and Tarina. Maia, Akmad and Adwin are only following him because they think it'll end better for them.'

'Where do the chains come into that?'

'Take Vitus and Tarina out of the equation, and this war will end. The gods are lazy. They don't care about this realm, only about avoiding Vitus's wrath.' Jaxon's grin grew. 'I think it's time we level the battlefield.'

There was a heartbeat of silence. I sensed Callum processing the information, understanding what Jaxon meant a moment before I did. 'You mean take one of them out.'

'Exactly. We'll turn Tarina's tricks against her. Draw her into a situation she can't resist. Attack and capture her with the chains.' Jaxon spread his hands as though he expected us to applaud. 'What can go wrong?'

Deana straightened, looking at Jaxon for the first time since his reappearance without a trace of his betrayal in her expression. 'So many things. How are we going to draw Tarina in?'

Jaxon clapped his hands together. 'I have the perfect bait in mind.' He grinned. 'Let's plan how we're going to trap a goddess.'

Chapter Twenty-Four

There were more souls than usual gathered at the Gates that night. I ushered them through, trying not to think of how many more would join them if our plan for the next night failed. The smoke and jasmine lingering in the air strengthened as though to comfort me, but it did little to help. Sighing as the last of the souls drifted towards what awaited, I placed my hand on the Gates, willing them to close. They hummed under my touch, seeming more energetic than normal. Almost anticipatory, as though sensing the deaths that would surely be coming to grace their arches.

They closed soundlessly, leaving me to the blankness of the other realm and the swirl of my own thoughts. I shut my eyes, for once not wanting to escape back to the mortal realm. Here, I could delay what was coming. Delay the possibility that Jaxon or Deana may not make it out.

We weren't facing mortals anymore, or even the creatures of the gods. When nightfall came the next day, it would be a god we hunted. There was no telling whether it would be her or us who would end up the prey.

'You're overthinking again, aren't you?' An arm slipped around my waist, warm and solid.

I smiled as I opened my eyes and tilted my head back, finding Callum staring down at me. 'It seems I have an intruder again.'

'This intruder was sleeping quite peacefully when I felt the bond call me.'

From the shadows under his eyes, the sleeping peacefully part was a lie.

As soon as I'd felt the pull of the Gates, I'd attempted to latch onto the bond as I had the last time I'd been drawn here. It seemed my plan to bring Callum to me had worked. 'I can send you back if your beauty rest is that important.'

'I've got plenty enough beauty already. I think I can forego a night of sleep.' He turned me around, tugging me against him as he stared up at the Gates. Their fathomless height left no shadows upon the ground. 'After all, it's not every day a man gets to court a beautiful woman in front of the Gates.'

I sighed. 'If it was up to me, we'd be together far, far away from here.'

'I don't care where we are.' Callum tilted my head back, his fingers leaving heat scorching my skin. 'We could meet on a battlefield for all I care.'

He leant down. Despite the thrill of desire that gathered in me, I slid my hand between us. Callum didn't let it stop him, his lips warm against my palm. I pulled away before I could give in to the temptation. I knew the moment I did, I would forget what I had called him here for. Forget everything but him.

'We should talk.'

Callum shifted a step closer again. I stepped back. 'We are talking.'

'Talk *without* any distractions.'

The smile he gave was wickedness given beautiful form.

A shiver ran through me, my resolve wavering for a heartbeat. 'Are you saying I'm distracting, Captain?'

Gods, even if I closed my eyes and blocked my ears his mere presence would be distracting. 'I'm saying I'm facing a goddess tomorrow, and if you touch me one more time, neither of us will be doing much talking at all.'

Light gleamed in Callum's eyes. 'Is that a challenge?'

'It's a promise.'

Callum held his hands out in front of him. I eyed him mistrustfully and he laughed. 'I'll keep my hands to myself. I swear it.'

'Good.' A smile crept back onto my face. All it took was being in his presence and my anxiety over Tarina was melting away. I sat down, leaning against the Gates. Callum raised his brows. 'What is it?'

He shook his head ruefully. 'Only you would use the Gates of Death as a backrest.'

I rapped my knuckles on the Gates, the sound hollow. 'It's sturdy enough.'

'I'm sure it is.' Still smiling, Callum seated himself across from me. 'What is it we're talking about?'

'You.' At his fading smile, I narrowed my eyes. 'You told me we'd talk about how you're handling everything after we'd dealt with Jaxon. We've dealt with him. So, talk.'

'I also recall we were going to talk about your power.'

I folded my arms. A stray soul flitted onto my shoulder, resting there. Murmurs of a child's voice whispered through the air, the words too muffled to pick out. It buzzed as though nervous before flying over to Callum instead. There, it settled, its light calm. 'We'll deal with that later.' The power flickered briefly to my skin, as though in protest at being dealt with. 'You're not all right, are you?'

Callum's fingers curled on his knees. 'I'm fine. Naruzia needs a king, and I'm handling it.'

'Handling it isn't the same as being all right.' I shifted, studying him intently. The shadows under his eyes. The tension that never seemed to quite leave his shoulders. 'People are dying. People from your kingdom.'

His flinch was so small I almost missed it. 'It's a part of war. People will die.'

'Just because it's natural doesn't make it easy to bear.'

Callum's gaze dropped to where his hands had fisted. The soul nuzzled his cheek as though in comfort. 'I am fine. I can deal with it.'

'Callum,' I said gently. 'I understand your people need you to be strong in front of them. You can lie to everyone else. Tell them you're all right. But you don't need to lie to me.'

The soul drifted to Callum's knee as he lifted his head. My heart squeezed at the sight of his eyes, shadows cracking through the green. His throat worked in a swallow before he whispered, 'I'm not fine.'

It hurt to see the pain in his face. Hurt to know that he'd been feeling this alone, and I hadn't been there for him. But I didn't speak. Not yet, when I could see all the words struggling to come out. Instead, I just gave him the time he needed.

'I've taken on my father's crown because I thought I could be better than him. But more people are dying under me than they ever did under him. He was a tyrant. What does that make me?' His eyes pressed shut, grief written in the harsh lines of his jaw. 'One of our scouting units didn't return today. We haven't found them yet, but...'

There were just a few reasons a loyal unit would fail to return. None of them were good.

'Every day, more pyres are lit for the bodies we find. It's like all

The Divine

I'm doing is fighting against the inevitable.' Callum laughed, the sound laced with bitterness so intense it echoed in me. 'What sort of leader sends out his men, day after day, knowing most won't return? Knowing it's the damned gods we face, and we're probably going to fail?'

I didn't let my gaze waver. 'The sort of leader who hasn't given up hope.'

Hope. Such a fragile word. One I'd crushed year after year until I'd forgotten what it was. But Callum had taught me its shape and light again. I wasn't going to let him lose it now.

Callum shook his head. 'Hope is for fools, and all it's doing is leading us all to our ends.' He opened his eyes, the pain stark. 'What am I supposed to do?'

I reached for him, grasping his hand in mine. His skin was far warmer than mine, but I didn't let that deter me. I held him tight as I said, 'You lead. You lead, and you don't ever give up. *You* are what our people need. You, not your father. Not the gods. There is no one more capable of this than you are.'

He blinked. '*Our* people?'

'Don't get sidetracked.' I shifted onto my knees, leaning towards him. 'You are enough.'

'And if I'm not?' he said softly, holding onto me as tightly as I did to him. 'If I fail, then this realm will be destroyed. There will be no—'

I thumped the top of his head with my fist.

His lips twitched. 'What was that for?'

'For being an idiot.' My hand dropped, curling around the side of his face. 'As long as you and I are here, there's hope. But the moment you let go of that, the gods win. *Vitus* wins.'

Some of the darkness lifted, but it didn't vanish entirely. 'If I misstep, everyone will die.'

'If *we* misstep. You're not alone, Callum. Stop pretending you are.' I gripped him tight when he started to look away. 'You don't need to handle it all. If there's too much, then I'll step up. If I can't, Deana and Jaxon will.' I curled my hand around the back of his neck, needing him to hear me. Needing him to understand. 'You are doing everything you can. Use those lives as reason to sharpen your blade for Vitus, not to turn it onto yourself. If the realms decide what you do is not enough, let them fall. They'd deserve nothing less.'

Callum drew me onto his lap. He didn't try to pull my mouth to his. Didn't do anything except press his face to my shoulder, his breathing ragged, and hold tight. I let him. Sometimes, I knew, this was all that was needed. A reminder that there was something tethering him to the mortal realm. That he wasn't alone, even if I wasn't physically by his side.

At last, he pulled away, though he didn't entirely relinquish his hold. He sucked in a breath and squared his shoulders. 'All right.'

I tangled my fingers in his hair, eyes scanning his features. Their sharpness hadn't become any less breathtaking since I'd first seen him, his smile no less wicked. But the shadows in his eyes hadn't completely disappeared, either. He'd heard me, but it didn't seem he quite believed me yet.

'What happened to not touching?' he asked.

I only held on tighter. 'I'm a god, remember?' The title was bitter in my mouth, but I didn't let myself falter. 'Gods are entitled to break a rule or two.'

'Speaking of which,' Callum said, looking physically pained as he settled me back on the ground. His amusement brightened as I huffed, letting go of him. 'Tarina's your mother.'

I wrinkled my nose. 'Do we have to talk about that?'

'Yes,' he said firmly. I sighed, recognising the look in his eyes. There'd be no escaping until we'd spoken. 'How do you feel about that?'

I flexed my fingers, aching to do something with them. Callum reached to his side where a knife was strapped next to where his sword would usually hang, manifesting here as it would be with his physical body. He withdrew it, handing it over.

I flipped it in the air. 'I don't know. How am I supposed to feel about it?'

Callum smiled wryly. 'I'm afraid I can't help you with that one. But whatever you feel is okay.'

The knife flipping quickened. 'I don't want to be a god. I hate most of the gods. Even those I don't hate, I resent. But now I find out I'm one of them. I'm sure I'm meant to think it's a good thing. That it'll put me on a level with the rest. But … I can't shake what I feel. That being like them is the very last thing I want to be.'

'Then don't. Don't be like them, Chiara.'

I huffed out a breath. 'It's not that simple. I can't wish away my blood.'

'I'm not talking about you being a god. That's what you've been since birth, even if you didn't know it.' His steady gaze was the only thing that kept me from losing myself to the fears I'd been staunchly ignoring since Jaxon had told me who my mother was. Fears I could only breathe to life with Callum. 'I'm talking about being *you*. You are brilliant – more so than any of the divine. Cruel and wicked. Kind and strong. You're many contradictions bundled into one extraordinary woman. No parentage or blood is going to change that. So, if you don't want to be like the gods, then don't be. Just be as unapologetically yourself as you've always been.'

I caught the knife before it could crash into the ground. 'You make it sound so easy.'

'It's not,' he said. 'I've struggled with losing myself to my role as king countless times. But do you know what keeps me from crumbling under all that burden of what I think I should be?'

I considered. 'Your overwhelming arrogance meaning you'd never lose yourself to what others think?'

His chuckle curled its way through me, warmth spreading at the sound. 'Rude, Captain. But no. It's the people around me. Deana. Lena. Jakob. Even Jaxon, to a degree. And you. The person who loves me as a man instead of a king. So, tell me – who do you want to be?'

I hesitated. Who did I want to be? He'd asked me something similar once before. And my answer was the same now as it had been then. 'Yours,' I whispered. 'Always yours.'

'That's a given,' he said, watching me carefully. 'But what else?'

Such a simple question for such a complex answer. 'I want to be the one to bring Vitus down.'

He grinned. I passed the dagger over to him and he slid it back into its place. 'Then that's what we'll do. First, though, we need to figure this reticent power of yours out.'

'Or we could spend the time we have here doing something more enjoyable,' I said, gaze dropping to his lips.

Callum sighed. 'As much as I'd love to do exactly that, you might be facing Tarina tomorrow. I'd feel far calmer if I knew you could access your power.'

'I can access my power.' I held up my hand, calling on the unruly beast. My hand lit up almost immediately, the silver bright and angry against my skin. It sparked, its light turning blinding around us. The souls hummed as smoke and jasmine intensified, the whisper of their voices becoming more distinct. The one that nestled near Callum called out for a mother who wouldn't come. Another screamed in defiance of their end, a third muttering incoherent words. The silver lashed out at the one screaming. There was a harsh pop, then the silver vanished, the soul vanishing with the light. 'See?'

'Poor wording choice. *Use* your power.'

'I used—'

'You prodded it. Actually try to put it into use.'

Slumping back, I sighed, lifting my hand again. The angry energy of the power slithered under my skin, whispering stubborn refusal to heed my command. I scowled at my palm, hoping the power felt the vitriol behind it. 'It refuses to be controlled.'

Callum shifted forward, his knees brushing mine. I tried not to focus on how tantalisingly close he was. 'Why?'

'Because it's stubborn and wild—' I cut off at Callum's arched brows. 'I don't know.'

'You said it speaks to you. Have you talked back to it?'

My brows pinched. 'I've told it what to do, just like I would with my Gift.'

Callum shifted. The soul on his shoulder clung stubbornly to him. I glanced at it – her, I thought it might be – pitying the poor thing. It wasn't like the other souls that didn't pass, stubbornly refusing to accept their fate. She only wished for her mother.

Wishes rarely mattered for the living or dead, though. If her mother lived, there was no telling when they'd be reunited. If she'd died, she must have already passed the Gates.

'Try having a conversation with it.'

The words were an echo of Dearil's and Evania's. They had both told me to listen. Their words, though, had been filled with the superior command of gods.

Callum's were patient. Warm.

I sighed. 'Fine.'

Feeling like somewhat of an idiot, I closed my eyes. Sensations became sharper without sight, the tickle of hair on my neck more pronounced, each of Callum's and my breaths clearer. Letting Callum's presence settle me, I reached for the stubborn power.

What do you want? I asked it.

I could have sworn I saw a silver eye crack open in the darkness. It stared back at me, narrow and filled with ice. Ice, and fear. *I will not obey.*

You've said that before. Why? I asked, my patience already thinning. There was something in its sharpness that rankled.

I kneel to no one.

Gritting my teeth, I clung to that shred of patience, resisting the urge to point out it didn't kneel at all. Under the irritation, though, a thread of unease grew. Those words were familiar. Unerringly so. *Why not?*

I am no one's to command.

The shred of patience disintegrated. With a frustrated curse, I reached for the power, grasping it tight. It wriggled wildly, its screams of fury echoing in my ears. I grasped it tighter. My skin burning under its fury, the scent of death chokingly thick.

Fingers curled around mine. The power's rage vanished in an instant, and my eyes snapped open to the last fragments of silver in the air.

'I take it your conversation didn't go so well?' Callum asked. Shadows swirled on his skin, his Gift reacting to my own. Only once I'd nodded that I was fine did he let go, the shadows retreating.

'It went fantastically. I've figured out that the power is useless and I'm better off without it.' I clenched my hands, narrowing my eyes at the streaks of silver breaking through the wards.

'Did it talk?'

My eyes narrowed further. 'It did.'

'What did it say?'

'That it wasn't mine to command, it doesn't kneel before anyone. All the usual pleasantries.'

Callum's brows quirked. He stared for a second before an

unfiltered laugh ripped through the air. I placed a hand on my hip, narrowing my eyes at him. 'What is it?'

'I think I've figured it out.' He grinned, and my glower softened. I could never hold out against that smile. 'Gods, that's perfect.'

'Tell me,' I demanded, but he shook his head.

'I suspect this is one of those things you have to figure out for yourself.' I started to frown once more. Before it could fully form, he tipped my head back, pressing his lips to mine and stealing most of my irritation away. 'Have I ever told you how damned stubborn you are?' he murmured against me.

I pulled away, frowning. 'I'm not sure what that has to do with the power.'

'Oh, I suspect it has everything to do with it.' He tugged me to my feet. 'Those words sound an awful lot like someone else I know.'

'Wh—' I blinked as his grin widened. 'Oh.'

He was right. The refusal to submit. The rage any time I tried to control it. The fury when it had said it wouldn't kneel. The unease of familiarity.

I had heard those words before. Countless times. Spat out in fury, whispered in defiance. Often in the confines of my own mind.

They were *my* words. My refusal. My defiance. My rage and fear.

'That wild, unpredictable, magnificent power,' Callum said, his hand curling around the back of my neck, eyes bright with awe, 'is a reflection of *you*.'

I scowled, even as the power shivered as if in agreement. The word struck a chord. The sharpness of its voice, how familiar it felt. If it was me, it made perfect sense.

Even so, irritation buzzed, because I couldn't see how that helped. I'd never been great at managing my own emotions, giving in to my rage far more often than I should. I glared down at my hand and the power that lurked beneath the surface. As though feeling my anger, it sparked upon my skin in defiance. 'And if you're right? What do we do now?'

'Now, Captain,' Callum said with a smile, 'we practise.'

I collapsed back onto the ground, batting away a few curious souls as they came to investigate. Sweat pooled on my skin, my chest rising and falling in pants. Callum stood over me, irritatingly sweat-free.

'Again,' he ordered.

'Gods, you're worse than the men who trained me,' I muttered, grasping his offered hand. He hauled me to my feet. 'At least they granted me the courtesy of unconsciousness instead of this cruelty.'

Callum shrugged. 'If you just use your power, we wouldn't have to go through this.'

I sighed, shaking out my hands. He was right.

The problem was, no matter how much I tried to reach for it, I couldn't quite grasp the elusive power.

'Let's get this over with.' We'd been sparring for some time.

Rather, *Callum* had been sparring. I'd been desperately trying to gather some flicker of silver. So far, I'd found nothing but frustration and exhaustion from constantly dodging his blows.

Callum gave no warning as he lunged for me, his fist thrusting towards my temple. I whirled past it, reaching for my side as the air shifted around. Callum launched a kick at me before I could, his grin sharp. 'No weapons, remember?'

'*You* have a weapon.' I glared pointedly at the knife in his hand. 'Seems a little unfair.'

'When have you ever let things like fairness dictate whether you win?' Callum threw the knife. I dropped under its sharp curve. He launched forward, catching it by the hilt before it could clatter to the ground. I spun, eyeing him warily. 'You can do this. Just trust yourself. Trust your power.'

'That's impossible,' I gritted out, dodging a brutal blow. Souls buzzed their excitement at our show, the Gates emitting a low hum of approval as Callum came at me again. His own Gift swirled over his skin, replenishing him and preventing fatigue. 'It's a stubborn asshole of a—'

My words cut off as Callum sliced the blade at my throat. I slammed my fist up on instinct. He caught it with his free hand, fingers grazing the underside of my wrist. He smirked. 'Breaking the rules again?'

I grinned back, every bit of vicious delight in his eyes matched in my smile. 'I've never been a fan of them.'

'No,' he said, his grip tightening. My pulse skittered under his touch, his gaze growing more heated as it dropped to my lips. 'You haven't.'

The power writhed under my skin in agreement. *No rules*, it hissed. *No commands*.

Callum twisted, pulling me in so that my back rested against his chest. Heat seeped into me from him. His knife lifted up, pricking at my throat. 'I win.'

It was first time he'd spoken the words aloud since we'd begun. My eyes narrowed. The power twisted and surged, its heat intoxicating in my veins. It had heard the words as well as I had. The claiming of victory.

I had never liked losing, even to Callum. Neither, it seemed, did the power.

Will you come? I asked.

There was a hesitation, and then, *We will not lose*.

Silver shot to my skin, swirling in light so blinding that, for a moment, I couldn't even see the Gates. Voices lifted around us, the remaining souls drawn to the power. They swarmed me, taking form as children and the elderly, men and women. Fingers brushed me, yanked on me, tugged me.

And the power grew.

It crackled down the knife, turning the blade into contained starlight. Callum dropped it before it could touch him. It might not be deadly to him with his Gift, but it could still sting.

I didn't waste the opportunity. I jerked my arm as I twisted my body, breaking his hold on me. Whirling, I raised my hands, and silver raised with them. It leapt through the air in eager strides, stretching for the top of the Gates. The Gates themselves lit up and the remaining souls didn't hesitate to go through, any previous hesitation eased by the power.

The power lessened, breaking into millions of shimmering drops. Smoke and jasmine filled the air around us. The power was not mine in the way my Gift had once been, but we had perhaps shifted a small step towards alliance.

If I call, will you aid me? I asked.

Yes, the power whispered back, and I heard my own voice in its depths. *I will come and I will destroy*.

Not a sharp weapon, then. A blunt one. The sort that could level a battlefield, regardless of who fought.

A last resort, but one that I could rely on far more than I had before.

Callum grinned as he stepped towards me, his eyes brightening at the sight of the silver sparks in the air between us. They flickered before launching back to my skin, Callum's own shadowy Gift hiding itself away. 'I told you you could do it.'

The power held in my hands for a handful of seconds before disappearing in crackling silver. I frowned. It was a stubborn Gift. Stubborn, and irritatingly rebellious.

But it was far easier to draw out now than it had been before.

'Will it be enough?' I asked, lifting my hand up and narrowing my eyes at the back of it. 'We're facing Tarina tomorrow.'

Callum laced his fingers through mine, pulling my hand down. 'You'll make sure it is.'

He didn't speak what we both knew. This meagre control I'd gained had to be enough. If it wasn't, then tomorrow's encounter with Tarina would end in blood.

Chapter Twenty-Five

I crouched in the shadows, trying to ignore the stench of decaying food drifting from nearby houses. Night had fallen quickly, the stars remaining unseen behind heavy clouds. Even the moon was hesitant to make itself known. Every breath seemed too loud in the quiet of the air, the alleyway leading to The Den free from the muffled cheers that had once reigned within.

Beside me, Deana leant in to me, her voice barely a whisper as she asked, 'I'm not the only one who thinks this is a terrible idea, am I?'

'No, but it was our only one, and Jaxon's right – if this doesn't work, our chances of success are going to be far lower.'

She shifted, leaning against the wall behind. Even the insects were gone, as though they, too, sensed the calamity that might be descending. 'And what does our esteemed leader think about all of this?'

'He thinks if you've agreed to go, it can't be completely reckless.'

'Only mostly reckless?' Deana sighed and I smiled. 'Great. If this all goes to shit, it's my fault, then.'

'Precisely,' I said, grinning into the darkness.

'I still think we should've brought more. Lena, maybe. Or Kailey and Corin – I could've stopped them joining the soldiers headed for the frontlines to help with this. They'd be of some help.'

General Jade had headed off a few days before, taking those who'd been guarding Alluvite with her. Callum had asked me to relay the need for more soldiers. They planned to meet with the forces still fighting on the frontline, allowing the injured and exhausted to head back for the city. Kailey and Corin had volunteered to join them.

'Not against Tarina.' I glanced towards the closed door of The Den. 'She killed hundreds of soldiers in one go by casting them into Illusions. They drove their blades through their own chests without any hesitation. Anyone else would just be more bodies for her to puppeteer.' I eyed what I could make out of her. 'I'm still not sold on you needing to be present.'

Deana made a noncommittal sound. We'd spent an entire day trying to strategise, going back and forth with ideas that were ultimately pulled apart by their flaws. In the end, there was one barrier we kept coming up against.

Tarina was a god. One whose powers weren't tethered as Vitus's had been when we'd faced him in Kane's body. Even Jaxon seemed uncertain as to the full extent of her abilities.

A sudden burst of music startled us both. Deana grasped hold of my arm, and I almost flung my dagger at the closed door. The tones were unlike anything I'd ever heard before – light, yet discordant, as though all the notes were trying to be something they were not. I pressed my free hand to my ear, wincing as the melody sent shocks of pain through my skull.

Deana's grip on my arm lessened. She began to rise. 'That sound – it's beautiful. We should—'

I grabbed her hand and yanked her back down. She tugged

against my hold in protest, but I only held her tighter. 'Don't trust anything you encounter – remember?'

Her fingers jerked in mine, hair brushing my bare arm as she shook her head. 'It's so ... *enchanting*.'

'I'll take your word for it.' I studied the door. The music rose and fell, the crescendos at odds with the tempo. 'It seems Jaxon has managed to entice Tarina here.'

Jaxon claimed he'd had a way to contact Tarina – a place to the north of Alluvite where a few Ankurans Vitus had lent her gathered. Despite his thieving, it seemed none of the gods had caught on to his duplicity, their egos too large to consider such mundane methods of sabotage. He'd been certain Tarina wouldn't doubt him if he brought up a compelling reason for why he'd left her stronghold.

After all, he'd said, *why would a pitiful halfling like me ever dare to leave a goddess's side for a second time?*

I'd been sceptical. It seemed I now owed him an apology, though I was unlikely to give it to him. He'd find some way to wrangle an opportunity out of that.

A figure dropped down in front of us from the roof above. My heart thudded. I launched to my feet, whipping my dagger out and shoving the man against the wall opposite. My blade pressed to his throat.

'It's just me!' Jaxon hissed.

'I know,' I whispered back, 'and we agreed to meet ten minutes ago. I also made it very clear that you were not to surprise us like that.'

He grasped my wrist and eased my dagger away from his neck. I shoved the dagger into the scabbard. 'Are we ready?'

'We are.' I looked at the closed door, considering it and the discordant music within.

Jaxon stepped forward, his feet light against the ground. There was a fluidity to his movements that suggested many nights spent prowling the dark, watching all sorts of shady happenings from the cover of shadows. His arm linked with mine, tightening until I'd have to truly yank away from him. 'Then let's go, my dear bait.'

It was, as Deana had said earlier, a terrible idea. So hideously simple that it wouldn't take much for the plan to crumble. Offer me as bait. Jaxon and I attack before Tarina realises Jaxon's truly changed sides, Deana bringing the chains when they were needed.

Hideously simple plans were my forte, though – a blade and some violence, and I usually came out on top.

A saccharine scent saturated the air as Jaxon pushed open the door. We paused at the sight that greeted us.

The Den was not the same as when I'd last seen it.

Where there had once been an arena, surrounded by high walls and chairs for observers to watch, there was now bright, sparkling lights, tables set up filled with food, ornate sculptures and pure marble floors and walls. Jewels dripped along the walls and from the ceiling, a lavish show of wealth. All shows of extreme mortal opulence – the sort that even kings would struggle to obtain.

It wasn't that which had me inhaling sharply and Jaxon stilling, though. It was the mortals filling the space where I'd bled and killed not too long ago. They milled around, wandering aimlessly as they placed small, delicate bites of bright yellow food into their mouths, not seeming to notice how it disappeared before it ever hit their tongues. I stepped forward, going to speak to the closest one. Jaxon tugged me back.

'Don't,' he breathed, his fingers cold where they pressed to my skin. 'You're resistant to Illusions, but not immune. If you touch them, you might be drawn in.'

The music crept insidiously amongst the mortals, lulling them to sway along with it. A few had given in to the urge to dance, smiling vacantly as they were swung around the room by their partners. They were all covered with the finest fabrics, the best jewels. And yet, despite the noise and festivity, not a single person met another's eyes. They didn't talk as they moved, synchronised around a single point in the room. Every time someone faltered or hesitated, they were drawn back into the orbit.

The back of my neck prickled. The disquiet of the scene could only come from gods playing in the mortal realm. Jaxon nudged my side, motioning towards that central point. My fingers were already firming around my daggers before I saw her.

Tarina had been stunning when I'd first met her in her true form. Now, she was utterly captivating. There was no denying it, just as there was no denying the severe perfection of Vitus, or the dark beauty Dearil had possessed. She sat upon a throne of velvet, long legs crossed, chin propped on her hand with a bored look upon her face.

I tried not to focus too much on her features – to see which parts of her matched mine. I found them, anyway. The slight upturn of her nose. The curls of dark hair, though hers were far better kept than my own. The thickness of her lashes and the shape of her eyes.

My mother, I thought, and found the words as detestable as when I'd used them with Madame Tussant. That woman was no mother. She was a creature who shared blood with me. Nothing more.

'Mother.' Jaxon's voice cut through the cacophony of noise. Immediately, every single person stopped as Tarina turned. She slipped the vial away, rising to her feet.

It was like he'd interrupted a puppet show midway through. Dancers stood with one foot raised. Those drinking had thick red wine juice dribbling from their lips, staining their gowns and floor.

Tarina waved a hand, and the stains instantly disappeared. Her lips spread into a full smile as she looked at him, not seeming to notice me.

The Divine

'Jaxon, darling.' Tarina's arms lifted, opening wide. 'Come and give your mother a hug.'

Jaxon gave me a warning look before moving forward, letting her take his hands in hers, then pull him into a hug, The saccharine scent strengthened as the mortals' faces split in wide grins, the adoration in their smiles not meeting their eyes. Jaxon didn't attempt to pull away.

'Let these people go,' Jaxon said, his voice wholly different to the one I knew. It was meek, that of a child come for a scolding. A perfect lie crafted for a goddess. 'Please.'

Finally, Tarina pulled back. The smile of hers did not drop, but a sliver of the Illusion she had held in place slipped, revealing the razor-sharp edges of it.

'But my dear, what would be my guarantee you would not run from here as soon as I did? You've been so disobedient recently. And not long ago you vanished. Why, I didn't even notice you were gone until you triggered one of my Illusions!'

She waved her hand, and the music started up again, each person moving with practised patterns. 'Perhaps this will keep you in line. I had to beg Vitus to allow me to bring these toys here, only to find out someone has rudely set up wards. Do you know how tedious it is to force ungrateful mortals to follow me through dirty streets?' Tarina pouted. It should have looked foolish on her lips, but she had a talent for turning the ugly into something that appeared to be lovely. 'Such a nasty trick. And so unnecessary when you know you will be returning with me. But it will keep you here with me, so I am satisfied. I know how much you detest me killing your little mortals.'

I bristled at the disdain dripping from her voice at the last word. Jaxon's hands clenched at his sides even as his head bowed.

'I brought the girl.' Jaxon stepped away from Tarina. Her lips twitched with displeasure, and the dancing grew more intense. 'Come here, Chiara.'

As we'd practised earlier, I let the subtle touch of his Gift curl over me. If it happened as it had in the palace, my eyes would take on the same vacant sheen as those of the mortals around us. My steps turned jerky, my arms slack by my side.

Tarina stared at me, her yellow eyes far crueller than Jaxon's had the capacity to be. 'This is Dearil's halfling? She looks even more hideous now than she did in Vitus's care.' She clicked her tongue. 'Why, her mother must have been something awful to dull down Dearil's beauty so drastically.'

I strangled the laugh that nearly broke free into submission. Yes, my mother *was* something awful. Just not in the way Tarina meant.

'So?' Jaxon prompted with an expectant smile. 'Does this mean you forgive my brief disappearance? I thought I'd fetch you an apology gift for all those years I spent away from you.'

Tarina sighed. 'I suppose so. You are at that rebellious age, after all. What are you now – six … or eight hundred?'

Jaxon's smile stiffened a fraction. 'Three hundred.'

'Precisely.' Tarina flicked her fingers at me. 'She holds a weapon. Make her get rid of it.'

Jaxon waved his hand sharply, and as though tugged by a string, I lifted my arm and flung the dagger I'd made sure to leave in a place easily spotted. The blade glinted in Illusioned light as it whirled before slamming into the limestone wall I knew to surround the fighting pits we stood in, even if I couldn't see it. It clattered to the ground.

Tarina didn't bother asking if I had any more. It likely didn't even occur to her that I might.

The goddess lifted a finger, spinning it in the air. The music slowed down, a sensuous tune designed to make pulses quicken and bodies warm. Around us, any who had been talking ceased their chatter and began to dance. Everyone still avoided looking at their partner, each person seeing some Illusioned sight crafted up by Tarina. Curves moved beneath swathes of fabric, partners stepping closer to one another. There was no longer a distinction between each partner, fabric and skin meeting.

'Stop it.' Jaxon looked away from the scene, staring up at the ceiling. I nearly did the same, almost ruining our ruse. I'd seen plenty of scenes before, between people of all varieties. I was no blushing maiden exposed to the wonders of human flesh for the first time.

But this was different. It was that every one of these people was seeing someone else – a lover, a husband, a wife – whom they were pressed against. It sickened me.

'Why?' Tarina pouted. 'Humans are so *delicious* with their desires.'

'Mother,' Jaxon warned, shifting. She let out a sigh, letting her head fall back. Her dark locks spilt over her shoulders, a dark contrast to the red of her dress.

'You're no fun anymore, darling.' But she snapped her finger. The tempo picked up into a jauntier beat, dance partners pulling apart. Sweat clung to their skin, hair mussed and Illusioned clothes askew. 'Sit, my darling boy.'

Jaxon sat, folding his legs as he planted himself on the ground. Was this what he'd been forced to be before he'd escaped the godly realm? An obedient dog for his own mother. 'We should finish this quickly. Chiara's well known in the palace. People will notice her missing soon.'

Tarina eyed me. 'I do not like the way your pet is looking at me. Make her kneel next to you.'

Jaxon's shoulders tensed. He twisted, meeting my eyes in silent plea. Anger wrapped around me, turning my skin hot. I hated kneeling. Hated the people who'd made me do it. I swallowed the rage, keeping my hands from curling into fists as I slowly walked over to Jaxon's side.

As though feeling my rage, the power swirled up inside me, nearly breaking free.

Not yet, I whispered to it. If I unleashed it here, with Jaxon so close, there was no telling what destruction might be wrought.

Soon, it whispered back.

Soon, I promised it.

I forced myself to my knees next to Jaxon, fighting to keep my rage from my face. We just had to hold on until Tarina fully let her guard down. Then, we could signal to where Deana waited outside. I could last that long.

Tarina smelt of sugar and decay as she crouched before us both, the scarlet silk of her gown pooling at her feet. She lifted both hands, pressing her palms almost lovingly to our cheeks. It might've looked an almost maternal scene to an onlooker. A mockery of a mother before her children. Her fingers curled, nails digging into flesh, as she asked mildly, 'Did you truly think this would work?'

My breath stalled. Jaxon stilled. 'I don't know—'

'Oh, my darling child. You are *mine*.' Jaxon inhaled sharply as though she'd pinched him. I didn't dare look to see if she had as my hand crept for the dagger I'd strapped under my shirt. 'You have always been disobedient. Perhaps you thought that would make me believe those wards you placed were nothing more than a game. Once, I might have.' Her fingers slid down, curling around my chin. She twisted, and I met Jaxon's eyes as she did the same to him. 'Is this the girl who has changed your cowardice? A pity. I suppose I shall have to find a way to remove her taint from your life. Perhaps Vitus will forgive me her death.'

If this was what a god was, I definitely didn't want to be one.

No, a small voice, different from the power's yet startlingly alike in its sharpness, whispered. *If this is what a god is, then I will remake what it means to be divine.*

'No one changed me,' Jaxon gritted out. Yellow tendrils were creeping over his skin from his mother's hand. From the panic in his eyes, the same was happening to me. 'I'm—'

'Do not lie. I see the same signs of love in you as I did with Garrett. The lies. The rebellion.'

The panic diminished, and I barely kept the wrinkle from my nose. Disgust at both the insinuation that there'd be anything between me and Jaxon, and at the way she'd flaunt the name of his dead soul-bonded with such a smile.

'Don't speak his name,' Jaxon said, his voice low. 'Not when you were the one to kill him.'

Wait for a moment, I reminded myself and my power, disgust and fury pounding through me. I'd been foolish with Vitus. Waited too long, and Dearil had paid the price for it. But with the yellow crawling over Jaxon's skin, a tingling of power creeping over my own, I suspected a wrong move too early would prove fatal for both of us.

Tarina laughed. 'You know very well that *I* didn't kill him, my darling boy.'

Droplets of blood appeared under Tarina's nails as Jaxon tried to jerk free. It looked far more out of place on his skin than the bruises Deana had given him did. 'No, but you made damned well sure that your king did.'

'Oh, do not be so dramatic, Jaxon. I did it for you. He was nothing more than a halfling.'

'*I* am a halfling, and he was mine. You took him from me.'

Tarina sighed, the sound filled with heavy regret. 'It seems you are set on being obstinate. Perhaps some time considering your actions will do you some good. You have been such a disappointment recently.'

She removed her hand from his jaw, tapping her nail upon his temple. Terror flared in his expression, his body jolting as the tangle of yellow on his body glowed bright. Then, his features slackened, his eyes shuttering with muted yellow.

The press of his Gift upon my skin disappeared. I tore away from Tarina, whipping out the knife and pointing it at her. The power within rose, eager for blood. Jaxon was here, though. Deana somewhere outside, likely trying to listen in to see if there was any danger. Unleashing that power here would kill them with the amount of control I possessed.

'Excellent. You brought your own blade.' Tarina rose to her feet, sweeping a hand down her skirts to smooth them out. 'That makes things far easier. I will tell Vitus that you realised how hopeless things were.'

A sharp scream rang from outside.

'He'd never believe that.'

Tarina arched a brow, her expression an eerie mimicry of the look Jaxon had given me when suggesting we try to trap her. 'Of course he would. You are a halfling, prone to all the frivolity of mortals. This is what mortals do – fight against the inevitable, and then give up when they accept their fate.'

But I was not mortal. Not a halfling, either. Neither of those was what this realm needed right now.

I was a god – not because of the power passed onto me, but because of the blood in my veins. And I would fight against the inevitable all the same. Fight against the goddess who'd given me life, unwilling though she might've been, oblivious as she was. Fight against the ruler of the gods.

All for those mortals she deemed to be playthings. For the people Callum loved. The people I was beginning to want to protect.

'Your Illusions haven't worked on me so far. Why would you think they'd work on me now?'

'Because now, I will not be going easy on you.' Tarina smiled serenely. 'Goodbye, child.'

She snapped her fingers. Something tightened around me, constricting all my senses until all I could see was yellow, all I could smell was that saccharine sweetness. I tried to move my arm. To throw the dagger and pray it landed.

But Tarina was right. Her attempts at Illusions before were nothing compared to this. I gasped for air, reaching for something, *anything*, to grasp onto. For a moment, I thought my fingers touched something sharp and hot, cold and blunt. Something that smelt of smoke and jasmine, cedar and the coming rain.

It was too late to pull myself free, though. Tarina's power consumed me, and I fell.

Chapter Twenty-Six

'Chiara.' A hand pressed to my shoulder, shaking me from sleep. 'Chiara, wake up.'

I blinked open eyes heavy with sleep. I was lying on a bed of soft white, the blanket cocooned around me. The air was warm, inching towards humid, and smelt faintly of the cinnamon rolls I used to pilfer from a street stall.

A small, round face leant over me, green eyes bright with anticipation, and red hair – a stark contrast to the black mess that was crushed beneath me. 'Wake up, Chiara.' Cassie flopped herself down, driving the air from my chest. 'We need to go.'

'Go where?'

'Silly.' She teased, poking at my arm with her finger. Something about her touch sent a shock through me, as though a deep, hidden part of me hadn't expected to feel something anything at all. 'To the seamstress, of course. For your wedding gown.'

'Wedding gown?' I echoed, slowly swinging my legs over the edge of the bed.

Cassie's smile was wide as she nodded eagerly. She wore a

simple but well-made dress of lacy white that hung loosely on her skinny frame. Her hair, apart from the tendrils that had brushed against me before, was pulled back into a bun. She looked sweet. Innocent.

Wrong.

The word crashed through me as I rose to my feet, but I shook it off. It was a silly thought. There was nothing wrong with Cassie. She was my sister. I loved her, and all was as it should be.

I looked around at the small house we called home. The simple table, a bowl of oranges sitting atop it. The bed I had been sleeping in that lay opposite the fireplace, with another on the other side of the room. On my side, clothes and shoes lay strewn across the floor. On Cassie's side, there was nothing but piles of neatly folded clothes.

This isn't real, Captain, a voice – a painfully familiar one, one that curled around me tighter than any set of arms could – whispered. *You need to wake up.*

My lips curled downwards. Cassie was there in an instant, thrusting something shiny into my face, and I shook the voice away as if I was ridding myself of a bad dream. I stared at the silver necklace. The chain was fine, with a single scarlet pendant on the end.

'Here, Chiara.' Cassie's hand was small and warm against my own as she slipped it there. 'Put this on.'

'I—' I stared down at the necklace. It was a pretty thing in its simplicity, and I did rather like it. There was something about it, though, that didn't seem right. Something too bright and too heavy about the way it sat in my hand.

'Put it on,' Cassie insisted, her fingers gripping tighter. 'I got it just for you. Please, Chiara?'

My fingers curled around the necklace, bringing it closer to my neck, but my other hand didn't wrap around Cassie's. It wasn't that I didn't want to.

No, it was because I couldn't. And I couldn't because … because—

Wake up, Chiara, the voice from earlier urged, urgency thrumming through it. *Please. I need you to wake up.*

I wrenched my hand away from my neck, turning to face those vivid green eyes. 'I'm sorry, Cass.' I whispered, my throat tight. 'I can't.'

Cassie's lips puckered into a frown. I saw, then, the undertone of yellow to her skin that didn't seem quite right. 'Why not?'

'Because you're dead.'

The pretty scene Tarina had painted in my mind and those false memories she'd laid there disintegrated into nothing but yellow dust. I had time to catch a glimpse of bloodstained stone beneath my feet, the high walls of The Den looming around, and a blade in my hand instead of a necklace, and I was falling again.

'You are radiant.' A hand brushed away a stray lock of hair that had fallen across my cheek. I blinked then stared up into eyes the shade of the finest of emeralds. Callum's lips were tipped up in a soft smile that he used only for me. There were no scars on his skin, not even across his lips.

My eyes tracked down to where his hand held mine. My own hands – both of them – were soft, the skin free of any mark or marring. A beautiful ring on one finger, a simple band of silver that matched the one Callum wore.

'You're a shameless flirt,' I replied, ducking away when Callum leant forward to kiss me.

'And you're a tease.' Callum's hand caught the back of my head, bringing my face to his. His lips were soft and I let myself melt into him. We stood upon a grassy hill past the outskirts of Alluvite, looking upon what was ours. Our kingdom. Our people.

Callum's father had passed only a year earlier, handing Callum the crown he'd been raised for. The people loved him. They always had, ever since he had been a child, and they had grown to adore me. Just as I was sure they would grow to adore the little one who was likely to come any day now.

This is not a world I want to bring a child into, my own voice clanged through me.

Glancing away to hide my frown at the unwanted thought, I stared over the city once more. There was no reason to think such a thing. Peace had reigned in Naruzia since when we had won the war against Archin a few years ago, with minimal losses on either side. Pulling away from Callum, I rested a hand on the bump of my stomach. Callum's hand covered mine, both of us staring with awe at where life was flourishing.

'Princess Cassandra.' Callum whispered. An old pang of sadness hit me. My sister had died young, taken by a plague that had racked the kingdom, but she had lived as full a life as any.

Don't listen to him. That's not me.

I blinked. That voice was like the one coming from Callum, but it was rougher. Less polished. Warmer. And filled with far more concern than the man appearing before me.

'What do you think?' Callum prompted, and I shook away the thought. This was my Callum. I was imagining things.

'If it's a girl.' I walked, as gracefully as someone eight months pregnant could, to a nearby tree. The shadow fell over my skin, giving relief from the sun. Small flowers bloomed nearby, the buds beginning to open to reveal bright colours within. 'And if it's a boy...'

'It's a girl.'

I rolled my eyes but could not hide the smile growing on my lips. Callum was always so sure of himself. It was what drew me to him when we first met as young children, when I was summoned to the court due to my mother's status.

'What a life we've built for ourselves.' Callum murmured as he came up next to me. He carefully tucked a daisy in the curls of my unbound hair, his smile sweet and gentle.

It truly was a life. A happy, unburdened one, despite the crowns we wore. We were loved by our people, and we lived in a time of peace.

You will be loved by our people if that's what you desire, but only if we win this war. Please, Captain. Wake up.

My breath caught at the words. My skin began to itch and I raised it towards the light, a perturbed frown catching on my lips. For a moment, ridges and pale scars lined my flesh, like a nightmare breaking through a dream. 'What—'

Callum caught my raised hand in his, pressing a kiss to my skin. 'Don't worry about that, my love.'

I tilted my head. 'That's not what you call me.'

'Of course it is.' His thumb traced circles on the back of my hand. 'This is what we want. A life without worry or fear. A life without scars.'

The words were like a blast of icy water skating down my skin. I shook my head, narrowing my eyes at the skin. The claws of the Illusion loosened, allowing the truth of my body, of the blood I bathed in, to show. 'No.'

'Yes, my queen. We are free. We are untroubled. We can stay here for eternity, unblemished by hard lives.'

I love your scars. Every one of them. That voice – gods, I loved that voice. Needed that voice. *That* was my Callum. Sharp, but warm. Not this falsehood before me.

'No,' I bit out again, and there was none of the sweetness or gentleness that had been forced into my tone through falsehood. 'I don't want that. I don't want to forget what happened. He wouldn't want to forget what happened. My scars are mine, and not even you can take them away from me, Tarina.'

Callum's eyes hardened, rage lighting his green eyes. No, not green. Yellow. *Her* yellow eyes. 'Fine.' Her voice was all wrong coming from between the lips I loved to feel against my skin. 'I thought we would do this the easy way. A nice gentle Illusion before your death at my king's hand. If you insist on making this difficult, though, we will make it difficult.'

The world shimmered around me, melting away in drips of colour that muddled into yellow. Sound wavered, the discordant music from before returning, the air shifting to that suffocatingly sweet scent. There was no sun on my skin, no breeze playing with my hair. Even the ballroom Tarina had created fell away. Instead, I stood upon stone ground, several spots darkened by stains of blood. Limestone walls stretched high, rows of benches behind, empty of the audience I'd always seen crammed into them.

'You could have died painlessly.' Tarina's red gown was now starkly out of place, its finery disturbing in the simplicity of The Den. She'd shifted to stand beside Jaxon, her hand on his shoulder. The position could've been mistaken as loving. To me, it only seemed possessive.

Jaxon was pale, his skin beading with sweat, his lips twisted into a grimace. Whatever Illusion Tarina was showing him, it was nothing like the ones I'd been cast into. It was some sort of punishment.

Chiara? Are you all right?

I startled at Callum's voice. Fear's hold slipped. *You're here.*

I couldn't let you be fooled by such a poor version of me, could I? We both know I'm far more handsome than that impostor. Amusement flickered and my lips curled upwards. *Now go capture yourself a goddess, my queen.*

'You dare smile at my offer of mercy?' Tarina bit out.

I dragged my focus back to the goddess. 'You offer nothing but lies.'

Tarina laughed. 'That is the very thing mortals crave. Lies to turn drudgery into excitement. To convince lovers that they are better than they are. You are no different. What lies do you tell your false king to keep him by your side?'

She meant the words to hit hard. Instead, my smile grew. 'Callum knows me. All of me. And he loves me anyway. Did Dearil know all of *you*, Tarina? Did he love you even when you sided with Vitus to lock him up?'

Tarina's expression twisted. 'You know nothing of that.'

'Oh, I think I do. I know you were soul-bonded. That you betrayed Dearil, yet still seemed to return to him time and time again.' There was a telling twitch to her lips that betrayed her displeasure. 'And I know you birthed his child.'

Her lips spread into a cold smile. 'I did, and I made sure that child died.'

'I'm sure you did,' I said with an equally cold smile.

I shifted a step forward. Tarina's eyes glowed yellow, and a mortal ambled forward, reaching for me. They were no longer dressed in finery, nor did they carry the flush of health in their cheeks. No, this mortal was pale and gaunt, her rags hanging off bones that were barely protected by any flesh. As the woman reached for me with dirt-coated fingers, I took her wrist and twisted, forcing her body away from me. Expressionless, the woman fought against my hold, shoving as her free hand reached for my throat.

'Careful, girl,' Tarina warned, her amusement coiling through her voice. 'These mortals are not like Vitus's Ankurans. They still live. If you do not want to harm them, you will—'

The woman's wrist cracked as I violently twisted it, fracturing bone and forcing her back to me. I wrapped my arm around her neck, pulling tight. Her body jerked in my hold, but I didn't let go until she fell limp.

Easing her onto the ground, I met Tarina's shocked stare. 'Don't mistake me for soft. I'd rather these mortals live, but they don't need to. If their deaths save countless others, so be it.'

'If your goal is me, you have no hope in—'

I lunged forward, seizing hold of her distraction. She stumbled back a step, nostrils flaring and a choked scream rattling from her lips. Around us, the mortals cried out in united agony. Her eyes pulsed with furious power as she tipped her head down to where my dagger sunk into her chest, yellow-threaded blood swallowed up by her gown.

Somewhere outside, a wail rang out, its sharp cry not of this realm. I didn't pay it any heed as I smiled, Tarina's blood soaking my skin.

'Y-you stabbed me.'

I withdrew a third blade. I'd packed as many as I could hide on my person. Entering a fight with a goddess unarmed was foolish. 'It might not kill you, but even goddesses aren't impervious to pain.'

Her cheeks darkened with rage as she yanked the blade free. More blood spurted, some of it spattering over where Jaxon sat. He didn't react to it. 'Your insolence has gone too far,' she snarled, blood painting her lips. 'I will grant you no freedom from death. No mercy from suffering. I will—'

The third dagger pierced her throat, hard enough to send her tumbling back onto the stone. Her scream was little more than a wheeze as she lay there, eyes filled with pain and fury. Another wail rose from outside, then another, far-off sounds of fighting filtering into the chaos inside.

Again, I ignored it. Ignored everything but the ailing goddess before me.

Her hand rose weakly, fingers snapping. Mortals rushed at me.

I sighed, not bothering to reach for where a small knife was stashed in my boot. This was going to be tedious. I reached for the soul-bond. *I hope you realise I'm making this harder for myself because of you.*

Liar. I think you're growing to care about our kingdom.

It wasn't fear that raced through me at Callum's use of *our kingdom*. It was a possessiveness I hadn't known I was capable of. He was right. These mortals were mine to protect against the gods. I might not be at all adept at lawmaking and political manoeuvring, but this – fighting to protect instead of simply to kill – I could do.

They were all weak, likely from the months they must've spent under Vitus's captivity. The first three fell with a solid blow to the head. The fourth, a burlier man whose girth hadn't quite left him with the malnutrition, lunged at me with yellow-coated eyes while I dealt with another. I slammed my arm into his throat, driving him down so that his head cracked against the stone.

I winced at the sharp sound of it. *How angry will you be if I give some of these mortals slightly more permanent injuries?*

As long as you remain unharmed, then I'll forgive anything.

I drove my fist into the nose of a dark-haired woman, bone cracking and blood flying as she fell back. An adolescent took her place, fingers reaching for my throat. I got to him first, elbow driving into his temple. *And if I am harmed?*

There was a chuckle of amusement. *You can't expect me to believe you're in any danger from a group of half-starved mortals.*

A little more concern might be nice, I grumbled back, my disobedient lips still smiling.

I am very concerned, Captain. I took down another, slamming my foot into their knee before driving their face downwards. I felt slightly guilty at the way they seemed to bounce at the impact. *After all, I'm missing out on quite a show. My wellbeing might take a toll.*

I meant concerned for me.

Another ripple of amusement. The last mortal fell easily as I drove their head into the limestone wall, their eyes rolling upwards as they collapsed. The amusement faded as I turned back to Tarina, who was struggling up onto her elbow, her hand closed around the dagger in her throat. *I'm always concerned for you. Especially when you enter dangerous situations with no backup.*

You knew I was coming here.

I thought you were going with a legion of soldiers at your back. Where's your backup?

I might have left parts of our plan out when I'd relayed it to Callum. *Jaxon was my backup.*

Is that why you were just fighting alone? Doesn't seem like he did his job.

I really needed to find out how much he could see through the bond. *Quiet. You're distracting me.*

Tarina's eyes locked with mine, burning with fury. Her mouth opened, but nothing except choked sounds came out. I strode over to her, slamming my boot onto her shoulder and knocking her back down. Bending, I closed my fingers over where hers held the dagger, driving it deeper as I smiled. 'Rather shameful to be brought down by a mortal weapon, isn't it?'

Her eyes blazed with power, hand lifting to reach for me. Yellow flared over her skin. Before she could cast me into another Illusion, I grasped hold of a handful of her hair, lifting her head and slamming it down three times. Something crunched on the third blow, her features slackening and eyes rolling back.

'Deana,' I called, not rising from Tarina's side. I inspected her wounds – the daggers driven through her, the blood beginning to pool beneath her head. She was still definitely alive, the power in me buzzing at the feel of another god's power. Could I survive a wound like that? Both would've been fatal, even for a halfling.

But for a god, unless they were made with the god-killer Vitus possessed, or if the balance between powers was unsettled, they would recover. Slowly, painfully, but it would happen. A chill skated over me, forming goose bumps on my skin. All those wounds I'd suffered. The battles I'd fought and the scars I'd collected. The fear I'd battled against until death was simply a fact of life rather than something to avoid. If I was the same as Tarina and the rest of the gods, then that death that had plagued me every time I'd stepped onto the battlefield had never been real.

Perhaps that was why I'd always found it so difficult to fear. At least, until it was someone else whose life was in danger.

I glanced towards the door. It remained tightly shut, no sign of Deana. Frowning, I stepped towards it, the sounds of fighting closer now. The wails of what must have been one of the gods' creatures were more frenzied, but it wasn't just those cries that rang free. There were mortal shouts out there, too.

And if Deana was caught up in it, there was no telling how long it would take her to reach us. Tarina would regain consciousness at some point. I didn't think I'd take her down so easily again. I started for the exit, careful not to tread on any of the unconscious bodies.

A sharp inhale halted my steps. Whirling, my eyes found Jaxon. He still sat, legs crossed and eyes coated with hazy yellow, every part of him taut. Tears wet his cheeks as his chest rose and fell in desperate breaths. Whatever Illusion Tarina had trapped him in, he didn't seem capable of breaking free as I had.

Pain lanced through his expression. I hesitated. I needed to find Deana – to get those chains onto Tarina. That was the priority. Once Tarina was sorted, I could help Jaxon.

I almost started for the door again when I spied his hand. It was moving, creeping towards the ground towards the dagger I'd thrown earlier. His fingers closed around the hilt. Muscles strained in his body, as though he were fighting himself for control.

This was different from those I'd seen slice their own throat. Jaxon didn't seem to be lulled into a sense of safety by the Illusion, ending his life as he dreamt of being wrapped in a lover's arms. No, this seemed more like he was fighting the Illusion to pick up that blade. Like whatever he saw was too painful, and the only way he could think to get out of it was to drive that dagger through his own chest.

The blade rose. My pulse quickened. Jaxon might've been less prone to injuries than full mortals, but he was only a halfling. A knife to the heart would kill him as surely as it would a mortal.

'Dammit,' I hissed as I lunged for him. I'd have to trust Deana to fend for herself. 'You'd better hope Tarina doesn't wake up anytime soon.'

My body slammed into his, both of us toppling to the ground. He didn't let go of the dagger. I reached for his hand, grasping hold of his.

Too late, I remembered his warning – not to touch anyone in an Illusion, lest I be drawn into it myself. Yellow light flashed. There was a flaring of Callum's concern, an annoyed exhale from me, and I was yanked into Jaxon's Illusion.

Chapter Twenty-Seven

I stood in the middle of a marketplace. It was quiet, the crowds that usually populated Alluvite marketplaces nowhere to be seen. Everything was different from what I'd grown up around. Instead of narrow streets opening into a large square, water lapped at the sides of docks, stone buildings keeping low to the ground. Salt laced itself through the wind as the sun shone down.

It was easy to find Jaxon. He was in front of a stall, where the young, pink-cheeked stall owner stood before the rows of fruit that decorated her stall.

I edged past a group of laughing children and tried to call to him. My words were swallowed by the Illusion, dying before they could make a sound.

'How much for these?' I heard Jaxon say as I came closer. He tossed a strange fruit up in the air before catching it. I could see its white flesh, speckled with black seeds, glistening with juice.

'For you?' The girl leant forward, her eyes keen. 'Ten silvers for twelve.'

'How about we say four silvers and call it a day?' Jaxon countered.

The girl tilted her head. 'How about we say ten silvers, and...' Her eyes dropped to the sword at his side. Interest sparked. 'Oh, that's *beautiful*. How much?'

Jaxon's hand dropped to the hilt. I recognised the blade. It was the only one I'd seen him use since the day I'd met him. 'Not for sale, I'm afraid.'

'Gods, I'd sell my whole stall for a piece of work like that.' She looked briefly disappointed before perking back up. 'Is it from the blacksmith's? The one over the eastern hills?'

'It is. The head blacksmith himself made it for me.' Jaxon's tone was fond. 'My husband's nothing short of extraordinary.'

The girl stared at the sword with awestruck eyes. Then, she waved her hand through the air. 'Fine. Take that fruit for free, and I'll consider you putting in a good word for me if I ever come along as payment. I've heard he rarely takes commissions anymore.'

Tossing the fruit again, I saw Jaxon nod. 'You'll want to come before the season's at an end. We'll be moving on to the next town soon enough.'

The girl's shoulders sagged. 'Really? I was hoping to save up for another year or so to get a nice knife for myself.'

Jaxon leant in conspiratorially. 'I'll let you in on a secret. Garrett has a soft spot for sincerity. Tell him why you want it and make it believable. He'll drop the price for you.'

The girl clapped her hands together in delight as Jaxon turned, beginning to whistle a soft tune. 'Thank you, sir!'

He waved a hand over his shoulder. 'Don't worry about it. I'll consider these'—his other hand raised, filled with three more of the fruit—'as payment for the advice.'

I followed behind Jaxon, trying to beat back the Illusion's consumption of my voice as the girl let out a squawk of outrage. It seemed he'd been a swindler even when he'd still retained some semblance of innocence. Every time I attempted to close the distance between us, it only seemed to widen.

Callum? I tried experimentally. Maybe if I could wrench myself out of this Illusion, I could drag Jaxon with me. But there was no reply. The bond was still there, but it was as though Jaxon's Illusion had clamped down on it.

If I couldn't use that to tether me to reality, then I'd have to find a way to force Jaxon to break the Illusion himself.

We walked a trail through wide streets that opened up onto a wider dirt road. It led through rolling hills, farmland filled with lush greenery stretching everywhere. Birds sang their cheerful tunes, the sound raking over my skin. With the view of the sea stretching out to the west and the greenery around us, this seemed as pleasant an Illusion as they came.

But Jaxon hadn't been finding it pleasant. That meant something else was coming.

A small cottage appeared at the bottom of the next hill we climbed. It was a neatly kept structure, white walls surrounded by tidy gardens. Flowers bloomed in varying colours, though purple and yellow seemed to populate most of the garden beds. A stone building out the back billowed smoke from a high chimney. Jaxon's steps quickened as we neared, his whistling switching into excited humming.

We were almost at the front gate when he stopped. The fruit dropped from his hand, bouncing on the dirt before coming to a rest. His hand pressed to his chest as he uttered a single whispered, '*No.*'

And then he was running, his boots kicking up small clumps of dirt. I followed behind, my hand falling to a dagger I knew would be of no help here.

'Garrett!' Jaxon screamed as he pounded up the three steps that led to a partially ajar door. 'Garrett, where are—'

This time, the Illusion didn't keep us separate as Jaxon pulled to a stop. I crashed into his back. He didn't seem to notice as he stood in the doorway, staring down. I looked with him. Red pooled beneath his boots, seeping into the floor.

Jaxon pushed at the door. It creaked as it opened, and gold spilt out to sweep over the blood soaking the ground. I inhaled, nearly stumbling back a step. I knew that light. Knew the rancid scent of roses forced to cover the stench of decay. I instinctively grabbed Jaxon's arm, trying to yank him backwards. To pull him away from whatever lay inside.

But this wasn't just an Illusion. This was a memory – his worst one, dragged from the depths of his mind, so that he would be forced to relive it. And he was in too deep for me to change anything about it.

Jaxon stepped into the golden light. 'Garrett?'

A gurgled gasp met his words. I looked over his shoulder, finding the gods first. Tarina, her yellow eyes sunk deep into the hollow face of an elderly woman. And Vitus, his body belonging to a far more able man, his arm thrust out before him, fingers sunk deep into a man's chest.

The man twisted his head, lilac eyes meeting Jaxon's. Blood dribbled from his mouth as his lips formed the word, *run*.

This, I realised as horror built, was Garrett. And this was the moment Jaxon lost him.

'Never,' Jaxon snarled.

'Darling.' Both Jaxon and I shuddered at his mother's voice, but he didn't take his eyes off Garrett. My heart twisted at the sight, too similar to the moment my own soul-bond had frayed. 'We didn't expect you home just yet. Be a dear and wait a minute while we clean up this little mess.'

'Put Garrett down and get out of our house.' Jaxon's skin began to glow with a yellow light, paler yet brighter than what Tarina conjured. 'Now.'

The body Vitus held was cracked through with golden lines, much like Kane's had been towards the end.

I couldn't stop the soaking of fear and hatred that dripped over me.

The god looked down at Jaxon, then Garrett. 'I do not listen to halflings.' His hand tightened. Garrett spasmed on the end of it, a choked scream coming from between bloody lips. 'Kyrah refused to divine the way to my future success. I warned her I would take her son as payment for her disobedience.' Garrett's mouth opened and closed uselessly. Vitus's smile crept upwards. 'Do not fret, halfling. Your death is not just Kyrah's punishment. It is also the price Tarina requested for her loyalty – freeing her son from the enslavement of his soul-bond.'

'Please, Mother.' Jaxon turned to Tarina. She smiled back at him as he sank to his knees. 'Please. I'll go back with you to your realm. I'll leave Garrett here. Just let him live.'

'Jaxon,' I whispered, but he still did not hear.

Tarina watched him for a few moments, her gaze softening slightly. There was something gentle in her eyes, like a mother telling a child why the dead bird they found wasn't going to fly again. 'This is for the best. You'll see.'

Jaxon whirled. Garrett was so close to us. Enough so that when Vitus ripped his hand free of Garrett's chest, blood spattered over my cheeks. Nausea rose at the bones poking through the hole in Garrett's chest as he collapsed, his body twitching as though it hadn't yet realised what it was missing. The smile did not fall from Vitus's face as he slowly, deliberately, held Jaxon's stare. Fingers bent inwards, the heart he held in his hand crushed in a second.

Jaxon screamed as though it had been his heart in Vitus's hand. There was a burst of light, and then the mortal forms the gods had inhabited dropped to the floor, free of their divine inhabitants.

A cloth lay over the side of a chair, hanging there. Jaxon

launched himself towards it, then towards Garrett's body. He bundled him into his arms as he tried to clean him off. Each wipe smeared blood further down Garrett's cheek, the mess spreading.

My hand fell away from my dagger. This was not the sort of problem I could cut down.

'No,' Jaxon whispered, fingers curling into the cloth as he tried again to clean the mess. A streak of red followed in the cloth's wake. 'This isn't ... it isn't right.'

He tried again and again and again, until the cloth was stained red. I could see the desperation in the movement – the refusal to accept what had happened, even as his soul crumbled to pieces. But no matter how hard Jaxon tried, the blood still remained.

'I'm sorry,' Jaxon moaned, his words broken up by sobs. 'I'm so, so sorry.'

I approached on quiet feet, kneeling by Jaxon's side. 'He's gone, Jaxon.'

This time, the Illusion didn't bother to swallow my words. Jaxon's head whipped up, his eyes flashing furiously. 'Don't you say that. He's fine! He's—'

'He's gone,' I repeated quietly, easing the cloth out of Jaxon's grip. 'It doesn't matter how many times you live through this memory. Garrett is dead. This is all an Illusion.'

Jaxon's body shuddered. 'You're lying. I can do this again. I can be better.'

'You can't. He's been dead for centuries. We need to—'

Jaxon clung tighter to Garrett's body. 'He can't be dead. I can't have existed without him. If I just—'

'Jaxon, stop!' The words rang through the air, startling Jaxon into silence.

I released a frustrated breath. I didn't know what to say to drag him out of his sorrow. This wasn't a physical enemy to fight and break apart. It was Jaxon's own mind. His grief. And I couldn't blame him. How many times would I relive a moment that ended in Callum's death if I thought I might change things?

'I can stay here and make things better.' Hope shone on Jaxon's face as he gently laid Garrett down. 'We'll move to the next town. Find a better place to live.'

The world around us began to shimmer – not with Tarina's painfully bright yellow, but with Jaxon's. As though he was taking this Illusion and twisting it into his own. Into one he could lose himself in for an eternity.

'I'm going to give you a good beating for this when we get out of here,' I muttered, but Jaxon didn't hear me.

The sounds of the marketplace started to trickle back into hearing, accompanied by the salt of the sea. I sensed that if it manifested completely, then it'd be impossible to drag Jaxon back out until we'd seen Garrett's death again. Or, if he did manage to change what had happened, impossible to drag him out at all.

I needed something, anything, to snap him out of this. But I was too similar to Jaxon. Too prone to my own selfishness to know what to say. It would've been far better if another was here. Someone like—

'If you do this, you'll be leaving Deana alone,' I told him.

The marketplace wavered. Jaxon blinked, finally meeting my eyes. 'Deana?'

I nodded. 'She didn't come when I called for her. I've subdued Tarina, but needed the chains. There were sounds of fighting outside. What if something's happened?'

Jaxon hesitated, then glanced down at where his hands were still covered with blood. 'Garrett…'

I made sure to soften my voice this time. 'You know he's dead, Jaxon. But Deana isn't. She's out there. Alive. Are you really going to leave her alone?'

Jaxon flexed his fingers. His shoulders sagged. 'All I wanted was to live peacefully with him. Tarina took that from me.'

I gripped his hand fiercely. 'Then you need to break out of here; you need to show her what—'

Something collided painfully with my side. The world around me broke into pieces as I flew through the air, The Den coming back into existence. I slammed into a wall behind, pain shooting through my shoulder as I crumpled to the ground.

I blinked, struggling to get my bearings. A shadow fell over me, the skirt of a red gown filling my vision. A dagger clattered to the ground before me, soaked in blood. I only had a moment to look at it before it was kicked away from me.

'You are a fool for believing that would be enough to hold me.' Tarina raised the second dagger I'd left buried in her high. 'But there will be plenty to end you.'

The dagger began to move. I braced myself to launch forward. The blade would still drive through me, but I'd knock Tarina off balance at the same time. Then, it'd be a matter of who could bear their pain for the longest. My money was on myself.

Before either of us could do anything, though, a hand clamped around Tarina's wrist. Her nostrils flared with indignation as Jaxon, his expression built with rage and sorrow, twisted sharply. The dagger clattered to the ground as Tarina whirled. I edged around her, coming to stand by Jaxon's side. Surprise flared in her eyes. 'You should not have been able to break free.'

Jaxon's lips twisted into a smile. 'And yet, I did. Tell me, Mother, am I still a disappointment?'

There was something almost sad in Tarina's eyes as she looked at him. 'No, my darling boy.' Her voice was soft. 'You are not a disappointment.'

'I am so relieved to hear that,' Jaxon replied with a smile that said the exact opposite.

Tarina's hand dropped away. Her expression turned from melancholy to bitter regret. Her fingers lifted, and a dusting of harsh yellow washed over them.

'You foolish boy. You should have just stayed in that memory. At least that way, I would have known my power was still greater than yours.' She sighed. 'But now, you are a threat. I despise threats. A pity. I thought I would have at least one of my children remain alive.'

'You're in luck.' Jaxon unsheathed his sword, its ring clear in the quiet air. I didn't gather any weapons. I'd had my moment with Tarina. This was not my revenge to take. 'You're going to have two who survive this war.'

Tarina blinked, her forehead crinkling. 'You speak nonsense. I eliminated all other threats. There were none as weak as you.'

Jaxon's smile was a vicious thing. I smiled with him as I shifted back, giving him space. 'Oh, I'm not talking about the weakest of your children. The very opposite.' He swung his free hand towards me. 'I haven't formally introduced you. This is Chiara Halnea.'

'I know who it is, insolent ch—'

'Did you not question how she broke your Illusions?'

Tarina frowned. 'She belongs to Dearil. He must have taught her some trick. Wards, perhaps.'

'Except we both know Dearil knew no wards to counteract your Illusions. The only ones who've ever been able to consistently break them are your own blood.' Jaxon's smile grew at the growing fury in Tarina's face. 'This, Mother dearest, is my sister. Your daughter.'

I saw the exact moment she recognised the traits she shared with me. It was in the way her eyes tightened at the corners, the tensing of her jaw. The utter hatred as she met my gaze.

'No,' she seethed, staggering back a step as yellow flickered at her hands.

Jaxon's own Gift rose, and the power in me tried to rise with it. It seemed calmer, somehow – still not settled, but perhaps more comfortable in my skin. As though it would follow most of my commands, provided it found them agreeable.

'No,' Tarina said again, her voice rising in a shriek. '*No*. That is not possible! That child is *dead*. I would not have allowed a child of mine to live. This cannot be!'

Yellow spindled under our feet, curling over the prone bodies on the ground. My nose wrinkled at the stench of sugar that rose with the power. Neither Jaxon nor I were yanked into Illusions, though. Tarina's power was faltering under her rage. And Jaxon had his own power. Where Tarina's power pulsated, his glowed steadily, sheets of bright light washing over the cracks of yellow. Yet it wasn't with that power that he attacked – the power he'd gained through the mother he detested.

Instead, he launched forward, thrusting his sword through Tarina's chest. She screamed, her hands pulling in vain at the blade, blood dripping from the wounds in her hands as he shoved her to the floor.

'That,' Jaxon said, voice hard with hatred, 'was for Garrett.' He wrenched the sword out before plunging it down again. This time, it speared her throat, and Tarina lost consciousness.

I stared at the goddess's body, nudging her leg with my toes. 'I thought I was the violent one.'

'Don't worry,' Jaxon said, fatigue slowing his words as he knelt and carefully wiped his sword – the one Garrett had crafted him – upon her dress. 'I remember you tearing out Liam's throat with your bare hands. I'm sure you can still claim the title.'

'We should find De—'

The door burst open behind. I spun as Jaxon jumped to his feet, both of us tensing. Deana rushed in, chains wrapped around her arms and panic on her face. She stumbled to a halt at the sight of us, took one look at the bodies between us and sighed. 'I thought you said this would be easy.'

'Surprisingly, it was,' Jaxon said with a grimace, placing his sword back in its scabbard.

'Easy is not two dozen bodies.' She stepped over one of them, careful not to tread on their outflung limbs. 'This looks like Chiara's handiwork. Am I right?'

I folded my arms defensively. 'They're not dead.'

The shock in her face was almost insulting. She wove her way through the unconscious mortals. I shifted away as she neared, the sickly power emanating from the chains rolling over my skin in oily waves. They were as horrific as I remembered them being, filled with a warped portion of the gods' powers. Like the bars to Dearil's cell in the godly realm or the god-killer Vitus possessed, there was an unnatural feel to the air in their presence. Deana made quick work of wrapping Tarina in the chains.

'If it's this easy to subdue a god, we should have no problem,' she said once she'd finished, the chains clinking as she let Tarina fall back to the ground. The goddess's head cracked against the ground. With the amount of blood seeping from her wounds and that nasty blow, I doubted she'd be rising anytime soon, particularly with the chains in place.

'It was this easy because Tarina didn't know the whole truth. She thought her previous failures with the Illusions were nothing more than a temporary problem with her power. Her arrogance got her caught. That, and she underestimated the efficiency of a dagger.' I bent, gathering one of the bloodied daggers from the ground. 'The next time we face a god, it won't be so easy.'

'Won't Vitus underestimate us, too?'

'No.' I slid the dagger away. 'He's arrogant, and he thinks mortals are weak, but he learns quickly. He's more powerful than Tarina. He'd never have come with so few under his control, either. When we face Vitus, we'll be doing so with far more enemies to contend with.'

'Ah.' She turned to Jaxon, then frowned.

The Divine

He flinched as she stormed towards him, her eyes scanning over the blood soaking his clothes. 'I can explain. It's all from—'

'Be quiet,' she snapped. She grasped him by the back of his neck and yanked him down, their lips connecting. I busied myself with pretending to check on one of the unconscious mortals as Jaxon melted into her kiss. He needed someone like Deana – a person who'd call him out on his bullshit rather than let it slide.

It seemed we were the same in that.

Only when I heard Deana beginning to launch into a lecture about the state of him did I turn back around. 'What took you so long?'

She winced, one of her hands fisting the collar of Jaxon's tunic as though she intended to haul him back to the palace. 'I ran into some unexpected trouble.'

'Ankurans?' I guessed, spotting a few golden stains upon her pale skin. 'I heard fighting.'

'No. Well, yes, but they were easy enough to handle. It was the ones who came after that were more ... difficult.' She shoved back strands of hair matted with golden blood. Her expression had worry curdling in me. The mixture of concern and consternation. 'We have a problem at the palace. Lena came to fetch me.'

I frowned. We'd provided Lena with our location only in case of absolute emergency. Given what I knew about the commander, she wasn't the sort to come find us unless it was a true crisis. 'Has the palace been attacked? Ankurans? Scythes? Something else?'

'Not quite,' Deana hedged, her consternation growing. 'It seems we have guests.' She met my eyes. 'Three of the divine variety. All here to see you.'

Chapter Twenty-Eight

We waited for reinforcements to arrive from the palace before heading back. Jaxon took charge of hauling Tarina to the palace cells, where he'd carve an extra set of wards around to make certain there was no chance of anyone slipping in to help free her. Commander Lena went with him, eyeing the unconscious goddess with a mixture of disbelief, awe and fear in her eyes. That same look was present as she glanced between me, Jaxon and Deana. It seemed bringing down a goddess had significantly raised our standing.

I quickened my steps to come up to Deana's side as we walked the length of a corridor. Most people were asleep, the night seeming heavy with all that'd happened. More than a few cries or whimpers crawled out from behind closed doors.

'Nightmares are a common plague amongst most here,' Deana explained as we rounded a corner. 'Though hopefully some will lessen once we reveal we've removed our first god from the playing board.'

I nodded, but I wasn't hopeful. Even if word was spread about Tarina being brought down, most wouldn't believe it. Gods were storybook legends. Creatures made of unimaginable power. And we were mortals.

Or, *they* were mortals. I was ... something else.

Callum? I whispered down the bond.

There was no reply. *He must be asleep*, I told myself sternly. He'd be exhausted out on the frontlines, and he'd spent most of the previous night with me. Jumping to extreme conclusions would only make things worse.

Even so, a sense of disquiet chased me down the corridors as Deana led the way. After our third turn, I asked, 'You didn't have them taken to Callum's receiving chambers?'

'Lena had them wait outside the palace.'

I grinned. 'I bet Evania loved that.'

'Given how pale Lena was when she found me, I can only imagine. I asked her to lead them to the throne room. Figured you'd rather not have them in the receiving chambers. Which, as you should be aware, also belong to *you* as the future queen.'

I sighed in lieu of arguing as we strode down a wide corridor ending in a set of double doors. Six guards stood in front of them, each paler than the last. They clutched their weapons with trembling hands, staring at the doors with fear.

Deana fell a half step back. Instead of summoning one of her weapons, she adjusted the fine garrotte she always wore around her neck. She likely didn't trust her Gift when the one who'd given it to her was in the room. 'I think it best we treat them as nobility.'

'Meaning?' I asked as I glanced over my shoulder at her, raising my brows.

'Meaning that you need to remind them who's in charge of this kingdom, and I'll be there to remind them who's guarding your back.'

I hesitated before the doors, staring up at their looming height. 'I don't have Callum's patience.'

Deana snorted, and one of the guards glanced at her with surprise. 'Callum doesn't have patience.'

'Exactly.'

She prodded me in the back, pushing me closer to the doors. 'Please don't pretend you're concerned about insulting a few goddesses.'

I folded my fingers around the dagger still wet with Tarina's blood. 'Oh, I'm not concerned about that. I'm more worried I might do something we'll regret, like take out the few potential allies we have.' Even though Evania had already made it clear there would be no allying with mortals.

'Go ahead. I've already made a bet with Jaxon that at least one of them will be leaving with some bruises.'

I placed my hand on the door. 'When did you even have time to do that?'

'Just before Lena came to help with transporting Tarina. I plan to win this bet, though, so try to hold off for a few minutes.'

I shoved the door open and strode into the room before I gave in to the urge to ask what else the pair had bet on. Something told me I really didn't want to know.

The throne room was as hideously large as I remembered it, with its white walls and floors, alcoves covered with draped red curtains. The chandelier hung high above, sending dancing arrays of candlelight over the floors. I didn't look down. If I did, I might've found myself checking for the remnants of blood from the massacre that'd occurred here – the one that had started with Cassie's death and ended with Vitus imprisoning my father.

My boots clacked against the marble as I strode for the dais, ignoring the pointed cough that came from the left. The goddesses were visitors in Callum's kingdom. *My* kingdom. They would wait until I deigned to grant them my attention. Deana followed behind, her steps quiet to my purposefully loud ones. A shadow to my presence. A ruler and her guard.

The Divine

The thought no longer choked me. The interactions with those in the infirmary and battle with Tarina had cemented things for me. This kingdom belonged to me and Callum. It didn't matter if I was a god or mortal, or something else entirely. No one had a right to dictate what happened to the people in this kingdom except for us.

I planted myself in one of the two thrones. From what Callum had told me, King Kane had intended for the smaller one to be more submissive. For the queen who'd been forced into a marriage she didn't want to remain as a possession rather than a ruler in her own right.

Callum had switched out that throne at some point during my absence. Gone was the dusty seat that'd remained vacant for too long. This throne was made of silver, the back formed by twisted strands of metal that speared into the air. A throne of wickedness, designed for a ruler made of the same.

It was perfect.

I twisted my lips into a smile, crossing my legs and reclining in the throne. I didn't look at the second. Didn't let myself think about the quiet of the bond.

'Well?' The word cut through the space, its echo almost as sharp as the daggers at my side. My eyes fell upon Evania first. Her features were ridged with indignation, her power pulsing upon her skin.

'Is this how mortals greet the divine?' she demanded as she strode forward, stopping when Deana shifted.

My smile grew sharper. 'This is how a queen greets guests.' I tilted my head as I stared down at her. 'If you'd prefer, I could greet you as enemies. I can assure you that you would not enjoy that.'

Evania inhaled sharply, her hands fisting at her side. 'You dare to—'

A firm hand on her shoulder quieted her, the skin there twisted and malformed from long-healed burns. Evania bristled as Kerta stepped forward. Her long hair sparked flames along their lengths. She let go of Evania, inclining her head in a far more respectful greeting than her soul-bonded, before she began to swiftly move her hands through a series of shapes.

A third woman stood a distance away from Kerta and Evania. Her hair, the colour of wheat, hung in fine braids almost to her waist. She was shorter than the other two goddesses, but was broad of shoulder and strong featured. Her eyes, a gentle lilac – the same colour as Garrett's had been in the Illusion, I realised – seemed to ripple like water might as they met mine. She wasn't anyone I'd met, but the power in me whispered through my body in quiet recognition of its kin.

This was the goddess who had refused Vitus's order to divine the future for him, who had paid the price with her son.

'You must be Kyrah?'

The goddess inclined her head. 'I am.' Her voice sounded like hundreds of whispers woven together, filled with unimaginable power and hidden depths. 'And you are the child that should not be.'

I raised my brows as Kerta's signing stopped abruptly, the other two goddesses turning to stare at Kyrah with furrowed brows.

Deana spoke before I could, her voice the same icy tone I'd often heard her use whenever Jaxon disrespected Callum. 'You will address her as Your Majesty.'

I didn't protest the title or point out that Callum and I weren't married. Now was not the time to shy away from what my future might be, if I was to survive this war.

Evania scoffed. 'If you think the divine will ever address a mortal like—'

Kyrah's skirts rustled as she dropped to a knee, her arm crossing her chest and head bowing. In the folds of her dress, far less extravagant than that which Evania wore, tiny specks of violet light seemed to pulse. 'I apologise. I meant no offence, Your Majesty.'

I stared at the top of her bowed head. This was ... unexpected.

'Kyrah,' Evania hissed, reaching for the other goddess. 'This is not acceptable. We are gods. She is a halfling.'

'I rather like it.' I withdrew one of my daggers, pressing its tip to the arm of the throne and beginning to twist it. I'd had enough of the gods looking down on me. If we were going to have a productive conversation, they needed to know who was in charge. 'You're in my kingdom. If you wish to speak, you can do the same.'

Evania's cheeks flushed, her hands balling at her sides. Kerta watched me carefully from behind, her flame-red eyes seeming to test me as Evania says, 'This impertinence will not—'

The dagger stopped. 'Kneel,' I said, voice dropping as the air seemed to chill with the cold ire in it. 'Or you will leave this kingdom.'

Her flush crawled down her neck. 'We are *gods*. We bow to no halfling.'

My smile fell away. It seemed some encouragement was needed. I reached inside for the power I'd been reluctant to touch until now. This time, it didn't rush forward in a wave of fury, desperate to crush any in sight. It curled around my fingers, the sting of the wards little more than a distant scalding now. Silver spread through the room in sharp lines, spearing straight for Evania. It didn't touch her – not yet. Instead, it wrapped in a tight circle around her. A cage fit for a goddess.

The sight thrilled me. I hadn't realised how much I'd missed wielding my Gift – the sensation of rightness that rolled through me. And now that the power wasn't fighting against me and I wasn't fighting against it – it felt exactly the same as my Gift did. Still violent. Still a little feral. But then, so was I.

Kerta shifted, a sword materialising in her hand, her hair igniting. Deana shifted with her, her fingers curling around the sword at her side. A warning that she wouldn't stand idly by if anyone attacked – even if that attacker was the goddess who'd granted her power.

'I do not care what you are,' I said as I rose to my feet, my steps the only sound other than the ring of my voice as I strode down the stairs. 'Nor do I care who you think you bow to. This is my kingdom. My realm. The realm *you* abandoned with your apathy. You should be grateful to kiss the feet of the lowest amongst us for what your inaction has cost.' I smiled, cold and sharp. 'So, you will kneel. You will obey my commands while you are here. And you will not speak of mortals or halflings with that sort of disdain again.'

A floral scent rose, chokingly strong. Before it could overtake the room, though, that of smoke and jasmine swallowed it whole. The silver intensified and Kerta made a sound that might've been a curse if she'd had the ability to speak. Her sword disappeared in a blaze of light as she reached for Evania.

All it took was a single touch from Kerta for Evania's power to dwindle, the pink that had failed to overtake my silver disappearing. Rapid signs were exchanged, Kerta's sharp and urgent, Evania's angry and abrupt. Kerta signed something that had Evania's hands dropping as she swung towards me, her eyes wide as she looked down at the wards.

Wards that were no longer golden, but completely silver.

I could have sworn the power felt smug at the goddesses' shock.

'That's impossible,' Evania breathed, shaking her head as Kerta sank to a knee. 'You are a halfling. Even if you claim Dearil's power, those wards cannot be destroyed by one with mortal blood. You are—'

'A child who should not exist,' Kyrah finished as she rose to her feet. Of the three goddesses, she was the only one who did not look shocked. 'One whose birth was set in fate, but who cheated the end that was to come for her. A girl born of death and lies.'

'You can't mean to suggest that she is a child of two gods.' Evania frowned. 'That is impossible. Gods cannot bear children with each other.'

'Gods do not bear children. It does not mean they cannot. They simply fear the changes a new god might bring. The balances that might be upset.' Kyrah's gaze turned far away, as though she were staring into fragments of the past that no one else could see. 'But Dearil was old and tired. He did not wish to continue in this world for much longer, and he sensed change must come. He made certain that the daughter born of his blood and that of Tarina lived.'

Evania trembled. Whether it was with shock or rage, I didn't know. But she slowly sank to the ground as Kerta reached up to brush her fingers on her arm.

Before I could command them to rise, Jaxon burst into the room with his usual dramatics. He looked around the throne room, brows raised at the goddesses kneeling before me. 'This is a welcome sight.'

Evania launched to her feet, swinging to him and jabbing a finger his way. 'You will speak of this to no one!'

'Don't worry, Evie,' Jaxon said as he moved past, patting her shoulder. He hurried up to my side as her skin sparked with rose power. 'This will be our little secret.'

I strode back up to the throne, sitting down. I didn't turn my attention to the goddesses yet. 'Tarina's secure?'

Jaxon nodded, taking a seat on one of the bottom steps and stretching his arms towards the ceiling. He'd got changed into fresh clothes that might've made me feel embarrassed by my own state of dress were I not used to being dressed in blood. 'All locked up. Still unconscious, too – hopefully she'll stay that way for some time. It'll save the sanity of the guards watching over her.'

'And you're certain the chains will be enough to hold her?'

'They held Dearil, didn't they? Mother's power is nothing compared to his.'

'Good.' I shifted my focus back to the goddesses. 'Speak. What have you come here for?'

Evania looked away, her hands fisted by her side. Kerta stepped forward to sign, Jaxon acting as translator. 'We have come to offer our aid.'

I didn't allow the shock or hope to blossom on my features. 'Oh? What happened to not getting involved with mortals?'

Kerta smiled, her fires subsiding into a warm flickering as she looked to Evania. Her hands moved in complicated patterns. 'Someone reminded us of those that paid the price for our apathy.'

She lifted a hand out. Red light flashed as she reached through the fabric of the realms, withdrawing her hand from the red to reveal the bloodstained doll I'd given Evania. She handed it to Evania, who still refused to look at me like a belligerent child who refused to admit they'd been wrong.

She continued signing, Jaxon keeping up his translations with ease. 'We have lived for so long that living became enduring. We had forgotten that there is more to existence than rules. That those mortal lives, even if they are far shorter than our own, are no less worthy of all the years they should have to live.'

I blinked, shifting my focus to Evania. 'You were the one to change their minds?'

Her rose power curled around her arms, almost seeming to comfort her as she met my eyes. 'I am the goddess of peace. I will find no peace if you manage to survive this and continue with your insolent reminders of the children who died.'

Jaxon twisted, looking up at me from where he sat. 'I'll act as her translator, too. Evania says, "*I was wrong, you were right, and I*

The Divine

actually care quite a bit about the mortal children who—'" He yelped as a rose spark flung into his bare arm, whirling back around to Evania. 'Don't attack me just because I'm exposing the truth!'

Evania sniffed. 'No one asked for your insolent input, boy.'

'Enough,' I said sharply before Jaxon could rile Evania further. 'It's all well and good that you're offering your aid, but we still have no idea where Vitus or any of the other gods are. He's not going to be drawn in by any tricks.'

'I believe I can help with that,' Kyrah offered. 'It may take me some time with the wards Vitus has surely put in place, but I should be able to divine where he will be in the near future.'

'At least one of you has some use, then.' I ignored Evania's bristling as I met Kyrah's lilac gaze. 'What do you need?'

'A quiet space and a sizable bowl of water.'

I nodded. 'That's easy enough to supply. Deana, would you be able to take her up to Callum and my wing? It should be quiet enough there.'

Deana crossed her arm over her chest and bowed her head. 'As you command.' She showed no signs of trepidation of being left alone with a goddess as she moved towards the door, gesturing to Kyrah. 'This way.'

Kyrah turned to follow Deana out, but hesitated, glancing back at Jaxon. 'I am glad you are well, Jaxon. And that you have found someone new.' The goddess looked over at where Deana waited. When she turned back, a soft smile curled her lips. 'I believe Garrett would have liked her.'

Jaxon shifted before quietly saying, 'I think he would've, too.'

Kyrah followed Deana out of the throne room. I turned to Kerta and Evania. 'What do you know of wards?'

'More than you,' Evania said, her haughty tone firmly back in place.

Silver sparked in the air. I bit back a curse. That time, I hadn't meant to release anything. 'I'm sure. And I'm also sure you will be ever so kind as to divulge that information, won't you?'

Evania opened her mouth, likely about to snap something that would break my fraying hold on my temper and power. She met my eyes, however, and snapped her mouth shut, throat working on a swallow, before she said, 'As you wish. What do you need to know?'

'These.' I held up my arms, gesturing to the now silver wards encircling my wrists. 'Explain exactly what they do to a god.'

Kerta nudged Evania forward when the goddess scowled. Not for the first time, I wondered if the realms had somehow mixed them up – Kerta always seemed the far more peaceable of the pair, while Evania's quick temper was perfectly suited to war.

Evania strode over. Jaxon, one foot up on the step, knee bent, grinned up at her from where he held a sword out to block her path. She glared. 'What do you think you are doing?'

'You can't approach my queen without permission.'

Evania's jaw tightened. I didn't interfere. Jaxon might act flippantly most of the time, but he knew how to manipulate like no one else. I suspected he was doing this to make sure the power in the room was firmly established. At last, the goddess looked to me. 'Well?'

I raised my brows at the impatience in her tone. 'I will allow it.'

Evania huffed, her usual light movements more grounded as she stomped her way to me. I held out my arm. Despite her foul mood, she held my wrist gingerly, turning it over to inspect the wards there. At last she said, 'They're almost destroyed.'

'Really?' I pulled my arm back, staring down at them. I could only make out the barest glimmer of gold beneath the silver. 'How?'

'You know nothing, do you?'

'Oh, I don't know about nothing,' I said mildly, tapping the hilt of my dagger. 'I know quite a bit about putting arrogant gods in their place. Just ask Tarina.'

Evania paled and fled back to Kerta's side before saying, 'Wards restrict a god's power for a time, but they always work to maintain balance. If carved onto something that does not live, like a stone wall, it is almost impossible to break them as you do not inject the power *into* the wards, but are instead trying to break through them. But when the wards are carved into flesh, they meld with your blood. For any mortal or halfling, they would need to be burned away within days of being applied, or they would become permanent.'

'And for a god?'

'It is different. Wards will meld with your blood, but they can only dampen a god's power for so long. It is like covering water with a cloth. The cloth will shield the water for only so long before it is soaked and sinks to the bottom. Wards cannot fully restrain a god's power as that would upset the balance for too long.' She eyed the markings. 'I suspect they began to crumble the day they were carved into you. Using your power would have quickened that breaking.'

I nodded. The first time I'd noticed the silver had been when I'd accidentally accessed the soul-bond to drag myself out of the Illusion. It was my divinity that had allowed me to break through them before Dearil had even done anything to make me believe they could be broken. Every time that I'd used my power since – when Dearil had died, when I'd fought with the army and later with Tarina – the silver had grown.

'If you had accepted Dearil's power as your own straight away, the wards would have broken on the spot,' Kerta signed.

'Then I can access my power now?' I flexed my fingers, hope building. Perhaps reuniting with Callum would happen sooner than I'd thought. The power was friendlier, though it still hadn't quite settled. It might be enough to take me to him. 'Travel through the fabric of the realms?'

'*No,*' Evania snapped, so sharply that I jerked in surprise. She huffed, running her hands down her pristinely kept gown. 'You should not do that.'

Kerta's fingers moved in quick patterns. 'The transfer of a god's power takes time to settle. To use it now is … inadvisable. Give it a week or so. It seems you have only recently begun to accept the power. If you were to try now, it would act unpredictably. You might end up buried underground, or in the middle of the sea. Worst case, you might end up in the more dangerous parts of the godly realms or at Vitus's feet.'

A chill swept through me as I remembered the rocks I'd seen the time I'd visited the godly realm, their grey surfaces melded with the bleached bones of forgotten gods.

Evania shook her head before I could speak. 'No. The worst case is you become unravelled by the fabric of the realm instead, if you become stuck between the godly and mortal realm. Until you are sure you have a full grasp on your power, you must not try to shift yourself using it.'

I eyed the silver wards. 'Fine. I will wait for Kyrah to divine Vitus's location.'

'She said a week,' Evania snapped. 'Kyrah will have the location in days.'

'I will wait for Kyrah to divine the location,' I repeated, more firmly. 'A week is time we don't have to spare. Once she has that, we will meet with the army on the frontlines. I trust you both have access to enough power to transport yourselves?'

'We can take one more each,' Kerta signed.

I nodded. 'Good. Jaxon and Deana will come.'

A few days. That was all I had to wait, and then I'd be with Callum again.

Chapter Twenty-Nine

The gentle calling of my name roused me from my sleep. I jerked upwards, yanking a dagger from under my pillow and shoving the blankets off my legs. The bedchamber was saturated in darkness, making even the small table next to the bed difficult to see. Calming my breathing, I listened for any warning sounds of where the intruder was. There were none.

The rug tickled my bare feet as I crept across the room. There was still a trace of incense in the room, the candle that burned it only recently gone out. Yanking the curtain open, I whirled, arm cocking back to throw the dagger at the intruder as moonlight and torchlight from below streamed in.

Exhaling, I scanned the room once more. A remnant of a dream that had chased me into wakefulness, perhaps? It had been a long night, sleep as elusive as always. Running a hand over my face, I sighed before heading back to the bed.

I was just about to settle in when it came again. *Chiara, are you awake?*

This time, I didn't yank the dagger back out. Instead, I smiled. *I am now.*

I'm sorry. I shouldn't have called.

I shifted onto my side, folding an arm under my head as I stared across the moon-dappled room. *No. I don't need sleep. I need you.*

Even you need sleep, Captain. I can practically hear you yawning.

I clamped my lips closed as a yawn threatened to burst out at that moment. Skirting past my tiredness, I asked, *Tell me you're safe.*

I'm fine. We engaged with Tizan's soldiers.

I frowned. *You didn't tell me you were going into a battle.*

I figured you had enough to worry about with Tarina.

I made sure to send every piece of my disapproval down the bond.

Callum ignored it. *They're all either dead or captured, him included.* He sighed, the sound heavy. *We lost half of our forces.*

The guilt that weighed down his words settled heavily on my shoulders. *You'd better not be blaming yourself for that again.*

A sigh whispered down the bond, and the ache in my chest grew. I wanted that sigh to rustle my hair. For his arm to curl around my waist and pull me to his chest. For me to smooth away the lines I could picture carving themselves into his brow as he took on deaths that weren't his to bear.

A few more days, I reminded myself. We could last that long.

I'm the king. Every death is because of some miscalculation I made. A failure for something I didn't put in place. It is my responsibility to take on all these deaths so no one else has to.

I was quiet for some time, Callum's words occupying my mind. There was a darkness leaking down the bond – a sense of despondency I hadn't sensed from Callum before. At last, I said, *I lost over four hundred of our soldiers that day I almost lost control, remember?*

I know, he whispered.

The Divine

If I'd accepted Dearil's power earlier, then we might not have lost any of those lives. There was a girl – Amara – who died. She was no older than sixteen, with a brother waiting for her at home. She'd thanked me a few days before. Apparently, I'd saved her town when I was Captain. In the end, though, she still died, right in front of my eyes. I curled my fingers into the fabric of my pillow, remembering Amara's brilliant smile and innocent features. How quickly that light in her eyes had faded when the Ankurans snapped her neck. *And I couldn't save her because I didn't allow myself to take Dearil's power as my own.*

A burst of anger came down the bond, its edgings of concern enough to let me know Callum wasn't truly angry at me. *It wasn't your fault.*

Perhaps. Perhaps not. I rolled onto my back, eyes finding the ceiling. It was painted in shadows, the carved cornices hidden from view. *My point is, we remember their faces. Remember their names and their stories. But we do not allow ourselves to drown in their deaths. Not when there are living people who need you – need us – to be at our best. Those deaths belong to the gods who caused them, but the living – their lives belong to us.*

Quiet fell, broken only by my breaths and the far-off murmur of the guards on patrol. Then Callum spoke. *When did you become so wise?*

Maybe it came with Dearil's power. I've never been particularly wise in the past.

I can attest to that. I pictured flicking him hard on his nose. The answering chuckle told me he'd received the image. *There were no problems after you captured Tarina?*

None. Tarina's currently enjoying the finest accommodation Naruzia has to offer.

Has anyone told you you're rather impressive? Callum asked. *That's the first goddess to go down in this war.*

I slung an arm over my eyes – finding the absolute darkness allowed me to picture Callum's face better. *Jaxon was of some use.*

That's more of a shock than you bringing down Tarina.

I laughed, but my amusement faded quickly. *We'll have to face Vitus soon.*

I know, Callum said. *And we will win.*

If confidence alone was enough to win a battle, we'd already be the victors.

After the war is done, what do you want to do? Callum asked.

I blinked. 'After' was a concept I'd never let myself think about. It had always been the next battle. The next enemy. The next war.

But if we did bring Vitus down, then after would be waiting. The thought sent a chill through me. I removed my arm from my eyes, blinking haziness away from the pressure I'd been applying.

Callum must have felt my unease because he asked, *What is it?*

I struggled to string the words into a sentence, but Callum waited, as he always had. *It was terrifying having centuries as a halfling – years stretching out that I'd have to fill. But now ... as a god, it's closer to eternity. What if we don't defeat Vitus? What if you never inherit his power, and I'm forced to face it all alone? If you don't take on his power, you'll die even if Vitus doesn't kill you. And I ... I will live.* I swallowed, terror drying the inside of my mouth. *I've never been good at living. Surviving. Enduring. But never living.*

You have the time to figure it out. Don't dwell on all the what-ifs. We will win this war, and we will both survive. His tone shifted to teasing. *Think of all the havoc you could wreak in that time. All the new adventures you can have.*

I pursed my lips, considering for a few moments before saying, *It seems terribly boring.*

I'm sure you would find spectacular new ways to wind up in trouble.

I sighed, my arm flopping out to the side of the bed Callum

should've occupied with me. There were traces of him scattered about the room – in the books left on the table to the left that I'd never touched. The neat lining up of a wardrobe I know I'd left a mess. The faintest traces of cedar and the coming rain that lingered in the air. But it still wasn't enough. *I don't want a future without you in it. If you fall, I fall.*

Chiara—

No. I jerked upright, a burst of fury clenching my hands into fists. *Don't tell me to keep on living. To exist in whatever ruins are left if Vitus wins. Not when I'm certain you'd make the same choice if you were in my place.*

That power you have – it's unlikely there's another suitable host for it. At least Vitus Gifted mortals. Dearil never did the same.

The realms can fall to ruins, balance be damned. I love you, Callum, and I have no desire to see a world without you in it.

The silence stretched on for so long that I reached for the bond, my pulse threatening to quicken until I managed to grasp onto it. *Damn. I was going to wait until we'd reunited and things have settled down like normal people do, but now I don't think I can wait. Patience isn't amongst either of our virtues.*

No. I drew out the word slowly, my heart beginning to pound for an entirely different reason. *It isn't.*

Besides, I don't need any more time to think about this. There was a nervousness to Callum's voice that curled my lips into a smile. I liked his vulnerability as much as I did his wickedness. More, perhaps, because I knew this was a side of him he'd only ever shown me. *I have admired you since before you looked at me with anything but hatred. And I have loved you since the moment you drove a dagger into my shoulder that night in the tavern and smiled.*

I laughed. *I think that's the moment I realised something was very wrong with you. That's not a normal reaction to getting stabbed.*

I think it is when it's done so spectacularly. I loved the amusement in his voice, yet I hated the way it drew out my desire when he was so far away from me. *I will love you tonight, and tomorrow, and for whatever eternity we have left.* My breath caught. *Chiara Halnea, will you do me the honour of becoming my queen?*

The sheets I held crinkled as my fingers tightened. *From what I've seen in the palace, most seem to believe I'm Naruzia's queen already. Which I suspect you played a large part in.*

I didn't ask you to become a queen, I asked you to become my *queen, whatever that means. If this all finishes and you decide you want a life away from Naruzia, I'll abdicate the throne and run away with you. If you decide you want to join the gods, I will... Well, I'm not sure what role I can play, but I'll be by your side. Whatever you want, I will do it, so long as it is with you.*

A flush spread over my cheeks and down my neck, my chest burning with emotions I'd once never dreamt I could feel – terror, anticipation, elation, hope. Love. All because of one man. All for one man.

There was only one answer I could give. *Yes*, I breathed. *Yes, I will be yours. Now and for however long we have left.* I paused before adding, *And I don't want to run away. Not anymore. I want to learn to rule.*

An exhaled breath met my answer, followed by laughter that teetered on nervous. I imagined Callum raking his fingers through his hair, his eyes bright with relief and the same love that glowed down the bond. *Thank the gods. It would've been rather embarrassing for you to say no after I've told every soldier I've come across that you are to be coronated once this is over.*

I blinked. *You what?*

You. As queen. Imagine all the documents I'd have to rewrite if you decided to—

Idiot, I said with fond exasperation.

Only when it comes to you.

I shifted, turning to stare out at the moon. It lit Alluvite in a pearly glow, the streets' shadows standing little chance against it. Wisps of clouds drifted in a lazy meander, having no rush to get anywhere. *I expect a ring.*

Giving orders already? There was a smile in his words. *And what sort of ring shall I be bestowing upon Your Majesty?*

Anything but gold. The only place I could stand that colour was in his hair. I wouldn't have our betrothal marked with a golden band.

Silver, then, he said resolutely. *My favourite colour.*

And a crown, I added on, more teasing than serious.

Only the best for you. I fell back onto the bed, closing my eyes and smiling as he continued on. *Now this battle with Tizan is over, I'll be heading back. We should be at Undia in three days. That's where General Jakob is camped. From there, it'll be mainly strategising on how to bring Vitus down.*

I'll meet you there, I answered straight away. Callum made a sound of protest, but I ignored it. *I refuse to wait a day longer, Callum. I will meet you in Undia, and that's the end of it. The moment Kyrah divines where Vitus is, I'm coming for you.*

He sighed, but there was a thread of relief in the sound as though he, too, couldn't stand to be apart for much longer. *As long as it's safe.*

Perfectly, I replied without a hint of the lie. He didn't need to know about Evania's warning.

Callum saw through it as he always did. *Chiara.*

Callum, I mimicked. Then, before he could try to convince me not to risk myself, I said, *Can you ... talk?*

Isn't that what I'm doing?

I huffed, folding my arms across my chest. *Well, yes, but I mean ... just talk.* It didn't matter how many times I heard it – nothing could soothe me quite as well as his voice.

All right, Captain.

And he did. He spoke of the parts of the kingdom he'd had the chance to explore. Of his mother, who'd died too young. Of those he'd met in the army, and tales of his and Deana's exploits as children. He spoke until my eyelids grew heavy and sleep claimed me, the gentle warmth of him following me into dreams of what awaited after the war.

Chapter Thirty

My fingers were currently in the process of strangling a tiny wood carving.

The carving, no bigger than my thumb, was that of a rat-faced creature that was known to lurk in the grassy plains to the east of Archin. I'd chosen it specially to represent Vitus. It hovered at the outskirts of Alluvite, where the black markings were edging towards looking like scribbles the longer this meeting drew on.

'There have been fewer sightings of Ankurans in Alluvite's streets,' Commander Lena explained as she leant over the map, indicating the twisting lines representing the slums. 'A few of the shadow wraiths – one of our men was brought into the infirmary this morning from a nasty surprise from one – but nowhere near the number that initially chased people into our two strongholds.'

'Isn't that a good sign?' a hawk-nosed woman who'd been introduced to me as Lady Rebekah asked. She was dressed in a gown that made my black trousers and white shirt shabby in comparison. 'Perhaps we have repented for our ways and they are pulling back.'

I tapped the base of the carving against the table. 'The gods don't care about us repenting. At least, Vitus doesn't. He wants mortals dead, and I imagine he's been waiting for the right moment to strike.' I shifted the carving to Perryth, where Callum had told me he was camped the night before. 'Tizan's been defeated. It's possible Vitus is nervous, but he's not the type to retreat. Something's happening.'

'And how would you know about that?' The ruddy-cheeked General Olisker leant in, dabbing at the sweat on his forehead with a cloth. 'His Majesty didn't set out more than a week ago. A missive could not have travelled here that fast.'

My eyes met Deana's. 'Remind me why we had to include him?'

'Because General Olisker commands much of the remaining forces, and we don't have time to replace him.'

The general bristled as I nodded and turned back to the map, ignoring his irritation. I shoved my sleeves back to my elbows as they began to slip down. 'I'll put up with it for today, then. Elijah, you bring news from the western front?'

General Elijah was older than the other generals I'd met, his greying hair and creased features placing him somewhere in his sixties. That he'd lived that long heading King Kane's army spoke highly of his skills. He pressed his hands to the table, studying the map with a frown. 'We encountered those shadow wraiths you spoke of, as well as creatures made of vines.'

'Scythes,' Jaxon supplied from where he lounged across two chairs shoved to one side, perfectly positioned under the lone window's light.

'Right.' Elijah rapped a finger at the northern edge of the Niguran forest, where trees bled into plains belonging to Archin. 'There was battle here against a lone woman. An archer. She brought down half of our men, and we didn't lay a scratch on her.'

'Maia,' I guessed, studying the plains. The goddess of the hunt – one of those whom Jaxon seemed to believe would cease fighting were Vitus and Tarina to disappear. 'Why didn't she kill you all?'

Elijah rubbed his bearded chin. 'There was another who appeared. A second woman. Dressed entirely inappropriately for battle. They just … stood there for a while, then both vanished.'

'What colour did she wear?' I asked.

Elijah gave me a bemused look. 'Ah … pink?'

I smiled. Despite her prickly nature, it seemed Evania had been helping before she'd come to the palace to offer her assistance. Perhaps she wasn't as awful as she pretended to be. 'Any other signs of gods?'

'None. If there were, I suspect we'd all be dead.'

'Right. Lena, where are you at with training—'

'Why are *you* running this meeting?' Lady Rebekah cut in.

Jaxon snorted, grinning as I forced myself to inhale slowly. 'You have objections?'

Lady Rebekah folded her hands on her lap, the perfect picture of nobility. 'You are a commoner.'

'And?'

She frowned, Olisker and Lord Lukas frowning alongside her. 'Does there need to be anything else? Commoners are not fit to lead.'

Gods, I hated nobility and their belief in their entitlement. It was almost as bad as the gods.

I placed a single finger to the table. Silver crackled over my skin and sliced through the wood, turning the brown into fractured starlight. Rebekah yelped, her chair clattering as she jumped to her feet. Lukas turned white.

'Let me make two things clear.' I rose to my feet, my shadow stretching towards where the nobles sat on the other side. 'Your king is the only one who has a say in what I am or am not fit to do. No one else. And if you ever think about questioning his decision again, I won't hold myself back.'

Silver arced off the table, sparking in the air in front of their faces. Smoke and jasmine filled the room as Jaxon clasped his hands together in delight, looking rather like a proud sibling might.

'Second,' I said calmly, still smiling at the rapidly paling nobility, 'I am perhaps our best chance at winning this war. Do you know what that makes me?'

Isla blinked rapidly, speaking for the first time. 'Strong?'

'Irreplaceable. Something that you are not.' I called my power back to me, letting it curl under my skin. Still not completely mine, but very close to it. Sitting back down, I folded my hands in front of me. 'Any further objections?'

Heads shook so fast I thought they might have fallen off shoulders.

Making friends, are we? Callum's voice coiled around me, warming my skin and soothing my fury.

I almost rolled my eyes. *Please. I was gentle on them.*

That you were. If I were there … well. We'd be having to choose three new members of nobility.

I think we'll need to do that anyway, I said back, eyeing the trio critically. *Olisker, too. Nobility like this … they're of little use. Better to find some distant relatives of theirs and give them the title.*

Then we will do that, as soon as— Callum broke off. I waited, ignoring the eyes on me. *I have to go.*

I frowned. *Where—*

But he was already gone, the bond absent of his voice. Sighing, I shifted my focus back to the room. 'Elijah, we're going to need to mobilise your forces, too, once we know where Vitus is. There'll be no holding back. We have one shot to bring him down, and—'

The doors burst opening, a harried looking Steward Terrion rushing in. His moustache twitched with fright as I turned towards him, his vest tight across his heaving chest.

'I thought I said we weren't to be interrupted.'

The Divine

'A-apologies, Lady Chiara,' Terrion said, bowing low at the hips. 'But the woman said it was urgent.'

'Which woman?' I prompted when Terrion didn't speak, still bent over. The man was as timid as I remembered. It was a miracle he'd survived Kane's reign.

'The one with—' His eyes flickered over the full room. He shuffled closer, lowering his voice so that only Deana and I could hear. Jaxon rose and meandered over. 'Goddess Kyrah. She said she has discovered what you were looking for.'

Deana, Jaxon and I exchanged a look. I turned to the room, smiling sharply enough that Rebekah pressed her hand to her chest with a gasp. 'I have things to attend to. I will be back once they're done.'

We strode from the room, the protests at the sudden departure cut off by the doors closing behind us. I reached out for Callum again, trying to grasp onto some sense of what was happening.

The bond was silent.

Unease began to rattle. I tried to shake it away, to convince myself that it was as it had been the day before – Callum simply had things to tend to. My fingers closed into fists. Yes. That had to be it. He'd told me he had to go, after all. It wasn't like our connection had suddenly been cut off.

Even so, the sooner we were reunited, the better.

Terrion led us to Callum's receiving chambers, opening the doors and swiftly disappearing as we entered. Evania sat primly upon the chaise, eyeing it with disdain, while Kerta looked far more relaxed seated beside her. I ignored them, turning to where Kyrah stood over a large bowl of water, a perplexed expression on her face.

'Well?' I asked as Kyrah looked up, the water before her wavering in shades of violet and lilac.

She waved a hand over its surface, the water returning to clear. 'It is difficult to make out. There are too many involved. Too many possible pasts and futures, muddling together until it is impossible to tell one from another. And Vitus's current location is … murky. Surrounded by too many wards to see through.'

'But you've narrowed down the possibilities?'

'Not as much as I would like,' she admitted, coming out from behind the desk. 'But there is one future I have divined. Two battles I believe are to come, and the end of war to come after. The decider of fates. If we intervene before the first battle, then there is a slim possibility we shall gain the victory you seek.'

'Easy,' Jaxon said, the clap of his hands startling Evania. She twisted to glare at him. 'Then we intervene. When's this battle happening?'

'It is less a when, and more a who. The passage of time is muddied by the changes to the realm. Sometimes the past becomes the future, and the future the present.'

'And if we don't intervene?' Deana asked.

'The second battle will come, and Vitus will be present. Those who are to face the god will fall. Every one of them, down to the last soldier.' She hesitated, glancing down at the water before looking back to me, her expression bordering on pitying. 'The price will be paid for a soul bound to this world. A life for a life.'

My heart thudded. I must've staggered forward a step, because Deana laid her hand on my shoulder, righting me. 'You mean Callum?'

'The mortal king shall fall to a god, and the god who should not be will ruin the realms.' She walked over to me, pressing her hand to my cheek. Despite its warmth, there was nothing but a chill that sunk to my bones. 'For it is not life that will destroy all that exists. It is death in all her glory. For the realms might demand a price for balance not maintained, but death shall wreak her vengeance if the price taken is too much. Even the realms cannot stop what will unfold.'

I stepped away from her touch. Where each of the gods

seemed to hold a distinct scent to them, Kyrah's flickered between all others. Roses over decaying flesh. Flowers freshly bloomed. Soil dampened by a winter's storm. The charring of a war-torn land.

But it was that of smoke and jasmine that reigned.

'Again – we intervene so that doesn't happen.' Jaxon turned to me. 'Not that it would, anyway. Right?'

I didn't look at him. Didn't break the knowing stare of Kyrah, who knew the truth as I did.

Death and life weren't opposites. They were the sun and moon – two existences who cohabited the same plane. Who were capable of drawing forth the same clear skies or ruinous storms if given the right circumstances.

Vitus, who'd loved Alexia, to the point of hating all mortals for her end.

Dearil, who'd loved the mortals enough to damn the gods to a miserable realm.

And me, who loved Callum enough to seek vengeance for his death.

Only, it wouldn't be the mortals who bore the brunt of my rage. It wouldn't even be the gods. It would be the realms who'd insisted time and time again on keeping us apart. On breaking us each down until we became something we were never meant to be.

'The first battle,' I said, not letting the rampage of my heart seep into my voice. I dug my nails into my palm, steadying myself. I needed calm, not to break apart at the thought of Callum dying. 'Who will be involved?'

'An army of mortals and a king to lead, and one of creatures led by a long-corrupted mortal.'

Hair raised at the back of my neck at her words. 'This is in the future?'

She tilted her head, her gaze turning far away as she

considered. 'The future stems from the past, and the past feeds the future. They belong as one and as one they shall remain.'

'She has no clue,' Evania explained. 'Kyrah is what too many years and not enough sanity looks like in the divine.'

'I speak the truth, even if you do not like it, Evania, goddess of peace,' Kyrah said, her gaze turning sharp as she looked at her. 'Time does not meld to linearity as we believe. It exists in a—'

'The battle,' I cut in sharply, stepping back into Kyrah's line of sight. The divine were worse than nobility when it came to straying from the topic. 'The mortal leading the gods' side. Do you know who it is?'

'No.' My shoulders dropped. 'But I can show you.'

I all but shoved Kyrah in the direction of the divination bowl. She waved her hand over its surface, hues of purple twining together into an ethereal mix. Tiny images burst forth – a mother and child sitting by a hearth; the same mother and child, dead. A babe in a crib, and an empty space where that crib should be.

'I must sift to find the fragment I had before,' Kyrah explained as she dipped a finger into the water, light twirling in fine lines from where she touched it. Faint hums of noise emanated from the bowl, each whisked away before I could make sense of any of them.

My focus fell to the desk as I waited for her to find what she searched for. The missives still sat there. I touched my pocket, where the one I'd taken sat. A connection to Callum that I wouldn't rid myself of.

Callum? I tried, reaching for the bond.

Silence.

I forced my breathing to remain steady. They'd be making preparations to come back. He was busy. He might not have heard, or he might be in the middle of meeting with his commanding officers. There were plenty of reasons for why he didn't immediately answer my call.

Wrong, my power whispered under my skin. *Wrong, wrong, wrong.*

'Can you hurry it up?' I snapped, tapping on the edge of the desk.

Kyrah raised her eyes to mine. 'Time does not follow the command of any god or entity. Even death.'

I stopped my tapping, dragging my hand through my hair as I fought the urge to pace the room. I needed to see who led that army. To confirm my suspicions were wrong.

'Everything all right?' Jaxon asked as he placed his hand on my shoulder.

I flexed my fingers, then drew one of my daggers. 'I don't know. Something just feels...' *Wrong,* the power whispered again. Silver sparked on the dagger's edge.

'Here,' Kyrah announced, before I could put the drenching of unease enveloping me into words. 'This is the mortal who leads Vitus's side. He will not fall in this battle, and the gods shall descend the day after.'

I leant forward. A man stared back at me.

Bulbous nose, veins seeming to split the skin. Beady nose. Thin, cruel lips.

Deana inhaled sharply as she recognised him. 'Tizan.'

I reared back.

'Perryth,' I snapped. 'Evania, take Deana. Kerta, Jaxon. Kyrah'—I looked at her half-focused eyes, still lost in the fragments of time—'if you won't be able to fight, don't come.'

Evania jumped to her feet as silver began to thread around me, her eyes blazing. 'Girl, I told you it was dangerous to step between the realms before the power settled. You risk being deposited—'

I pictured Callum, yanked my power to swallow me whole, and stepped through the fabric of the realms.

Chapter Thirty-One

The world did not exist as it should. Sights and sounds passed me by, my useless attempts to clutch hold of reality futile. I was dragged through the space between the realms, hurtling through colours and lights with nauseating speed. No matter how much I tugged on my power, no matter how much I willed myself to appear at Callum's side, the realms did not listen.

My heart pounded in a frantic rhythm to my fear. There was no sense of where I was. No direction or solidity to what surrounded me. All I knew was that Callum was not here, and I could not reach his side.

Something grasped hold of me, seizing my momentum. My desperate flight stalled, colours and light convalescing into a magnificent spectrum that coiled around me. It shifted with every frantic beat of my heart, the kaleidoscope far more radiant than anything I'd encountered in either godly or mortal realm. It should have been beautiful.

Yet it was not awe but terror that gripped at me. I was suspended, somewhere beyond the mortal realm. There were no

The Divine

smells. No sounds. Just the brilliant light and me, trapped far away from where I needed to be. Far from Callum.

I yanked on my stubborn power. Silver flared in furious strands, crackling over my skin. Not quite rebelling, but not yet giving in.

'Damn you,' I spat out, flexing my fingers in front of me. They felt strange. Numb, as though they were unravelling at the tips, becoming one with the in-between of the realms. 'I need to get to him. *Now*.'

'You will not reach your king until you listen.'

I yanked my hand back to my chest, eyes widening at the rich tones of the familiar voice. I scoured the space around me, searching for Dearil's features. There was nothing but a slight brightening of the silver, like a pet greeting its owner.

I tugged on it, and it slunk back to me. The colours around started to swirl in a dizzying array, matching the panic striking through my chest. 'Where are you?'

'I am where I began. A thread in the fabric of the realms. You cannot see me, my daughter, but you must listen.'

Fear turned my words sharp. 'The only thing I must do is reach Callum's side! He needs me!'

The same sensation that had hauled me to a stop brushed my cheek. It was warm, like a summer's breeze come to steal away winter's chill. 'You have travelled before your power was ready to. You will pay the price if you do not do as I say.'

I tried to move, to will myself onwards, but it was like ropes were attached to my limbs, holding me in place. The numbness at my fingers crept further upwards, the power growing frenetic in its crackling. 'Then I'll pay the price. I don't care about that.' I held out my hands impatiently. 'The realms can take whatever they need.'

'They will unravel you, child.' Gentle pressure pushed my

arms back down. 'It has already begun. You must make the power your own if you intend to leave.'

The numbness grew into a prickling. I swallowed, ice drenching me. If I … *unravelled*, as he said, then what would happen to those who fought? What would happen to Callum?

I wanted to smash my fist against the garish colours. To grasp whatever threads of Dearil remained and squeeze them until he let me out of this place. As if sensing this, Dearil sighed. 'Do not be impatient. You must do this if you are to succeed.' The air warmed around me, the scent of smoke and jasmine breaking through the space. The silver in the kaleidoscope around intensified, shining like shattered stars. 'Breathe, child. And *listen*.'

Frustration knotted nearly as fiercely around my throat as fear did. 'I've tried that! I know the power's a reflection of me. I know I need to listen to it. But it doesn't listen to me!'

'Do not listen to it as others tell you to.' What felt like a whisper of a breeze sliced through the numbness, nudging my hand over so my palm was facing upwards. 'Listen to it in the way that you have always understood others.'

I frowned. Understanding others had never been my strong point. I'd always been too wrapped up in myself and my own suffering to spare time for everyone else.

I looked down at my hands. Stared at the silver weaving through my fingers. It was quieter than it had once been, but it was far from settled. Instead, it seemed to watch me as intently as I watched it. Waiting for something.

'I don't understand,' I said softly, and I didn't know if I spoke to the power or to Dearil. The power shivered as though in a shrug.

'How did you come to understand your king's intentions? Jaxon's? Deana's?'

My frown grew. Everything in me screamed to yank at the power until it took me to where Callum was, but I couldn't be reckless now. Not when a misstep might mean I never made it to Callum's side. I considered Dearil's words, trying to ignore the creeping numbness as it crawled over my elbows. Instinct warned me that if it reached my chest, I would become as Dearil now was – nothing more than loose threads in the fabric of the realm, present only in fragmented parts.

I'd hated Callum at first. Desired him. Raged at him.

Eventually, though, I had loved him. It had never been his words that won me over. It had been his actions. How unfailingly he gave me choices where I never had them before. How he stood by me even as I spat back at him. How he didn't cower from me as so many had.

I'd always understood actions far better than words. A sword raised at me was a clearer sign of intentions than pretty words might be. A hand outstretched spoke higher than bitter insults.

And my power – it had been spiteful, flaring too bright or showing too little. Angry, in the same way I so often had. But it hadn't hidden away and left me to die with Tarina's Illusion. It had never struck out at Callum, Jaxon or Deana.

It hated control. Hated everything I tried to force it to do. Because *I* hated being under another's control.

As though sensing my realisation, the power shuddered. It spindled out of my hands, leaping over my skin to form a light brighter than any of the colours around. My breathing turned ragged as I stared at it. Stared at *me* as it took form, features growing sharp, hair growing curly and wild. Its eyes were pure silver, no white or pupils to be seen, but I saw the hardness in them, all the same. A hardness honed by years of suffering. Years I had survived when I could have given up.

'Good,' Dearil said, and warmth crept over me at his approval.

I lifted a hand, and the replica did the same. Its fingers brushed mine, a shock passing between us. It curled its silvery hand around mine, holding tight.

I saw it then. All the broken, ugly pieces of me, pushed into the silver power. The despair. The rage. The hurt that sank far deeper than anything else. The terror that I had shoved down, time and time again, until it festered.

But it wasn't just the ugly. There were other pieces. The silver mirror of me wore the smile I saved for Callum. It was hardened with experience. Strong because of it. A god raised as a mortal. A scared girl who'd become a bitter woman. Something sharp. Something fierce.

It was horrifying. It was beautiful.

It was *me*.

And I knew exactly what it needed.

'Will you work with me?' I asked. Not a command. Not a threat.

A request, just like the request Callum had once given when I'd been in the depths of darkness, stretching an offer to work together to find our way to the godly realm to bring down Vitus. A request that had grasped hold of me and dragged me out of the shadows.

My power inclined its head. That was all it took for it to rush forward. It slammed into me, filling my body with an intensity far greater than what it had possessed before. If I could have moved in the in-between space, I might have stumbled back under the weight of it. Might have floated higher with the elation of it. Where before there had been numbness, there was now a riot of sensations. Heat and ice intermingling, the hair raising on my skin. It was terrifyingly magnificent.

And it wanted the exact same thing as me. *Callum*, it whispered, and I smiled a promise of savage violence in response.

Callum, I agreed, willing it to take me to him.

That was all the power needed. The invisible binds that had kept me stationary snapped, the colours starting to whip by once more. My fear for what I might find upon landing returned, accompanied by resolve to cut down everything in the way.

But before I could go, I whispered into the in-between, 'I won't find you again, will I?'

'Not until death calls your name, child.' There was a trace of sadness in Dearil's voice. Sadness, and hope. 'Protect your realm well. And protect yourself. I do not want to find your threads here for a long, long time.'

'Thank you,' I said back, my hands squeezing into fists as I started to plummet through the colours, my destination clear in my mind. 'Father.'

I thought I caught a glimpse of a smile, wide and bright, amongst the shards of brightness, but it was gone before I could make anything else out. In a violent burst, the fabric of the realms spat me out.

There was nothing under me but air. I stared into a sky swathed in smoke, the sun turned brown by its cover. For a heartbeat, the realms allowed me to exist that way – suspended in the moments before I faced what was to come. That moment was snatched away before I could claim it for my own. I plummeted, slamming into the ground.

My breath punched out of me. It took me a few moments to reclaim it. As soon as I did, I shoved to my feet. Around, chaos reigned. Soldiers shouted and scrambled, weapons held in trembling hands. Some raced for the mess of tents, their tops ablaze and blowing smoke into the sky. Most raced in the opposite direction. A few simply ran, seeming so lost to their fear that they had no direction.

'Enemy!' a soldier screamed as he spotted me, silver sparking upon my skin. His pupils were blown with fear. 'Enemy in the camp! Ene—'

'Quiet.' His mouth opened again and I clamped my hand over it before he could start shouting again. 'My name is Chiara

Halnea.' I waited for a flicker of recognition to shoot through his eyes. 'The king. Where is he?' I peeled back my hand.

'He's—'

The air shifted beside me. Evania, Deana, Jaxon and Kerta appeared with far more grace than I had. The man paled.

'Th-they just appeared out of nowhere! All of them! This is—'

Deana took stock of the situation and came to my side. She snapped her fingers in front of the soldier's face, waiting until his eyes met hers before saying, 'Report, soldier.'

The soldier began to look back to Evania and Kerta as though sensing something was different about them. I dug the dagger in a little deeper. 'Ignore them. Do as Deana said. Report.'

His throat bobbed. Soldiers slowed as they rushed past us, but Deana was a recognisable enough figure that they quickly hurried on, not daring to question why we were all there, huddled around one of their own with clothes entirely unsuited to battle. 'Ti-Tizan. There were spies in the camp. They killed his guards and set him free. His Majesty found him carving in the ground. He was executed on the spot, but His Majesty—'

'Carving?' Evania interrupted, stepping forward with a sweep of her skirts. The air seemed to quiet as she approached, the clamour of the soldiers fading into peaceful silence. Even the man I'd pinned stilled, his expression slackening into one of calm. 'Explain.'

'Evania,' I said, rising from the man. 'Your questions can wait. I need to know—'

'—what you're walking into,' Deana finished for me.

Evania smiled, turning back to the soldier. Even through the smoke, sunlight seemed drawn to her, her pale hair shimmering with its glow. 'Well?'

'G-golden marks,' the soldier stammered, his eyes hazy. 'Ones looping around in a circle.'

A clicking drew our attention to where Kerta had wandered to the side. She pointed downwards, her boot swiping over the ground to reveal golden wards shining in the mud. They stretched out in a long line, heading in the same direction the soldiers were running. This was why I'd landed here, I realised, rather than by Callum's side.

Jaxon crouched, running his fingers over the golden lines. 'Why have Tizan ward a place where a battle will be taking place? It limits Vitus's own movements.'

Evania eyed the wards distastefully. 'Horrid things.'

'And why was Tizan the one to do it?' Deana asked. She straightened, looking around. The campsite was all but abandoned to the flames, the numbers of soldiers dwindling as the last disappeared down a hill to the right. 'Surely, Vitus could've done it himself.'

Kerta's fingers moved through rapid signs, Evania translating them. 'Vitus must have sent the mortal general out knowing your armies would come for him and be unlikely to kill him straight away. It was not a location he waited to draw the wards around, but a person. Someone who he had not yet been able to hunt down, and so waited for them to find his forces.'

'It's a trap,' I surmised, catching on to where her mind was going. There was only one person I could imagine Vitus going to the effort of building such a trap for. My heart lurched, and I took two steps forward, the wards briefly pressing down on my power as I crossed them. The heat of the air suffocated me as I stared at the hill the soldiers had disappeared down. 'Callum.'

'Wait!' Deana shot forward, grasping my arm as I tightened my grip on my dagger, fury beginning to build. 'That makes no sense. Why the wards? They wouldn't affect Callum's Gift unless they're applied directly to his skin. This trap can't be for him.'

I stared at where something that might've been a battle cry rose, its fury spearing towards the smoke-strewn sky. My pulse quickened. I needed to be there. Needed to be with him.

'It is not,' Evania said. 'The king is the bait. The prize is—'

'It doesn't matter,' I cut in before she could speak of what I'd realised the moment Kerta had unveiled the wards. This was Vitus's final grand move – his way of taking any opponents off the board. I'd be confined to this space, unable to get myself out if things went wrong. And it would be the same for Evania and Kerta. 'I'm not leaving Callum to fight this alone.'

'You are being reckless again,' Evania warned.

The smile I gave was harder than any scowl could be as I reached for my power. 'This isn't recklessness. This is protecting what is mine.' And I was not going to let Kyrah's prediction come to pass.

My boots barely had a chance to sink into the soft mud as I yanked away from Deana, racing for where the sounds of battles were becoming more certain of themselves, screams and shouts melding with the clang of blades and wet tearing of flesh. There was a curse – Jaxon, I thought – and then footsteps were following behind. I paused at the top of the hill, scanning the chaos below. Ankurans leapt at mortals, many already feasting upon the bodies on the ground. Vines curled around legs while shadow wraiths cut through flesh. It was an anarchy of blood and suffering, the mortals losing badly. Here, the smoke was cut through by the scent of iron, the ground watered by lifeblood.

Where are you? I whispered down the bond, searching desperately for my king amongst the soldiers. For him, or for the golden god I'd come to cut down. I could see nothing but glints of armour and injuries that too many would not recover from.

There was no response down the bond. The air seemed heavier, filled with too much power. Power that belonged to other gods. It buzzed across my skin, seeming to swarm along the bond every time I reached for it. It was as though a blanket had been thrown over the connection between us, just as it had been when the wards had been carved into my skin.

I forced myself to keep my breathing steady. He was still there. Still alive. I'd know if he wasn't.

Kyrah's words rang in my mind. *Those who are to face the god will fall.*

'Gods,' Deana breathed. 'This is—'

'Madness,' Jaxon finished. He drew his sword – the one Garrett had crafted him, the gentle curve of it a stark contrast to the viciousness it was capable of. 'Good thing we're the sort who enjoy a little bit of insanity.'

A short sword appeared in Deana's hand, the surface gleaming red. 'Let's teach our enemy fear.'

'We will stay back,' Evania said. Before I could snap a reminder at her of the aid she'd promised, she held up a hand. 'It is not because we will not help. It is because the other gods have not yet interfered with the battle. The moment we intervene, they will also step into the fray. For now, they will avoid dirtying their hands for as long as possible.'

I pointed at an Ankuran. 'That's not interfering?'

'No,' Evania said, her expression darkening. 'They are mere foot soldiers. You have seen a glimpse of Vitus's power. Do you truly think so many mortals would still live if he'd used it to its full extent? It is best we delay that for as long as possible.'

I grudgingly nodded my understanding before taking a calming breath. I would find Callum, even if I had to cut down every creature before me to do so. And the best way to do that was to bury myself deep in the violent chaos below.

I reached the first Ankuran, its golden eyes fixing on me with chilling eagerness. It fell quickly, my dagger driving through its eye. My next opponent, a shadow wraith, wailed its death as I thrust my blade into its chest. An enemy mortal fell to a slashed throat, and I took their sword as payment. Two more fell in quick succession, their warm blood spattering over my face.

And then it was nothing but bodies around me, fingers and

blades reaching for me, grappling to pull me down as the true portion of the enemy forces crashed into me like a wave. Eyes of gold and light, of hollowed-out darkness and mortal cruelty, turned to me as though recognising that I was the true enemy they faced.

They came at me, again and again, fingers catching in my tunic or attempting to grasp hold of my hair. I sliced with my blade, the elation of my power singing through me. A hand flew free of its body to my left, another enemy nearly taking my blade with it as it fell down from a thrust to its throat. A mortal stumbled into me, a vine shoved through her chest. I offered her the mercy of a quick death before turning to my next victim.

The world existed as a cacophony of screams. I twisted as a soldier to my left fell to one knee, an Ankuran's fingers clawing at the armour. Shifting the sword to a one-handed grip, I yanked out a throwing knife. I whipped it in the Ankuran's direction. The creature fell. The soldier had enough time to turn his eyes on me before three more Ankurans took him down.

This time, I didn't try to save him. Warmth gathered in my veins from the nearing death. Underneath the churning mass of wretched limbs and scrambling fingers, the man's screams cut off abruptly.

I spun, still searching for Callum.

The bond, muted though it was, tugged at me, warming, as though letting me know he was close by. That he lived for the time being. A scythe sent its vines shooting for my neck. I twisted, cutting through them as I tried to sense where he might be. I caught sight of Jade slicing through three Ankurans in quick succession, unfazed by the spray of golden blood. She looked up, meeting my eyes briefly before throwing herself back into the carnage.

Focus, I reminded myself as I whipped a knife into a shadow wraith whose long fingers were sunk into a woman's chest. The creature wailed. I didn't wait to see it dissipate, turning my dagger onto an Ankuran to my left. My blade caught it in the chest. The victory didn't last long. Something heavy collided with my side, sending me flying into the chaos.

Idiot, I berated myself, even as I flew through the air.

I reached for my power. I'd been trying to save it for facing Vitus – but I needed to remain conscious to do so. The silver sparked at my fingertips, humming with anticipation.

An arm wrapped around my midsection. My power only hummed more – this time, in contentment at the presence of its two favourite things. Death, and my soul-bonded.

'Careful,' Callum murmured in my ear, arm still wrapped around me as he sank his sword into the midsection of a mortal man. The man's snarl vanished as he died, only having time for a brief gasp of agony before his soul untethered from his body.

My soul sung with his literal presence, even as screams continued to pierce the air around us. *He was here. He was alive.*

I sent my sword into a shadow creature as it sank its clawed fingers into my skin, raking red lines before it shattered into wisps of black. The pain barely registered. Every part of me wanted to wrap my arms around Callum, to spirit us both away so no one could take him from me again.

But I'd promised to be queen. Not just his queen, but that of a mortal kingdom. I had more to protect now than just him.

'I'm always careful,' I said, guarding his back as he did mine.

'Liar.' Gods, the sound of his voice – not just in my head, but in the air, slicing through the sounds of suffering around us – was the most beautiful thing I'd ever heard. 'I'd hate to win so easily. Which I will do, if you don't make sure to keep your feet under you.'

'Win?' I pulled myself free, sending a boot into the stomach of a mortal who had thought to approach me from my side. Ribs cracked.

'Kill more than you.' Callum grunted as he twisted, driving his sword through a scythe as I took down the shadow wraith next to it.

Twisted delight filled me. I'd missed this – how perfectly we fought together. In any other situation, I would've enjoyed it almost as much as sparring with him.

'Not this again. I can't believe'—I shoved my sword through the back of a mortal and threw a dagger past Callum's head and into a scythe, attempting to shoot its vines towards him—'we're having this conversation right now.'

Gold arced through the air, splattering my face and arms as Callum severed an Ankuran's head. I kicked it away as I grasped the wrist of an attacker, twisting sharply until I heard a crack. The woman, a young mortal the same age as me, gaped at me. There was fear in her eyes as she found death staring her down.

'Please,' she whispered, the single word wavering.

I cut her throat.

'Don't lie,' Callum grinned as he killed an Ankuran. 'You enjoy this.'

I did not wish for war, but he was right. This – this was a part of me I'd never been able to deny. The part that lived for mindless carnage and the anarchy of my blade. The way any other concerns or worries faded away, the only law that mattered being the one decided upon by death.

And death could be beautiful, particularly when delivered as quickly and viciously as this.

I cut through more enemies. Iron and smoke began to meld with the stench of decay as the bodies piled higher. 'What I meant is, I can't believe you'd think you'd have a chance after the last two times I won.'

'Not this time.' Callum didn't bother to lift his sword as a man came at him, batting away his bow. Two of our other soldiers

The Divine

finished him off. 'I'm determined to win this time. How many do you think killing a god is worth?'

'At least a hundred.'

'Then all I have to do is kill more gods than you. Should be easy enough.'

'I—' The words died on my tongue as a second wave of bodies crashed into us.

The sudden crush forced me back. I lost Callum in the tangle of bodies, and fear purged any sense of delight from my veins.

There were enemies everywhere, pushing in from left and right. The air was thick, heavy with the fire's wavering heat and the crush of too many in one place. Hands and blades reached for me, and I spun past them, letting my blade carve through skin and muscle, cutting to the bone. Blood splattered my face as I lost myself to the dance of death.

I could not fully unleash my power here, not with so many mortals surrounding me, but I allowed it to crackle over my blade, slicing up my fingers and across my skin. The blade gouged through decaying flesh and shadows, and the healthier flesh of the mortals. As soon as it hit, that silver spread and crackled, taking down whoever was in its way.

Sweat clung to my neck and gathered beneath my armour despite the chill in the air. There was blood everywhere. It was on my face, splattering in crimson and gold across my armour. It was on the ground, beneath my feet, in my mouth. My feet trampled over bodies, several of which let out weak moans before a creature or mortal ended them.

And everywhere inside me, from my toes to the strands of my hair, all I felt was the warmth of death.

Slim, dark shadows flicked over us as arrows flew through the air. They struck beyond where I stood at the front of our soldiers. Many missed, driving through the air and quivering in the ground. Others hit their targets, a wet, meaty *thud* sounding as the pointed tips drove into flesh.

In the corner of my vision, a blade sliced through the air. I whirled towards it, but General Jade got there first. She thrust her weapon through my would-be attacker's neck. The mortal choked, red blood spurting as she ripped her blade free before he collapsed.

'Thanks.' I snapped my arm out to the left, catching an Ankuran in the throat and knocking her to the floor before driving my sword through her heart.

'There's too many,' Jade replied grimly, as more and more bodies came, filling up spaces left by the fallen. To one side of me, a foolishly brave soldier, no older than twenty, raced past me and Jade, who cursed, lunging towards the girl to haul her back.

She was too late.

A vine caught around the soldier's ankle, wrapping itself tightly. The girl had enough time to widen her eyes with surprise before the scythe yanked and she fell to the blood-soaked ground.

The Ankurans were on her in a second.

'Fucking gods,' Jade muttered, her skin pale.

I gritted my teeth, driving my blade again and again through flesh as I considered. Jade was right. There were too many, and our soldiers were going to tire quicker than the gods' soldiers were. If we continued as we were, then we would be decimated before the day ended.

We needed to even the odds.

A particularly brutal cut across a throat sent blood spraying into my eyes, hot and stinging. I swiped a hand across them, blinking away the red. 'Get your soldiers to fall back,' I ordered Jade.

Her eyes widened. 'What?'

'Get your soldiers to fall back. Now.'

Jade stared at me for a second before abruptly snapping into

The Divine

attention. 'Yes, ma'am.' She took a few steps back, head twisting to the men and women who followed her. 'Retreat!' she yelled, her voice cleaving through the sounds of the dying. 'Fall back now!'

The pressure of bodies around me eased as those who had been cutting their way forward began to cut their way back. The call was taken up, spreading along the ranks. Through a haze of blood and bodies, emerald eyes locked on mine and my chest loosened a fraction.

Callum's face was grim as he wrapped an arm around the throat of a man, letting an Ankuran drive a spear into the man's leg before Callum dropped the body and twisted his sword deep into the Ankuran's chest. I jerked my head towards where our forces were retreating. He nodded once, his trust in me unwavering.

While everyone fell back, retreating to safer ground, I carved a path forward. Enemies fell. Blood spurted. But I did not stop.

Three scythes coordinated their movements, sending vines creeping for me between the feet of their forces. Our soldiers had mostly fallen back. My smile grew as I called upon my power. Silver energy coursed over me, as hungry and vicious as I was.

It was no longer rebellious. It was mine, powered by fury and vengeance, love and fierce protection. It filled my body with its energy, twining with my will until they were one and the same.

I met the shadowed hollows of the scythe's eyes as I brought my boot down on the roots.

The green browned, the vine withering. There was a cry of anger from somewhere behind the mass of bodies that shook the grass beneath my feet. Not the cry of the creature, but of a god who'd sensed his creations had fallen. Adwin.

Coward, I thought. The gods hid behind their forces, letting their soldiers fall for them.

It seemed I'd have to teach the divine what it was to truly fight.

The ground began to splinter, the grass growing longer and wilder around me. The Ankurans' eyes gleamed a brighter gold as their skin cracked with the colour. They became more frenzied, pushing closer and closer to me. Vitus's focus, finally latching onto the one he'd sought to trap.

It was time he realised I wasn't the only one trapped in by his wards.

I spared a glance behind me. Most of the soldiers had retreated far enough back, but there were a few who had either not heard or been unable to heed the command. There was nothing I could do for them now. To try would be to damn all the rest.

I faced the enemy once more, baring my teeth as I gathered the power that roared through me, letting it seep onto my fingers, spiralling out and across the ground. What had once been a well of power – deep, but with a clear ending – now seemed endless and infinite, coming to me as easily as breathing. The world turned silver as my vision embraced the power's might.

I shifted my attention, beyond the Ankurans and mortals, to where gods watched, my eyes finding a pair of gold ones. My lips lifted into a brutal smile.

And I let that power do what it was made to do.

I let it bring death.

Chapter Thirty-Two

The death that came was a beautiful creation, crafted of starlight and polished with vengeance. It twisted and arced, crept and lunged, seeking all those who lay before me. Creatures and mortal fell to our wrath. Bodies were reduced to nothing but ash, their screams swallowed by silence.

I couldn't stop it sweeping for the mortals who fought for us – those too injured to move, or too deafened by battle to hear the call of retreat. But my power was not without mercy. It saw their terror – their pain and cowering – and it curled around them, gentling the agony in their eyes, sending them to the Gates with a softer touch than it did the rest. Death came for all, but it did not treat them as equals.

My silver chased away the smell of blood, replacing it with smoke and jasmine. Death delivered in its full glory.

It was over in seconds. Half the battlefield, turned to ash.

But I was not done.

I lifted a finger, raising it to the gods who stood in a line, content to watch the massacre play out without their intervention. Adwin, whose beard crept with vines fresh for harvesting. Maia, complete with her bow; and Fortuna, who flicked the coin of luck in the air. The shadowy form of Akmad, his cruelty the same apathetic kind that King Kane had possessed.

But I swept past them, pointing at my target. At Vitus.

I had not seen him before in his godly form, yet it was impossible to mistake him for any other. His hair hang in long strands around his shoulders, golden tunic shifting into a coat and back again. His golden skin, blank of flaws, was free of blood or sweat. He was a statue carved of precious metal, any trace of sunlight worshipping his form.

But his eyes – they were as I remembered. Cold. Malicious. Filled with ancient hate.

I smiled, and he snarled back.

The silver lunged.

It crashed into a wall of brilliant gold, the two battling for dominion over the land. Grass grew and shrivelled, bodies shaking then stilling. Neither of us giving to the other.

Someone cried out behind. I thought I saw Maia stumble through the brilliant light.

As quickly as it attacked, the gold pulled back. I did the same with my power. They were too well matched, and I could already sense the drain. This wasn't the way I'd win against Vitus. And I suspected he'd realised the same about me.

His end would have to come in bloody retribution. The thought of it curled my lips upwards.

'Fucking *gods*,' Jade said into the quiet. I twisted, glancing over my shoulder to check that most of the army still stood, as tendrils of silver wove through my fingers. 'What is she?'

Callum's lips curved into a grin. 'She's exactly that. A god.'

Even the bodies from before had disappeared. Soldiers shifted uneasily.

Callum was the first to stride forward, pushing past others who were unsure whether to be more afraid of the gods on the other side of the field or the god right in front of them. He paid no mind to the shifting of ash underfoot. He did not look at the several patches of land where even the mud seemed to have dulled, turning dry and cracked. He only looked at me as gods and mortals alike watched on.

'That,' he murmured into the silence, 'was incredible.'

'We have a war to win,' I said back, pointing my blade in the direction of the gods. My eyes, though, remained fixed on him. 'And some gods to kill. Your admiration can wait.'

'It most certainly cannot.' Nonetheless, he pulled away, turning his eyes back to the gods.

Their army wasn't destroyed. The creatures who'd been protected by Vitus's barrier lurked, their inhuman eyes fixed on us. But they were diminished, their stillness a mark of their wariness.

I locked eyes with Vitus again. 'You're next.'

Those two words were all it took for the soldiers behind to emit a cry, boots slamming on the earth as they raced forward. Vitus waved his hand and his surviving creatures launched forward at the same time. This time, when the forces met, there was no fear or fumbling, no wide eyes or uncertain steps. There was only room for steadfast focus and determination.

Callum and I fought as one, filling each other's gaps. Bodies dropped around us. Some, from blade. Others, from a stray tendril of silver that turned my opponents to ash. My smile sharpened, Callum's echoing it. We were no gentle rulers, content to sit on our thrones and rule from afar. We were those forged by a realm that wanted us gone. Those who'd learnt suffering and knew how to give it in turn. And we would give every piece of agony we could to save our kingdom.

'Lady Chiara!' someone shouted. I turned, finding Kailey supporting a wounded Corin. He blinked blood from his eyes, his smile carrying the haze of a head injury. Kailey held his arm tightly, a sword shaking in her other hand. 'We need to—'

She choked, hands flying to her neck.

'Kailey!' Corin cried, a shard of clarity coming into his eyes. He whirled as Kailey's legs weakened, and bore her weight despite his injury.

'Watch yourself!' I snapped, driving my sword through the chest of a shadow wraith that had aimed at him. The creature writhed on the length of it before crumbling away. I twisted, glancing down at where Kailey had slumped to the ground, Corin standing protectively over her. 'Dammit. Callum!'

Callum turned, his face paling as his eyes fell on what mine had – a thin band of shadows wrapped around Kailey's neck. A band that had once curled around my sister's neck, a warning of what would happen if I disobeyed King Kane. This, though, was far darker and thicker than Kane's cruel restraints had been.

Her lips were parted, desperately trying to seek air that wouldn't come. Callum was as familiar with those shadows as I was. Akmad's power.

He rushed to her side. Shadows wreathed his hands, grazing Kailey's skin. Cuts healed and bruises vanished as his Gift washed over her. Corin's injury also disappeared, though the lesser of Callum's remained.

But the black band stayed.

More cries came from around us. I whirled, sword raising, only to find another soldier on their knees, another black band around his neck. More fell. Each clawed at the shadows, but none were able to get it off.

A strange chortling came from the nearest shadow wraiths. They paused their attacks, watching with a pleasure that seemed to shine from their bright eyes.

'I'll get it off!' Corin cried as he dropped to his knees by Kailey's side. My skin warmed at looming death. Kailey met

Corin's eyes, fear turning her young. Corin's attempts became more frenzied. 'Hold on. I'm going to—'

A sharp *snap* sliced through the sounds of the battle. Every soldier affected by the shadows collapsed. A hush blanketed us as I looked down at Kailey. At the way her head bent unnaturally to one side, fear gone from her eyes.

'No!' Corin's scream broke through the moment of disbelief. His fingers curled around Kailey's shoulders, sword forgotten by his side. 'Come on, Kailey. You can't – you're fine. We need to—'

I turned away, throat tight.

'A pity. I thought I might catch a king with my little trick,' a voice as cold and calm as Kane's had once been reached us, raking icy claws across my skin.

Callum pulled me to his side as a man appeared before us. His skin was the pale white of bone bleached by the sun, hair the colour of depthless waters on the darkest night. Flat eyes met mine before swinging across to Callum, interest sparking.

'Akmad, I presume,' Callum said calmly.

Akmad's colourless lips peeled into a grin. Screams began to break out in earnest around us, the sounds of our people dying enveloping us. My power bristled in recognition of the calamity that'd found us.

The mortals had had their moment of victory on this battlefield.

Now the gods had decided it was time to play.

Chapter Thirty-Three

I stepped towards Akmad, sword raised. Callum caught my hand and tugged me back.

'Let me handle this one,' he whispered.

I was shaking my head before he'd finished. 'He's a god. I can't—'

'You can, and you will. Remember your goal, Chiara. Kill Vitus, and this ends.'

Akmad laughed, the sound abrasive. 'You are amusing for mortals. You really believe you can achieve the impossible.'

Callum's fingers tightened on mine as anger surged. There were so many dead around us. Too many were from this god. My power rolled hungrily. It could feel it – the discrepancy between our power. That it could crush this god if I wished it.

And gods, did I wish it.

'Chiara. You can't,' Callum said when I made no move to back away. Akmad's smile grew as I tore my focus away from him and turned to Callum. 'You need to save your power. Trust me with this,' he said.

I dipped my head in reluctant agreement. He was right. Killing creatures was one thing. Ending a god was another entirely – a use of power I couldn't spare. And if I fell, so did Callum.

But leaving him here...

'Trust me,' Callum said again, as though sensing my thoughts. There was no uncertainty in his words.

'Make it hurt,' I said as I studied the chaos around for any signs of the golden god. 'And don't die.'

I didn't need to look at Callum to sense his smirk. 'As you command.'

Akmad's laughter chased me. 'Fly away, little raven, and leave your king to me.'

My fingers tightened on my sword, but I didn't look back. Callum had asked me to trust him, and I did. He would emerge victorious. Not just because he knew death nearly as intimately as I did, nor because he was the only person who'd ever brought me to my knees during sparring.

It was because he fought to protect something. Akmad protected nothing but himself.

I had my own protecting to do. My own god to end.

That meant I'd need to cut a path through the battle before me.

Mortals and god-created creatures fell before me like dominoes. Some, I left as bloody carcasses upon the barren ground. Others, I left as nothing but dust and ash. I did not pause to take a breath or steady my heart. I was unstoppable.

I smiled at a mortal as I stalked towards him. His eyes widened in terror. Silver sparked at my fingertips, but I did not touch him. I simply willed him out of existence, and he was gone. Creature after creature crumbled into ash before me as my blood sang with power. Several enemy soldiers saw me coming. Swords fell to the ground as two sank to their knees. Three more turned and bolted. They did not get far.

The gods did not take well to cowards.

A ropey length of brown vine wrapped around one man's legs,

spiralling up to encase him. Leaves sprouted from the bare branch as bones crunched underneath. Another fell beneath a shadow creature's claws, which ripped through his chest in a matter of seconds. The third was downed by an impossible shot from an arrow that seemed to swerve to strike the woman dead centre in her forehead. There was no pity in me as the three corpses lay discarded, a few Ankurans falling upon the warm remains. They chose their death when they sided with a being who would see his own brethren slaughtered just for a taste of power.

I dragged a hand over my face, failing to clear my eyes of the stinging blood. The ground was densely covered by bodies here, as it had been near where Callum and I fought. It wasn't hard to see why.

Jaxon and Deana fought in tandem, Deana's weapons shifting and changing in her hands, switching from a sword that thrust through a scythe's body to a knife that slashed a mortal's throat. Any that her Gifted weapons missed, Jaxon's Illusions found. His eyes gleamed with his Gift, creatures falling upon each other with an almost frightening wildness, their eyes glazed over. Those that emerged from the chaos victorious, fell swiftly to Jaxon's sword.

'Kerta and Evania?' I called, shoving past a quaking soldier and cutting down a shadow wraith.

'Occupying Maia and Fortuna,' Jaxon replied. He waved a hand to the left, where swirls of grey and rose speared up in the sky, shoving at each other. Beside the ethereal beams, flames sparked in the air, copper crackling as it attempted to bring the other power down.

My power leapt at the sight, then sank as I kept hold of it. Those were not the gods we were after.

'Then Adwin and Vitus are all that remain unoccupied.'

Deana grasped a mortal by her hair, a crimson blade appearing in her hand. She sliced the woman's throat without looking down. 'Adwin's split away from Vitus. We'll offer him our company.'

'And Vitus will be mine.'

Jaxon smiled grimly. His hand shook with its next flick, a shadow wraith screeching as it turned its sharpened limbs onto its yellow-stained eyes. 'Better hurry. I don't think our soldiers can withstand much more fighting.'

He was right. Our side was weakening again, their momentary spur of energy fading quickly under the constant onslaught of the gods' side. Where mortals fell, Ankurans rose with frightening speed, their vacant eyes turned gold and hungry.

If I didn't move, then our army would become nothing more than walking corpses.

I forced myself to not give Jaxon and Deana a backwards glance as I ploughed through creatures. The scent of my power had faded, allowing that of blood and sweat to reclaim its hold on the air. Sweat coated my neck, blood soaked my skin. My garments were ruined, and fatigue weighed upon me.

But I was not done yet. I wouldn't be until I held the heart of a god in my hand.

'Stop.' The voice forced its way between cracked lips as an Ankuran with eyes of molten gold stepped in front of me. Its fissures were far deeper than others', a mark of its inhuman life coming to an end. 'End this now, little raven, and we will be merciful.'

I answered with a thrust of my blade through the creature's throat. It fell, its spot taken by another. The creature who had once been a woman held up a hand. 'We shall grant your mortals quick deaths.'

My blade dug deep into her chest, ribs cracking. The Ankuran's smile didn't fade in death. Staring at the woman's blank eyes, I let a tendril of my power slip over her, turning her to ash.

'We—' I didn't allow the next to finish its message. The silver tendril that had wrapped around the woman shot forward, spearing the Ankuran.

More Ankurans crowded forward, lips parted as they began to speak as their god had commanded them to. Words tumbled together, ancient power forcing limbs in need of eternal rest to move.

'Come, little raven,' one spoke, chestnut hair red from blood. 'Join my side. Let us work together.'

Another moved, jostling past its brethren. This one was further gone, the gold spreading past its irises, over skin and down its body. There was barely a hint of flesh to be seen. 'We could be more powerful than anything this world has seen.'

My brows lifted. Ever since he had first lain eyes on me, Vitus had promised either my death or eternal captivity. 'No,' I replied, smiling as I brought death to the creatures of false life.

The way cleared before me, lined by silver ash. Before I could step forward, a terrible scream split the air. I whipped around. Flames burned a path, threatening to consume enemy and ally as Kerta stalked forward. Her hair flowed behind her, eyes molten with rage. At the end of her destructive path, Maia planted her feet, arrow pointed at Kerta's chest. Behind, Fortuna held Evania by her hair.

Kerta did not even look at the huntress as that arrow flew. She plucked it from the air. Her fist clenched, and the arrow broke. Fear paled Maya's skin. Fortuna dragged Evania back a step.

More Ankurans appeared, dragging my attention from the goddesses. With a snarl, I drove my blade straight through muscle and tendons, letting the hand of the Ankuran fall to the ground before eviscerating him. To one side, a dome of shadows rose, mortal soldiers attempting to beat it down. The darkness didn't so much as flicker.

Callum was in there, I realised. Trapped with Akmad, the god who'd Gifted his father.

The Divine

My next victim fell in a particularly bloody mess.

He'd be fine. There was no time to think anything else.

I looked in the other direction. Peered past the Ankurans, their golden skin jarring against the brown hues of smoke. But even their brightness faded in comparison to Vitus.

The god carried the cold perfection of carved jewels, his eyes equally sharp as they met mine. Golden threads wove around him. Whenever they touched a body, it rose, the eyes shifting to gold. And with each rising of an Ankuran, the scent of the air deepened, that of decay and flowers taking hold.

'Shit,' I muttered. I sent two throwing knives into the skulls of a man and woman, lunging to retrieve the blades before popping back to my feet and sending my sword thrusting into the gut of another. I was down to very few weapons to throw. Blades were a valuable resource I couldn't afford to waste.

Blood sprayed left and right, drenching me. It clung to my skin and hair, golden streaks forming a work of art on my ruined clothes. Where there'd been three Ankurans, five took their place. Every death was an opportunity for more twisted life to grow.

Just like that, I had had enough. They were in my way. Callum was in danger, fighting a god. I wanted them gone.

I raised a hand, letting the silver gather on my fingertips. All it took was a single thought. No, not even a thought – a desire. One to see them all vanished.

Silver sprang to life. It shot forward, far quicker than any blade could, coating all in its path. Smoke and jasmine rose. My fingers curled. The silver snapped back to me.

Only ash remained.

More Ankurans poured in from gods only knew where, but I did not leash my Gift as I strode through them. As each reached me, they fell. The power rolled over me, holding me in its embrace. I did not shy from it.

I was made for this. Made for death.

'You have come.' The melodic voice rose over the cries of the battle around us, its sound hollow beauty. 'That was foolish of you. But then, you were always as foolish as your father.'

In a burst of gold, Vitus was in front of me.

He stood amongst a mass of bodies, a ring of Ankurans around him. The god-killer hummed its discordant tune at his side, the blade yet undrawn.

'I've come.' I tilted my head. Sunlight attempted to reach us through the smoke, turning the world into a dusty haze. Where my feet hit the ground, it dried and cracked, any weeds or insects dying in my presence. The silver-dusted brown stood in stark contrast to the vibrant green around Vitus.

'You should have convinced your father to lower the barrier and saved yourself an eternity of suffering.' Vitus's eyes flicked over me.

'And you should've killed me when you had the chance.' I let the death around my feet expand, reaching for the neat circle at Vitus's feet. 'It's far too late for that now.'

Vitus tracked the movement of death crawling towards him. He smiled. The green shot forward, overtaking the darkness of death.

Faint, dark amusement rose, momentarily breaking through the rage. We were in the middle of thousands battling for survival. Two gods, one ancient and one newly forged, fighting over a patch of grass.

It was pathetic. Laughable.

Gritting my teeth, the invasion of the green stopped, death and life at an impasse.

'Your resistance is futile, little raven.' Vitus lifted a hand to the bodies that remained amongst the ash. The corpses trembled, bodies contorting as they rose to their feet. Gold seeped through their veins. With a flick of his fingers, the newly formed Ankurans turned on me.

The Divine

I didn't shift my eyes away from Vitus, my hand mirroring his. The golden corruption shifted into silver, then into nothingness as each of the creatures crumbled.

Vitus's lips twitched. His other hand raised, golden light stirring on the tips of his fingers. This time, I was faster. Before the bodies to our right could shift upon the bloody ground, silver met gold, and those bodies crumbled as well.

The wind stirred the ashes left behind, picking them up and sprinkling them around me and Vitus. Soldiers from both sides gave us a wide berth. Even the mindless Ankurans seemed reluctant to near, skirting around the edges of the bodies that hadn't yet turned to ash.

'I will give you one last chance. Kneel before me and you can have a place in our new world. One outside of a cage.'

My heels dug deeper into the ground. *We do not kneel*, my power whispered, and I let its strength fill me. 'No.'

'No?' Golden eyebrows arched, and light flickered along Vitus's skin. His power flowed smoothly, in thick, winding bands of golden light. The power that jumped to my own skin did not flow. It crackled, pulsating as it leapt across my body. Where Vitus's was calm control, mine was a wildness that none had ever managed to beat out of me.

'No.' I stepped forward. 'But you may kneel before me. I can't promise that you will live to see how I remake your little godly realm, though.'

No, he would be long gone. Vitus had sealed his fate the moment he had driven Liam to slice Cassie's throat. And he'd added kindling to the flames of his end in every horrific moment since, from sending the Ankurans to the palace to my father's death.

Vitus didn't wear anger well, the expression twisting his features into something ugly as he snarled, 'You dare speak to me in such a way? I am the king of gods. This is the justice the mortals deserve for what they did to my Alexia. You will bow or you will die.'

'Even gods and kings can fall.' Where Vitus struggled to contain his anger, I welcomed it, letting it form a vicious smile. 'And today, you will fall. Fall so terribly that there will be nothing left of your soul to find Alexia after death.'

Vitus snapped, just as I'd intended. Gold slammed into my chest, sending intense heat and pain spiralling through. I invited it in.

'Is that all?' I stared at the god. 'Pathetic.'

The gold in his cheeks deepened. 'You're insignificant,' he snarled, another beam of power catching me in the arm. 'Weak.' He took another step, the power hitting my thigh. The pain roared through me, but I endured it. Let him waste his power in trying to subdue me. 'A waste.'

This time, when the gold made its way to me, it met silver. Burning light filled the sky. The colours clashed together, each winding around the other in a stranglehold as it spread out around us, encompassing a space of nearly fifty metres either side.

The few fools close to us tried to run as clashing powers swept towards them. None got more than a single step before that light touched them. Bloody wounds healed moments before their bodies disintegrated into ash. The gold kept pushing, wrapping around the crackling silver, edging towards the mass of fighting bodies beyond.

Stop, I commanded my power as it raced away with the gold. Twelve more, a mix of mortals and Ankurans, succumbed. Death was hungry, and it had found what it craved.

'Your pitiful power will not be enough to save you.' Vitus waved his hand. The gold pulled inwards, aiming right for me.

It hit me hard, stronger than before. The pain stole my breath. My legs buckled, body pitching forward. I managed to get an arm under me as I collapsed, barely preventing a face-first collision with the ground. I didn't stay down.

I tightened my fingers on my sword. Silver jerked forward, crackling like streaks of lightning. It slammed into Vitus's arm. His lips contorted into a grimace of pain, body convulsing slightly as he fell to one knee. Above, clouds gathered quickly, casting us in deep shadow. The air brimmed with coming violence.

Lunging forward, I angled my blade at his exposed back. He twisted, his features turned ugly by his snarl. I slammed into the ground and twisted with him, slicing at his throat. His hand shot out. Gold-stained fingers closed on the blade, tightening until the metal snapped in two.

Cursing, I tossed the useless weapon aside, withdrawing one of my remaining daggers.

Vitus eyed me. 'That weapon will not kill me. You must know that.'

'Death is far from the worst ending a person can have,' I said, stepping back to reclaim some space between us. The sounds of fighting were distant.

'I am well aware of that.' There was a moment of something that might've been humanity on his face – a flicker of pain, as though he was remembering anew the absence of his soul-bonded. 'And you will be familiar with the same before this day is through.' He smiled, his gaze turning past me. 'Or perhaps you already are. Tell me, little raven, is your soul-bond still there?'

I froze. Spun in the direction Akmad and Callum were as I reached for the bond. The dome of shadows still stood, but light was beginning to splinter through, stretching for the sky. Whatever was happening in the shadows was almost over, and only one would emerge victorious – either mortal or god.

The bond was still there. Muted, each of us focused on our own opponents, but there. I didn't dare call for Callum. A distraction might cost him his life.

But he was still alive.

I began to turn. A golden hand shot out, fingers curling around my throat. 'You think you are enough to protect him? You are nothing. In the end, you and I are the same. You will lose your soul-bonded, and you will destroy whatever is left of this realm if I do not chain you.'

I drove my dagger upwards, driving it into the fragile skin of Vitus's wrist. Blood sprayed. He howled, staggering away from me. 'You're right. I would destroy this realm if Callum died.' I batted away a spear of golden power with a swipe of my hand, my silver consuming it. 'But there's one difference between us. I will not allow him to be taken from me. He is not Alexia, and I am not you.'

Vitus's wrist glowed golden. His wound disappeared, but his rage did not. 'I have changed my mind. I thought to keep you as a pet – chained at my feet, so I knew where that wretched power was housed. But you do not deserve that mercy. You shall die.'

I smiled. 'What about your precious balance? My power might not find—'

'It is not *your* power!' Vitus's voice slammed through the air, setting the ground shaking. I could no longer hear the battle around us, the silver and gold acting as a barrier. In here, there was nothing that could protect Vitus from me, and nothing to protect him from me. 'It belongs to the gods, not to a halfling like you! It will find another host because I command it to.'

My power buzzed angrily, as though it sensed that if I were to fall, the balance of the realms would tip, the power unable to find any willing or able to take it on.

And if that happened, it wouldn't just be the mortals that died. It would be everyone. Everything. Complete destruction.

'You do not command death,' I said, raising my hand as Vitus raised his. Power crackled between us, two snakes ready to strike to see which held more venom. 'And this power is mine. It was always destined to be.'

'Dearil was a god. You are—'

'The one who will end you.' Sparks flickered. Smoke and jasmine wrapped around me.

'Enough,' Vitus growled, that gold light swinging towards me with a ferocity that was almost impressive as my power turned on him.

Gold and silver met mid-air, each one fighting the other for dominance. Pain racketed through my body as gold slipped past my shield of silver. Fire surged through my veins, knives digging into my flesh. I didn't make a noise as I reached inside for that power and pushed.

Vitus staggered back a step. His golden skin paled, the veins under his skin bulging as though ready to burst, but his power did not give.

'Give up,' he snarled.

'Never,' I snarled back, with every bit as much hatred.

'You're nothing compared to me.'

I lunged at Vitus, slicing deep into his arm. Another flare of gold, and only a silver line remained. Vitus hissed, the ugly ring of metal sounding as he yanked out the god-killer. Exhaustion weighed heavily on me, turning my movements sluggish as his power pressed down. I did not let myself give in, though.

'You have it around the wrong way.' I spun under a swipe of the god-killer. Its nearness sent ice prickling over me. 'You're nothing but a pathetic creature so caught up in your own greed that you would seek to destroy an entire realm to satiate it.'

I didn't have time to spin past the backhanded blow Vitus sent my way. It caught my cheek, the weight of his fist lifting my feet from the ground. Warmth spilt down my cheek from where skin had split. I swiped it away.

'Who are you to call me pathetic?'

I rolled, losing my sword as I went. Vitus drove the god-killer downwards. Dirt flung into the air. I staggered to my feet, eyeing the fissures of power formed where Vitus had struck, each colour reflecting a different power of the gods.

Yanking out my last dagger, I flicked it towards Vitus. It sunk deep into his shoulder. 'I will be the queen of this kingdom.'

Vitus roared his fury. Thunder met his call, rain beginning to fall around us. He wrapped golden fingers around the small blade, his blood watering the earth. 'You will be the queen of nothing.'

The god-killer swiped for my side. I twisted in response. Instead of sinking in between two ribs, the blade cut through the flesh of my arm instead.

The wave of agony that came from that wound was like nothing I had felt before. It rippled outwards, as though my whole body was being forced onto shard upon shard of broken glass. Strands of colours cut through my skin, silver rising to beat it back. My blood dripped, silver flecks littering the crimson.

Vitus smiled. 'It is agonising, is it not?' He stalked forward. I tried to tear my mind from the pain, but between that and making sure that his rising wall of power didn't crash down, all I could do was stagger backwards. 'The only blade in existence to kill a god. It should handle a halfling fine.'

Most of my strength went into maintaining that silver aura in the air. As soon as I let it go, the world around me would fold to the power of twisted life. I could not let that happen. I would not, not when Deana and Jaxon stood out there, facing down a god of their own. Not when soldiers fought so bravely, despite the hopelessness of it all. Not when Callum was out there, still trapped in that dome of darkness, fighting for me as desperately as I did for him.

I scanned the ground, searching for something, anything, as Vitus approached. All I saw was crackling silver and gold energy, dust and ash on the floor, patches of fresh grass warring with dead shoots.

Vitus's voice lashed through the air. 'Kneel.'

'I will not.'

'You will, little raven, or you will fall into nothingness.'

The world shuddered, and I didn't know if it was our power or one of the other gods that did it. If it was Akmad unleashing his fury on Callum.

But the bond was still there. Stronger than it had been before, even, as the battles between gods used up much of the power saturating the air. I could feel him at the end, now. We both still breathed, and I would not give in.

I slammed my blade upwards, catching him on the underside of his jaw. Silver-lined metal sunk through soft flesh. 'I will do neither of those things,' I snarled, letting warm gold blood trickle over my fingertips.

Vitus's eyes blazed. Slowly, deliberately, he reached up, curling his fingers round mine. My bones groaned in his hold as he wrenched the blade free. The spurt of blood lasted for no more than a second.

'So be it,' Vitus spat, his teeth gold flecked as his blade swung for my head. I met the god-killer with my dagger. Gold and silver flashed through the sky. He withdrew once more, his next blow vicious and quick.

I let the dagger drop. My free hand snapped forward, catching it as I used Vitus's momentary startlement to spin around him. My arm hooked around his neck. He choked as I tightened my hold, a lifetime of training and divine blood strengthening my hold. His fingers clawed. I was relentless. A beast with her prey between her teeth.

Vitus sank to his knees, the grass around us lengthening with his desperation. He gave up at clawing, reaching upwards instead. I reacted too late. His finger caught on my hair, wrenching forward. Stinging pain erupted. My grip loosened and he twisted free, staggering to his feet.

The bond between Callum and I turned hot, agony lancing down it. Agony that was not mine.

Panic reared. My head whipped in the direction I'd last seen him, heart thudding until a trickle of calm slipped through to me. I didn't see the blow coming until it slammed into my cheek. Air punched out of my lungs as I fell backwards, colliding with the ground. For a moment, all I did was blink at a sky I could not see. The world was made of gold and silver and little else. One god's vengeance and another's retribution.

'It is almost a pity,' Vitus said. He pressed a knee into my chest and angled the god-killer at my throat. Pressure clamped down on my wrists, its oily touch telling me it was Vitus's power. 'If you had been more malleable, perhaps you could have lived to see a new age. An age where even halflings could have lived and thrived.'

I choked out a laugh. I didn't know if it was his blow, or simply the press of the power building around us that speckled my lips with blood.

'I would never let you bend me to your will,' I bit out. 'Never.'

Vitus sighed. 'As stubborn as your father, though without any of his decorum and restraint. A distasteful combination.'

I snarled back. I'd show him restraint. I twisted my body forward, attempting to send my head colliding with his. Vitus did nothing but lift a single finger, pressing it to the middle of my forehead.

Where I had raw power, Vitus had centuries of practice and experience. A single thread wove around that pointed finger, driving straight through me. For a moment, my vision blackened. When it cleared, black spots lingered.

'Your mortals will die. Your friends will die. Your king will

The Divine

die,' Vitus told me. 'You will die. This will all have been for nothing.'

'You disgrace your title,' I hissed back, straining against his hold despite the pain. Pain, I could endure. This sense of helplessness, of being able to do nothing as he stared down at me – not so much. 'You call yourself the god of life, and yet you know nothing of it. All you crave is death.' I smiled then, letting him see what the machinations of men and gods had created over the years. 'In the end, even you bow before me.'

Vitus paled as though he saw the monstrous thing that lurked beneath my skin. Not something to be feared by my allies, but to my enemies, the sort of beast that made nightmares seem tame.

'I bow before no one, and particularly not you, little raven. You are nothing but a weak halfling playing at being divine.'

'And all you are is a cowering god,' I spat back. 'At least I don't shy from what I am.'

Chiara. The word punched through my focus, the silver softening slightly against the cruel blows of the gold, as Callum's voice filled me. The bond was back, which meant some of the godly power saturating this area must have lessened. *Where are you?*

I'm fine, I sent back, smiling as Vitus used his fist to vent his rage. *Just a little occupied.*

If Callum replied, I didn't hear it as Vitus's hand wrapped around my throat. He leant in close, forcing my head back into the ground, lips pulled away from his teeth. 'You're nothing.' He echoed his earlier words. 'You were born to be no one. Do you think yourself worthy of being anything more than a mortal-made monster?'

I stared up at the god, a creature made to emulate perfection. A monster. I'd never shied from what I was before. My scars told the tapestry of all I'd endured. All this realm and its people had created.

A monster, and a queen.

'I—' I began, eyes meeting Vitus's cold ones.

I did not get a chance to finish my sentence.

Vitus made that choice for me as he plunged the god-killing dagger deep through me.

Then, there was only pain.

It consumed me. But what raced through me with far more force was my rage. Rage that I'd let myself fall. Fury that Vitus – the god who'd taken too much from me already – was the one holding the knife driven into my abdomen. And a realms-ending wrath that I'd been reunited with Callum only to yet again be forced apart from him. Only, this time, with that blade stuck in me and Vitus triumphant above me, that separation would be far more permanent.

My power simmered with it all as that fury built beside the pain. Built until there was nowhere else to go but *out*.

The world paused. Power crackled, and an entire army fell into silence. Vitus tilted his head.

And then the world exploded in a flash of silver and gold.

Chapter Thirty-Four

My ears were filled with ringing.

There were bodies everywhere. Bodies under me, limbs pressing painfully into my back. Bodies on top of me, suffocatingly heavy. The blood … oh, gods. The blood was everywhere. It drenched my skin, stinging my eyes and blocking my nose. And I … I couldn't move. I was trapped in a mass grave of my own making. I must've flown backwards, the armour of my own allies holding onto lingering remnants of my power. Not enough to reduce them to ash, but enough to end them.

Beneath the crush of bodies, I began to calculate my pain. The sting was one above my left eyebrow, small but fierce. A near identical pain lancing my right cheek. A sharp throb in my right arm. The most concerning, though, was the fiery agony that shot through my abdomen. I didn't know if the dagger remained in there, or if it had been dislodged.

If it had dislodged, I suspected it wouldn't be long till I bled out. The thought sent fear coursing through me.

A sound that might have been a laugh had I enough air to do

so wheezed from my lips. This was a fitting end. Death, the one thing I'd brought again and again, was to be my burial ground.

Chiara, Callum's voice whispered down the bond.

My mind was a haze of pain, but I managed to latch onto the sound of his voice. Callum was alive. That was all that mattered. *Are you all right?*

Fine, he said, and I wondered if he was shielding the bond from his pain as much as I was. I hoped not. Callum had had enough suffering in his life.

Agony pulsed in sharp rebuke as I managed to get out, *Never been better.* I tried to shift. Tried to open my eyes. All I found was pain.

I must not have had as good a grasp at shielding the bond as I thought I did. There was a moment's silence, then a burst of fear so violent I nearly bit my tongue as it slammed into me. *What's happened?*

I swallowed, my mouth dry. Sounds of fighting filtered through the buzz in my ears, and I thought I heard Callum's voice – his actual voice, not just the bond – roaring my name. But it was too far, and I was too tired to rise. *Nothin—*

Do not lie to me.

I thought my lips might have curved into a smile. Of course, he knew I was lying. My fingers twitched, shifting onto the dampness spreading over my midsection. I barely felt them. Barely felt anything but cold. *I have to finish Vitus.* I could feel him close by. Sense the shift of bodies around me as though someone were flinging them away.

I needed to convince my body to move before he found me buried here.

Chiara—

The wound didn't hurt as much as the break in my name did. *It's just a flesh wound*, I promised, the words steadier in their lie than they had been before. I didn't let the grief of knowing I

The Divine

wouldn't get a life with Callum break through. Even if I wasn't here, I needed to make sure he survived. The only way to do that was to ensure the power in his body beat back the death that had once come for him.

He needed to inherit Vitus's power before I died.

Of course it is. There's nothing strong enough to take you down. His voice was firm. Forceful. A king commanding the realm to bend to his will.

But the warmth in my veins told me the realm had already decided my fate. Death was coming for me, and I was running out of time.

Show me what we're facing, I ordered Callum.

Images flashed down the bond.

Three Ankurans, falling in quick succession to Callum's blade, gold blood spraying.

Deana and Jaxon fighting back-to-back some distance off, creatures swarming them.

Evania, standing over an injured Kerta, with teeth bared and swords of pure white glowing in her hands, as Maia approached.

And finally, of Vitus. Gold blood streaked down his face, his eyes wild and movements manic as he tore away at a pile of bodies. Bodies that I suspected were currently my only protection from him. With the blood-soaked golden strands and skin, he did not seem beautiful or noble. He merely seemed cold and lifeless. A god who'd moved too far from that which he was meant to represent.

He would find me soon, and he would make sure I died.

I could not let that happen. The gods all followed Vitus simply because they were creatures designed to bow before power. The Ankurans only existed because of Vitus. Callum's life was only threatened because Vitus lived.

If Vitus were to fall, his army would fall with him.

I braced myself, willing strength into my limbs. My breathing settled. My shoulders tensed.

If I asked you to rest – to leave this to me – would you? Callum asked. Again, I thought I heard his actual voice, closer this time. I let it centre me, tether me to this realm for just a little longer. *If not for yourself, for me? I can't lose you.*

Pain lanced through my chest, matched by that in my abdomen. I wanted to agree. To rest. Gods knew I needed it. Had needed it for a long time.

But that was not who I was, and we both knew that.

I enslaved myself for my sister, I said as a body to my left shifted. Rain fell onto my hand, and Vitus's laugh broke through, triumph filling the sound. He'd found me. *I made myself survive for months for you. And I would do both a thousand times over for anyone I love.* Power twisted, gathering under my skin and warming my veins. *But this fight is mine.* I paused, then added, *Though I might need you to watch my back.*

Always.

I didn't need to tell him what to do. He'd carve his path to me and cut down any who would try to interfere.

The crush above me disappeared as my final shield was torn away from me. I readied myself. Shoved aside the pain and focused on what I'd have to do.

'Pathetic,' Vitus sneered. 'All it took was a single wound to kill a halfling.'

I opened my eyes. For a moment, the world was a hazy mess of gold. It took several heartbeats to sharpen. Vitus crouched over me, no blade in hand, his face split with victory. I was weak. Injured. Prey not worth the effort.

Blades clashed nearby. I didn't need to look to know Callum had made his way nearby and fought to protect me. No Ankuran would make it close.

My grin was something that came from nightmares.

The Divine

And that was what I was. A nightmare made flesh. A monster given form. All the blood-soaked terrors of apathetic gods given reality.

His victory faltered as I asked, 'But would it be enough to kill a god?'

'It matters not. You are a halfling, and you will die.'

'I'm no halfling.' Silver power flickered at my fingertips. A knife made of pure death. 'I'm the god of death.'

For the first time since we had met on the battlefield, Vitus finally realised that there was something more fearsome than him. He started to pull backwards. He was far too late.

I lunged upwards, drawing the silver blade across his chest. He hissed in a mixture of pain and fury as the silver latched onto him, spreading outwards in a fine webbing for a few seconds before dissipating underneath the flow of golden power from the god.

The gold swamped the cut before receding, but the cut remained, a silver glow infecting the gold blood that slowly oozed from the wound at his side. Vitus's power would not reverse the effects of my own, the two too different to interact.

I forced myself to my feet, grinning my feral smile.

His eyes narrowed. 'You will regret that.'

His head jerked and I stepped backwards, the movement pulling at the wound on my abdomen. Sweat clung to my skin as surely as the blood did, dampening my hair. A raindrop fell from the sky, splattering against my forehead.

But Vitus did not move. He didn't even draw on my power as a sudden wave of pain crashed through the bond. Pain that did not belong to me.

Comprehension bowled into me as I whirled around, leaving my back exposed. Callum was still upright, but his swings were slower, more laboured, and his side was soaked in blood. There were no shadows caressing his skin, seeking out the wound. His

Gift was that of a mortal, and it had already been used too much.

He grunted as an Ankuran drove into his injured side. The Ankuran died quickly, Callum's sword plunging through its back. But his strength couldn't last forever, especially with the amount of blood seeping through his armour.

All it would take is a single falter, and I might lose him.

Don't worry about me, Callum said down the bond as he gripped an Ankuran's throat with one hand, cutting down a mortal with his other. *I'm doing just fine.*

He was a beautiful liar. He was not doing fine, and he would not be standing for much longer.

I had enough power to take a good portion of the enemy, and Callum could deal with the rest. But if I did that, I'd have nothing left for Vitus.

Trust me, Captain, Callum said.

Always, I replied.

'That,' I breathed, whirling at the god who watched with cruel satisfaction, 'was a grievous mistake.'

'No, little raven. I don't think it was.' His eyes turned knowingly to the silver blade in my hand, the way it flickered like a candle caught in a gust of wind. 'You have a choice, now.'

Another burst of pain, thick and vicious, across my thigh. Again, no blood stained me, but that silver blade – it was near translucent, the power flickering.

'A choice?' I ground out.

'Your king's soul is so desperate to break free right now, as is your own. You can choose to let him go, to let him fall and finally release that soul you have been clutching. Or, you can fall to me.'

'If I fall to you, he dies anyway,' I snarled, willing the blade back into being. It wavered. My strength shook with it.

'Perhaps.' Vitus smiled. 'Perhaps I will offer him my mercy.'

'I...' My words trailed off as the blade in my hand flickered once, twice, then disappeared entirely. Those black dots that had been threatening rushed in. I stumbled, falling to one knee. 'I…'

Where the blade had met flesh, the pain no longer existed. There was only an icy numbness that belied the warmth of death.

'Yes, little raven?'

'I…' The words were a whisper accompanied by blood dripping from my mouth. Silver-freckled red splattered the ashy ground. I could feel death, feel its talons reaching. If I lost to unconsciousness, Vitus wouldn't need to do anything for my end to come.

He crouched before me, his cold fingers reaching up to cup my chin. It would be easy for him to end me. To take the god-killer and drive it through my heart. But Vitus was the sort who enjoyed prolonging suffering. This was to be his final victory over Dearil.

'Speak your final words, little raven. I will allow you that.'

I forced my head back. There was blood on my lips, on my chin, as I smiled at him. 'I win.'

I ripped my hand away from where I'd clutched my wound. The god-killer came with it. Any numbness that existed fell into fiery, terrible agony that tore up my insides with claws of iron. I pushed that aside.

Vitus reared back. He was too slow, and I too filled with desperation for Callum. I shoved the god-killer through his abdomen, the positioning a mirror to my own wound. Gold flared on his skin. It struck at the wound, trying to wrap around it. But this was a weapon made to decide the fates of gods. Even his power couldn't overcome the effects.

'That,' I hissed, 'was for my father.'

I drove my arm down again as Vitus made to move. His movements were slow, more sluggish than mine. He was unused to pain, and it made him weak. Unprepared.

The blade met his shoulder, sinking through the flesh and

cracking against bone. He fell backwards, and I fell with him. 'That was for my sister.'

His golden skin was pale, eyes hazy. Golden blood bubbled between his lips. He did not speak, though. He likely did not know how. By his side, his arms twitched uselessly as rain began to fall in earnest, plastering my hair to my neck and sending Vitus's blood cascading down him in watery rivulets.

'And this,' I said as Vitus's expression shifted to, for perhaps the first time in his miserable existence, genuine fear for his life, 'is for me.'

I plunged the blade deep into the god's heart.

Chapter Thirty-Five

The world stilled. There was a second of surprise flaring in Vitus's eyes. Around us, silence blanketed everything. Creatures and mortals were frozen, the rain halting mid-fall. But I didn't freeze. I twisted the knife deeper. Let my power seep into the blade – into him – until he let out a choked sound, and then slumped, the rage and shock flickering out of existence.

I exhaled. The god of life was dead.

The gold of his irises leeched outwards, stretching past his eyes and onto his cheeks, winding its way through his hair and over his body. His power was ravenous. It consumed him, wrapping every centimetre of his body in tight tendrils of power. I didn't move from where I straddled him, god-killer still in hand. Even if I'd wanted to, I couldn't, my body beginning to give in to exhaustion.

But I also wanted to watch this. To feel his death under my hands.

I'd done what I needed to. And with this, Callum could live.

There was a flare of light more brilliant than the sun itself. This time, it wasn't the scent of flowers and decay that surrounded us, but the promise of coming rain and cedar. A sign of the successor of the power. As quickly as silence had fallen, noise started back up – a wind whistling through the air, the laughter of children and the call of birds. All the life that Vitus had threatened to destroy. The brilliant light collapsed in on itself, taking Vitus's body with it.

The sudden cacophony of noise stopped as quickly as it had started. Silence reigned, the sound of my own breath seeming muffled and far away. The screams and cries that had surrounded me only a moment before had fallen into the same heavy quiet, the weight of the stillness oppressive.

And then, all at once, the silence shattered. Thousands of bodies fell, crashing to the ground as corpses forced by Vitus to fight were allowed to rest. Souls fluttered free, brushing their warm shapes past me as they sped off to wherever they were destined to go.

Those who remained upright began to let out a cry of victory. At first, only one or two voices held the cheer, but it was quickly passed on, soldier after soldier roaring their triumph to the skies. The ground shook with the violent euphoria. Weapons beat against armour, feet thudded on the ground as, one by one, any mortals who had chosen the wrong side dropped their weapons.

I did not turn to soak in the noise. Instead, I lifted my head, eyes seeking out the one person I needed to be all right.

Callum was already there, resplendent in his blood-soaked armour, his eyes fixed only on me. He smiled. His golden blond hair brushed against his brow, collecting raindrops that were already beginning to cease falling from the skies. And his wounds…

My own eyes widened at the speed with which they closed, his shadows more fierce than they'd been before. Where it had taken time for me to accept my power, that of life latched onto Callum with startling intensity. The dark tendrils entwined

The Divine

themselves over his limbs, brushing away bruising and cuts within the space of a breath, leaving nothing but unblemished skin in its wake. When they reached his side, the darkness softened. A scar would be left, I knew. A reminder of what he had overcome.

'Your—' I choked on the words, shifting my arm to hide the severity with which blood was leaving my body. Callum deserved at least this moment of relief. Of happiness. 'Your Gift. It's ... you're amazing.'

He crouched before me, pressing a hand to my cheek. Shadows brushed across his skin, skimming over my cheek gently. Even if they couldn't heal me, I felt their warmth, as reassuring as a summer's breeze.

'I'm amazing?' He quirked an eyebrow. 'I'm not the one who just killed a god and saved this realm.'

My lips tugged upwards, the slight curve as much as I could manage. 'I did do that, didn't I?'

Callum pressed his lips to my forehead, not seeming to care about the blood or dirt that soaked the skin there, just as he never had before – he'd never paid any mind to what blemished my skin or my soul. 'You did.'

'Your Gift—' I paused, letting my words trail off like I meant them to as I sucked in as much air as I could handle, feeling each breath rattling through my chest. 'Does that mean Vitus's...' Again, I trailed off, the words coming too slow and laboriously to my lips.

Callum finished my sentence for me. 'His power flowed into me as we suspected.' He frowned, turning his free hand over. Other than the shadows there, a little thicker and stronger than they had been before, there were no differences to his skin. 'I'm a little underwhelmed so far. I was expecting something more ... flashy.'

I choked out a laugh. 'Of course you were.'

Callum flicked his gaze back to me, his expression turning concerned. 'Your wound. We should get you to—'

I wrapped my arm around the nape of his neck, pulling him down to me. When our lips met, it tasted like salt and sorrow. Like a goodbye. I held onto him desperately even as I weakened. I needed this moment. Needed him for however many heartbeats I had left.

But I was cold, and I could barely feel anything anymore, even him.

I pulled away, pressing my forehead to his. 'I'm sorry, Callum.'

'Sorry? Why are you—' He pulled back, his eyes searching mine. I saw the moment he understood. The moment he felt what I allowed to slip down the bond, no longer able to hold it back. 'No. No, Chiara.'

'I had to – end this,' I managed to get out. My hand fell to his shoulder as my knees weakened. I didn't have long. 'Had to – see him – dead.'

'Dammit, Chiara.' Callum's voice was soft. Broken. 'You're a godsdamned stubborn fool. The realm could've fallen. If you'd rested, then—'

'It wouldn't change anything. I'm—' My words ended in a gasp as the world spun around me. Callum caught me as I fell, lifting me into his arms. The grey of the sky commanded my vision. I stared up at the sky, the last of the raindrops falling to break upon my cheeks, wetting them like tears. It was beautiful, that mess of sun and cloud spread across the sky.

This power would find a new host. I had to believe that – that there was a mortal out there who could manage its viciousness. Callum could help them to make sure the realms would live. That he would, too.

And I would be gone.

The frantic thrum of a heartbeat beat against my skin. Callum held me tightly as he turned, then began to move towards the campsite. There was no adrenaline now to bring sweet numbness. Every one of his steps or brush of the wind brought a fresh sharp spike of pain that had me curling inwards.

'I'm sorry, my love,' he murmured into my blood-soaked hair. 'But we need to get you somewhere you can get help.'

I didn't know how long I existed in the hazy world of pain, the grey of the sky often blotted out by blackness. When we stopped, the remnants of smoke clung to the air around us, the remains of the camp filled with activity. There were screams and moans from the dying as non-Gifted healers rushed amongst them. I blinked back the darkness threatening to take hold, turning my head as much as I could. There were so many. Near as many bodies here as those left standing on the field, laid out on the ground or in whichever tents had survived. Too many made no sound at all.

'Alannah!' Callum barked. A tall woman bustled over. Her face was freer of blood than mine or Callum's. Her arms, though, were covered in it, as though she had just been elbow-deep in someone's insides. 'We need you.'

Alannah's pale eyes flicked to me, fingers twisting and features paling as her gaze dropped to my abdomen. 'Your Majesty, a wound like that... I'm sorry, but resources are precious enough as it is. Even if she only received it a moment ago—'

'Your aid. Now.' Callum leant forward, his arms curling tighter around me. 'It wasn't a request.'

I watched the woman's throat bob nervously, but she stood firm. 'I'm sorry, Your Majesty, but we simply don't have the resources to spend on a dead woman.'

I let out a weak laugh that sounded more like a rattle of a breath. 'Hear that?' I rasped, hand lifting to hold weakly onto Callum's arm. 'I'm dead already, apparently.'

His glare switched to me. 'Save your strength for things other than an absurd sense of humour.' He looked past Alannah. 'How many of these need to be healed before you listen to your godsdamned king?'

Alannah's mouth set into a hard line. I thought I might have liked her, if I had had time to get to know her better. 'All of them. They all need the resources. Everyone else … they've already faded.'

Callum nodded once, and darkness exploded from him. Shadows flew through the air like little spears, each sinking into the flesh of the men and women on the floor. Within moments, all screams had stopped.

Beautiful, I thought, smiling faintly.

Alannah gaped up at Callum. 'What-how—'

'Your aid,' he repeated.

Alannah swallowed, then nodded. 'Yes, Your Majesty.'

Callum looked down, his eyes the only thing bright that I could see. 'You're ice-cold.'

'It's okay,' I murmured, my head tilting back to take in the grey of the skies again as he took long strides after Alannah. 'I'm warm enough.'

I had faded into that numbness from before. It cocooned my skin just as surely as Callum's arms wrapped around my body. It was easy, now, to block out the concern in his eyes as he stared down at me, and to ignore the way his fingers curled just a little deeper into my skin as though he refused to let any part of me go.

'Your soul is safe,' I whispered, and Callum cocked his head.

'What?'

'Your soul.' I thought I smiled up at him, but perhaps I didn't. It was hard to tell, now, what parts of my body still obeyed my command. 'Vitus's powers.' The grey sky was replaced with the cream-coloured tarp of a tent roof, the canvas billowing softly. I was placed onto something hard. If I'd had the strength, I might've reached for the warmth of Callum's arms again. 'Should be enough to keep your soul in.'

It would be life that maintained the balance for saving it in the first place. Everything was as it should be.

'I don't care about my soul, Chiara. I care about you.' I thought maybe Callum held my hand, but I wasn't entirely sure. Sensations were odd pricklings now, rather than lucid feelings.

Alannah murmured something to Callum. The pressure at my hand tightened. He turned his face from me, but not quickly enough for me to miss the rage and grief. 'Callum.'

When he looked back, his eyes were too bright. 'I'm damned useless.' He pressed his mouth to my hand, eyes closing for a moment. 'All this power of Vitus's, and it can't save the one person it should.'

That numbness was creeping now, as was the black. I wasn't sure what the hazy shapes around me were anymore, aside from Callum's eyes. Those, I would recognise in utter darkness. Those, I would hold onto until I died.

'Callum?' I whispered again, my breath almost choking me. There was no pain. No cold. No warmth. Nothing.

I didn't think I'd ever been afraid of this before. Of ending up on a table like this, those around me unable to help. Of finding the fate that I had always been sure I was destined for from the first moment I set foot on a battlefield.

But here I was. Terrified.

'Save your strength, my love.' Callum leant over me, pressing his forehead to mine. And I – I couldn't feel it. There was something in my throat, something metallic tasting that made it difficult to get the words out. I could barely breathe around it. Barely think around the haziness that I waded through.

Callum. There was no strength left in me to speak the words, so I sent them down the bond instead, trying to keep my grasp on it. His eyes were fixed on mine. *I don't want to die.*

For a moment, it seemed like Callum was the one choking on his own blood as he cupped my cheek.

I— It was an effort to even see that bond between us, now, to hold onto it. The invisible hands I used to grasp it seemed as slippery as the blood-soaked ones that lay by my side. I could no longer see the tent. I could no longer see Alannah.

I could no longer see Callum.

I could see nothing but blackness and the thinnest sliver of shadow threaded silver.

I don't want to go.

Then don't. The words that came to me were adamant. Set in stone.

He didn't feel that pull, though. The thing that tugged me to beyond, to wherever gods ended up.

It struck me then.

Callum might be like a god now, imbued with the power of one, and he might have the immortal lifespan of one, but if he died – he was born as mortal as the soldiers on the battlefield. And mortal souls did not end up where gods did.

I was about to lose him forever.

I had not even really got to have him, yet, not truly, and I would never have him again.

I love you. I wish I could have been your queen.

I did not know if he heard it, did not know if he sent anything back. The silver was murky, now, and so thin I could cut it with my teeth if it were a corporeal thing.

It was getting harder to cling to the thread. I wanted to, so badly. I wanted time with Callum, as long or short as it might have been. I wanted to explore the world, to taste freedom, to learn who I was when killing was not demanded of me, when drawing blood was a choice. I wanted to rule a kingdom by his side, and one day pass that kingdom on to someone else. I wanted to have adventures, and to find out all the small things I had not yet discovered about him.

The Divine

I wanted life. I wanted it so much that it hurt more than the wound had.

My heart beat loudly in that blackness, the only sound that reached me anymore. It was little more than a flutter, a pitiful attempt at claiming life.

I don't want to die. I wanted to wail the words, to rage with them against the cards fate had dealt me. I didn't want to die – and it wasn't just because of the grief it would bring in my friends and in Callum, or the mess my death would leave behind.

It was for me. I simply hadn't lived enough yet.

But death was a fickle creature and did not always bow to its master.

My heart beat once. Twice. Three times.

That silver thread slipped, and my unseen hands did not catch the end as it whipped away from me.

And then … then there was silence.

Chapter Thirty-Six

Callum

Callum was unmoored. He wanted no part in the power filling him. In all that life buzzing around him. Not when the person he truly lived for, that he would gladly die for, was gone.

The bond had torn free from his grip and cut a gash open in his soul that he knew could never be healed. And now ... now his forehead was pressed to her too-still chest, fists bunched in the cloth of her shirt. His fingers were sticky with blood that was cooling too quickly.

Blackness exploded around them, spearing out from him. The power he'd only accepted because it would help Chiara. The healer, Alannah, shrieked. Something crashed – a vial, perhaps – and cries echoed outside the tent.

Callum didn't care.

He didn't think he would care about much ever again.

'Godsdamn you, Chiara,' he breathed into her skin. She was

still warm, her skin clinging to a facsimile of life. 'Open your eyes. Breathe.'

Everything that made her *her* – every beautiful, sharp, wicked part – he couldn't feel it. The bond between them hung, loose as a cut thread. And at its end, there was no trace of her.

'Callum,' a voice gasped, breaking through the shadows and reaching his ears. The word might have been one of relief or of pain as a familiar set of hands somehow found his shoulders in the dark. 'Thank the gods. You're fine.'

Callum didn't turn, his fingers pressing into Chiara's skin as though sheer will alone would be enough to save her. He didn't acknowledge Deana, barely registered her presence even as the blackness receded. The power was too untested and untried to exist out in the open for too long.

He wished it would. Then he could grasp hold of the fragile hope that the stillness beneath his hold was a trick of the mind.

'Dammit, Chiara. Don't do this,' Callum bit out as he took her in. 'Breathe. You do not get to leave me.'

Alannah quietly made her way out of the tent.

'Where's Chiara?' Callum turned his head just enough to see the anger in Jaxon's eyes as they fell on him, and then dropped to … to… 'No. No.'

'Oh, gods.' Deana stumbled back, hand covering her mouth. 'This can't be real.'

'She was supposed to be safe,' Jaxon whispered. He looked more god than mortal in that moment, the yellow of his eyes flaring violently as they locked onto Callum. 'You were supposed to keep my sister safe.'

Callum's jaw clenched. The anger was easy to latch onto. It was far better than the hollow emptiness that threatened beneath. 'She'll be fine. Someone just needs – where is that damned healer? If we work quickly, there has to be something that can—'

'Callum.' Deana's voice was too soft, as though she had already given up.

'Why aren't either of you helping?' Callum curled his hands into fists, the material of Chiara's shirt wet with blood and rain. Paper in his pocket crinkled as he twisted towards them. The missives he'd taken with him, a link he'd been sure would keep them together even when apart. He should've left them behind. Severed that link between him and Chiara if it would've meant she'd live. 'Help her.'

Jaxon's anger seemed to fade as he came to stand on the other side of the table Chiara was laid upon. The gentleness that replaced the hard lines was all wrong.

Callum wished he'd be angry. He wished Jaxon would try to cut him down.

The sympathy – the pity – was far worse, because if it was there, that meant there was something to pity him for.

'Cal, she's gone.' Jaxon reached forward with one hand, his other arm bent at an odd angle.

Callum's head shot up as Jaxon's hand neared his. 'Don't fucking touch me,' he snarled, and Jaxon raised his hands, palms facing outwards. Callum returned his gaze to Chiara's face. She looked far too peaceful, her features too soft for the woman he knew she was. Even in sleep, there always seemed to be a curve to her lips that hinted at wicked thoughts. Now, there was none of that sharpness. 'She's not gone. She can't be.'

He didn't let his gaze drift lower than her face, did not let himself think about the ruin of her body.

'She's gone,' Jaxon whispered again. 'Let her go.'

'I—' Callum rasped out, but the word was thick and heavy. 'I can't do this without her.'

'I know.' Jaxon rested a hand on Callum's back. This time, Callum didn't shrug it away.

'She's my everything.' Callum leant in close to Chiara, his

words whispered just for her ears. There were no tears in his eyes. But they would come, he knew, and he would drown in that sorrow. 'You hear that, you brave, foolish woman? You're mine, and I'm yours, and you cannot leave. Not now, not when there's so much for you to live for.'

But the woman he loved did not respond.

Chapter Thirty-Seven

I was lost. Gone. Nothing more than ash left to drift darkness.
The realms demanded a price for Callum's soul to remain in the realm of the living. A soul for a soul. A life for a life.
Balance was righted.

Chapter Thirty-Eight

Perhaps I was not quite gone, not quite lost yet. There was enough awareness within me to scream out, to rage against the cards fate had dealt me.

I didn't want to be dead.

I refused to be.

And there, cracking through the warm darkness that had swept me away from those I loved, I saw it. A glimmer of silver.

It was so faint that I could barely make it out, too far away for me to grab, but it was there.

If I had a body, I would have gritted my teeth as I willed myself towards it. The silver seemed to tease me, darting in and out of existence.

Stop, I ordered it with whatever consciousness existed right now, and it did. *Come.*

I was Chiara Halnea. I'd been born a nobody. I'd suffered years of abuse and misuse, allowed myself to be enslaved and tortured. I'd raged against the world, and let my wrath be painted in blood. I'd fought, tooth and nail, for the chance at life. I loved a king, and he loved me. I was to be queen of a kingdom that had suffered alongside me.

I had not suffered and survived, not hated and loved with such passion, to allow my end to come like this.

I stretched out whatever remained of me towards that silver, letting myself feel its familiar pull. The silver seemed to wrap around me, tightening and anchoring.

And there, in the blackness, this part of me that remained smiled. It remembered what I was. Who I was.

I was a god, and I bowed to no one.

Not even death itself.

Chapter Thirty-Nine

Everything hurt. Not just the sting of cuts or the ache of bruises, but the pain of bones cracking and flesh splitting. And gods, did it feel good to know I was alive.

Hands pressed into my shoulders, clutching me as though I was a tether to this realm, another weight resting on my chest. My power, slow to rise, hummed in happy recognition. It took some time for my body to remember how to obey my mind, but I didn't need my eyes to open to identify the smell curling around me – cedar and the coming rain.

'I don't know what to do.' I knew that voice, even if it was hoarser than I'd ever heard it. Deana, whispering off to one side. 'Kyrah's arrived, and she's helping Kerta and Evania take the other gods back to their realm, but the mortals … they need…' She trailed off, her words heavy with grief and shame.

'I know.' Jaxon, his voice almost too quiet to hear. 'They need their king. But he's on the edge. His power's too new, and this … this is too fresh. For all of us. There's every chance he might lash out without meaning to.'

Unlikely. If you lashed out, I'm sure it'd be with very careful deliberation, I said, the bond easier to speak with than my mouth.

The weight on my chest jerked. I finally forced my eyes open, the space around me hazy. A canvas ceiling wavered above, the constant patter of light rainfall spilling the space.

'What is it?' Deana asked. Footsteps sounded. 'Callum, did something—'

'This is all rather morose,' I croaked out. My throat ached as though I hadn't drunk water in days, but breath was easier to come by than it had been before. 'Haven't we just won a war?'

There was a breath of silence. Then Callum's face appeared in my vision, his eyes wide and shot through with terror. His hands cupped my face. 'Chiara? I – how—'

I had no words to give him. Not yet.

Instead, I lifted a too-heavy hand, curling it around the back of his neck and using what little strength I had to pull him to me.

He tasted of blood and salt, his lips gentler than I would've liked. Tentative, as though he feared I might crumble if he kissed me too hard. I had no such reservations. I clung to him, pressing my lips to his. My other hand pressed to his chest, his heart thrumming beneath.

I needed him. The man I loved, the person I'd lived for. Callum started to pull back, his breath grazing my skin, but I was far from done. I curled my fingers in blood-matted hair, dragging him back to me. My skin was too warm, my heart too fast and my body riddled with pain, but none of it mattered.

All that mattered was that we both lived.

'Chiara,' Callum whispered against my lips, and his voice sent a shuddering need through me. But I relinquished my hold on him as he gently pried himself away, his hand pressing back to my cheek. 'You're ... you weren't breathing. I couldn't *feel* you, Chiara. I thought you were—'

I lifted my hand, curling it over his. There was still pain, but it was less than it had been – agonising rather than life-ending. 'I know. I'm sorry.'

Callum's eyes shut, his head bowing. He exhaled raggedly. 'Don't you ever do that to me again.'

'I won't.'

'You can't leave me.' His eyes opened again. 'You hear me?'

'I won't.' He continued to stare down at me, the terror not quite leaving his eyes, and I firmed my hold on him. 'I promise. I'm not going anywhere.'

'This past month has been torture. And just when we'd won – when I'd thought we'd finally have peace—' He inhaled sharply, attempting to turn away. I lurched upwards. Pain shot through me, and I fell back with a grimace. Callum whirled, reaching for me. 'Can you not rest for one godsdamned moment?'

The warmth from our kiss was beginning to fade, pain making its return. 'Not when you insist on being a stubborn ass.'

He laughed, a bark of anger that had my own irritation rising. '*I'm* the stubborn one? You insisted on fighting when you had a godsdamned *knife* sticking out of you.'

'Because Vitus needed to die!'

'And I needed you to live!' Callum snapped back.

The tent fell quiet, Deana and Jaxon conveniently finding themselves occupied with the shadows on the wall of the tent.

'I needed you to live,' Callum said again, quieter this time. 'If that cost me this kingdom, so be it.'

'But this way, you have both,' I said gently. 'A kingdom, and me.'

'I almost lost everything.'

'But you didn't.'

'I don't think I'd survive without you.'

'You don't need to.'

'I—' He dropped to his knees by the table, grasping my hand

and pulling it to his forehead. 'Gods, Chiara. You're everything to me.'

I shoved aside the pain, twisting to reach for him with my free hand. I tilted his head back, forcing his eyes to meet mine. Letting him see that I wasn't going anywhere. 'And you're everything to me. We survived, Callum. Together.'

Some of his anger softened, the relief finally given permission to take hold. He turned my hand over, pressing a kiss to my bloodied palm. 'We did.'

'Not that I'm ungrateful,' Jaxon said, turning to look at us and I smiled as irritation flickered over Callum's features at the interruption, 'but how *did* we all survive? Because I'm pretty sure you were dead, Chiara.'

'I'm fairly certain I was, too.' A chill ran over me as I recalled the blackness I'd drifted in. I'd almost lost myself to that darkness. 'But the soul-bond … it was still there. So I grabbed onto it.'

Jaxon's eyes met mine. There was a moment of grief – likely a remembrance of the soul-bond he hadn't managed to catch hold of – but it was gone in seconds, relief replacing it. 'I suppose the combination of your power and a convenient bond with the newest member of divinity might've been enough to overpower the knife.' He glanced at my midsection. 'Even so, you were stabbed. You should probably have that seen to.'

I shifted, going to rise to my elbows. Callum was on his feet in a second. He placed his hands on my shoulders, firmly keeping me down before shifting his focus to my midsection. 'It's stopped bleeding.'

'Still hurts,' I muttered.

Callum's brow creased. He reached for the wound, then stopped, fingers flexing as shadows wreathed them.

It's all right, I said down the bond, cursing my thoughtless words. *Really.*

I can't do anything.

I grasped his hand once more. *You do enough just by being here.*

'I've told you before, it's rude to have silent conversations,' Jaxon huffed, relief filling the sound as he strode forward and leant in. He studied the wound for a few moments, oblivious to the glare I was sending towards the top of his head for his disregard for personal space. 'That's an impressive wound. It'll need stitching.'

He turned, heading for a small table of medical instruments. Callum's hand snapped out, grasping him by the collar.

'I will be handling any stitching,' Callum ground out.

Jaxon opened his mouth, a twitch of amusement curling one corner up. Deana wisely shifted forward and hauled him away. There'd been enough violence today. Jaxon's careless words stoking Callum's anger could very well add more.

The flap to the tent opened, hazy light and a gust of wind bursting in alongside General Jade. She was drenched in blood – most golden, some black – a visor tucked under one arm. Blood dripped down one arm. Her eyes darted around before falling on Callum and then me, the tension in her shoulders easing. 'You're both alive.'

'Mostly,' I said, waving a hand to the throbbing wound in my midsection.

Jade blanched. 'How did you survive...' She shook her head. 'Never mind. I should know to expect the impossible from you by now.' She glanced between me and Callum. 'I was looking for ... well, anyone with more authority than me, I suppose, to make a report. But I can wait?'

Callum opened his mouth, his intention to send her off written across his face. I snatched his hand, squeezing tightly. 'No need to wait. Report now.'

Callum levelled a stern look at me. I levelled one back.

You wanted me to be queen. Well, this is me being queen. Our soldiers need commanding.

His gaze softened. *I like that. Our soldiers.*

Good. Then you can listen to the report, and stop fussing over me. Chiara—

'How many dead?' I asked, cutting Callum's sigh off.

Jade's lips flattened. 'We lost ... too many. At least three thousand. Likely closer to four. General Jakob was one of them. A few of the captains, too. Deidre. Alec. And—'

'Kailey,' I rasped, a stab of sorrow piercing me at the memory of her sightless eyes, and of Corin crumpling beside her.

Deana paled. Jaxon laced his fingers through hers, squeezing tightly. 'What about Corin?'

'Alive last we saw,' Callum said, shooting me a stern glare when I attempted to talk again. *Rest*, he said down the bond.

I'm—

You weren't breathing minutes ago, Chiara. His hand tightened on mine, a small tremble in it. *Please.*

It was the fear in his voice that did it for me, the echo of it still haunting our bond. I remembered what those few moments he'd died at Liam's hands had done to me. What it still did to me if I let myself think about it for too long.

I settled back.

'Which one's Corin?' Jade asked.

'The one with the offensively bright hair,' Jaxon said.

'Ah.' Jade glanced over her shoulder at where healers tended to those whom Callum's initial burst of power hadn't healed. 'He's ... alive.'

'Poor Corin,' Deana whispered, leaning into Jaxon. A cut ran along her cheek, still trickling blood. 'He and Kailey have been inseparable since they first joined the guard. I don't know what he'll do now.'

'He'll survive,' Callum said. He waved a hand, and Deana's cut closed. His shadows, though, weren't as obedient as they'd once been. They leapt from her to Jaxon, setting his arm, before enveloping a startled Jade and healing her wounds too. 'And he'll grieve, as will most others. This victory … its price was high. But, when he's ready, he'll remember again what it is to live.' Even as he looked to the others, his thumb brushed over the back of my hand. A reminder of what I'd chosen to live for. What we both had.

'And what about Naruzia? The mortal realm? The kingdom is mostly destroyed. Crops withered. Archin is gone.' Jade shook her head. 'This doesn't feel like a victory should.'

'Victory rarely tastes as sweet as we expect it,' Jaxon said, Deana's back to his chest and his arm wrapped around her waist. Neither seemed to have any inclination to move. 'So? What will it be now, Your Majesties?'

'Now,' Callum said, turning to smile down at me with a new light to his eyes, 'We rebuild.'

Chapter Forty

'Gods should be exempt from all mortal rules of healing.' I scowled at Callum as he held me down, cursing my weakness. The bed was a rather comfortable cage of soft blankets and his scent, but I was growing tired of its habit of lulling me into sleep.

'If the god in question had not allowed themselves to get stabbed, then that wouldn't be an issue.' His tone was stern, as it had been every time we had had this argument over the past month. 'Besides, this particular god would have been able to get out of her bed considerably sooner if she didn't keep sneaking out to the training ring and ripping her stitches.'

'Stupid logical bastard,' I grumbled as Callum grinned.

'I think you mean stupid logical husband.'

My scowl shifted into something softer. The handfasting ceremony had been small and without fanfare, done as soon as I was well enough to sit upright without losing myself to unconsciousness from the pain. Deana and Jaxon were our witnesses. Deana grumbled that I should've been wearing something fancier than the bedclothes I'd been in, but she'd been smiling as she did so. Jaxon had not when he'd told me the same.

Callum leant in for a slow, lingering kiss. I curled my hand around his neck, deepening it. A thrill ran through me, no duller than the first time we'd kissed. That this was my life still seemed like a fragile dream to me.

Callum broke away first. 'You know we'll have to have a proper ceremony once you're well enough.'

I returned to glaring. 'We will not.'

His lip quirked, pushing at his scar. 'We absolutely will. Once we get through the coronation, I'll have Deana plan for it. There will be feasting and dancing and revelry. It's part of being queen, my love.' He leant back in, his lips tantalisingly close. 'And we both know you'll love it even as you scowl your way through it.'

I managed to steal another kiss before he leant back. 'I won't be leaving my daggers behind.' When I shifted again, Callum sighed, easing an arm under my shoulders to help me upright.

'Of course not. I have Deana working on something more to your style.' His fingers slipped to mine, shadows curling around them as silver sparked on my own. Our Gifts had developed a habit of doing that – rising from within whenever we were in close contact with each other. Which was a lot. 'A gown with plenty of places to stash a blade.'

I smiled, a full-blown grin that made my cheeks ache. 'I do love my blades.'

'Just your blades?' He lay down next to me, propping his head up with one hand.

I tilted my head. 'I suppose I do also love chocolate.'

'And?' He prompted.

'And my brother.' I paused. 'On rare occasions.'

'Have a good, long think.' Callum's fingers curled around my jaw, angling my face towards his. His lips hovered a few centimetres from my own as a teasing smile curled the corner of his mouth.

'Deana.' I nodded decisively. 'I love her company.'

Callum's fingers toyed with the edge of the nightgown I was wearing. He'd become a tease, always offering and then pulling away. He claimed he was worried he'd worsen the almost-healed wound. I was certain he found the teasing amusing. 'I believe you're missing someone.'

'I don't think so.' I smiled up at him, admiring the way the golden morning light picked up the strands in his hair that were lighter than others. There were less shadows to his features now, his smiles and teasing coming easier than they had before.

But the nightmares – they still came. Sometimes, it was me they hunted. Visions of golden eyes and cruel smiles. Of Callum, dead before me.

Other times, I awoke to Callum crying out my name, his expression twisted with grief.

I suspected those nightmares – those memories – would chase us for a good long while.

'I'll just have to remind you, then.'

When Callum looked up at me, his smile was filled with desire and mischief as he pulled at the hem of the nightgown. I raised my brows, the corners of my lips twitching. 'I guess so.'

Callum's hand slid under the thin, gauzy material just as the door swung open.

'Rise and shine!' a too-cheery voice called.

With a sound of annoyance, Callum pulled his hand away from my skin. I immediately missed his touch, my body humming with desire. 'What were you saying about your brother?'

'She was saying how great I am.' Jaxon launched himself onto the bed, unconcerned about Callum's glare as he landed beside me, one leg crossing over another. He held a slice of bread slathered in jam in one hand. Grinning at me, he took a bite.

'Brother dearest,' I said sweetly, leaning into him and tearing the piece of bread out of his hand before he could spill any more crumbs through our bedchambers, 'You have exactly ten seconds before you end up being tossed through that window over there.'

Jaxon snorted in amusement, arms folding behind his head as he leant back on the pillows. 'Why is your bed so much more comfortable than mine?'

'That would be because these are Callum's quarters, and a bedchamber isn't something even you could steal. Eight seconds.'

'Please, Cal is a big softie now. He would never throw me out of a window.' Jaxon cracked open his eyes, leaning forward far enough to give Callum a smirk. Callum rolled his eyes.

'I wasn't talking about Callum,' I replied mildly. 'We're down to four seconds.'

'If you make her tear her stitches again, a window won't be all you have to worry about,' Callum warned. He rose, neatening his clothes.

In the weeks after the battle, Jaxon had developed a habit of repetitively checking on me, where I lay in a state of semi-consciousness, which had evolved into a habit of bursting in on me at any given moment. There had been three times when he'd been bodily thrown out the door by Callum in the past week, Callum having had enough of the constant interruptions.

'It wouldn't be my fault if Chiara decides to throw me out the window!' Jaxon protested, reaching for the jam bread. The glare I sent him stopped his sticky fingers in their tracks.

'One second, Jaxon, and I don't make idle threats.'

'He was coming to tell you a delegation from the godly realm has arrived.' Deana, who was more cautious in checking she didn't walk into anything she shouldn't, peered around the doorway.

'Was I?' Jaxon raised his eyebrows. 'I thought I was checking that Cal here wasn't doing anything he shouldn't.'

'Gods,' I muttered, clambering over Jaxon to get off the bed and sending a deliberate elbow into his midsection. 'We're not children for you to chaperone.'

Jaxon caught me before I could fully get off the bed, his sticky fingers mussing my hair more than it already was. I was beginning to question any of the joy I'd felt at having a brother after I had got over the shock of it. A brother, I quickly learnt, was a no-good, nosy creature whose sole purpose was to annoy me. 'Of course not, but you two do have a habit of getting ... passionate.'

'That was one time!' I protested. 'And the only reason I threatened to cut off his hands was because he said he was going to tie me to this bed if I didn't stay put.'

Callum offered one of those hands to me now, helping me rise to my feet. His lips twitched, fighting between a smile and frown, as though he was debating whether to threaten to do so now. The digging of my nails into his flesh and my narrowed eyes was enough for him to sigh, offering me a loose shirt and flowing pants. I stepped behind a panel, tugging my nightgown over my head and throwing it over the top of the panel.

There was the sound of feet against the floor as someone moved to pick it up. It had been an adjustment, me learning to live within Callum's precise organisation and him learning to suffer my chaos, but it worked.

Most of the time, at least.

'And what happened after?' Jaxon called out, and I hid a smile.

What happened after... Well, passionate didn't quite encapsulate it.

I ran a finger over the ridge on my stomach as Jaxon continued needling Callum, Callum giving very little reaction in return. The mark left by the god-killer was thick and ropey, the flesh paler than that surrounding it. Of all the scars on my body, this one was the biggest and most hideous. The centre was nearly as thick as the width of my finger. Every so often, it sparked with a glimmer of colour from the power that had been imbued in the blade – sometimes rose-pink, other times violet, even black. The worst days were when the colour shifted to gold. On those days – and only those days – I avoided looking at it at all.

Despite Callum's concerns, the flesh had sealed over. It was that which lay underneath that was still healing, and there was a pain when I pushed at it that would likely always be there. All in all, the scar was quite a disturbing sight.

I rather liked it.

After the men had been ushered from the room, Deana helped me ease a severe, black dress over my head, its brutal simplicity fractured by glittering strands of silver threads. The neck rose high, wrapping around my throat in silver-fractured obsidian, while my arms remained untouched by any fabric. It allowed full view of my scars, and the weapons belt Deana strapped on gave easy access to a sword and two knives.

'Beautiful,' she said as she finished with my hair, leaving it unbound in its wild curls.

I smiled. I felt dressed for a different kind of battle to the one that had ended the war.

A knock came at the door, Callum sticking his head in. He stared for a moment, then broke into a grin, crossing the room in a handful of strides. His hand curled around my neck, the other one tilting my face towards his.

'Magnificent,' he murmured, and a shiver ran through me at the deep sincerity in that word.

Deana's hand appeared between us as Callum began to lean in. 'No.'

Callum halted, his brows raising. 'No?'

'She has gods to meet, and then a coronation to attend. I will not have you messing up my masterpiece.' Callum seemed about to ignore her. She snapped her fingers in front of his face. 'No.'

I smiled, stepping back and making the decision for them both. 'We should go.'

'Fine,' Callum said, 'but I'll be taking my payment for this cruelty later.'

'Cruelty?' I asked as he offered his hand.

'If you're going to look so divine, then you shouldn't expect me to stay away from you. It's a wicked form of torture, Captain.'

I scoffed, taking his hand. 'You told me I looked divine yesterday.'

He nodded. 'You did.'

'I'd just woken up and was an absolute mess.'

'A divine mess,' he said with a beatific smile.

'Stop delaying us,' I said, turning my face from his to hide my own grin. 'We have gods to put in their place.'

Together, we strode down the hall towards the throne room.

The throne room remained my least favourite place in the palace. I still sometimes saw the blood that had once stained the tiles, saw the too-small body I had wrapped so tightly in my arms. Callum had offered to tear it down and rebuild, but I had refused. It was a reminder, of what I had lost and what I had fought to keep. Of what we had both conquered.

Outside the throne room doors, Olisker awaited, nervously wringing his hands. I despised the man, as did Callum, but Callum had little experience running a kingdom, and I had none. The nobility were slow to cull and replace, and we needed to maintain control while we rebuilt. As much as we might hate him, he was terrified enough of us to be best of the worst options.

For now.

Beside him, Commander Lena stood, hands folded in front of her as she watched the greying man with amusement. At the sight of us, she straightened, bowing at the waist.

'Your Majesties.' At Callum's nod, she straightened, returning to her amused watch of the advisor.

After the battle, Lena had been granted full authority over the king's and city guard. Deana happily moved aside for her, instead taking up a position on the council as our right hand, and regent should we both fall. Jaxon had taken up another more ... secretive position. One that he delighted in, particularly given it meant mingling with his old criminal cohorts to commit the black deeds the Crown didn't need on record. And, following the war, there were plenty enough of those.

Some, though, Callum or I attended to personally.

'Your Majesty,' General Olisker hastily bent a knee, bowing his head. A second later, and through gritted teeth, he turned that bow to me and echoed the title.

I smiled. The man had never warmed to me. He likely never would. That was fine by me. He didn't have to love me, and he feared me plenty enough to at least feign respect.

'I trust our guests have been behaving themselves?'

Olisker nodded, eyeing me warily as he rose. Just to see the terror in his eyes, I let a little of my power slip to the surface. He balked, backing away and nearly crashing into the wall behind.

I'd visited the godly realm shortly after Vitus's fall, staying as long as my injury would allow. The gods who'd been dragged to the godly realm had switched their loyalty quickly. Tarina currently occupied the cell my father once had – a fitting end, after her betrayal of him. Jaxon had been given full permission to do with her as he wished. He hadn't visited her yet. However, I suspected there would come a day where Tarina met her end, and a new god rose in her place. Akmad was also under the watch of Kerta, as were the other three.

The goddesses who'd sided with us had come intermittently since then to update on their realm. The gods held no interest in the mortal realm, finding it dirty and wild compared to the godly realm. Vitus only wanted it for his revenge. There had been no rebellions, no uprisings. The gods were rather content to stay where they were.

Or rather, they were content to stay where they were after Callum and I had made a joint appearance and shown them exactly what we were capable of.

I nodded to Lena, who moved to push open the great doors before us. Callum and I strode into the throne room, our footsteps echoing. Deana and Jaxon walked behind. Lena slipped in, pulling the door shut and standing guard.

There were already twenty guards in the room, each standing stoic and tall with a hand resting on their blade. Corin was amongst them. He didn't smile when we entered. Just knelt with the rest until Callum told them to rise, his grief over losing Kailey turning him haggard.

But he was alive. Surviving. And one day, he'd remember how to live.

Evania stood in the middle of the room, as resplendent as ever. Her foot tapped impatiently on the floor, wearing the same rose-gold she always did. Today, she was dressed in a cropped shirt with lacy sleeves that cuffed at the wrist and a matching skirt that flowed to her feet. Her silver hair was braided into a coronet, and her light blue eyes glared at us with impatience.

At her side, Kerta seemed much calmer, though her red hair was loose and untamed, matching the wildness in her crimson eyes. She wore fully black clothing that clung to her body.

The two made quite the pair.

'We've been waiting for hours,' Evania snapped, one set of fingers tapping against her leg.

Kerta signed something back. I'd learnt enough of her language to recognise the word love, but nothing else. Jaxon leant in close, whispering an interpretation. 'We've been waiting for minutes, Eva. Nothing more, nothing less.'

At least Evania's haughtiness hadn't changed.

The Divine

Evania curled her lip. 'Any length of time is below me.'

'And yet, here you are. Still waiting.' I passed the goddess, taking the steps up to the set of thrones and sitting down on the silver one with its sharpened edges. My lips curled into a smirk as the goddess's lips thinned. 'It must not have been completely beneath you.'

The throne that had once been King Kane's had been replaced entirely. Gone was the gaudy gold creation, replaced by a simple black throne with a back of shadowy, ropey vines that wove together. There was little gold in the palace anymore, other than in the coffers. We'd all developed a deep repulsion for the colour.

Except, of course, for Callum's hair.

Deana came to stand behind Callum, Jaxon behind me as several guards moved in closer. They were not a threat, merely a reminder. Kerta and Evania might be our allies, and we would treat them as such, but were they to be as fickle in their loyalties as any of their brethren … well, they were in my realm now, and I did not suffer traitors.

'Your Majesties,' Kerta signed as she inclined her head, the red of her eyes catching the gleam of the light hovering above us. 'We trust all has been good and the rebuilding has been going well. Apologies for timing our visit on such an important day.'

My smirk relaxed into a genuine smile at the goddess of war. Evania was a creature I would tolerate. Kerta, I actually liked. 'It's been slow, but most of the houses in Alluvite have been repaired, and we've begun to work on some of the towns.' With the influx of those seeking shelter after entire towns were demolished by the gods, the capital had been the first priority. 'Archin is…' I trailed off, lips turning downwards.

'Archin is going to take a long time to heal,' Callum finished, reaching over to curl his fingers around mine where they lay on the arm of the throne.

The last missive we had had from Brayden, now the king of

the massacred kingdom, had detailed the homes in ruin and the number of bodies left by Vitus. So far, there'd been two thousand living mortals discovered out of the towns and cities, smart enough to hide where an arrogant god could not lower himself to look in. Two thousand, out of the two hundred thousand who had lived there. The number of dead counted seemed to rise with each day.

'I am sorry to hear that.' From the slowness of Kerta's signs and her furrowed brow, I thought she might mean it.

'Yes, yes, it's very sad,' Evania snapped, her lovely features pulled into a frown. 'But I rather wish to go back home, so can we hurry this along?'

Kerta seemed to hold back a sigh as she sent a look to her soul-bonded. I forced back my smile. The look reminded me of the one Deana often gave Jaxon when he was being particularly obnoxious. Her hands began moving, though, the words given life by Jaxon as he watched the signs she made. 'We have come about the rule of the gods.' Her unfathomable eyes turned onto me, burning with the heat of a thousand fires. 'Now things have been ... contained, there is a spot empty. We need a ruler, and quickly, before chaos comes.'

'Really?' Deana muttered behind Callum, voice too low to reach the goddess's ears. 'They're ancient beings and they can't sort out a power dispute themselves?'

'You are wrong, little one.' Evania's gaze flicked to Deana, her expression sombre. 'It is not a power dispute, but a basic, instinctual need. Gods are, at our very core, primal beings led by instinct. Almost every creature in the world bows to another.'

'And how is this our problem?' Callum asked, spreading his hands wide. 'I mean no offence, but we have plenty of our own issues in this realm without adding yours on top of it.'

Kerta stilled, body rigid as she faced Callum. Her moves grew quicker. 'It is your problem, Your Majesty. My soul-bonded is correct. We are driven by instinct, and instinct demands that we bow to the most powerful amongst us.' Her eyes flicked from Callum to me and back again. 'Once, that would have been Dearil, before Vitus had turned the gods against him. Then it was Vitus. Now both gods are gone, their power fleeing to new hosts.'

Evania's smile held a little malice, as though she expected one or both of us to balk at her next words. 'The boy king holds a great deal of power from Vitus. But you, girl, hold not only the power of Dearil, but also the power Gifted to you upon birth by your divine heritage. You might be a silly little creature, but the laws of the gods demand that you sit upon our throne.'

I froze, staring at Evania as I took in her words. Her smile grew, her gaze shrewd as she watched for any flicker of unease, any sign I might run.

She didn't know me well enough.

I knew what I was, now. I knew every bit of power in my veins, every bit of darkness and all the shadowed, cruel things that made me. At night, as I slept, I was still called to the Gates, fulfilling my father's old obligations of ushering the dead to their rest in the Light or the Dark. I had not balked from that. I would not balk at this.

But ... to wear two crowns at once, to govern the mortals as I governed the gods... 'No.'

Evania's smile froze, her blue eyes glittering like twin shards of ice. 'No?' She glanced at Kerta, who watched me. 'This was not an offer, child. This was what you were made for.'

I smiled back. 'That may be so, but it's a no, nonetheless.' Evania's mouth opened, and I held up a hand. 'Not forever. Just for now.' Callum's hand had found mine again, wrapping around it and providing me with every bit of strength I needed. 'I have lived a half-life ever since I could remember, bound by the whims of everyone around me. Gods, kings, mortals. I want to live a mortal life. I want to find out what it means to be human, to live amongst the mortals, to engrave it so deep into my memory that no amount of time passing will cause me to become as callous to this realm as you gods have become. I want to live as many mortal lives as I wish to, and then, and only then, will I settle for being your ruler. And I will not allow you or what your gods want to take even a centimetre of freedom or choice from me.'

Evania's cheeks reddened, but Kerta stilled her with a single hand on her shoulder.

'I will be the queen of your gods one day, but today is not that day.'

'You cannot do that!' Evania's skin sparked with rose-gold power. She reached a hand up into the air before her as though to grab me and topple me from my throne. The look I returned dared her to try, to see where she ended up. 'You cannot deny this.'

My lips twisted as I moved my gaze away from her, turning them to the silver slithering under my skin. The scent of smoke and jasmine filled the room. The power that grew restless with each day I spent confined to my bed. 'Can't I?' I lifted my eyes once more. 'I'm the queen, right?'

Kerta nodded, her lips curling upwards just a little. Evania scowled.

'Perhaps you could help me out, Your Majesty.' I turned to Callum, whose eyes glittered with amusement. 'As queen, I can appoint a regent, correct?'

'Most definitely.'

'Fantastic.' I smiled widely, turning back to the goddesses. 'In that case, I appoint you, Kerta, to be acting regent until I deem it time to take up the throne in the godly realm.'

'You—' Evania's words died off as she processed what I had said. She folded her arms, unfolded them and then folded them again. Her lips puckered. 'That would be fine, I suppose.'

Kerta's lips pressed together, holding back what seemed to be a mixture of silent amusement and shock. Regardless, she bowed her head towards me, arm crossed over her chest before standing straight. Her signs flowed smoothly. 'Thank you, Your Majesty. I shall serve you well.'

'Fine. We're done here,' Evania announced and, with a wave of her hand and a shower of rose-gold sparks, both vanished from the room.

Silence fell in the throne room at the disappearance of the goddesses. If the guards had any reaction to the conversation, their blank faces showed nothing. There was little movement from anyone as we all absorbed that little conversation.

A laugh broke the silence. A loud, deep laugh that had me turning and glaring at the man it came from.

'What?' I snapped, eyes narrowing at the king at my side.

'Only you, my queen,' Callum grinned, 'would somehow manage to both infuriate a goddess to the point where I thought she might try to chain you to her realm, and placate her so completely within the space of a single conversation.'

My lips twitched back. 'That's probably not the queenliest thing to do, is it?'

'On the contrary,' Callum stood, and I did the same, 'I think that only a queen could have managed that so well.' He looked towards the throne room doors. 'And your kingdom awaits you, Your Majesty.'

My heart thudded – with excitement and fear, anticipation and worry. Today, my place would finally be cemented as queen of this kingdom. I would be a leader – not just to the soldiers, but to everyone else. To the old and young, the strong and defenceless.

And I would do it with my friends by my side. With Jaxon and Deana.

With Callum.

Another set of chains, a voice whispered. *That's all this coronation is. All that being queen is.*

I recognised that voice. The me that had once existed before I'd met Callum.

I smiled as I crushed that little voice. She was still there – the hardened parts of me. The bits that knew how to cut and do little else. And I would never let her disappear, not entirely. Because she was who made me. Her hatred of others. Of the realms. Of me. A memory I would keep close, to remind myself what I'd conquered.

But I wasn't her. Not anymore.

I looked to Callum. To his steady presence, always by my side. The person who'd rescued me from what I might have been, and taught me what I might become.

A monster. A weapon. A queen. A god.

I would be any of those for him. For this kingdom of ours, too.

Callum offered his hand. 'Well, my queen?'

I smiled, laying my fingers in his. 'Let's show this realm exactly what it has created.'

Acknowledgments

Thank you to my family, who have always been my biggest supports – mum, I couldn't have done any of this without you, and dad, your encouragement means the world to me. To my friends, both in the writing community and out, who've supported me from the very first drafts.

A massive thank you to the One More Chapter team. From draft manuscript to final edits, the whole team have been such a huge support in turning these books into the series they are. And thank you to the reader – I couldn't have done this without you!

The author and One More Chapter would like to thank everyone who contributed to the publication of this story...

Analytics
Imogen Wolstencroft

Audio
Fionnuala Barrett
Ciara Briggs

Contracts
Laura Amos
Inigo Vyvyan

Design
Lucy Bennett
Fiona Greenway
Liane Payne
Dean Russell

Digital Sales
Laura Daley
Lydia Grainge
Hannah Lismore

eCommerce
Laura Carpenter
Madeline ODonovan
Charlotte Stevens
Christina Storey
Jo Surman
Rachel Ward

Editorial
Janet Marie Adkins
Rosie Best
Kara Daniel
Charlotte Ledger
Jennie Rothwell
Sofia Salazar Studer
Emily Thomas
Helen Williams

Harper360
Emily Gerbner
Ariana Juarez
Jean Marie Kelly
emma sullivan
Sophia Wilhelm

International Sales
Peter Borcsok
Ruth Burrow
Bethan Moore
Colleen Simpson

Inventory
Sarah Callaghan
Kirsty Norman

Marketing & Publicity
Chloe Cummings
Grace Edwards
Katie Sadler

Operations
Melissa Okusanya
Hannah Stamp

Production
Denis Manson
Simon Moore
Francesca Tuzzeo

Rights
Ashton Mucha
Alisah Saghir
Zoe Shine
Aisling Smyth
Lucy Vanderbilt

Trade Marketing
Ben Hurd
Eleanor Slater

The HarperCollins Distribution Team

The HarperCollins Finance & Royalties Team

The HarperCollins Legal Team

The HarperCollins Technology Team

UK Sales
Isabel Coburn
Jay Cochrane
Sabina Lewis
Holly Martin
Harriet Williams
Leah Woods

And every other essential link in the chain from delivery drivers to booksellers to librarians and beyond!